THE
FORTUNE
HUNTER

THE
FORTUNE
HUNTER

Jasmine Haynes

BERKLEY SENSATION, NEW YORK

THE BERKLEY PUBLISHING GROUP
Published by the Penguin Group
Penguin Group (USA) Inc.
375 Hudson Street, New York, New York 10014, USA
Penguin Group (Canada), 90 Eglinton Avenue East, Suite 700, Toronto, Ontario M4P 2Y3, Canada
(a division of Pearson Penguin Canada Inc.)
Penguin Books Ltd., 80 Strand, London WC2R 0RL, England
Penguin Group Ireland, 25 St. Stephen's Green, Dublin 2, Ireland (a division of Penguin Books Ltd.)
Penguin Group (Australia), 250 Camberwell Road, Camberwell, Victoria 3124, Australia
(a division of Pearson Australia Group Pty. Ltd.)
Penguin Books India Pvt. Ltd., 11 Community Centre, Panchsheel Park, New Delhi—110 017, India
Penguin Group (NZ), 67 Apollo Drive, Rosedale, North Shore 0632, New Zealand
(a division of Pearson New Zealand Ltd.)
Penguin Books (South Africa) (Pty.) Ltd., 24 Sturdee Avenue, Rosebank, Johannesburg 2196, South Africa

Penguin Books Ltd., Registered Offices: 80 Strand, London WC2R 0RL, England

This is an original publication of The Berkley Publishing Group.

PRINTED IN THE UNITED STATES OF AMERICA

ISBN-13: 978-0-7394-9004-4

To Terri Schaefer
For always being a straight shooter and
saying it like it is

ACKNOWLEDGMENTS

Thanks to Jenn Cummings, Terri Schaefer, and Rose Lerma, for endless hours of reading. To Nancy Cochran, Elda Minger, and Rose, again, for all their brainstorming when the story was just a germ of an idea. To Christine Zika, for talking me through the rough spots. And to my agent, Lucienne Diver, and my editor, Wendy McCurdy.

1

"FAITH. Over here." Trinity Green waved frantically from the other side of the ballroom, her voice falling into a sudden hush as the dance number ended.

Faith cringed as she suddenly felt every eye on her, the party-goers around her stepping back slightly so that she was in a little circle all her own. The indisputable center of attention.

Trinity would never understand why any woman in her right mind *wouldn't* want to be the center of attention.

Faith, obviously not in her right mind, loathed it. Her friend was now skirting the dance floor, a dark-haired man in tow. Faith smiled. Men loved being towed by Trinity. In addition to her blond hair, Aphrodite looks, and flawless body, she was quite a lovable person.

They'd been best friends since the seventh grade when Trinity had rescued Faith from a spiteful group of girls. Middle school girls could be terrors on anyone different. Though their fathers had known each other for years up to that point, Trinity hadn't seemed to notice Faith existed. Yet Trinity stood by her that day, and Faith would forever love her for it.

"Sweetie, there's someone I'm dying for you to meet." Trinity grabbed Faith's hand, then seized her companion's, and forced their handshake. "This is my best friend in all the world, Faith Castle. And Faith, this is Connor Kingston. He's working with Lance at Daddy's company." Lance was Trinity's brother and heir to the Green company throne.

"It's nice to meet you, Miss Castle."

Out of force of habit due to her short stature, Faith tended to look at hands instead of faces during introductions. But something in Connor Kingston's voice, the husky quality of it, like a rhythm guitar strumming a deep chord, made her look up. And up. She was five foot four in the heels she wore tonight, five foot two without them. Connor was over six.

He had the blackest hair she'd ever seen, so black the chandelier lighting gleamed off it. Charcoal eyes gazed down at her—though charcoal seemed such a boring color. His were the shade of a moonlit midnight.

He and Trinity made a perfect couple.

"And it's nice to meet you, Mr. Kingston."

Trinity snorted. "Give me a break. It's Faith and Connor, okay? No more of that *Mr.* Kingston and *Miss* Castle stuff."

Faith almost laughed hearing the names said so closely together. His king to her castle. Like a chess move. Or a statement on male to female relations.

Introductions done, Trinity stroked his black tuxedo-clad arm. "Connor, would you get us some champagne? I'm parched." Not that Trinity would drink the whole glass. Too many calories.

Connor smiled. A wolf, tamed for the moment, grinning at a cute little bunny. "Of course." He turned the smile on Faith, something flickered in his eyes, then his mouth crooked a little higher on one side.

If she didn't know better, she'd have thought she'd made the wolf comment aloud.

"Isn't he divine?" Trinity whispered as they watched him until he was swallowed up by the crowd at the bar.

"Absolutely."

Then Trinity sighed. "It's too bad he doesn't have a cent to his name other than what Daddy's paying him."

"At least he has a job."

Their small community of Silicon Valley elite, those left after the dot-com crash and the economic downturn a few years ago, could be broken down into two categories: those who had, and those who didn't. Most of the didn't-haves lived off the did-haves, not by working but by being charming and getting their entertainment written off as a tax-deductible business expense by the other half. Or, they married into the class they coveted.

"That's the worst part," Trinity moaned. "Everyone *knows* he works. Daddy would have a hissy fit if I even *mentioned* marrying an employee." She tapped her chin thoughtfully. "But we could have a wild affair." She fluttered her eyelashes. "You know, all that unbridled passion, the fear of being *caught*." She shivered dramatically. "It sounds so intense."

Agreeing completely, Faith wanted to shiver herself. With his dark good looks, Connor Kingston incited many a delicious fantasy. Trinity winked, and they scanned the crowd for him.

Faith spotted the back of his head. My, his shoulders were broad in the tuxedo. "I'll leave you alone to work your magic."

Trinity grabbed her arm. "You can't run off. He wanted to meet you since I talk about you all the time."

Faith gasped. "You do not."

"Close your mouth, sweetie. I told him you're the only one in the whole dissolute lot of us who has a calling."

"What calling?"

Trinity huffed. "As a kindergarten teacher, of course, shaping young minds. You're producing a better next generation."

Faith taught because she loved children. And because she was sometimes terrified she'd never have any of her own. She was twenty-nine years old, thirty by the end of the year, and unless she married one of the didn't-haves looking for a did-have wife, teaching might be the sum total exposure she had to children.

Yet Trinity was right, being a teacher was her calling. Which reminded her. Faith smiled to herself. "Do you know what little Roger Weederman said the other day?"

"That's what I adore about you. You *love* the little monsters. When I have children, you have to quit your job and become their nanny. You'll raise them to be little presidents." Trinity spread her hands. "President of the company, president of the United States, president of the United Nations."

Faith laughed. Heads turned. She sometimes laughed too bois-terously, but when she was with Trinity, she couldn't help herself. Trinity didn't mean half of what she said. She liked to talk, espe-cially at big bashes, saying outrageous things to anyone who would listen. She had, however, graduated from college with honors and would one day make a perfect first lady.

But Faith wasn't going to be anyone's nanny. She wanted chil-dren of her own.

Over the crowd, Faith spied Connor fast approaching. She wasn't jealous of Trinity's sleekness when matched against her own relative plumpness, but for some reason, she didn't want to watch *him* do the usual mental comparison. "I really have to go before Mr. Stud-Muffin returns. He's all yours."

"I can't have him. Unbridled passion doesn't outrank one of Daddy's hissy attacks. And Connor got you champagne." Trinity clasped her hands. "Come on, Faith. Pretty please, don't go."

"Ladies' room," Faith whispered as she slipped away.

"Spoilsport," Trinity returned, just before creasing her lips with a smile any man would die for.

Handsome men made Faith nervous. Connor Kingston did worse. For the first time, he made her wish for cosmetic surgery to turn herself into a Trinity clone.

*   *   *

FAITH grimaced. This was a humiliating position to find herself in, sitting in a ladies' room stall, minding her own business, while being forced to listen to mean-spirited gossip.

"Lisa is so dumpy, she deserves to have him cheat. I mean, really, she wore stripes. No one wears stripes to a formal."

"Not only that," the other girl joined in, "they were going the wrong way. Everyone knows stripes make you look fatter when they're horizontal instead of vertical. What possessed her?"

Poor Lisa. Faith commiserated though she was secretly thankful she wasn't the subject of the nasty gossip. She'd chosen a basic black cocktail dress for the evening.

One of them sighed without an ounce of sympathy for the hapless Lisa. "Well, he got exactly what he wanted. A frumpy little heiress and all the afternoon delight he can handle."

Faith couldn't remember the husband's name, only that he was one of the have-nots before he married Lisa. *Afternoon delight.* What a lovely term for adultery. Poor Lisa.

"Do tell. Who's he doing the do with?"

"Kitchum's wife."

Gasp. "That slut. She's twenty years older than him."

"She just had her face done and looks younger than Lisa."

"Well, that's what old man Kitchum gets for marrying a gold digger half his age."

They laughed in unison, then, thank God, their voices faded as the ladies' room door snicked closed behind them.

Faith was now blessedly alone. Which was worse? The cheating, or the humiliation of having it discussed in the restroom? Maybe she was in danger of lumping all those in her own social circle into one neat ziplock Baggie, but gossip did seem to be a favorite pastime amongst them.

What on earth was she doing attending one gala after another? Searching for Mr. Right? That's what her father hoped for her, bless his heart, though he did seem to find something lacking in the few prospects Faith had brought home.

To tell the truth, she didn't need Mr. Right. She only needed children. Her heart ached she wanted them so badly. Yet she grew up without a mother, and she firmly believed kids needed both parents. So, being good potential father material was the only requirement on her list. Amongst her peers, she had serious doubts of finding a man who fit the bill.

Slipping out of the now empty ladies' room, Faith headed into the club's gardens for a respite from the activity. Blooms perfumed the spring night, the garden resplendent with camellias and azaleas, and the crescent moon reflected off the still waters of the man-made lake in the center of the club grounds.

She wandered down the incline through the trees and bushes, and she would have made it to the water's edge if she hadn't suddenly heard a voice on the other side of the hedge.

"Suck it, please, honey. I'm dying here."

Dear Lord, with another few steps, she would have passed the hedge and stumbled right on top of the couple. Faith knew she should find another route to the lake, but something, a devil on her shoulder perhaps, kept her rooted to the spot.

The woman didn't say a word. There was only the rasp of a zipper on the night breeze.

Faith, that devil whispering in her ear, peeked around the end of the hedge. Seated on a stone bench, the woman had a firm grip on her partner's penis, slowly pumping him as his head fell back in total ecstasy.

"Christ, yes. Suck it, sweetheart."

"Don't rush me." The voice was soft with seduction, husky with desire, sultry with power.

The couple cavorted in the shelter of the overhanging trees, and Faith couldn't make out faces. Somehow, their very anonymity fueled her own fantasies.

"Please," he begged.

Faith's nipples beaded against the soft fabric of her dress, and a throb started low in her belly, streaking down between her legs. In an instant, she was damp.

Oh yes, she could almost feel her own hand wrapped around his erection, hard flesh begging her to caress the tip, to suck the tiny drop of come.

She wasn't a virgin. She'd had moments when she'd almost believed she was desirable. Those moments hadn't become anything lasting, and the few men she'd been with had gotten bored quickly. Or they were after her money. Just as her father said.

This, however, was the stuff of her sexually explicit fantasies, where she could have everything done to her and do everything in return. Where she asked for what she wanted without fear of rejection and indulged in all the erotic, sensual acts she'd never done but wanted desperately to experience.

The woman bent her head. Faith could almost taste him, feel him between her lips. Without conscious thought, her hand lifted to her breast, her palm fondling one tight nipple as she watched. Watching was naughty but so incredibly sexy.

Then the woman took his penis all the way, her mouth fusing to him, his fingers tangling in her hair. Whispers, groans, sounds all around her, making Faith almost a participant in what they were doing. Her hand slid down the front of her dress, over her abdomen until her fingers lightly pressed her mound.

She should have walked away. But her feet wouldn't move. Nothing on heaven and earth could make her stop watching.

CONNOR followed Faith Castle into the moonlit gardens, giving her plenty of lead to disguise the fact he was tailing her. When he caught up, the meeting would appear accidental.

Over the past few weeks, as he'd dutifully squired her around town, Trinity Green told him everything there was to know about Faith. She was almost thirty, a schoolteacher, and she loved chil-

dren beyond anything. She also happened to be the heiress to
Castle Heavy Mining. According to the Trinity gospel, Faith was
a paragon. Could there actually be such a thing? Trinity had ex-
tolled her virtues as if she were putting the woman on the auc-
tioning block. The question was why. What was the benefit in
touting Faith?

Whatever her reasons, Trinity had told him everything important about Faith. Or so he thought. She hadn't mentioned Faith's
abundant body. Far from a model-thin beauty queen, Faith was
round and curvy. A man could hold Faith in his arms and not
worry about breaking her. Her breasts were a bounty. Her derriere
begged for a man's caress. Her hair, cascading past her shoulders,
was the color of an exploding sun, all reds and golds.

Faith lacked the classic aristocratic features revered in today's
world. Her face was round, her nose a tad snub, and her mouth
small, but beauty was so much more than bone structure. It was
the whole package, inside and out. Trinity had given him a hint of
Faith's soft center, but her full impact hit him when she laughed.
From across the dance floor, the throaty sound shot straight to his
cock. That's when he started imagining her on her knees taking
him into her mouth, when he'd envisioned sinking his fingers into
her hair and holding her to him as he came.

Yes, Faith Castle was a pleasant surprise. A lush creature begging for him to plumb the depths others casually dismissed. He
hadn't imagined that seducing her would be so pleasurable.

Ahead of him, she stopped at a hedge, leaning forward slightly
to peer around it.

Connor stole closer. Hushed voices reached him, then indistin-
guishable sounds. Faith seemed rooted to the spot like a statue
hewn in place. She didn't hear him as he circled, coming up on
her left. The fingers of her right hand found purchase in the hedge
branches, as if to steady herself.

Then he saw what so fascinated her.

Well, well, well, Faith Castle was indeed a bundle of contrasts.

Knee-length cocktail dress, well-hidden cleavage, moderate heels on her shoes. One thought prim and proper.

But there she was, standing in the flower-scented garden watching a woman go down on her lover. A breath whispered from Faith's lips as the man drove his cock deep. Her hand left the hedge and skated down the front of her dress, brushing her abdomen, then pressed between her legs.

The sight sucked Connor's breath from his lungs, and his cock surged. Her breasts crested against her dress. Diamond-tipped nipples begged for his mouth. That luscious body was meant for loving, and if Trinity was to be believed, Faith hadn't seen much of that lately. Fucking idiots, the men who passed her over because of a mere body-type fad. She wanted passion. Hell yes, she wanted it badly.

He wanted to give it to her. He'd stumbled onto the perfect supplement to his plan, the ideal stratagem to draw her in.

He hadn't imagined securing his future could be this sweet.

IN her fantasies, Faith felt an arm wrap around her waist, pulling her against hard male thighs and a raging erection. Warm, enticing breath bathed her hair.

"You like watching, don't you?"

"Yes," she murmured.

Her own voice snapped her out of her reverie. Her body stiffened in his embrace. The touch was tangible, his words real, her orgasm on the horizon.

"Let me watch with you."

Smooth and sultry, his pitch seduced her as easily as the tableau in front of them. All she had to do was permit his caress, his nearness. She didn't have to act, simply allow him to do as he would. It was so effortless. He pulled her closer, rubbing his body sinuously against her back, bottom, and thighs.

His hand slipped down her abdomen and covered her own. He moved his fingers over hers, rotating gently, caressing her.

"He's going to blow in her mouth," he murmured.

Faith's breath rasped in her throat. She was dizzy and drunk on sex, on the kinkiness of watching, of letting some stranger take liberties with her body.

Under the trees in front of them, the man groaned louder, his hips pumping frantically. He held his partner's head, taking her mouth with his body rather than the other way around. He clenched, held, then cried out.

Lips dropped to Faith's neck, bit gently. Fingers rolled her nipple, pinched. Between her legs, he guided her hand rhythmically back and forth across her covered pussy.

She almost came when he pressed up and in, hard. Ripples of pleasure shot out from her clitoris. She bit her lip, closed her eyes, and savored the sensation.

Then he yanked her back into hiding on the other side of the hedge just as the male half of the tableau before them spoke.

"Jesus, that was good."

The woman's answer was smug, as was her voice. "I know."

"Let me fuck you."

"You'll get my dress dirty. Tomorrow. Doesn't your wife have tennis lessons or something? Meet me at the usual place."

Behind the hedge, Faith's mystery man held her close in the circle of his arms.

"Shh," he whispered.

As if he knew she was about to twist away and say . . . something. Such as, *How dare you?*

There was the rustle of clothing and what sounded like a belt buckle, then the man's voice again. "You're such a fucking tease."

"You love it. And Lisa doesn't swallow."

"And Kitchum wouldn't be able to fill your mouth with that much come. Don't tell me you don't love it."

God. It was old man Kitchum's wife with the face-lift and Lisa's had-none-of-his-own husband.

And just who was the man holding her?

"Thank you," he whispered, "for letting me join you."

She knew his voice then, the seductive, rough tones she'd first heard not a half hour ago.

Connor Kingston. Trinity's new dish.

She struggled a little in his arms as the lovers drifted off in the opposite direction. They'd part soon and head back to the ballroom. To Lisa with her horizontal stripes, and Kitchum, well, who knew if he was even here? Faith hadn't seen him.

"Let me go."

He shook his head as he once again dropped his lips to her neck. Did he even realize who she was? Or had he merely been turned on by the sight of a woman watching a sex scene played out in the moonlight?

Then he stroked her chin and turned her face to his. For a fraction of a second, his eyes locked with hers. No surprise, no horror. He had known exactly who he was touching. Faith almost drowned in his glittering gaze a moment before he took her lips with his. He tasted of the evening's champagne and something else—hot, hungry male. Greedy, ravenous, his tongue swooped in and stole her breath.

With a kiss like that, he could make a woman do anything.

His touch, then his kiss had her so hot, restless, and bothered, she had to battle her own needs far more than she had to fight him. She tried to wriggle away. "I have to go."

"Not before we make a date."

That made her stop. "A date?"

"Tomorrow evening."

"Why on earth would you want to go out with me?" Screw her, maybe. But a date?

He chuckled, his chest rumbling against her back. "Because I like the way you laugh."

"The way I laugh?" She was repeating like an idiot.

"In the ballroom. Trinity made you laugh."

No one had *ever* thought her laugh was special. She wanted to accept his invitation, but the whole incident was a fluke. And she was the one who'd get hurt. "You think I'm easy because of what just happened. But that was a strange combination of events, and it'll never happen again." Except in her fantasies.

"Not a date, then. Coffee."

"No." She squirmed against him once more.

"I'm not letting you go until you agree."

"Why?" It was the dumbest thing to ask, making it sound as if she couldn't understand why a man like him would want to see a woman like her again. But really, she *didn't* understand.

"I like your laugh, and I like the way you feel in my arms."

He was seducing her with just a few wonderful, tremendous, unbelievable words. He couldn't mean them.

"Meet me. Say yes. Please."

Dammit, the please did it. "Just coffee. And this will be the only time."

He sighed, his breath fluttering her unbound hair.

She said it would be the only time, but she knew without much pressure, she'd do anything he asked. That's how frighteningly hungry *she* was.

HE had a King Kong–sized hard-on for her. She'd been equally affected. He could have made her come with one more touch. A woman hadn't felt that good in his arms since . . . not since he was teenager and still believed in love.

Step one complete. He'd secured the first date. Connor had a plan for Faith Castle, a mutually advantageous plan.

He'd considered Trinity Green for a few short weeks, but while she was beautiful, sweet, and loyal, she was a little too absorbed with outward appearances, not to mention she'd probably freak if she perspired during sex. Besides, he had nothing to offer Trinity in return for what he asked, and he didn't intend making a one-sided deal that benefited only him. But with Faith, he had the one thing she wanted, and, according to Trinity, the thing Faith wasn't sure she'd ever get.

Yet, instead of pulling together a strategy for his campaign, all Connor could think of was the exquisite taste of her on his lips. That was a boon he hadn't anticipated.

Oh yeah, Faith was the one he wanted to marry. The moment he touched her, no other woman would do.

2

"DO you want dessert?" Connor slid her coffee cup over to her.

Faith made a production of adding cream and sugar. "No, thanks. Now, why did you want to meet me?" There, that was businesslike. Not as if this were a real date.

After getting their coffee and snagging a small table in the middle of the café, he'd sat in the chair closest to hers instead of across like a civilized person would do. She was terribly conscious of his thigh only inches from hers. On top of that, she'd been awake all night thinking about what they'd witnessed, what he'd done, the way he'd touched her. That kiss. Oh yes, that delicious, unforgettable kiss.

Faith put up a hand before Connor could answer. "And don't say anything about my laugh or last night."

He chuckled. "How about saying I want to get to know you better?"

At seven on Sunday evening, the little café was bursting at the seams with couples and small groups getting in their last bit of weekend socializing. The place served specialty coffees and tantalizing desserts. The sugary scents unsettled her stomach.

Actually, *he* unsettled her. She'd been jittery all day. Then she'd taken an extraordinary amount of time deciding what to wear, finally choosing a slimming skirt—Trinity wouldn't let her buy any other kind—and a fitted sweater. Spring was definitely here, but the nights could still be cool even in late April.

And the sweater nicely defined her breasts, which were her best feature.

Connor would look good in anything. Jeez, she thought too much about other people's comparisons. That's why she didn't like going out with good-looking men.

The three young women two tables away stared at him as if he were a chocolate truffle without any calories. Faith dipped her head as they looked at her and started whispering.

"Trinity tells me you're a kindergarten teacher."

Faith realized she hadn't said a word for half a minute. And that Connor hadn't given the gaggle of beauties a single glance since he sat down. Trinity, he was talking about Trinity. "Are you and she dating?" she blurted. Despite Trinity's disclaimer, it was only polite to confirm up front that she wasn't stepping on toes.

"She doesn't like to attend parties alone. So I take her. It's not dating."

She, too, had often attended events with Trinity when an available male couldn't be found at the last minute. Though Trinity usually managed to find one soon after they arrived.

"I haven't seen you at any functions." She almost made it sound like an accusation.

Which didn't seem to bother Connor. "I haven't seen you, either. Must be on different evenings."

What was there about him that made her feel bitchy? Maybe it was that niggling doubt that he could actually be interested in her. "So tell me, why does Trinity talk about me?" She didn't consider herself scintillating party discussion.

Connor looked at her as if she were as cute and silly as her students could sometimes be. "You're the only one of her friends who does anything meaningful, she says. Including herself."

Trinity said things like that to Faith herself, but to tell someone else, especially a hunky guy . . . well, it warmed her heart.

He touched her hand, just a gentle stroke across the back. "It's admirable on your part."

She didn't know what to say. Her skin was warm and her insides gooey like the truffle she'd thought of. "Thanks."

"Why do you do it? Teach, I mean."

"I like children." She loved feeling a part of their lives, knowing she, in some small way, helped mold their futures.

"But you want kids of your own, too, don't you?"

She swirled her spoon in her coffee, the conversation lagging. Talking about herself wasn't easy. "Someday."

Connor pushed his coffee forward and leaned his elbows on the table. His hair glistened blue black under the lights as he focused his smoky gaze on her. "I know this is early in our relationship, but I have a proposition for you."

Her heart did a little lurch. She was sure his leg was closer than it had been. His heat singed her. "What?" She felt trapped by his gaze like a mouse in a cat's paw.

"I have a goal. And I don't want to wait fifteen years or more to achieve it."

That wasn't what she'd thought he'd say. A proposition usually meant something sexual. Didn't it? "What goal?"

He didn't answer that. "You have a goal, too. You want a big family. Together we can achieve our goals faster than we could alone."

Her hands were suddenly numb, cold. The spoon tipped sideways out of her cup, splattering milky coffee across the table. "What's your goal?" She was afraid to hear it.

He sopped her mess up with a couple of napkins. "I want to climb the corporate ladder. Be a CEO. Run the company. Make the important decisions. Your father doesn't have anyone to fill his shoes at Castle Heavy Mining."

Her father. Whose only heir was a kindergarten teacher uninterested in his business. Of course, there was Cousin Preston, but he wouldn't do, according to her father, who'd been looking for an acceptable protégé for a long time and, as Connor correctly stated, had yet to find the perfect candidate.

Trinity had been talking. *A lot.*

"What's that got to do with me?" The words were a painful whisper that hurt her throat. And her heart.

Connor covered her hand with his, giving her back some of the warmth she'd lost. "We can marry; I can help your father. We'll have that big family you want, and I can pass his legacy on to his grandchildren. To *our* children."

His eyes burned with a passion far beyond the physical, but his proposition slammed into her like a huge tree crashing down on a tiny one-room cottage. She yanked her hand away. He needed an heiress. A frumpy heiress barefoot and pregnant at home while he had his afternoon delight with beautiful, sexy women.

Her skin prickled, her eyes ached, and her head started to pound with the need to hold in a vast ocean of tears. "No."

He traced her jaw with the pad of his finger. "Just think about it."

She jerked her head away. "No." She'd have run out of the café if her legs hadn't felt so weak. She thought they'd buckle if she even tried to stand.

He tipped his head, his eyes softening to a light gray. "I've hurt you. That's not what I meant to do."

No way would she let him think that. "You don't have the power to hurt me. Besides, why would I marry a stranger?"

"What do you want to know about me so I'm not a stranger?"

She shook her head so hard her brain seemed to rattle. "Nothing. I'm not interested. I wouldn't even consider marrying you." She leaned forward. "Especially after the way we met."

"We met when Trinity introduced us."

He knew she was talking about the garden, but he just had to go and remind her that wasn't their first meeting. He had to remind her about Trinity's part. "Did Trinity tell you I needed a husband?" That she was desperate for a husband. For children.

"No. She doesn't know anything about what I want."

It was one thing to *be* desperate, quite another to have the fact broadcast. Her best friend wouldn't be that cruel. Except that sometimes Trinity didn't know when she was doing more harm than good. She knew how much Faith wanted to be a mother.

Faith chose indignation over blubbering in front of Connor. "The nerve. I can't believe you'd just come right out and tell me you want to marry me for my money."

"Not your money. And would you prefer I romance you, make you fall in love with me, and *not* tell you my intentions?"

She remembered Lisa and her have-not husband's romance. Starry-eyed Lisa, unsuspecting Lisa. Now unhappy Lisa. No, she didn't want that, either. "I wouldn't fall in love with you if you were the last man on earth." Last night, even fifteen minutes ago, maybe, but now? No way.

Why didn't she just get up and leave?

She noticed he'd stopped touching her, the heat of his leg no longer penetrating her skirt. "Anyway, how do I even know you'd make a good father?"

"Children are a man's most important legacy. I'm an orphan. My mom died when I was seven, and I lost my dad a couple of years later. I know how important a father is."

She felt sorry for him, losing both his parents so young. She almost wanted to know more. Almost. But his proposition was absurd. It would never work. "If you run a company, you'd never be home. Your children wouldn't even know you."

He reached for the cup he'd pushed away earlier. "Was *your* father gone all the time?" The question was a challenge.

"He's special. My mom died when I was young, too. He tried to make up for that by being there when I needed him. Most men with powerful careers think bringing home the bacon is enough."

"I'll be there for my children."

She couldn't shake him, and the way he said it, with an uncompromising glint in his eye, made her believe he meant it. Or maybe she was just blinded by her attraction to him, by what had happened between them last night. She didn't want to admire him, yet she was starting to, for more than his black hair, good looks, and distracting body. Dammit, she was starting to *like* him, and that just couldn't happen.

"Fine. But what kind of husband would you make? If we're not marrying for love, then how do I know you wouldn't be running around behind my back? I won't be a laughingstock whose husband cheats on her." She wouldn't budge on that issue. Ever.

"That won't be a problem." He paused, studied her, his head tipped. "As long as you don't shut me out of the bedroom when you're not trying to get pregnant." Lowering his voice, he moved in on her, his big, wholly male body close, closer, his knee pressing hers. "After the way you reacted last night, I have a feeling great sex won't be an issue."

She didn't move, as if his touch beneath the table had no effect on her. "Do *not* bring up last night. That was an aberration." She mourned the sweet memory. It had been wonderful in a kinky, extraordinary way. His offer tainted it.

Still, he had a way of looking at her, searching her face with his gaze for long, silent moments, his perusal unnerving her. She fidgeted with her coffee cup.

Finishing his assessment, he backed off a few inches. "I'm sorry. I thought you'd prefer honesty right from the get-go. I'd make a good father, a good husband, and a good son-in-law."

"Gee," she quipped. "What more could a girl ask for?"

He gave her face that consuming scrutiny again. "I take it a girl could ask for a lot more."

Like wild declarations of undying love. But Connor was right; she preferred honesty. If love was nothing more than a lie, what good was it in the long run? The lie always came to light in the end and with a lot more pain attached to it. And he wasn't offering love. "Why did you pick me?"

"Why *not* you?" He pulled his chair closer until only a slight bend of his head would bring his cheek to hers.

"Well . . ." She wouldn't say it. She would not mention her weight or her looks. "You met Trinity first." Which got her point across. Why would he choose her over Trinity?

He smoothed flyaway strands behind her ear, his brief touch sending sparks right through her. Her hair was her second-best feature. It wasn't carrottop red, but a rich ginger that shone with blond highlights after she'd been in the summer sun.

"You're sexier than Trinity."

She snorted. It was very inelegant, but really, sexier than Trinity was going too far. She had more in common with Lisa-the-cuckolded-wife. Trinity oozed sex appeal.

His eyes traveled her face, taking in every feature, almost as if he were memorizing. As if . . . of course, he didn't find her beautiful, it was more like . . . well, she didn't know. She'd never had a man look at her that way.

"What about last night? Don't you think I found you sexy?"

She waved a hand, punctuating with an eye roll. "That wasn't me; that was what we were watching."

He shook his head, one corner of his mouth curving. "It was watching you watch them."

"With another woman, you'd have had the same reaction."

He took her chin in his hand and forced her to look at him. "It was *you*. You got hot. And that made *me* hot."

"But—"

He covered her lips with two fingers. "One more *but* and I'll drag you onto my lap to prove it to you."

She almost asked how, but instead managed to say, "I mean really, be serious—why me? There are plenty of heiresses out there to choose from."

He dropped his hand to the top of hers. "I am serious. Besides making me hot, you don't appear to be shallow."

She really should tell him to stop all the touching. But she didn't. "Don't forget that you like the way I laugh."

"I didn't forget that. Or how good you felt pressed up against me last night. You have passion and sensuality, and there's nothing hotter than sex with a passionate woman."

She laughed, a real laugh, not one of horror or disbelief. His compliments warmed her, made her sit straighter in her chair. God. Was he starting to win her over? "I've never met anyone like you. You just say what you're thinking, don't you, without worrying how the other person is going to judge you."

He leaned back in his chair and spread his hands. "What you see is what you get."

The girls at the next table turned saucer-eyed like one of her little kindergartners. He continued to ignore them. Rather, he didn't even appear to notice them.

What you see is what you get. What Faith saw was extremely appealing. Broad chest with nicely defined muscles tapering down to a hard abdomen showcased by a formfitting polo shirt. She just didn't know that what she saw was the same as what she'd get. With a jolt, she realized she was actually considering his outrageous proposal. "So, I get children and a husband who promises not to wander as long as I have sex with him as often as . . ." She tilted her head. "How often?"

"At least once a day if I'm stressed. It's a good tension reliever." He didn't even crack a smile. "How about you?"

Gee, once a year would be nice. She had low expectations. "I've never really thought about it. But we're talking about the bargain here. Lots of children, no infidelity, as long as there's sex once a day." She started to tingle. "And all you want is to run my father's company."

He didn't address the last comment but went back to the sex issue. "Not just wham-bam sex. Real sex."

She couldn't believe she was having this conversation. She glanced around to see if anyone was listening, but except for the table of young women too far away to eavesdrop, they weren't the center of attention. Far from it, they were just another couple in a crowd talking about sex. "Define *real sex*, please."

His breath whispered across her hair. "Mind-blowing sex. Last night doesn't count since neither of us had an orgasm, but it was a damn good hint of things to come."

She had to swallow and not let her erotic thoughts rule her emotions. "What if you get tired of the same woman every day?"

"We won't get tired if we're willing to try anything. To experiment. To let our inhibitions go and no limits."

His use of "we" was so terribly seductive. She tried to appear unmoved. "Anything? I'm not into bondage or stuff that hurts." She tipped her head one way, then the other. The discussion had become almost a game. Except for the core of heat burgeoning inside her. "Or wife swapping. Or group sex."

"Just the two of us." He stroked her middle finger where her hand lay on the table. "No pain. Only ecstasy."

Her face flushed. "You're too agreeable. I must be missing something here."

He nodded gravely, as if her concerns meant something to him. "Think about it overnight and put any other conditions on it that you want." He was so close, he could have been talking dirty in her ear.

She'd almost lost the ability to think. "I have to give you my answer tomorrow?"

"You can give it to me whenever you're ready." The way he said the word, *it* could mean anything, marriage, an answer.

Or hot, sweaty sex and unbridled passion.

Her throat was completely dry. "You're too accommodating. There's a catch here. I know it."

He picked up her hand and threaded his fingers through hers. "If you think I haven't kept my part of the bargain, divorce me."

"You'd still get half of everything I have. California's a community-property state, remember?" She pulled her hand away, clasping both on her lap. Away from his magnetic pull.

"Draw up a prenuptial agreement. If I violate any of the conditions, I get nothing, not even a part of your father's company, and you get a divorce free and clear. Except for one thing." He put an arm along the back of her chair, casual. His tone, however, was anything but. "If we have children, you can't stop me from seeing them. I'm not going to father a child and walk away as if he or she doesn't exist."

It was the one thing she couldn't have predicted. An alimony payment, part of the company, but not simply that he would want to see his kids. "That's all? No cash settlement?"

He shook his head. "No cash. Will you think about my proposition?" He uttered the question in a husky tone, just the way he'd sounded last night. He had such a voice, such a way of looking at a woman. He'd get whatever he wanted from her, no strings attached, if she wasn't careful.

She worried her bottom lip. "What if you're planning to bump me off before I get a divorce or have children?" She had to be realistic; she didn't even know the man. Not one bit. Oh, he felt good wrapped around her body, and he was a great kisser, but he wanted something from her that required far more data.

"You can add that to the prenuptial agreement. In the event of your death, under any circumstances, I get nothing."

They were talking about her life, and her demise, as if it were just a mark in her grade book. Or maybe he was merely making a point that she didn't have anything to worry about.

He'd almost given her all the good cards to play with. "You know, I don't think you're getting anything out of this."

"Yes, I will. You're going to get your father to make me his successor at Castle Heavy Mining."

"What if he doesn't step down for years? More than fifteen years." Which was the number Connor had quoted in the beginning.

"He doesn't want to wait that long."

True. But she hadn't told Connor that. "How do you know?"

"I work with Lance Green, and Lance likes to talk."

Lance. She'd forgotten Connor worked at Green Industries. She'd had a marriage offer, from Trinity's brother, one she'd put out of her mind. Lance thought it was a good idea to merge romantically, but Faith suspected marriage wasn't the only merger he wanted. Green was a major contractor for Castle, exclusively providing some of the machined components for the multimillion-dollar mining equipment her father's company manufactured.

If Lance had been as honest about his intentions as Connor, would it have made a difference?

No. Lance oozed false charm. She hadn't liked him even when they were kids. In his marriage attempt, he'd made the moves on her, but she couldn't imagine letting him touch her. Ever. Not to mention having a child by him. She'd never figured out how he and Trinity could have sprung from the same gene pool.

Connor was nothing like Lance. He was certainly charming, but oddly sincere. His every compliment seemed to be genuine, meant especially for her. He made her believe that once he gave his word, he wouldn't break it. Maybe it was the intensity of his gaze. Liars couldn't look you in the eye when they lied.

Yet there was one big problem. "Daddy does want to retire, and he is looking for a trustworthy replacement. But he won't pick you because he'll believe you married me for my money."

"Your part of the bargain is to convince him to choose me."

Only Connor would be able to convince her father. He'd have to prove he was worthy, an impossible task with such a huge strike against him right from the get-go.

She shook her head and murmured to herself, "This just seems so wrong." Yet last night he'd seemed so right.

"Get to know me better before you decide. Have dinner with me tomorrow night."

"I don't know."

"Look at me, Faith."

He reached out to tip her chin when she didn't respond. "I'm not out to hurt you or take advantage of you. This will be good for both of us. All I want you to do is think about it and have dinner with me tomorrow night."

"And what will you do if I decide not to agree to your offer? Scope out another—" She'd almost uttered it. *Scope out another frumpy heiress.*

"I haven't asked anyone else what I'm asking you. And if you say no, I *won't* ask anyone else."

She looked at him, enthralled by his words' allure. "Why?"

"You're not like the rest of the women I've met at all the parties Trinity's taken me to. I intend to pledge myself to the woman I marry, even if what I'm proposing sounds more like a business deal than a marital match. And I wouldn't pledge myself to any one of them. Not even Trinity."

She felt his pull. That deep gaze taking in her every variation of expression. His eyes were dark and smoky, and his voice sincere in its urgency. If he was a liar, he was good.

Faith stared at the table, picking out each individual scratch and mar on the surface.

"Dinner tomorrow night and you can ask me anything you want," the object of her musings cajoled one more time.

"Just dinner?"

"Dinner. And questions. And anything else you want."

Another kiss? No. That would further screw up her faculties. That they *were* screwed up was evident in the fact that she was seriously considering his proposition. Yet she owed herself this chance. She wanted no regrets. Twenty years from now, she didn't want to be alone and childless, wishing she'd thought it over before she said no. "All right. Dinner."

She was twenty-nine. Her biological clock was tick-tick-ticking like a time bomb. She didn't have any viable marriage prospects on the horizon. She needed to hold her own children in her arms, carry them in her womb, but she wouldn't choose the single-mother route. Besides her own conviction that a child needed two parents, her father would have heart palpitations.

But how would he react if she told him she wanted to marry a fortune hunter?

STEP two of his plan had been achieved. Faith would have dinner with him. And by the end of their evening, step three, acceptance, would be in effect. He should be triumphant.

Instead, the moisture clouding her eyes had burned a hole clear through his gut and out the other side. He'd wanted to gather her close, tease the hair at her nape with his lips, and *show* her how hot she made him instead of merely murmuring words.

He'd wanted to take her home with him and plead his case with his hands, mouth, and body. For a moment, he'd desired her sweet, succulent pussy more than her father's firm. But sanity returned.

He had a goal. He didn't want to end up like his father, where the only person on the face of the planet who even knew he'd existed was Connor himself. Connor wanted his children to have what he'd never had, a family legacy, bred into them, part of them, something that would live from generation to generation, the glue that bound them all together.

It was the one thing he'd learned to appreciate almost as soon as he started work at Green Industries six months ago, the family atmosphere. He wanted it for himself and his children, his family. At thirty-four it was time to start that family, and he wasn't adverse to marrying into someone else's legacy. In the end, he would make it his own. While he'd first thought of Trinity, he'd soon realized she wasn't the woman for him and Green Industries wasn't the company. Lance Green was next in line to take over the helm, and Connor had quickly discovered that Lance's decision-making abilities sucked. Connor didn't have an ounce of respect for the man. In addition, Green was a stagnant company, with Herman Green unwilling to consider its health or growth potential.

Jarvis Castle was a whole different ball game. Connor had met him several times, found he had a keen mind, and in his tenure as chairman, he'd tripled his company's margins. In Connor's research on the company, which included many a conversation at the country club events to which Trinity dragged him, he came to realize that Jarvis Castle didn't find his pool of relatives to be adequate to handle the job of running the show.

And his daughter needed a husband to start the family she wanted badly. With every word Trinity said about Faith and the company information Connor found on the Internet, he knew Faith was the right woman and Castle Heavy Mining the right legacy.

The prenuptial wouldn't prove a problem. He had no intention of violating their agreement. Besides, after the way she'd reacted last night, he was sure that with encouragement, Faith would give him everything he needed.

Setting her passion completely free would be his pleasure.

3

"TRINITY, can I ask you a really important question?"

The phone crackled with a long pause. "No."

"Tri-in."

"Well, don't *ask* if you can ask me; just ask."

Sitting on the bed, Faith pulled her knees to her chest. She lived with her father, and after leaving Connor an hour ago, she'd snuck upstairs to her own suite of rooms. The house was so big, she barely saw her father if she didn't go looking for him, but tonight, she'd intentionally avoided him as if he might see something of her strange date with Connor written on her face.

Thank God Trinity couldn't see her face, either. "Are you sure you don't want to have an affair with Connor Kingston?"

"I was kidding about that, silly. You know Daddy would have conniptions." Trinity sighed. "Besides, Connor didn't ask."

Oh. "I'm sorry. Do you feel bad about that?"

Trinity laughed with a perfect musical note. Faith wondered how hers compared in Connor's mind.

"Faith, hon, he's not interested. My ego's over it. Plus, he's a total commitment type. He takes his job so *seriously*. I once asked him to escort me to an afternoon gallery showing, and he said he had a report due. I offered to ask Daddy to give him extra time, and he looked at me as if my hair were askew."

Trinity didn't value his dedication. Faith found it another thing to admire about the man. She was finding too many things to appreciate. "Your hair is never askew," was all she said.

"Why all these questions, as if I didn't know?"

Faith bit her lip and said a thank you prayer for the telephone's invention. Trinity wouldn't be able to see the flush on her cheeks. "He took me out for coffee tonight."

"Aha. I knew it." Faith could picture Trinity's happy dance. "I wasn't fibbing when I said he wanted to meet you. And I saw all those sparks flying when you shook hands and your eyes met and angels sang."

"Oh, quit, will you?" She didn't know about angels singing, but sparks had certainly flown later in the garden. She didn't mention that, though. Despite all the glib talk about passion, she and Trinity didn't get into sexual details. Not that Faith had a lot of sexual details to share.

"You weren't matchmaking, were you?" *Matchmaking* was the polite word. She wanted to make sure Trinity hadn't painted her as a hopeless basket case whose friend had to find her a date.

"I didn't have to. He soaked up everything I said like SpongeBob. He's perfect for you. He's so intense, and you're so . . . intense." Obviously, Trinity couldn't find another word. "Ooh," she gushed, "I feel like Cinderella's godmother."

"We just had coffee." And he made a marriage proposal, but she wouldn't tell Trinity about that yet. Not until she made her decision. Even then, the story would be a much-edited version.

"Did he ask you out again?"

"Dinner. Tomorrow."

"Yippee." Trinity clapped her hands in the background and dropped the phone. "Oops. Sorry."

"So I wouldn't be stepping on your toes or hurting your feelings if I went out with him?"

"You know, Faith, you're the only one of my best friends who would even bother to ask."

Faith took that as the highest compliment. "Thank you."

"Hmm. Does this mean he can't squire me around when all my other dates fall through? I mean, he really is so convenient."

"It's just dinner, Trinity. He might not ask me out again." The white lie bothered her only a bit. Honestly, she hadn't said yes to anything Connor proposed. Yet.

"Perish the thought. I'll find someone else. There's that delicious engineer down in Quality Control at the plant. He's always fiddling with test equipment when I walk through so I *know* what he can do with his hands." And Trinity was off making plans for Mr. Quality Control, though Faith often wondered, despite Trinity's talk of unbridled passion, if her friend was a lot more talk than action. She just never seemed serious about anyone.

Still, Faith offered up a prayer of thanks that her friend didn't want Connor Kingston, because he might very well be absolutely perfect for what *Faith* wanted from him.

HE took her to a semicasual Italian place with mood lighting, candles scenting the air, quiet conversation around them, and an unobtrusive waiter who seemed to appear only when they needed something.

The food was good, and she was glad Connor hadn't tried to impress her with a more showy setting.

"Would you like to go dancing at a club?" Connor asked.

Their dinner plates had long since been cleared away, and Faith had run out of questions. "I don't dance."

Connor smiled reassuringly. "Neither do I. But you don't have to know how to dance at most of these places. It's just a matter of shuffling your feet."

His arms would be around her, which would completely muddle her senses.

"Let's just go for a nightcap," he coaxed.

His marriage proposal didn't seem to have a hitch, he hadn't hesitated answering any of her questions, nor was she normally a distrusting person. Yet what he proposed was so . . . out there.

"I'm sure by the time we get to the nightclub, you'll have another question or two in mind."

She'd asked him everything she could think of. He had no family, and after his father's death, he'd gone through several foster homes. He'd graduated from high school, supported himself through junior college, then miracle of miracles, he'd won a college scholarship through the fast-food chain he worked for. University, a job in finance at some small manufacturing company in Silicon Valley, then the move to Green Industries.

She felt like she'd gotten a resume for a potential employee. How would he handle something more personal? She thought about asking if he'd ever been in love, but she didn't want to know. Their arrangement didn't involve love. She chose something entirely different. "What about venereal diseases?"

He laughed, as if he could actually trace her thought patterns from his suggestion of a nightcap to her question about STDs. The deep tenor affected her physically, hitting a soft spot around her heart and deep in her belly.

"Not that I know of. But I'll take all the tests you want."

"You're too agreeable."

"I'm determined." He dropped his voice. "I'll make it good for you, Faith."

That could mean a lot of things. Sex. Marriage. Childbearing. Life. "All right. A drink. But only one." She glanced at her watch. "I have to be up early for school."

He took her to the Bankers Club, which was loud but fairly tame. The music was eighties and nineties. A few dancers swayed on the dance floor, but most of the customers clustered around tables, drinking, laughing, and, Faith was sure, trying to score.

A booth freed up just as they were passing. Connor guided Faith into the seat, and a waitress stopped by promptly. Faith didn't have any illusions. The young woman had made a beeline for Connor, and her gaze never once touched on his "date."

"What do you want, sweetheart?"

Faith almost looked around as if Connor were addressing someone else. He stroked her knuckles with his thumb.

An obvious caress for the waitress's benefit, yet Faith still melted beneath the attention. "White wine is fine."

"What kind?" the waitress asked. "We have—"

Faith cut her off. "Just the house chardonnay." Connor had paid for dinner, and though they hadn't gone to the fanciest place in town, the bill would still have been quite a sum.

Connor ordered the same, then waited for the girl to leave. "I'm not destitute. You don't have to watch pennies for me."

"I wasn't."

He drew her hand to his lips and kissed her fingers lightly. "You were. It's nice. But I don't need your money. When we're married, I don't intend to sponge off you. I'll do a good job, and your father will pay me a decent salary."

"You mean *if* we get married." She shrugged, partly to keep him from assuming too much, partly to prove to herself that his touch didn't have an effect on her. "I'm not even thinking along those lines yet. I'm still getting to know you."

He sidled closer in the booth and put his arm around her.

She'd worn a different yet still slimming skirt, this one a jean-style with snaps down the front, accompanied by another of her formfitting sweaters. She felt good, almost attractive, especially when his gaze caressed her as it did now.

He put his mouth to her hair. "You know I can give you whatever you need." Then he nosed aside the strands and licked the shell of her ear.

A shiver shimmied down her legs. His breath and his lips made her squirm on the seat.

She pushed him away, which didn't amount to more than a few inches. "I can't think when you're doing that."

He opened his mouth, but the waitress's arrival with their drinks interrupted whatever he'd been about to say.

If Faith wasn't careful, he'd seduce her into doing whatever he wanted without any promises. He had charisma that most ordinary women wouldn't be able to withstand. And Faith was very ordinary. She hadn't dated much in the last year. Sex was even longer. Connor touched on all her needs. He knew it, too.

Alone again, he snuggled her into his embrace. "Next question, please. Do you want me to have a sperm count test?"

She couldn't help but smile. He was dogged, while at the same time teasing and putting her at ease. There was something about him that gave her the courage to step beyond her limits. That made her *want* to. What could she say to shock him?

"I'd rather know your measurements. Circumference and length." Her cheeks flamed at her temerity. She shocked herself more than him.

He grinned. When he laughed, he was scrumptious. When he smiled, he stopped her heart. But seeing that devilish grin, she was in danger of falling for his bullshit hook, line, and sinker.

"You want erect length or nonerect?"

She wasn't a sexual banterer for fear of sounding inept, but she liked how he made her feel—free to say or do anything. Being with him was incredibly liberating and unbelievably erotic. She let her fears go. "Erect is the only thing that counts."

"A touch is worth a thousand words." Before she realized his intention, he'd pulled her hand beneath the table and caressed his length with her palm. Up, down, the action hidden from the bar at large by the booth's white tablecloth. He was magnificent, ready to burst through his pants. For her. The touch took forever. Steel against her skin, the scent of male arousal swirling up to fog her mind. Her breath caught in her throat, and his gaze on her darkened to the night sky without a speck of moonlight to soften it.

"Big enough?"

She could only nod. He actually wanted her. The idea was amazing and new. And wonderful.

"I'm glad you approve." He moved his hand to her thigh, stroking up beneath her skirt. One snap popped all on its own.

She felt him throb beneath her hand on his crotch. He pulled her closer still, nuzzling her ear again, driving her absolutely mad even before he whispered, "Go into the bathroom and take off your panties."

She blinked. He robbed her of speech. Which didn't seem to matter one whit, since her thoughts were written on her face.

"I know you're wearing panties. It wouldn't occur to you not to wear them." He pushed gently, steering her out the other side of the booth.

She couldn't. She shouldn't. Yet she wanted to do exactly what he suggested more than anything in her entire life.

In the restroom, she splashed cold water on her face, not caring about her makeup. She dabbed dry, patting away the mascara smudges, and didn't bother to reapply her blusher. Her cheeks were stained with natural color. Embarrassment, but more than that, sexual heat suffused her skin, giving her a sexy glow.

Why, she almost looked beautiful.

In the stall, she rolled her panties down her bare legs and slipped them off over her sandals. As an afterthought, she unfastened her sweater and removed her bra. When she redid the buttons, she left the top two open, revealing ample bare flesh.

She'd been about to shove the utilitarian undies in her purse, but instead, she threw them in the trash, covering the offending articles with a paper towel. Made of too much white cotton, there wasn't a thing alluring about her underwear.

Whether she decided to marry Connor or not, he'd at least released her awareness of her own sensuality. She closed her eyes, remembering the touch of his tongue on her ear.

Maybe she'd have sex with him tonight. Faith had the feeling he'd be more than up to the idea of letting her test out the merchandise before making her decision.

Gazing at herself in the restroom mirror, it seemed like a great idea, but once back in the bar, sliding across the seat to his side, her confidence deserted her. Though her naked sex felt pouty beneath her skirt, and the soft sweater caressed her breasts, she'd lost some essential ingredient she'd felt in the ladies' room. Now, she couldn't utter a single sexual innuendo.

His gaze dropped to her burgeoning nipples. "You take direction well, then you improvise. I like it." His voice was husky and low with sexual intent. Thank God *he* had every intention of seducing *her*.

And Faith would let him.

When he put his hand on her thigh and slid under her skirt, she was powerless to stop him. She didn't even want to try. His touch brought her fantasies to life.

She held her breath as his fingers brushed her curls. Then he stopped.

She didn't realize she'd closed her eyes until he whispered, "Look at me."

He had the most mesmerizing gaze, like the snake oil salesman who got you to buy every last one of his bottles of so-called medicine. Closing his hand around her thigh, Connor guided her leg over the top of his knee, holding her open for his touch.

"Someone will see," she whispered. Protesting seemed the right thing to do, but she prayed he wouldn't stop.

"No one's noticing. Besides, the tablecloth is covering us." He leaned forward to put one elbow on the table and fully hide whatever he planned to do beneath the white cloth.

"It's kinky doing it here, though."

He grinned. "Yeah." Then he nuzzled her hair. "Tell me to stop, and I will. But you'll never know how good it could feel."

If she said yes, she couldn't later claim he'd gone too far. If she said no, he'd remove that exquisite touch from her thigh. Better to say nothing and let him convince her with more action.

"No other people, no wife swapping, no orgies, no pain, no humiliation," he listed. "But everything else goes." He lightly brushed her curls again, then stroked her thigh for a gentle probe against her flesh that didn't quite penetrate inside her cleft to her clitoris. But the promise was there.

She was wet, hot. Her breath seemed trapped in her chest, her nipples ached, and her fingers curled against the seat. Bearing down, she pushed against him, begging him without words, almost trying to force him to touch the hard bead of her clit.

With the hand not occupied beneath the table, he raised her wineglass. "Take a sip."

She did. He turned the glass and drank from the same spot, the wine glistening on his lips. She watched the slight bob of his Adam's apple as he swallowed.

"Say yes, Faith, and I'll give you anything you want." His fingers teased, flirted with her. "Everything you want."

"Not here," she managed to whisper.

While the kinkiness of letting him finger her in a bar raised her temperature to near combustion, she couldn't actually let him. If she did, she'd be under his complete control.

He stilled, cupping her thigh. "Are you starting to see how tantalizing and exciting we can be together?"

Unbearably tantalizing. But was it what they'd bargained for? "This is just supposed to be a business proposition. You give me babies, and I give you my father's company."

"That's before you asked for fidelity, Faith. For that, you have to give me more. All your sensuality and passion. All those kinky fantasies running around in your mind."

"I don't have kinky fantasies."

He backed off a taste and stared at her knowingly. "I saw how you watched that couple in the garden. I felt the heat between your legs. I tasted your mouth. You've got some pretty damn kinky fantasies, Faith, and if you want fidelity, then I want those fantasies."

She shivered at the thought. "Like what?"

"Like my hand surreptitiously up your skirt in a bar. Like taking advantage of a closet at the country club. Or an empty locker room. Like doing anything I suggest wherever we are because you're so fucking hot to get me inside you."

She did burn up then. If he'd had his hand two inches closer, she'd have come all over his fingers.

"I want it hot," he whispered, "I want it fun, and I want it a tad kinky. It'll be the best, Faith. I promise. Lust like you've never known it."

She could barely find her voice. "Lust dies eventually."

"You're wrong." His eyes were deep, dark, mesmerizing pools. "Love is what dies. It's messy and people get hurt. But lust"—he swooped in and took her with a quick hard kiss—"lust can last as long as we're both willing to try anything."

She wasn't so sure about that. Lust was like a drug. You got high, then *bam*, you hit bottom in the morning. Still, she'd never felt *this* with anyone. Ever. He might be right. For them, love would only complicate things. He obviously wasn't going to fall in love with her; she would almost bet he didn't even believe in love. But what he offered . . . maybe, just maybe it was something better. "No wife swapping, no orgies, no pain?"

"I'm the only one who'll touch you, and you're the only one who'll touch me. And I swear you'll love everything I do to you." He squeezed her thigh intimately. "Say yes."

"Yes." She whispered the word, afraid of it, exhilarated by it. And totally surprised by it.

He grabbed her hand, moved so that her leg fell from his, then pulled her out of the booth. She'd forgotten about the popped button of her skirt until she stood, but holding his hand, she couldn't bend down to fasten it.

"Are we going to your place?" He'd make love to her there.

He didn't answer, letting her go long enough to throw a few bills on the table. Sitting next to him, she'd forgotten how tall he was. Standing, the top of her head came to his shoulder. She felt small and engulfed.

God, had she just agreed to marry this man?

He'd parked in the back beneath a burned-out light. Pebbles crunched beneath her feet. The jean skirt roughly caressed her bare bottom, and her breasts bounced freely against her sweater, sweeping her nipples to hard nubs. Heat rushed between her legs. Connor unlocked the car door, helped her inside, then shut her in. If he didn't touch her again soon, she'd hyperventilate.

But he was there, and before he started the engine, he leaned over and took her mouth in a hungry kiss. A kiss even hotter than that night at the country club. His lips and tongue consumed her; the almost brutal taking pushed her head back against the seat. Faith arched into him, rubbed her aching nipples against his chest. Then his hand was between her legs.

He stroked up, parted her expertly, her knees falling open to allow him whatever access he wanted. Then his finger was inside, first one, slipping through all her heat and moisture, then another. She bucked against him, tried to tear her mouth away just so she could breathe. Finally he was on her clitoris, stroking, rubbing, gliding, driving her wild.

He withdrew slowly. Both his mouth and his fingers. "I knew you'd be totally wet, but I had to feel for myself."

She couldn't see his eyes in the darkness of the car's interior, but she could hear the triumph in his voice.

"Take me home with you," she begged.

He slipped loose two more buttons on her sweater, reaching inside to pinch her nipple, then lifted her breast in his hand. "You have gorgeous breasts." He bent, sucked a nipple between his lips, and teased with a soft bite. "And the most succulent nipples. They're like flowers, large and tight and needy."

God, *she* was needy. He didn't need to take her home. He could do her here. In the front seat. Or the back. She didn't care where. She just wanted him between her legs again. Now.

Connor buttoned her sweater, smoothed her skirt, snapping that pesky snap, then straightened in his own seat.

Okay, not here. His apartment. That was a question she'd forgotten to ask—where he lived. "We can go to your place. Now." She felt bold, risky, but she didn't care.

All she could see were his white teeth as he smiled. She felt like a puddle of jelly in the seat, her legs weak.

"Not tonight. We're not going to have sex until we're married." He started the engine.

"What?" She almost shrieked, then put a hand over her mouth when the sound echoed through the car.

"We're waiting for our wedding night."

"You're joking. Right?" *Please say you're joking.* Her body was on fire.

He looked at her, one side of his mouth higher than the other, revealing slightly more teeth. "Back in the bar, you said yes to marrying me when I had my hand between your legs and your thigh on my major hard-on, so it's prudent to wait until you've had a chance to think it over. Just like the three-day law when buying a car. You can change your mind for whatever reason."

"Fine. I can change my mind for whatever reason." She pulled in a deep breath, huffed it back out, and said exactly what she wanted. "But there's no reason you can't take me home and screw the hell out of me."

He chuckled. "Why Miss Castle, I'm shocked."

So was she. "I never say things like that."

"I know you well enough to be aware of that."

"But you've left me very frustrated."

He reached out to stroke a finger down her cheek. "I don't think you have any idea how frustrated *I* am."

"Hah," she puffed out.

He grabbed her hand and pressed her palm against his erection. The front of his slacks was damp.

"I didn't exactly cream in my pants, but I was this close." He gestured with his finger and thumb a half inch apart. "I'd like nothing better than to pull you on top of me right here, sink inside you, and come until I don't even know who I am anymore." He closed his eyes as she pressed her advantage on his pants. "I won't risk starting our child before the wedding."

Our child. It sounded so . . . beautiful on his lips. Faith stopped fighting him. "I don't think I'm going to change my mind. I meant it, even if your hand was up my skirt."

He sighed, a long breath tense with his frustration, yet rife with acceptance. "I'll take you to *your* home. But I'll call you before I go to sleep. We'll see what you think then."

She didn't think her answer would be any different.

She wanted to give Connor all her fantasies.

And she wanted a freaking orgasm, dammit.

HE wanted her so damn badly, he'd almost jacked off in the car on the way home just to relieve the excruciating throb in his balls. Coming inside her would have eased the sexual tension riding him, but he didn't want her accusing him of taking advantage and changing her mind in the morning because her thought processes were messed up when she agreed to his offer.

Problem was his own thinking was screwed up.

In every way, Faith Castle was far more woman than he'd ever imagined. Only time would tell whether that was a good or a bad thing for him.

4

LIGHTS blazed in her father's office as Faith entered the front hall. A crystal chandelier illuminated the marble floor and gleamed on the polished brass handrails of the staircase leading to the second floor. The house was far too large for two people, ostentatious in fact, but it had been in the family since the beginning of the last century.

Since her father hadn't arrived home from the plant by the time she left for her date with Connor, Faith had written him a note so he wouldn't worry. During the drive home, she'd prayed he'd already retired for the evening. She wanted at least one night to phrase in her mind how to tell him about Connor.

"Sweetheart, is that you?"

"Yes, Daddy." Faith stopped on the threshold of his inner sanctum. She wore neither panties nor bra. She *really* wished her father had gone to bed, but now, she'd have to tough it out.

He smiled at her, then waved her in. "So, you had a date. Tell me all about this new young man you've met."

With her desire banked, her brain had begun functioning again. She could view his proposition rationally. She appreciated that

Connor was honest about what he wanted. No one else had been. With another man, Lance for instance, she might be lied to, cheated on, and ignored once a baby came. That was another thing. She liked the way Connor thought about children: They weren't just something he'd give her. He actually wanted them. In short, Connor offered everything she could hope for. Except love. She could live without that.

Now, she just had to convince her father.

If she blew the date off tonight as nothing, she couldn't very well come back tomorrow and say she'd found the man she wanted to marry. "He's nice, Daddy. I think you'll like him."

Her father picked up his snifter of brandy, rounded the edge of his desk, and sat in his favorite chair. The fireplace was unlit, but in the wintertime, not that the San Francisco Bay Area had extremely cold winters, he'd get a fire going and sip his usual brandy before going to bed.

"Sit. Tell me all about him."

What was she supposed to say? *He wants to marry me so he can get a foothold in your company, and I'm so desperate for what he offers that I've agreed to everything he wants.*

Settling in the chair opposite him, she took the few spare moments to consider how to answer her father.

"How did you meet him?"

"Trinity introduced us at a country club party." She didn't say that had been on Saturday.

The lamp beside her father gleamed on his white hair. She adored him. She couldn't bear hurting him. He believed she deserved a marriage such as he'd had with her mother. Mutual love and affection. Total happiness and commitment.

But her mother had died. Maybe the best things in life weren't meant to last forever.

"You'll think this is fast and very weird, but he's asked me to marry him." She held her breath a moment, staring at the Persian carpet, then she raised her gaze to his. "I said yes."

Silence. Her father found love later in life with her mother, who was ten years younger than him. He'd been thirty-eight when Faith was born, and this year, he turned sixty-eight. Running Castle Heavy Mining was a monstrous task even for a young man, and her father wasn't young anymore.

In the last few seconds between them, he'd aged another five years. "Is this some sort of joke?"

"I'm not being funny. His name is Connor Kingston, and he wants to marry me. And I want children."

He rose abruptly, droplets of brandy spilling from his glass. His back to her, he said, "You've got your whole life ahead of you."

"I'm almost thirty."

"This is the first I've heard you mention the man." He turned to her. "How long have you known him?"

"Since Saturday." She sounded timid and hated it. The only way she could convince her father to take Connor into the company was if she remained strong. She mentally firmed up her spine. "That's long enough to know we have the same goals. Family."

He laughed without a single thread of humor in it. "I've never known you to be so stupid, Faith. He's after your money." He stared her down with a hard gaze foreign to his nature.

She winced, but didn't try to deny the truth of it. "Yes. And I don't care. This is more like a business arrangement."

He shook his head, his hair glimmering white and yellow in the different shafts of light. Once tall, he now stooped. Formerly slender, he now appeared gaunt and much too thin. She'd seen the changes, but ignored the implication. She didn't want to think of him as old, but so many creases lined his face, and age spots dotted his forehead, his hands, and his throat.

His usually fond gaze was dark with antagonism. "What's happened? Something must have made you lose your mind."

She set her feet flat on the floor and folded her hands in her lap, like a witness on the stand coming up against the tough questions. "I want a child. I've always wanted children. And I'm not willing to wait until someone comes along with whom I *might* fall in love and who *might* fall in love with me. Connor is willing to give me children now."

Her father narrowed his once-blue eyes, now faded to gray. "And what does he want in return?"

Her natural urge was to stare at the carpet again and whisper. Instead, she met his gaze, and her voice when it came was harder, stronger, and louder. "He wants to work for you. He wants you to teach him the ropes and let him step into your shoes, to be the chairman when you retire."

He slammed his delicate glass down on the sideboard, and splashed more brandy into the dregs of his previous drink.

"No." He didn't even face her when he refused.

"At least talk to Connor about it."

"How the hell could you even tell if this man you've known only *two* days is the right man? If he's any better than the possible replacements I already have?"

"You haven't got anyone."

Oddly enough, Faith didn't know Preston or her other family members well. Her father had never approved much of his cousins. Though the two family branches ran the company jointly, the *Castle* side held controlling interest, and since her father was chairman, he would decide who took over. It might actually be in her favor that he didn't approve of Preston Tybrook or anyone else. Here was his chance to keep the company on his side.

"You don't like Preston," she pushed on, "and you haven't found anyone else. You've told me that over and over."

He didn't bother to argue. "The answer is no."

Her stomach crimped, but she voiced her thoughts anyway. "You're not getting any younger, Daddy."

"Don't you think I know that? Don't you think I worry day and night about how you'll fare when I'm gone? You need someone to take care of you. I've hoped and prayed you'd find a man worthy of you, a man worthy of carrying on Castle for me."

"I don't need anyone to take care of me." It was so like him to treat her as a child. "But I have found a worthy man."

He threw his arm wide, brandy sloshing over the glass rim. "That is the most ridiculous thing I have *ever* heard you say. And you're the least ridiculous person I know." He brushed the droplets from his hand. "Tell me this is a farce, Faith."

"It's not." She rose from her chair. "You haven't approved of anyone I brought home." There hadn't been many. "You're making it impossible for me to get what I want. Children."

"I know you want a family, but I'm trying to protect you from getting hurt later on."

"You scare men off." She felt guilty putting the blame all on him, but she had to convince him. "I'm almost thirty years old. I can make a good decision. You taught me that."

"Honey." He used only that one word, pleading.

"I can't be hurt if I'm only in it for one thing, Daddy. A family. If you won't at least meet him and consider it, for me, then we don't have anything else to say to each other."

He took her arm gently, the way she'd hoped he would.

"There will be someone for you, Faith. I promise."

"What if there isn't? What if this is my last chance?" The thought terrified her. Life without babies would be unbearable.

He trailed a finger down her cheek, smiling at her as if she were ten years old and asking for a pony. "Sweetheart, you have years to find the right man."

From the vantage point of his age, maybe he thought she did. But in childbearing years, she was almost a has-been. "Daddy, please do this for me. I can't wait any longer." She had serious doubts love would happen for her the way he hoped. "Talk to Connor. Give him a chance. Give *me* a chance."

After a long moment, his eyes flicking from her face to the fireplace to somewhere deep inside his own mind, he offered a concession. "Let's talk. Who is he? How old? Is he just some no-good bum who's looking for an easy score?"

She winced but tried to hide it. "No. He went to San Jose State on a scholarship, and he's in his early thirties. He works for Hermie. Why don't you ask him about Connor?"

Something changed on her father's face. Someone who didn't know him as well as she did might have missed the subtle tensing of his jaw. "How long has he worked for Hermie?"

"I'm not sure. He's in the finance department. Budgets." Wasn't that what Connor had told her? She couldn't remember for sure. His work history had concerned her far less than the fact that he was an orphan with limited opportunity who'd gone on to graduate with an MBA. A pretty impressive feat.

"I think I've met him."

She held her breath. Was that good or bad?

Her father didn't say, staring at the unlit fireplace for a long moment. "Who are his people?" His softened voice lacked a certain amount of attention, as if he asked one thing but his mind was working on something else entirely.

"He doesn't have any people."

"Everyone has people." Still that distracted tone, the faraway look centered on something beyond the andirons.

"His parents died when he was young. He has no relatives. He's alone in the world."

He didn't comment. Faith sometimes saw this preoccupied side of her father when business weighed heavily on him. It wasn't his way to tell her all his problems. She knew little about the actual running of the company. She only knew he worried about keeping it healthy once he was gone. And keeping Castle healthy meant finding someone he could trust to run it.

Faith hoped she'd found that someone for him. But neither of them would know unless her father gave Connor a chance.

"Invite him for dinner tomorrow night. I'll talk to him."

She held in her gasp. "Thank you, Daddy." Something was missing, his change of heart too quick. Faith wanted him to take her hands in his and tell her he'd try his best to like Connor.

Instead, her father continued to stare at the fireplace as if it might spontaneously combust into a brilliant blaze.

"I'm going to bed now." She waited.

He merely raised a hand. "Good night, sweetheart."

"I love you, Daddy."

"Love you, too."

Faith waited a few moments out in the hall. Waited for him to call her back, something, anything.

He didn't. A large hole opened in her chest and engulfed all the euphoria she'd experienced in Connor's arms.

BASTARD. Who the hell did this Connor Kingston think he was? Faith was so naïve, so trusting. She didn't have a clue. No way would Jarvis allow some low-life fortune hunter to use her up, then throw her away like yesterday's garbage. Yet Jarvis had no choice but to agree to talk with the upstart. He had to at least look as if he'd done due diligence in the matter.

Thank God she hadn't said she was in love with the man. There was hope he could get her out of Kingston's scheme emotionally unscathed.

Jarvis set his brandy snifter down and laced his fingers behind his back. Thinking, he rocked back and forth, heel to toe. He'd met the man at a few meetings with Hermie, and while Kingston seemed capable and talked a good line, in the end, he was just another number cruncher. Nothing impressive.

Jarvis had known Hermie since their college days. He'd even loaned the cash to start Green Industries. Castle manufactured custom heavy mining equipment, blasthole drills, excavators, feeder-breakers, loaders, crushers, etc. Green Industries machined, die-cast, and plated many of the component parts. The partnership had worked well for forty-five years.

They'd also shared the grieving when their respective spouses passed on. Faith's mother had died in a car accident almost twenty years ago, and Hermie lost his wife to cancer ten years later. There was nothing that bonded two people together quite so much as a terrible loss.

His dream had been to unite the companies more permanently. He and Hermie had hoped that Lance would one day marry Faith.

Jarvis didn't want Preston Tybrook getting even a ghost of a chance to sell out or bring in outside investors. Castle Heavy Mining had been started by their great-grandfathers, two brothers, one hundred and fifty years ago. Preston's side had bred prodigiously, diluting the family name until there wasn't a real Castle left amongst them. Jarvis's side had kept things more pure, and maintained control of the company with the largest block of voting shares. Since Tybrook's daddy, old Rufus, had died twenty years ago, there wasn't a worthy contributor in the bunch. Jarvis was not letting his company be ruined, but God, he was tired of fighting the daily battles. Faith was right—he wasn't getting any younger.

Lance would be the solution, but despite claiming she wanted children and a family, Faith was the marriage holdout. Now there was hope. Jarvis had seen it the minute she'd said Kingston worked for Herman Green. A little compare and contrast might do the trick. Connor Kingston, who had to *marry* into a family business, versus Lance Green, who'd been born to it as his right.

Faith would soon see who was the more worthy once Jarvis pointed it out to her tomorrow night. Faith was the most important thing in the world. Everything Jarvis Castle did was for his daughter and the company.

If she wanted a family that badly, he'd pay for artificial insemination before he'd give her over to a fortune hunter.

"YOU'RE invited for dinner tomorrow night."

Faith lay in her bed, the lights out, the phone tucked close to her ear. Her suite of rooms was on the opposite end of the house from her father's and overlooked the garden. The conversation in the library had doused her earlier fit of desire, but with moonlight falling through the open curtains, silky sheets against her body, and Connor's voice intimately in her ear, passion sizzled once more through her veins.

"Did your father blow a gasket?"

Faith laughed. Her father was one of the most easygoing men she'd ever met. At least most of the time. "He wasn't terribly pleased, but he's willing to give you a chance." He'd been troubled, but what more had she expected? He needed time to digest Connor's proposal just as she had.

She worried her lip between her teeth. "This part is up to you, you know. If you want me, you'll have to impress him."

If you want me. She'd phrased the words deliberately.

Connor gave her exactly what she'd sought. "Oh, I want you, Faith. You felt that tonight. What are you wearing?"

She smiled, like a woman with a secret she'd been dying to share. "Nothing."

"Is that what you usually wear to bed?"

"My usual nightgown is long and flannel." Actually, she had a pair of soft baby dolls, but she wanted Connor to think she was making even bigger changes for him.

"Are you wet for me, too?"

"Yes." After climbing into bed, she'd relived those minutes in the front seat of his car all over again. She'd been wet and flushed waiting for his call.

"Tell me how wet."

His low voice and probing questions only added to her aroused state. "Very, very wet."

"Put your hand between your legs, and tell me more."

A kernel of unease lodged in her chest. She'd never done anything like this before. Let's face it, no one had been interested enough to have phone sex with her. Connor might want a foot in the door of her father's company, but the husky rasp of his voice over the phone seemed genuine. More than just part of a business deal. She wanted this experience despite her fears. Faith stroked down her abdomen and parted her legs.

"How wet?" he whispered.

"It's all over my fingers." She moaned.

"Where are you touching yourself?"

"My clitoris. And now I've got a finger inside." With her eyes closed and his voice inside her head, she could almost believe it was his touch on her. She stretched on the bed.

"How often do you masturbate, Faith?"

Not if, but how often. "Once a week," she told him.

"That's all?" His voice rose slightly with incredulity.

"How often do *you* do it? Wait, don't tell me, let me guess. At least once a day."

"At the *very* least." He laughed softly. "But not today."

"Oh, you're slipping." Her fingers stopped while they talked, and she rested her hand on her belly.

"I knew it would be better with you." His voice was like honey drizzled over her senses. "Do it with me now."

Yes. She wanted this. If nothing else ever happened between them again, she would have *this*. "Okay."

"That was easy."

"I need to finish what you started tonight," she admitted.

"That's exactly why I started it, so we could do this together." He was so good at seduction, the pure devil of his pitch, the lure in his words.

She wondered if he was as seduced as she. "What should we do?" She wasn't sure exactly how phone sex worked.

He sighed, a long, guttural pleasure sound. "How do you want me to touch myself? How hard? How fast? Tell me what you'd want me to be doing to you if I was there."

She melted on the inside with everything he asked for, but she wasn't good at this. "You tell me first."

"Take a chance," he seduced with a whisper. "You might like the idea of telling me what to do."

She sounded like an insecure teenager, and that wouldn't do. So she began the way he'd started. "What are you wearing?"

"I'm naked."

"Is your cock hard?" Being a kindergarten teacher, she didn't say the word often, and it felt strange on her lips. Naughty yet tempting.

"Yes, my cock is painfully hard."

"Stroke it." The act of telling him what to do intensified the heat between her legs.

"I've been stroking it all along."

The freedom in being on the other end of the phone suffused her. She could say whatever she wanted without embarrassment. She could become the sexy woman she'd always dreamed of being. She puffed out what she hoped sounded like an indignant breath. "You can only touch yourself when I say it's okay."

"I thought you said you weren't into bondage."

"I'm not. Bondage hurts."

"Sometimes it's just about who's in charge. You're going to love having me do your bidding."

She could learn to crave the power in it, though she could never do it face-to-face. "Do it faster."

"Yes, my little dominatrix."

Her hand rested on her belly. For the moment she wanted to savor the rasp of his breath in her ear. She lowered her voice, trying for husky, sultry. "Do it harder."

He groaned.

She gave him another order. "Now move your hand up to the tip of your cock and work just that."

His breath sighed across the phone. "I think you're much more experienced than I imagined."

"I'm not sheltered, if that's what you mean."

"I am so going to enjoy learning everything about you." Then the sound of his breath shivered down her spine. She spread her legs and delved into her pussy.

"Are you touching yourself, Faith?"

"Yes." She pushed her head into the pillow, her body thrusting against her fingers. "God, yes. It's so good."

"Christ, Faith, you're killing me. Pretend it's real. That I'm touching you and you're touching me."

With her eyes closed, the fingers caressing her clit became his. Thrusting deep, she felt *him* inside her. Her body undulated, begging for more.

She was breathing so hard, it was difficult to talk, yet she took command. It was so easy with the phone between them, and with Connor, she figured she'd have to learn to hold her own.

"Yes," she encouraged, "rub me there. Right there. Don't stop." She circled her clitoris, then moaned and squeezed her eyes so tight she saw stars.

"Come with me, Faith. Now." He growled low, then swore in her ear.

She hit her orgasm, hard, her body jerking and tears leaking from her eyes as he groaned with her and said her name as if it were a prayer.

"Christ." Long moments later, his voice was a lazy, satisfied whisper. "That was good."

It was. Incredible. "I'm not usually like that, telling men what to do."

"I want you to do things out of your norm. Like coming with me on the phone. You haven't done that with anyone, have you?"

"No."

"But you've fantasized about it." As if sure of her, he didn't wait for her answer. "There will be more firsts, Faith. A lot of them. And I swear you'll love every one."

She felt his vow, his sincerity, like a stroke of his hand down her breasts, a promise from his lips to hers.

But exactly how kinky would he want her to get? And how would he handle it if she said no?

*   *   *

SHE was so trusting. And so damn hot. Connor had scorched his fingers touching her in the car and blown sky-high on the phone. Even now, his breathing hadn't returned to normal, yet his limbs felt languid and spent. Ah God, the things he wanted to do with her. Desire for her still eddied through his veins. She'd stepped out of her comfort zone on the phone. Her orgasm had been as much a revelation to her as Connor's had been to him. She was perfect for him. She didn't expect love. There'd never be the ugly, messy emotions that went with it.

Could a man have it all? Wealth, family, security, dreams, and a sexy wife willing to do anything he asked waiting for him at home, all night, every night? Connor had never been so lucky. He'd always had to work hard for everything he wanted.

His father's long-ago voice murmured in his ear. "If you don't ask for the moon, Connor, you can't be disappointed when you don't get it." Dad hadn't asked for anything since the day Connor's mother died, and he'd gotten nothing but two years of endless grieving and an early grave.

Connor had learned you couldn't depend on another person for what you needed. You had to go for it yourself.

FAITH zipped her navy blue dress, fastened pearls at her throat, and stood before the full-length mirror in her bathroom. Did she look like a frump?

Pots of makeup lay strewn over the pink tile vanity. She'd abandoned two fluffy pink towels on the marble floor outside the shower door. In the bedroom, her walk-in closet looked as though a poltergeist had flown through. She wasn't usually so messy, hating to leave a bunch of crap lying around in her wake for Estelle to clean up. She didn't like anyone to think she expected to be treated as if she were a prima donna. Or the daughter of a rich man. Okay, she had to admit she didn't make her king-sized bed, do her own laundry, or clean her bathroom.

She glanced at her watch. Connor would be here in less than a half hour. Her heartbeat seemed to get louder with each minute that ticked by. Yanking off the navy dress, she threw it on the bed and pulled out the black number she'd worn to the country club on Saturday. Maybe Connor wouldn't notice.

What on earth did her clothes matter? They weren't dating.

They were . . . making a pact . . . contemplating parenthood . . . or something. Oh hell, she didn't know what they were doing. She didn't know what *she* was doing. Doubts had assailed her from the moment she woke up this morning. All it took was the light of day to highlight what an idiot she was.

"This is the dumbest thing you have ever done in your entire life," she told her reflection, clothed only in panties, bra, and control-top hosiery. "He doesn't care what you wear; he wants your father's company, and he'll do anything in order to get you to marry him, right down to pretending he finds you attractive."

A huge sigh slipped out, her shoulders sagged, her belly pooched. Oh God. *I can't do this.*

If you don't, you'll never have a baby.

Connor was Mr. Not-Perfect-But-One-Helluva-Good-Bargain. He offered her what she'd always wanted: a family. She liked his honesty. He didn't offer her pretty lies or hopes. He probably had her from the moment he said the only thing he'd never give up was the right to see his children. The statement rang with sincerity. She never imagined she'd fall head over heels with a man head over heels about her, too. Connor promised fidelity, or at the very least, no humiliation. She trusted him simply for the fact that he didn't romance her or offer her the fairy-tale ending. Not to mention that she truly believed he desired her. What more could the woman in the mirror ask for?

She was in the driver's seat. She held all the cards. She pulled all the strings. Gee, how many more clichés could she think of to emphasize that she had the advantage over Connor?

Faith straightened her shoulders, her breasts thrusting up and out, and sucked in her belly. "I want a baby," she told the mirror, "and I'm going to make sure I have one."

The problem was she liked the way Connor made her feel when they were together. What if she started wanting more, some emotion on his part other than lust? She narrowed her eyes at her reflection. *Don't expect anything from him on the emotional front and you'll be fine.*

Pulling the black dress over her head, she slid it down her thighs, smoothing it over her abdomen before she zipped it up. She gave herself a last look in the mirror, and a scolding to stop obsessing about her clothing. It wasn't as if she'd be at the country club.

The doorbell rang just as she started down the stairs from the upper landing. He was early. Butterflies swarmed in her stomach and flew up into her throat. *Come on, Faith, be cool.*

"I'll get it, Archie," she called. She didn't want it to look as though she were making an entrance. And she didn't want to appear that she was flaunting their English butler and their money right in Connor's face.

Then again, she and her father lived in a nine thousand square foot house. She had a suite of rooms all to herself. The painting above the long hall table was a genuine Lord Leighton. The pool was Olympic sized, a Jacuzzi on either end, and the guest cottage out back had three bedrooms. Wasn't this ostentation what Connor was buying into with his sperm?

She pulled on the handle, only it wasn't Connor framed in the doorway. "Lance, what are you doing here?"

"Your father invited me for dinner."

Her father? That double-crossing . . . She had to smile. He'd said he'd meet Connor; he never said he'd do it one-on-one. "Where's Trinity? And your dad?"

Lance crooked a half smile. His mustache twitched over his neatly trimmed goatee. "I don't think they were invited. At least, they didn't mention anything to me."

So that's what her father was up to, offering an alternative to Connor. But Lance was . . . Lance. When they were in their young teens, he'd teased her about her weight. Until Trinity gave him a black eye. He'd never taunted Faith again. Instead, he'd become excessively flattering, yet she recognized the glint in his eye that belied his compliments. At thirty-two, he was handsome in a polished, arrogant sort of way. Tonight he wore a casual jacket and pants with the pleat pressed down each leg. He never had a single dark hair out of place, worked out daily, and followed it up with an hour in the tanning booth. Trinity swore she wouldn't go near a tanning booth in case her skin turned to leather the day after she turned thirty.

"Your dress is lovely. New?"

Right. She lifted the waist of the dress away from her body. "This old thing? No. But thank you so much for the compliment." See, she could be sarcastically gracious, too.

"Lance, so glad you could make it." Coming from his study, her father was more elegantly dressed, in a three-piece suit, than Lance in his casual attire. He held out his hand.

"I wouldn't miss a dinner with just you and Faith. This way I don't have to share the limelight with Dad or Trinity."

Now *that* was the truth. Lance didn't like the word *share*. Ah, but he'd have to share dinner tonight with Connor. Faith wondered if her father had told Lance about that ahead of time.

"Let's go into my study for a drink." Jarvis extended an arm. "That whiskey your father loves, direct from Ireland."

"Can't wait, sir." Lance followed.

Once inside, her father poured two shots of the rich Irish whiskey and a glass of Riesling for Faith. She liked the sweeter wines. With an unobtrusive flick of her wrist, she checked the time. Connor would be here in two minutes. She had the feeling he would show up neither unfashionably early nor fashionably late, but right on time.

Her father fully intended to make him appear the outsider in the small, intimate group.

The bell echoed through the hall. This time she'd have to let Archie get it.

"Ah, there's our other guest." Her father raised his glass, looking first to Lance, then sliding his gaze to Faith. "You know him, Lance. He works for you. Connor . . ." He snapped his fingers and groaned. "Faith, what was his last name?"

"Kingston," Lance supplied, a congenial smile on his lips, and a semimalicious sparkle in his eye that confirmed he'd known Connor was also a guest tonight. "Yes, he works for me."

"He works for Green Industries," Faith couldn't help amending.

Lance smiled. "That's what I said."

Okay, so the name of the game for the evening would be "put Connor in his place."

Archie led him in, then departed with an inclination of his head. Unlike her father's, Connor's suit didn't cost a thousand dollars or bear a designer label, but he looked scrumptious.

Faith took his hand as if he were truly a beau she couldn't wait to introduce. Warm fingers closed around her own and squeezed. She looked up, up, up into his smoky eyes, and he gave her a killer smile.

"Daddy, this is Connor."

"Mr. Castle. I believe we've met." They shook hands.

"Please, call me Jarvis. You already know Lance Green."

Lance didn't offer his hand. And when her father poured a drink for Connor, she noticed it wasn't the aged whiskey, but something out of the decanter. He never kept anything good in the decanter in case Archie got into it, at least that's what her father claimed. Then again, Archie knew where the good bottles were. In ways, her father was an anachronism, viewing life and servants with an attitude born in another century.

Clearly, he viewed Connor with the same attitude, and really, Faith couldn't blame him. After all, she'd told him Connor was a fortune hunter. But her father had gone one step further and invited Lance over to help twist the knife.

"So, remind me, what do you do over at Green?" Her father tapped his head. "Getting forgetful, you know." Sure. He wanted to show Connor their previous meetings hadn't made an impression on him.

"Budgets," Lance answered for Connor. "Kingston rides us about wasting pencils and making too many copies of things he doesn't think we need to make copies of in the first place."

She expected Connor to slam Lance down, but Connor merely smiled. "Don't forget about the shredding cost when we have to destroy all those extra copies we don't need."

They went on in that vein for what seemed like an interminable amount of time but was probably only ten minutes, until Archie poked his bald head through the open door and announced dinner. Thank God.

Lance led the way to the dining room, showing that he knew where it was when obviously Connor didn't. Men. She thought they were supposed to compare the size of their penises, not play table manner games.

Connor took her wrist before she made it out the study door.

"Did you do that on purpose?" he whispered.

"Do what?" Allow her father and Lance to humiliate him?

"Wear that dress."

She didn't even have the urge to dissemble the way she had with Lance. "I know I wore it at the country club, but—"

He put his fingers to her lips and blew her circuits. "And you thought you'd drive me crazy by wearing it again tonight and reminding me how close I was to pulling it to your waist and taking you right there in the garden."

He didn't blow just a few circuits with that; he stole her ability to speak and took her breath away.

"How am I supposed to concentrate on impressing your father when all I want to do is beg you to let me have my way with you?"

He smelled good, some dark, mystical aftershave created by witches over a seething cauldron of love potion number nine. Or lust potion number ninety-nine. Her nipples were beaded tight and stark against the bodice of her dress. He was so good at seducing her. All that vulnerability overwhelming her as she'd dressed came rushing back.

"Don't worry," he murmured. "I'll be a good boy. But be warned, when you call me tonight—"

"Stop it." She didn't realize her whisper was so harsh until he pulled back. "You don't have to flatter me, Connor. You don't have to pretend. We both know what the bargain is. I get a baby, you get Daddy's company."

"Faith—"

She pulled away before he could finish. "We'll have sex. I'll do what you tell me to within the bounds of the agreement we made. But just stop all the false compliments."

Then she turned and followed her father into the dining room, her heart beating in her ears and an ache behind her eyes.

HE'D made a tactical error. Faith had a long way to go before she believed he meant what he said, that he *felt* what he said. She didn't know him well enough yet to understand he never gave a compliment he didn't mean.

She would learn; he could wait. Connor had the patience of a cat watching for a gopher to poke its head out of its hole.

He had little patience, however, for Lance. Connor didn't work for him; as director of Finance and Budgeting, he worked for the CFO, who wasn't a homegrown man, but he might as well have been because he sided with the Greens in every decision he made.

Lance Green had a quality about him that Connor recognized from his youth. There were always the people who'd crawl into your bed at night and take advantage of you if they thought you were weaker than they were and they could get away with it. Connor had learned early on not to show weakness.

"I'm curious, Kingston, if you were able to finish that report my father asked for."

It was an innocuous list of major suppliers, with their contract values, costs, and return rates pie-charted. Busy work designed to make Connor late for his dinner date with Jarvis Castle, he now realized.

"I e-mailed him the data before I left."

"I would have thought pulling together that kind of information would require a bit more effort on your part."

"The data's readily available to anyone who knows how to use the system." Connor couldn't help the cheap shot.

The small group took up one fifth of the twenty-seat dining table, Jarvis at the head, Faith on his right, Lance next to her, and Connor opposite, separated from Jarvis by one chair. The seating arrangements said a bit about the business relationship. Castle Heavy Mining was Green Industries' biggest customer. It was a wonder Jarvis Castle hadn't bought them out years ago. And between them sat Faith. If Lance married her, the two companies would have the familial tie as well as the business.

Is that what Jarvis Castle was angling for? Maybe. Trinity had, in her breezy way, flapped away any possibility of a relationship between Lance and Faith. The fact that Lance was here spoke volumes. He *did* have plans for Faith.

But so did Connor. At Green Industries, he'd learned to appreciate the autonomy in a family-run, family-owned company. *That* was the real legacy for his heirs, to determine their own futures, make their own decisions, without being at the mercy of another's whims, no matter how well-intentioned they were.

The bald butler set another fork by the side of Connor's plate. "For your main course, sir," he stage-whispered.

Connor realized he'd used the dinner fork for his salad.

"Thank you. I don't know what I would have done without it. God forbid I would have had to use my fingers."

The gentleman's lip twitched, and his gray eyes sparkled. Tall and thin-shouldered with a concave belly, he could have done with sitting down for a good meal, too.

Smiling, Faith covered her mouth to hide it. Lance merely looked down his nose.

Connor studied the Castle mogul as Jarvis sliced his greens. His gaze flicked from Faith, to Lance, and finally to Connor. "Tell me more about your experience at Green."

By God, this dinner was a job interview.

"I'm director of Finance. Which means I deal with every aspect of the company from sales to cost, analyzing variable and fixed expenses, ROI, strategic projections." He waved his hand in the air to indicate the on-and-on of his daily activities.

"It's a wonder, given you're *such* an important man, why Jarvis can't quite remember what your exact role is"—Lance did his own sarcastic air wave—"since he is our largest customer."

And so it went. It was almost amusing, figuring out how to raise Lance's hackles. A bit childish, though. He'd never been into one-upmanship before. Yet gazing at Faith across the table from him, watching the way her lips twitched every time he made a direct hit, Connor couldn't help himself. It was like a medieval joust with words instead of lances—pun intended—the winner taking the lady's hand.

He hadn't had so much fun in, well, hell, never. Faith was good for him. He could be good for her, too.

THE whippersnapper would be out of a job tomorrow, that was for sure. Didn't he get it?

Jarvis had to admit Kingston had won the verbal sparring with Lance. Barely needing to interject a word, Jarvis sat back to watch the spectacle, throughout dinner. He'd found it entertaining. He would have admired Kingston if it weren't for Faith. Kingston was smart, articulate, and unemotional. Jarvis liked that in a business associate. Except that the man wanted Faith in the bargain. She couldn't see she was a means to an end. Faced with broad shoulders, handsome features, and a rather earthy quality, women threw logic out the window. What she needed was someone of her own class. Well, not class— Jarvis wasn't classist—but someone who understood the world she lived in. She and Lance were suited. Which is why Jarvis had sent them out into the garden and taken Kingston into his study.

Jarvis poured two generous glasses of brandy, his favorite after-dinner drink. Then he took his customary wing chair before the fireplace without inviting Kingston to sit. Pulling up his pants leg, he crossed his knees.

"Let's not beat around the bush. You want to marry my daughter and take over my company when I retire."

Jarvis expected all sorts of hemming and hawing. What he got was a simple "Yes," which took the wind out of his sails. He'd felt like a grilling. How could you grill the truth?

Kingston then sat, minus the invitation. He, too, crossed one leg over the other. "You need someone to grow the company when you're ready to step down. Faith needs someone to father her children." He took a deliberate sip of brandy before continuing. "I'm offering a solution to both those issues."

"I don't know you," Jarvis said with a pleasant smile, as if they were talking about the wood carving on his mantelpiece. "You might intend to sell off Castle to the highest bidder."

"What I want is a legacy, not money. I want to grow into the future, not make the fast buck in the here and now."

"Yet you're taking the fast climb up the corporate ladder by marrying my daughter. Why not work for it like normal?"

Kingston cocked one brow. "Like you worked your way up?"

"I was in short pants when I started working for my father."

The whippersnapper smiled. So, he saw through the old expression, but Jarvis had damn well earned his chairmanship. And why was he suddenly feeling as if he were on the defensive? "All right, let's agree you're not out to make a fast buck, and you want a legacy"—he allowed a certain amount of disdain to lace the word—"why not marry Trinity Green for it? You've been dating her." He raised a brow, the implication being that Kingston was doing more than date the blond princess.

Kingston smiled. Jarvis was starting to dislike that smile.

"I don't want a woman like Trinity Green."

That started a slow boil in Jarvis's gut. The young asswipe. "No, you want a woman like my daughter. Someone you can manipulate, who'll be so grateful for your attention that she'll jump at the chance to marry you."

Kingston recrossed his legs, took another leisurely sip of too-good-for-him brandy, then leveled a steady gaze on Jarvis. "Actually, I want a wife with more depth than Trinity. A woman like *your* daughter. You undervalue Faith's assets. She's devoted to her students and has an admirable mothering instinct."

Jarvis almost slapped his brandy down on the side table, stopping himself at the last moment. Showing emotion now would indicate weakness. Who the hell was this . . . person to say Jarvis undervalued Faith? He worshiped the ground she walked on. Everything he did was for her. "What would you know about Faith? You met her Saturday night."

Kingston set aside his glass and laced his fingers over his abdomen. "I know a lot. You might call it hearsay, but her friends see her true strengths. She's kind and caring. Right now, she lavishes everything she has on children who don't belong to her. She has a helluva lot more to give to her own children."

"I know that, dammit."

The man raised one dark brow. "Do you?"

Jarvis felt himself splutter but nothing came out. He knew she was kind and generous. Too generous and too trusting. That's why he needed to protect her from fortune hunters.

Ah, finally he could say something. "I make sure no one takes advantage of her."

Quirking a half smile, Kingston slowly shook his head. "Yet you'd give her to Lance Green?"

"I've known Lance since he was a child. They're from the same world; they understand each other." And why the hell was he explaining himself to this upstart?

Kingston uncrossed his legs and leaned his elbows on his knees. "He won't make her happy. You know that."

"And you will?"

"I won't lie to her." He blinked. "I won't lie to you. The question is whether you trust her to make up her own mind."

"Of course I do." Jarvis was beginning to realize how many defensive statements he was throwing out. The truth was he didn't have confidence Faith would choose well. She was a woman and could therefore be blinded by a pretty face. She had a good heart, but kindness and generosity weren't valued these days.

Yet Connor Kingston, a goddamn fortune hunter, was the first man to even mention her inner beauty.

Lance never had. But Lance had known her so long, he didn't need to *say* it. "What about love? You're not offering that."

Kingston drummed two fingers on the armrest. "I've seen love matches. Most of them end up in divorce court or murder."

"That's cynical."

"Maybe. But since we're not going into it expecting romantic perfection, I'm offering Faith better odds at success."

Jarvis had to admit the man had a point. He'd loved Faith's mother to distraction, but their life had been a long series of ups and downs, fights and making up. At times, she'd wanted to leave him; at times, he'd hated her almost as much as he loved her. Yet when she died, he thought he'd never make it. Had it not been for Faith, he might never have survived the grief. He'd always given Faith the picture-perfect version of his life with her mother, but many a time, it had been far from that.

His breath felt heavy in his chest, and the weight of Faith's future sat on his shoulders like sandbags. There would come a time when Jarvis could no longer meet the battles head-on. He was tired of the infighting, the greedy, grabbing fingers of his relatives. He didn't trust a single one to keep Castle Heavy Mining thriving. He had two choices: find her a husband to take care of her or find someone to take care of the company.

Or, he could take a chance on a man who would do both. At least with Kingston, he could control things, ensure a prenuptial that protected Faith in every way. If he left it to the *love* route, he might not be able to protect her at all.

Then again, it was all academic. Right now, if Lance was doing his job out in the garden, Faith would see he was the better choice, and Kingston would be out on his ass. In the meantime, what was the harm in letting the young whippersnapper *think* he'd come out on top? Jarvis had to admit he was curious, and the way to bring out the man's plans was to play along.

"You hurt her in any way, Kingston," he whispered, "and I will break you."

"I wouldn't expect anything different, sir." It was the first time Kingston used the deferential term.

"And you damn well better keep your dick in your pants."

"Would it be feasible," Kingston said with a straight face, "to bring it out in the men's room? When appropriate, of course."

Jarvis couldn't help himself. He laughed. He felt an inkling of like and admiration. The man had a sense of humor. "I'll make sure that exclusion is in the prenuptial." He crossed a leg, his knee creaking. "Let's talk terms."

"You want to keep the company in your direct line. Your daughter wants children. And I want the chairmanship eventually. It seems to me that we can all have our needs met. And let's face it, you've got inbreeding in your management structure. You need fresh blood, fresh ideas."

True. But Jarvis wanted measurable goals for Kingston to meet. "You improve the after-tax bottom line by fifteen percent in three months, a total of twenty-five percent in six months, sign a prenuptial agreement, and impregnate my daughter by her birthday." Which was December fifteenth, seven months away.

15 percent was easy, Jarvis knew. There was always everyday waste that could be eliminated. It was the extra 10 percent that would give Kingston the trouble.

"Twenty-five percent in six months isn't reasonable."

Jarvis almost snickered. "So you're not up to the task?"

"I'm not cutting my own throat before I even start. It'll take that long to know the inner workings of your company in order to figure where the additional cutbacks would come from and probably a year to fully implement."

Jarvis waved a hand. "Fine. You've got one year."

"If I've got the responsibility," Kingston added, "then I want the authority to get it done, which means CEO. And as soon as I achieve the first profitability goal, I get a 2.5 percent share in the company and another 2.5 when I meet the second." He paused, smiling slightly. "And you retire as chairman when I make all my commitments. Including the child your daughter wants more than anything in the world."

What the man didn't know was that Jarvis wanted to hold his grandchild before he died. Yet he also wanted Faith to choose the right father. "You lose it all if Faith divorces you for *any* reason at *any* time. And I want that in writing."

Kingston leaned back, that sardonic smile on his face. Though maybe it was better described as a shit-eating grin. "Don't forget to add that I get nothing in the event of her death. Just in case you think I plan to murder her."

Jarvis flashed an equally mocking smile. "Good point. I'll make sure you don't get the gum off the bottom of Faith's shoe."

Kingston laughed, then the smile faded to total focus, a deep line bisecting the young man's eyebrows. "I've already told Faith this, but you better know it, too. I want one thing and one thing only that neither you nor she can take away from me." His brows dropped together as he put his head down, spearing Jarvis with his dark gaze. "If there's a divorce, I want the right to see my children. I'm not backing down on that."

An odd request. It made him see the young man in a slightly different light.

Jarvis steepled his fingers and damn near stared cross-eyed at them. Then he raised his gaze and experienced the oddest sensation as he surveyed Kingston's face. *Would* Faith do better with

Lance? Would the company do better? Only the Lord knew. Right now, she was probably deciding Lance was the one. Jarvis almost laughed. Wouldn't that frost Kingston's nuts? Hah.

But Lord, what if Jarvis was wrong? What if Lance made her unhappy? What if Kingston here *was* the superior option?

For the moment, Jarvis played the game to the hilt. "Deal." He pointed with his index fingers. "But Faith needs to agree."

"Of course."

Jarvis had the sudden, sickening feeling he was selling his daughter to the highest bidder. He just wasn't sure whether it would be his best friend's son or Kingston.

6

SHE'D led Lance along one of the garden paths. The night air was laden with the scent of blooms. Faith couldn't tell the difference between the perfumes except the lavender. She often picked the lavender, and used it for a sachet in her dresser.

"You need to talk to Trinity about him. He's already tried this whole thing with her."

Naturally. It wasn't as if Lance would even expect Connor to choose Faith first. "Trinity was the one who introduced us."

"She probably didn't expect you to fall for his bullshit lines so easily."

Faith pursed her lips. See, that was the thing about Lance. He could be insulting without even knowing he was. Or maybe he did know and didn't care. Then again, right before dinner, hadn't she accused Connor of using bullshit lines on her?

Obviously, her father and Lance had conspired to get in the way of what she wanted. And who she wanted it with. She folded her arms over her chest. "What did my father tell you about me and Connor when he invited you to dinner?"

"He said that it's my responsibility to make sure you don't get hurt since the guy works for my father's company. I have to agree. I feel responsible for what happens to you."

Right. Lance's caring was laughable. "Hmm." She let the sound hang a moment. "Just what did he *try* with Trinity?"

"I don't know for sure. That's why I want you to talk to her before you let this go any further."

Which meant Lance didn't know a thing about Connor and Trinity, but she was sure Trinity would get an earful when Lance went home tonight. "I really appreciate your concern—"

He put his fingers over her lips, and she recoiled. Lance didn't seem to notice. "We'd be good together, Faith. I've asked you before, you've always said no, but I can give you the same life you're accustomed to. I can take care of you. We're a perfect match in every way. Let's get married."

He sounded like her father's parrot. "Lance, we've been through this before." Except that back then he'd wanted her to believe he had "feelings" for her. "My answer's the same."

"I know you want children, and I want them more than anything in the world, too."

Faith heard Connor's rough voice saying that no matter what happened between them, he wouldn't leave his children behind. Lance didn't have a single note of sincerity.

"I've chosen Connor. You're too late with your offer."

His mustache twitched, and he narrowed his eyes. "I asked you to marry me long before he came on the scene." He sounded like a petulant boy, more a mouse than a man. The moonlight caught his eyes, and the glint there was nasty.

Faith shook her head slowly. "That's the first time you've offered me children."

He snorted, reminiscent of the thirteen-year-old boy who tormented her. Before Trinity blacked his eye. "Children went without saying."

"No, they didn't, Lance. They're very important. And you didn't figure that out."

"So, you were testing me?"

"No. I never intended to marry you." She didn't intend to argue with him or justify her actions. "Let's go inside now."

He took her arm, stopping her. "I hate to see you get hurt, Faith. And he *is* going to hurt you. Connor Kingston isn't like us. He doesn't play by our rules. He'll eat you up and spit you out. He's a liar and a manipulator."

Lance *wasn't*? "He'll sign a prenup guaranteeing everything." She raised her chin. "You never offered that."

"We wouldn't have needed that between us." He leaned in, lowering his voice. "I would have married you for free while Daddy had to *buy* Connor for you with the company."

She wanted to smack him, but that would be stooping to his level. "Did my father tell you that?"

"He didn't have to. A man like Kingston is only after power and money."

And a man like Connor couldn't be interested in a woman like her just for herself. She wouldn't let Lance see a single shred of emotion. "Thanks for the warning. My eyes are open now. You don't need to see me back to the house."

He held on to her arm when she would have walked away. "You're crazy if you think he won't cheat on you every chance he gets. He's a user. You'll find out, Faith. He thinks he knows everything, and everyone else is just a fucking idiot."

So that was it. If she probed deeper, she was sure she'd find a laundry list of things Lance resented Connor for. Lance didn't want *her* so much as he wanted to make sure Connor *didn't* get her. Or her father's company.

She jerked her arm out of his grip. "Go home, Lance."

From the beginning, Connor had told her honestly what he wanted. If her father thought Lance was a better choice either as her husband or chairman of Castle Mining, he was crazy.

*   *   *

SHE didn't knock, and she had the look of a Valkyrie about her as she burst through the double doors to her father's study. God, she was hot. Connor wasn't into dominance or submission in the classic sense of the terms, but he liked a woman who knew her own power. *This* Faith made him completely combustible. It was all he could do to control his rising libido.

"Are you two done talking yet?" she demanded to know.

"Yes," Jarvis said.

Connor let the old man answer without adding a comment.

Faith stood there in the door, a hand on each knob. "Good. Because I have a few things to say."

Damn, how he wanted her right now.

Something had happened during that stroll in the garden with good old Lance. It hadn't been to Lance's liking, he was sure. *You go, baby.* She was his. The company was his. His future lay ahead, bright. He couldn't wait to get inside her two seconds after he slipped his ring on her finger.

"We're getting married, Daddy, so I hope you've worked all the details out while you've been in here."

Jarvis's jaw dropped, and Connor's heart thudded in his chest. Faith's hazel eyes shone with battle light.

"Faith. Are you sure about this?" Jarvis's Adam's apple bobbed as he tried to swallow. Despite all the haggling, he still expected her to change her mind during a few minutes alone in the garden with Lance Green. Connor wouldn't let her.

"I'm absolutely sure, Daddy."

She was amazing. Once Faith Castle—soon to be Faith Kingston—made up her mind, there was no stopping her. Now all Connor had to do was get her to put that level of tenacity to their sex life.

"I want you to agree to the bargain."

"But Faith . . ." Jarvis trailed off. He'd read between the lines of what she said just as Connor had. If he *didn't* agree, Jarvis stood to lose her.

Connor almost put a stop to it. He'd never intended to come between father and daughter.

But Jarvis spoke first. "I hired him."

She didn't smile. "As chief executive officer?"

Jarvis eyed Connor. "Yes." Regaining his equilibrium, he tipped his nose eloquently. "But *I'll* still be chairman."

If that look meant anything, Jarvis could be a problem Connor would have to deal with. But that would come later.

"All right." Faith waved a hand dismissively. "We want the left wing of the house for ourselves."

Jarvis's eyebrow almost met his hairline. "All of it?"

It was time for Connor to add his two cents. "We're not living here. We're getting our own home."

"But—" Faith stopped, her lips slightly parted.

"We'll have our own house." There was something about having sex with a man's daughter in her father's house that was a little too kinky even for Connor. Especially with all the things Connor wanted to teach Faith.

"Can Daddy give us the down payment as a wedding gift?"

How much did he want to be bought and paid for? He intended to give Jarvis his money's worth at Castle Heavy Mining. He intended to give Faith her money's worth in the bedroom.

Things were different for the rich. They got cars for birthday presents and houses for wedding gifts. The last present Connor had gotten was a red fire engine on his seventh birthday. A week later, his mother was dead of a blood clot in her lung; two years later his dad finally managed to drink himself to death out of pure grief. Connor had worked for everything he'd gotten since.

"I have plenty for a down payment," he said.

No matter what anyone else thought, one way or another, he would pay for what Faith and her father gave him.

He rose and held out his hand to her. "Walk me to my car."

"I'll have the papers drawn up tomorrow," Jarvis said.

"I'll be by to sign them. Faith?"

She took his hand, her eyes wide. As if she'd only just realized what she'd committed herself to.

GOOD Lord, she was engaged. Connor's hand wrapped around her cold fingers as he led her out into the garden instead of to his car, following a different path through the flowers and foliage from the one she'd taken with Lance.

Hmm, was that a metaphor or what?

"What's so amusing?"

"I was thinking about Lance."

"You've just agreed to marry me, negotiated my job title, and tried to manage our living arrangements, yet you're thinking about another man?"

Despite the moonlight filtering through the trees, his eyes were dark, but she thought for sure one side of his mouth quirked in a smile. "I'm sorry. I didn't mean to direct things."

He stroked his thumb down her cheek. "I liked it."

"But I treated you like you were one of my students."

"No, you treated me as if you had a stake in the deal I made with your father." He feathered a finger across her lower lip. "You do have a stake."

Now that the *deal* had been made, she had so many questions, she didn't know where to start. And she was afraid. She hadn't thought past convincing her father. Now she had a fiancé.

"What did Lance say that made you charge into your father's study?" He raised one brow. She liked that devilish look.

"I didn't charge."

He tapped her nose. "You did. Like . . . a lioness. Did you know that the lionesses do all the hunting while the male just sits back and enjoys the spoils?"

"Is that how you felt?"

"Yes."

"Is that good or bad?" There were so many things she didn't

know about him. Scratch that, she didn't know *anything* about him. Yet she was going to marry him.

"It was good," he whispered. "Very good."

She had the feeling he was telling her something much more. "When are we going to do it? Get married, I mean," she added in case he thought she meant *it* as in sex.

"When's your birthday?"

"I . . . ? My birthday?"

"Your father says I need to have you barefoot and pregnant by then. I don't even know when your birthday is."

He didn't know anything about her at all. "December fifteenth."

"Then we better get married ASAP. As soon as we get a marriage license, blood tests, whatever else we need. And I have to get that sperm test. You don't want to marry me if my count is too low." He was making fun of her.

"I trust your count," she said before taking a breath and plunging in. "Where are we going to do it? Get married, I mean." She kept feeling the need to explain. Maybe because being so close to him, scenting him as if she were the lioness and he were the lion, *it*, sex, was on her brain.

"We can get the license and go down the hall to the judge's chambers, if you like. Or do you want a church?"

"Daddy and I don't really go to church. Do you?"

"No." He answered quickly, flatly.

"Then we can do it at City Hall. That's fine with me."

"I'll start the arrangements, as soon as your father draws up the prenuptial."

The agreement made her feel uncomfortable. She kept flitting from glowing to uncomfortable to ecstatic to tongue-tied in no particular order. "Tell me why you don't want to live with Daddy. It would save us money. And the house is so big." She fluttered a hand in that general direction.

He encircled her throat with his big hand, his warmth rippling through her body. "If I've got a mind to do you on the dinner table during the dessert course, I don't want to have to ask your father and your butler to vacate the room. And when I make you scream in ecstasy, I don't want you saying"—he raised his voice an octave—" 'ooh, Connor, but Daddy might hear.' "

This was when she felt most comfortable with Connor. When they were on a sexual footing. Which was odd because sex had always made her feel uncomfortable with men. What were the expectations? Would she perform well? With Connor, her anxiety seemed to melt away when he touched her, when they talked sex.

"And when I drag you into the backyard on a sultry summer evening to beg for a blow job in the moonlight, I don't want you saying"—he raised his pitch once more—" 'ooh, but Connor, Daddy might see us.' "

He set things tingling inside her even as his bad imitation coerced a laugh. The acre and a half surrounding the house didn't qualify as a backyard. It was a garden, paths weaving between flowering bushes and overhanging trees, two lily ponds, one with carp, one without, a gazebo tucked in the corner. A real backyard was a sandbox, a swing set, grass, a picnic table, and a barbecue. A place where children got dirty and the landscaping wouldn't get ruined if they played too hard.

More than anything she wanted Connor to beg for a blow job in her very own backyard. For a moment, she wished hard that he meant every word.

And scared herself half to death. Wanting that from a man who was marrying her for her inheritance was the surest way to drown in her own tears down the road.

She heard Lance's warning all over again. "I don't want you to humiliate me by bagging other women—"

"Bagging?" Connor tipped his face down until his forehead almost rested against hers.

Faith ignored him. "And no phony compliments, either. It'll be just sex, and I'll do it the best I can, but don't say a bunch of other stuff you don't mean." She glanced at him, but his eyes were unreadable.

"Okay." He tucked a lock of her hair behind her ear. "But it's not a lie to say I want you down on your knees right now."

Her heart seemed to fly into her throat, and once again he stole her breath.

"I want your luscious mouth"—he cut himself off—"sorry, that was an adjective. No adjectives because they can sound like phony compliments."

Though he was again teasing her, inside, her heart raced. Heat danced down between her thighs.

"I want you on your knees and your mouth on my cock. I want you to suck me down your throat so hard I explode." He feathered the fine hairs at her temple. "I want that so fucking badly—" He stopped again. "Sorry, that was an adjective *and* an adverb."

She wanted it just as much. "Yes." She tipped her head back to level a steady gaze on him. "What if I'm not good?"

"Haven't you heard the old proverb that the only *bad* blow job is *no* blow job?"

She laughed, and the tension eased from her belly. "I don't think that's exactly a proverb."

"Maybe not, but it's true. Trust me, Faith, you can't do it wrong." Then he pressed her hand to the front of his slacks. He was sweetly hot and hard in her palm. "This isn't a phony compliment. It's my cock hard for you and the thought of your mouth sucking me until I scream."

Connor Kingston was a dangerous man. She could want so many things from him. She could expect him to make her feel like a beautiful woman. That would only get her hurt, yet there was no turning back. She wanted babies. She wanted Connor.

Faith turned and pulled him. "Come into the gazebo."

"Said the spider to the fly," he whispered.

Just who was the spider and who was the fly?

The roof of the gazebo blocked out the moonlight and left them in a pool of darkness. She reached for his belt buckle. He held her hand still.

"Is this coercion? Or do you truly want to?"

She did feel a certain need to prove she was ready to hold up her end of the bargain, sex whenever he asked for it, but there was more to this. "I want it."

He tipped her head back with his thumb beneath her chin. "Remember, when you take me in your mouth, you have the power. In that moment, a woman can make a man do anything she wants."

Was he right? Could little Faith Castle hold all the control? She wanted to try. He made her feel bold and hot and risky. "Well, then, we're going to see if you can actually come for me. In my mouth."

His eyes blazed hot enough to light up the whole gazebo just before he grabbed her and crushed his lips down on hers. It was a kiss to end all kisses, at least any she'd received. Faith's toes curled in her pumps, and her heart raced beneath her breast. She clung to his arms and let him devour her. His tongue swept into her mouth and set her blood thrumming. He tasted of brandy and hot, needy male.

Then he let her go, only one hand remaining on her shoulder to keep her steady on her feet, his breathing harsh. "So far I've been all talk and no action, haven't I? Silly of me to forget I needed to prove to you I can do what I claim I can."

A thin five o'clock shadow darkened his skin. The roughness of his whiskers still shimmered on her skin and lips. His penis was hard against her belly, and she didn't have a doubt he could accomplish what she wanted.

"Unzip me. But leave the belt done."

Her fingers trembled as the rasp of his zipper disrupted the quiet of the night, but she kept his gaze. It wasn't so dark that she couldn't look into his eyes; she just couldn't see where the pupil ended and his iris began. Yet there was the slight reflection of her face, distorted, almost not her at all. Then she slipped inside the opening of his boxers and touched him.

Hot, hard, and pulsing.

"Rub me," he urged, wrapping an arm around her back to hold her in place.

She trailed the back of her fingers from tip to base, nestled his testicles, then rose back up to slide through a generous helping of pre-come at his tip. His nostrils flared.

"Wrap me in your fist and pump." He dropped his voice. "Just a little. I don't want to come yet."

She'd stroked a man before, but never made him come that way. She'd taken a man in her mouth, but darn near suffered lockjaw before she'd gotten him off. She wasn't an innocent by any means. She'd just never felt so powerful as Connor parted his lips to drag in a breath, closed his eyes, put his head back, and groaned from deep in his belly.

No one had ever groaned for her before.

"Too much," he whispered. "Don't make me come now."

She swirled her thumb in the moisture at his crown.

He looked down at her. "Blow me, baby. Now. I'm feeling out of control, and I want your mouth on me. Please, baby."

No one had begged with quite that note of need or called her baby. If Connor was faking it all, he deserved an Academy Award.

She went down on her knees, her hand still wrapped around him. Pushing his fingers through her hair, he pulled her closer.

"Take me, baby."

She didn't care that she was in her father's garden. She didn't care that she'd just sold her soul for the chance to have a child. All she cared about was the sweet sound of endearments on his tongue, the heady aroma of his sex, the tangy scent of his semen, and the inexorable grip of his fingers in her hair.

"You're so big," she whispered at that first glorious sight of him.

He curled one hand around the back of her head. "When the time comes, I'll be a perfect fit, baby." He guided her to him.

She took him in her mouth, salty and hot, thick and hard. Swirling her tongue around his tip, she delved into the tiny slit and reveled in the involuntary jerk of his body. She licked the rim on the underside of his crown, all around, and shuddered with his growl vibrating against her. He was almost too much to take all the way, but she slid down until her lips met the fist of her hand. With her pinkie, she caressed his sac, then held him in her hand, squeezing lightly.

His hips moved restlessly, forcing him deeper. In clipped words, between a gasp and a groan, he told her how good her mouth felt wrapped around him, how soft her hair was, how smooth her skin. Then he moved urgently, holding her head in his hands.

"Fuck me, Faith, please, fuck me. Make me come, baby."

She held on to his hips with her hands and let him take her mouth. He tightened, throbbed inside her, then said her name softly, almost reverently, and filled her mouth with his essence. So much, so good. He held her until he was done, then draped himself around her, his hands down her back, bunching her dress in his fingers as his body jerked one more time.

"Baby?" he whispered. "You all right?"

He straightened, pulling her to her feet with him as he tucked himself back in his pants, zipped, then finally wrapped her in his arms. "I need a nap," he murmured.

Faith licked her lips. She didn't have to ask if she'd done well. For the first time in her life, she was sure of herself, at least where a man was concerned. In the classroom, she was in control, but men had always made her uneasy.

Connor had given her a special notch on her belt. He'd loved what she'd done. She loved the taste of him still piquant in her mouth. His hands roamed up and down her back. Was it possible? Could she actually satisfy this gorgeous, perfect male specimen? She had. She could keep on doing it.

At least, that's how she felt right now.

Connor tugged gently on her hair until Faith looked up at him. "You've got my come at the corner of your mouth."

Her tongue darted out, and she licked the drop away.

He'd never seen a more beautiful sight in his life. Christ. The long, slow glide of his cock between her lips. The slippery sound of her mouth on him. The fast, hard pump to the finish. Her skin lightly flushed and her lipstick long gone. Her mouth still glistened with his come. Her glorious hair was a tangled mess, falling about her face, her shoulders. He could smell himself on her, a unique sexual musk that was unlike anything else in nature. He loved the scent of sex on a woman, could wallow in the curves of her body drinking it in. He adored the taste of sex, the commingling of flavors. He took her mouth now, still ripe with his come yet tamed with her sweet flavors, remnants of fresh fruit and flavored lip gloss.

She relaxed into him, folding both arms around his shoulders, a sigh falling into his mouth as he kissed her.

They'd do well together. She'd gone to her knees on her own. He hadn't pushed her. She'd swallowed his juice without pulling back, then sucked him dry. He didn't hold any illusions; she'd shy away from some of the things he'd ask her to do, but he would teach her how good sex could be if she let herself go, if she gave herself into his hands. He would test her limits, push her farther than she'd ever gone. And she would love it. Her insecurities would vanish and her self-esteem would soar.

He'd give her that in addition to the children he'd promised. Their marriage would be so fucking perfect, and all without the messy emotional involvement of so-called love. He should have thought of combining marriage and business years ago.

7

"DO you have a vibrator?" Connor's voice over the cell phone bore a husky edge.

The classroom was empty. In twenty minutes, the school day would begin, and Faith would have twenty screaming, squalling, lovable little five-year-olds each demanding all her attention, but for now, she was alone. Despite the fact that no one could see her, she felt her face heat.

"Because I want to hear you do yourself with your vibrator."

"I don't have one." She was burning up. "This is embarrassing." Her words were barely more than a whisper.

"You gave me the most magnificent orgasm and swallowed my come, Faith." He dropped his voice, almost as if he sank lower into his chair, getting comfy for the long haul. "It's too late to be embarrassed."

She shivered all the way to the center of her bones. God. Last night. She'd lain awake thinking about what she'd done to him in the garden, tasting him in her dreams, reveling in the power of it. "Where are you?"

"In my car in the Green parking lot. I've got a quarterly budget review to attend, but I'm hard just listening to your voice, so I need a few minutes before going in."

How did he know just the right thing to say? He wanted her, desired her. Just the sound of her voice made him hard.

"Here's what you're going to do," he went on. "There's a little shop I know. Lingerie in the front parlor, but in the back, there's exactly what you need. I want you to buy the vibrator that's just right for you. Okay?"

She gasped, the thought horrifying. "I can't do that."

"Faith," he said with mock sternness. "Wasn't it part of our bargain that you were going to do everything I told you to?"

"We aren't married yet."

He clucked his tongue at her. "Picky, picky. Didn't you like sucking me off last night?"

He turned her inside out, and her panties were actually damp. But was she ready for *everything* he wanted? "Connor, I can't walk into a store and ask to look at vibrators."

"You have to own your orgasms, Faith, own your sexuality." His voice dropped to a seductive note. "Do it. A man only enhances a woman's orgasm, but she's the one who creates it. You have to ask for what you want, baby; demand it as your right."

She let the stapler fall to the desk with a thump. Out in the hallway, she heard the slam of a locker, one of the older children. Soon, her students would be racing through the door, demanding, cajoling, screaming, playing.

For now, there was only Connor's voice. He seduced her, yet there was a part of her that balked. He wanted *too* much.

His voice was like that of a mesmerist trying to steal her will. She wanted to believe in what he offered so badly that if she wasn't careful, she wouldn't have a will left to call her own. And they weren't even married.

*   *   *

"SAY yes, Faith. Say you'll buy a new vibrator and let me listen to you. One day I want to watch you with it."

Still she said nothing. Dammit, he should have waited until a private moment together. When he could see her and touch her.

All he could hear was her breath, faster than normal. He made her hot. He knew it. "It'll feel good, Faith. You'll love it. I'm so damn hard just thinking about listening to that little hum over the phone. Say yes, baby, please."

"Yes." Her voice came so softly, he almost didn't hear it. But it was there. Thank God.

Yet she sounded a tad distant, and he disliked the phone between them. If she was at home in her bed, he could seduce her with words. Jesus, he was starting to sound obsessed. He had to keep the goal in sight. Faith's delectable body was icing on the cake, not the cake itself. If he didn't keep his head straight, he'd screw up what he was working for.

"I'll see you tonight, baby."

She whispered good-bye and cut the connection.

Baby? What's up with that? It had been fine to use the expression last night in the throes of orgasm, but now, the term of endearment was out of sync. As if he were getting possessive.

Connor climbed from his car, his cock still hard in his pants. He closed his eyes, sought the control he needed. It was harder to grab hold of than usual.

Yeah. He was obsessed. But it wasn't a bad thing. Lust was good, and that's all this was, signified by his almost painful erection. He was for damn sure looking forward to the day Faith truly owned her sexuality and started demanding her due as a gorgeous, luscious woman.

MORNING sun streamed across the letter of resignation Connor laid on Herman Green's desk amid a riot of file folders, computer printouts, and cigar ashes. Connor stood; he hadn't been invited to sit in one of Herman's expensive leather chairs.

Herman Green puffed up his chest. His belly was round and his face florid, and right now, his high blood pressure appeared to be getting the better of him.

"If you even think of taking proprietary information over there . . ." His bluster faded off, as if he couldn't come up with an appropriate threat. Herman was generally a jovial man; he didn't do confrontation well.

After Lance appeared at the Castle home last evening, the stage was set for this inevitable scene.

"I have no intention of taking anything over to Castle." Connor didn't have any propriety information to take. Herman Green played his cards close to his chest. Which was why Connor had a devil of a time doing his job. How could you come up with a strategic plan when you weren't given access to the strategy?

If there was one.

Herman shook his finger and the flesh on his arm jiggled. "You've got some scheme up your sleeve, Kingston."

Quite frankly, Connor didn't understand Herman. Green Industries was Castle Heavy Mining's sole supplier of machined, diecast, and plated parts. Not so bad for Castle—though no company should have *one* source—but for Green, it was disastrous. Castle was *their* primary revenue generator. That wasn't merely unsound business, but a catastrophe waiting to happen.

Herman refused to aggressively search out new markets. Connor had no idea why. Besides Lance being heir apparent, this was another of the reasons he'd discarded Green Industries as a candidate for his legacy building.

He wouldn't broach that subject again, but he did have other advice to offer. "There's no scheme, Herman, but you should take a look at the quality issues." They'd only just managed to reduce costs, and *bam*, quality had gone into the toilet.

Herman's cheeks puffed up like a blowfish. "Are you threatening me?"

Where the hell did he come up with that? "No," Connor said

patiently. "But you have mature products yet mysteriously your return rates have risen over the last few months." Yesterday he would have referred to *our* products; today, he was on the other side of the fence. "There's a problem that needs addressing."

Herman settled back into his chair, huffing out a breath, his anger deflating along with the exhale. "Thanks for the consideration, but Lance has a handle on that."

Yeah, sure. Lance was no longer Connor's problem.

"Well." Herman brushed cigar ash from his calendar. "There's no need for you to remain the last weeks." He waved a hand ceremoniously. "Go forth and prepare for the wedding."

A false note rang in Herman's tone that Connor had no idea how to interpret. Green and Castle had a symbiotic relationship, and he didn't want any burned bridges between them. "We're going to be working together, Herman. I have no ill will."

"Yes, yes, fine, fine." Herman wiped a hand across his mouth, his gaze focused on his desktop. "But it really is pointless for you to stay."

True. Connor had realized weeks ago that his days at Green Industries were numbered. He couldn't work in such a secretive atmosphere. His management philosophy centered around teamwork. The only team at Green Industries was comprised of Herman and Lance. Everyone else was simply an opponent.

He saluted Herman. "It's been a pleasure."

If it did turn out that Green Industries was experiencing irreversible quality issues, Connor's allegiance was now to Castle Heavy Mining. Herman would sink or swim on his own.

Swinging out of Herman's office, he almost ran into Lance in the hall. What, was the guy eavesdropping? Executive row at Green Industries was a wide hallway that dead-ended outside Herman's door. It wasn't what you'd call a normal traffic route, and Lance's office was at the other end.

For the moment, they were alone, and Lance's cologne was

overdone in the airless corridor. The man was on the pretty boy side, polished like a new penny. But still a penny. "Lance."

"She's going to regret it."

After the meeting with Herman, Connor felt like rolling his eyes and heaving a great sigh. The Greens were becoming a tiresome lot. Instead he smiled. "Who's going to regret what?"

"Faith. She'll regret marrying you when she sees what a total dick you are."

Lance's antipathy wasn't surprising. Connor'd had several run-ins with him, such as the time Lance signed them into an ill-advised supplier contract that Connor had to negotiate them out of. But that was business. Connor had never cared much about being liked. He cared about doing his job, and he wasn't about to let that deal go through just because the boss's son had made it. Lance, however, took Connor's actions as personal attacks. He'd go so far as to say Lance hated him at this point.

"Thanks for the warning," Connor said without inflection.

"She'll dump you on your ass, and I'll be there to watch."

Connor spread his suit jacket, his hands on his hips. "What's your issue, Lance?" Besides the fact that Connor had gotten the partnership Lance himself wanted with Jarvis Castle.

"I don't have an issue. I just want you to understand that when she tosses you out and Jarvis fires you, you can't slink over here asking for your job back."

Connor was a couple of inches taller and a few pounds heavier, but what was the point in using size to intimidate a buffoon? "Thanks for telling me. I never would have figured that out on my own."

Yeah, he didn't want to burn bridges, but as he walked away, he understood they'd gone up in flames the moment he decided he wanted Faith and Castle Heavy Mining. All that was left was to determine the repercussions and deal with them.

*   *   *

TRINITY picked the walnuts, avocado, and cheese off her salad. Thank God they'd put the dressing on the side or she'd have dipped her lettuce in the water glass to wash it off.

"Why didn't you just ask them to give you greens, carrots, and tomatoes?" Faith remarked. "That would have been easier."

They were seated at a table outside a small sidewalk café, and the midafternoon sun felt good on her arms. A week ago, she'd been a woman hopelessly without a man. Last night, she'd gotten engaged. It still didn't seem real. Not even after the intimate act she'd performed.

"I like the cucumbers," Trinity said defensively.

Faith giggled. Cucumbers and Connor. Oh God, she was losing it.

Trinity frowned. "What's so funny?"

"Nothing." Faith couldn't explain. "Eat your cucumbers."

Trinity wasn't a picky eater. She pretty much liked everything. Just about everything, though, had either fat or added sugar, which converted to fat. At a cocktail party, she treated herself to one glass of champagne that she'd nurse all night long until there wasn't any fizz left, and she'd carry around a plate of carrot sticks so she wouldn't dive on the cheese puffs. Trinity was a perfect size four. Her clothes were labeled size zero, but she claimed that over the last few years clothing manufacturers had been tinkering with women's dress sizes, labeling them as a lower size to make people feel better.

Faith had to admit she might be right. She'd gone down two dress sizes since she was twenty-five, but she could swear she hadn't lost weight. Then again, she rarely stepped on a scale. Weighing yourself could be demoralizing. And she liked being a size eight, or sometimes a ten on a bad day.

Finally, Trinity seemed satisfied with the undressed state of her salad. "Why didn't you tell me about Connor and his marriage proposal?"

That was getting to the point. "Lance has a big mouth."

Trinity flared her nostrils dramatically.

"I didn't want you to talk me out of it."

"*Could* I have talked you out of it, hon?"

"Maybe." Faith shrugged. "In the beginning."

"And"—Trinity arched an already perfectly arched brow—"when exactly was the beginning?"

"Which beginning?"

Trinity tapped the end of her fork on the tabletop. "You owe me the whole story."

Faith realized she did. She'd let her best friend find out from Lance. Faith knew that hurt Trinity's feelings.

She told the whole story, everything, minus the sex stuff. She and Trinity never got into specific sexual details, so how on earth was she supposed to tell Trinity that Connor wanted her to buy a vibrator so he could listen to her use it, *watch* her use it? Oh God. If she thought too much about all the things he *might* ask her to do, her nerves would snap. *You have to own your sexuality.* What did that really mean?

Trinity held out her hand. "Let me see your ring."

"My ring?" Faith's stomach plummeted.

"Your engagement ring, silly."

Good lord. She hadn't even thought about that. "We haven't picked one out yet."

"Faith." Trinity patted her hand. "I love you oodles and oodles, but you don't have to marry a man who didn't even go down on bended knee and put a ring on your finger."

"But I thought you liked Connor."

"I liked him *before* I knew he was after your father's company. I wouldn't have introduced you if I'd even suspected."

"But I'm glad you did. I want children. And I want to get married in order to have them."

"But you don't have to settle for someone who simply wants your money. There's a man out there who's going to love you for who you are just like there's a man out there who's going to love me just the way I am."

Faith almost laughed. Trinity was gorgeous. "Men drool over you."

"I'm the proverbial dumb blonde, and most of the time I don't mind. But men don't want to just *talk* to me." She leaned forward and shook her fork. "And you're doing that deliberately, trying to push the conversation back on me."

Faith smiled. "Busted."

Trinity speared another bare lettuce leaf. "Hold out for love, Faith. You deserve it. Connor's not good enough for you if he doesn't love you wholeheartedly. I have half a mind to tell him what I think of him, especially since he goaded me into introducing you."

Faith felt the words stick in her throat. Okay, okay. That wasn't really news. Connor said he'd soaked up everything Trinity said about Faith. He'd *chosen* Faith.

"You'll hate me for saying this, but Faith, honey, it's going to kill you the first time someone walks up to you at the country club and tells you what your husband's been up to with some skanky bimbo."

It was worse than a knife thrust. It was a chain saw dismembering her. She didn't expect it from Trinity, everyone else, yes, but not her friend. "Trinity, please."

Moisture glimmered in Trinity's eyes. "I'm sorry," she whispered. "That was mean. I thought he was special, but he's a scumbag like the rest of them. And I gave my best friend to him." She dabbed at the corner of her eye. "It's not fair."

"He's not going to cheat on me, Trinity. He promised."

Trinity gave an unladylike snort. "Men always *promise*."

"No. We're going to put it in a prenuptial agreement. He cheats, he's out. This isn't about sex, Trinity. It's about both of us getting what we want. I want a baby and Connor wants to run Daddy's company. If he cheats, he'll lose that, and it's worth more to him than . . . sex. Some men are like that, you know."

Except that Connor wanted both, the company and sex, with

her, whenever he chose. There was a certain buzz in knowing that, and yes, after last night, a thrill in believing it, too.

"It's not as bad as you think, Trin."

"It sounds like a business deal, not a marriage proposal. Your father is *buying* him for you."

Trinity viciously stabbed a cherry tomato, and Faith felt her words stab her own heart. That's what Lance had said. But Daddy wasn't *buying* Connor. He was . . . her chest hurt with a breath she couldn't drag in. Oh yes, he *had* bought her a husband.

"You're the nicest person I know," Trinity went on as if she had no idea of the wound she'd just inflicted, "and you deserve more than that. I can't believe I helped him."

Faith touched her hand. "Trin, I *like* what he's offering." She wouldn't let Lance's words get to her, even if they were out of Trinity's mouth. "Connor didn't lie. He gave me honesty. And I think the whole . . . sex thing will be . . ." She waved her hand in the air uselessly. Why couldn't she just spit it out?

He makes me so hot I almost cream my panties just listening to his voice on the phone, not to mention how good he tasted in my mouth.

"The whole sex thing," Trinity mimicked. "That's the main problem. You deserve someone who'll make love to you. Mad, passionate love all night long. *That's* what I wanted for you."

"He wants me, Trin. Honest to God, I think he wants me, and it doesn't seem like he's faking it, either."

Trinity stared at her with those gorgeous baby blues men went gaga over, and Faith read every skeptical thought. Trinity couldn't hide a single emotion. "He'd be crazy if he didn't want you," she said softly, a glimmer of moisture in her eyes. "Of the whole sorry lot of us, you're the only one worth having."

For the first time ever, Faith had an inkling that Trinity's life wasn't the perfect scenario she made it out to be. She was still searching for Mr. Future President. She was always smiling, flirting, super confident, and sweetly ditzy. But maybe what she wanted for Faith was what Trinity really wanted for herself. Someone to make mad passionate love to her and mean it.

"I want him, Trinity. I don't love him and he doesn't love me, but together we can make some pretty darn good babies, and that's all I care about. I trust him not to make a fool of me. And I can't say that about a lot of the men we know."

Trinity worried her bottom lip without messing her lipstick. "I support you because you're my best friend." Not *one* of her best friends but her *best* friend. Then she narrowed her eyes. "If he hurts you, I'll torture him with my curling iron. When it's turned on. And where I'll put it, it's gonna hurt badly."

Faith laughed. She could just imagine. "I never knew you had such a sadistic streak."

Trinity waggled her blond brows. "You better let him know he'll have me to deal with."

Faith's chest felt a little tight, and her head throbbed right above her left eye. That's how it always felt when she wanted to cry, but wouldn't allow herself. "Trinity, have I ever told you how much your friendship means to me?"

"A million times, hon"—Trinity waved aside the moment—"and same goes for me."

They didn't talk like this often, but Faith believed Trinity would brand Connor with her curling iron if he misbehaved.

What more could a friend ask for?

8

THE marriage contract, prenuptial, or whatever you called it, had squeezed his balls in a vise. Connor signed away his sperm, his sexual autonomy, and the right to name his firstborn child. Jarvis wanted the little tyke called *Jarvis*. Helluva name to saddle a baby with. Despite leaving Green Industries the day after his engagement, Jarvis had refused to take him into Castle. That would happen only after the wedding.

Today, two and a half weeks later, Connor had followed Jarvis's limousine to San Francisco's city hall in Friday afternoon commute traffic because he wasn't allowed to see the bride before the wedding. They didn't have to make the drive to San Francisco; they could have done it down on the Peninsula, but Jarvis had insisted his daughter should be married in the City.

Jarvis Castle controlled every aspect of the nuptials, a not-so-subtle message that he now controlled Connor's life. The old man's actions were almost laughable. He'd probably try to walk into the honeymoon suite and direct things there, too.

Yet Connor Kingston couldn't be happier as he dotted the *i* on the marriage certificate. The civil ceremony was brief, the judge reading the minimalist pitch quickly, with Jarvis and a clerk witnessing. After the ring exchange, the clerk had hustled them into a quaint antechamber for the signatures. The walls were paneled wood, no windows, just a desk, a chair, and a book, like one would find in a church rather than a clerk's office.

Faith was glorious in a cream-colored suit, a prim pale lipstick on her lips, her magnificent hair unbound, and a shell-shocked look in her eyes.

Taking her hand in his, he wrapped her fingers around the ballpoint pen. "Your turn," he murmured.

She licked her lips, her gloss glistening with the light moisture, then Faith signed away her father's company.

Connor had waited almost three weeks for the wedding, yet in many ways, he'd waited a lifetime. Everything he'd told himself he'd get out of life was within his reach.

Not to mention the added bonus. Tonight, he'd finally slide inside his wife's succulent body. He'd been dreaming about that night after night. To date, she hadn't purchased that vibrator as he'd instructed. He hadn't pushed. Yet. Over the phone, he'd coaxed her through multiple orgasms. He'd come with her. But he hadn't touched her again. He wanted her body signed, sealed, and delivered before he took her.

He also wanted to give Faith something special, a real wedding night with a few surprises. He didn't want any question that the child they made wasn't legitimate in every way possible. Faith would get her money's worth. He wasn't a taker. He would make marriage worth everything her father paid for it.

Faith laid down the pen and jutted out her cheek for her father's kiss. Jarvis hugged her hard, his gaze steady over her shoulder. Connor merely smiled. Jarvis Castle had an eye thing going. He'd shot Connor any number of meaningful glares, stares, glances, and steady gazes over the last half hour. And they all held one message. *Hurt my daughter, and I will annihilate you.*

Connor stretched out his hand, palm up, and Jarvis had no choice but to give over his daughter, gently placing her hand in that of her husband's. Connor chastely kissed her forehead. It was the last chaste kiss he'd give her for a long, long time.

"I've booked a table at the Top of the Mark," Jarvis said.

"Daddy, you didn't have to do that."

"I couldn't give you a big wedding, I didn't give you away, you don't want my help with buying a house, but I will give you a memorable send-off."

Any dig the old man could get in, he did. He didn't give in gracefully, that was for sure. But the restaurant was at the top of the Mark Hopkins Hotel on Nob Hill with a magnificent view, and it was a fitting place for Faith's wedding feast.

The hotel itself was a perfect setting for other things, too, once Connor got rid of Jarvis.

HER father secured a secluded table in the corner right next to the window overlooking San Francisco, and soon, as the sun started to set, the sky would streak with color if the fog didn't roll in. For now, it was still a bright, cloudless blue.

They were early and many of the tables were empty, others occupied by chattering women or couples starting on Happy Hour. While the Top of the Mark was actually a bar, her father had persuaded the staff to have dinner sent up from the restaurant. It was a civilized affair, but Faith couldn't wait for it to be over. Her father talked, about Connor's duties at work, his duty to Faith, the condo they'd rented until they found something to buy—an endless litany that made her want to scream. Yet throughout it all, Connor smiled and nodded, a glint in his eyes. A glint that turned wicked when he fastened his gaze on her.

She went to take a sip of wine, miscalculated the distance, and a drop splashed her cream suit. Her filet mignon tasted like horse meat and the dessert mousse was chalky. All right, it was her. She was so nervous, she felt nauseous.

What have I done?

She'd thought the evening would be dinner for two, but her father had decided it was better if three attended. There was something nerve-racking about sitting next to your father when you knew you were going to give the man right across from you carnal knowledge of your body in a couple of short hours.

She felt her cheeks flush.

Connor's mouth lifted on one side, and the devil winked in his eye.

"If you'll excuse me a moment." He pushed his chair back and tossed his napkin by the side of his coffee cup. Walking away, he had a flawless rear view in a tailored dark blue suit. A chorus of female gazes followed his progress.

"Thanks for the wonderful dinner, Daddy." *Now it's time for you to go.* "Connor's going to drive me back to our condo." *So there isn't any reason for you to stay.*

"I'll be watching every move he makes, Faith." Her father squeezed her hand. "You'll tell me if he upsets you."

Faith took a belly breath. "No, I won't. I'm married now. If Connor and I have any disagreements, they're between us."

"I'm only looking out for you, sweetheart."

"I know." She squeezed his hand back. She appreciated his concern, but . . . he'd bought Connor for her, and he was still orchestrating everything. If she was ever to let go of that raw nerve, she had to take a stand. "You need to butt out now, Daddy. Go home. If I've made a mistake, it's *my* mistake."

He let go of her, jerking his cup off the saucer and spilling coffee over the side. "It's my mistake, too. He starts work for me on Monday."

She smoothed a couple of crumbs aside on the tablecloth. "Daddy, I want this to work. And the only way it's going to is if you aren't constantly picking apart the things he does."

"I don't pick on him."

She shot him a look from the corner of her eye, then shook her head. "I love you. But I'm married to him, and you hired him. It's done. Now go home, Daddy, and let me run my life."

"But—"

She held up a finger. "No buts. I'm almost thirty."

The waiter arrived with the check, setting it by her father's elbow, then slid an envelope in front of Faith. She tipped her head up at him.

"The gentleman left it for you."

"He's gone?" Her father's voice was a note louder than necessary, and a few heads turned.

"He simply asked me to give this to the lady, sir." The man backed up two steps, turned on his heel, and walked away.

"I told you, Faith."

She rolled her eyes and yet . . . a tiny tremor ran through her body. Slipping her finger under the flap, she opened the envelope to find a room key in a pocket card. And Connor's neat writing. *Get rid of your father and meet me ASAP.*

She almost hugged the card key to her chest. "He's booked a room at the hotel for tonight."

"You didn't pack clothes." Her father sounded scandalized.

She leaned over and kissed his cheek. "Don't worry about it. I love you. Thanks for dinner. I'll call you tomorrow."

Then she rose from the table, tucked her purse under her arm, and left to meet her husband. When she turned the corner and was out of sight, she ran to the elevators.

She was nervous, afraid of how he'd look at her naked body, terrified she wouldn't measure up, her pulse pounding against her eardrums. What would he ask her to do? How far would he push her? But more than anything, she wanted finally, *finally* to know how Connor felt inside her.

"BUT I didn't pack any clothes."

Faith stood in the middle of a room done in gold tones from the burgundy and gold comforter on the queen-sized bed to the gold-striped wallpaper. The room was all-equipped: antique desk outfitted with the latest Internet hookups, a tallboy disguising the TV and small refrigerator, and a gorgeous view of Alcatraz. A champagne bucket sat on a small table next to an easy chair.

"You're not going to need clothes tonight. But I did get his and hers toothbrushes in the gift shop." Connor pointed to the bathroom. "You wanna see? They're on the counter."

There was something he wanted her to see in the bathroom, and she didn't think it was his and hers toothbrushes.

She stopped on the doorstep and gasped. "It's all mirrors." Two walls were mirrored floor to ceiling, more than enough to show off every crevice. Every bump. Every . . . imperfection. And Connor wasn't the one with the imperfections.

He came up behind her, pushing her inside with his body, his breath at her ear as he whispered, "I can lean you over the counter and watch my cock slide inside you from every angle."

"Pervert." She tried to joke, but her chocolate mousse had curdled in her stomach.

In the mirror, he quirked a smile. "Take your clothes off."

She needed to stall before she collapsed in a quivering heap. "Aren't you going to give me any champagne first?"

"I got the champagne so I could drizzle it all over you and lick it off."

Her nipples puckered against her wedding suit, but her fears and nervousness spiked. "You're rushing me."

He wrapped an arm beneath her breasts and pulled her against him, his erection nudging her spine. "If I don't rush, you'll balk and run. But I can get you drunk on champagne first."

He backed her up, turned, his hand sliding across her midriff, then grabbed her fingers and took her to the champagne. Pouring two glasses, he handed her one, tipped his own against it, and sipped. "Drink up."

He was moving too fast. She wanted to get off the merry-go-round he'd created inside her. "Can't we have some conversation before I take off my clothes?"

"You talk." He nuzzled her neck. "I want to bury my face in your pussy and lick you until you scream."

Oh. Oh. Her body tightened, and moisture gathered between her legs. "You certainly get right to the heart of the matter."

He took her glass, setting both on the table. Then he gathered her lapels in his fingers and drew her closer until her nipples rubbed the backs of his hands. "All I've thought about for the past seventeen days is touching you, tasting you, getting inside you, and coming in you." He undid the buttons on her jacket and dropped his voice. "Do you remember our first date? I rubbed my fingers in you, and later, after I dropped you off, I sucked them. Now I want that taste on my tongue again."

She could barely breathe, let alone answer him. Heat raced through her body, then blazed straight to her clitoris.

He stroked one hard nipple with his thumb. "So tell me, do you still want to have a little conversation first?"

She swallowed and shook her head.

"Good." He undid the buttons on her silk blouse, popped the front clasp of her bra, then bent at the knees and lifted her until her nipple nudged his lips. He sucked her inside, hard, and she felt it in her clitoris and right up into her womb.

Then he tossed her onto the bed. She bounced, squeaked, then laughed. "You're crazy."

"I'm just so fucking horny for you I can't see straight." Grabbing her foot, he raised it, tugged off her high-heeled white pump and threw it over his shoulder, where it hit the wall. Then he did the same with the other. Caressing her instep, he asked, "Are these hose or thigh-highs?"

"Panty hose," she answered.

He grinned, then slid both hands down the outsides of her legs, forcing them apart with his body, and pushed up beneath her skirt. "Lift," he whispered.

She did. Plucking the waistband, he slid everything back down the way he'd come. "Hey. Got the panties, too."

She'd worn black lace, thinking he'd rip them off with his teeth, but now she was just glad they were gone.

Pulling her to the edge of the bed, he went down on his knees between her legs. Her skirt had ridden to her waist, and he pushed her thighs wider to accommodate his body.

She felt exposed and vulnerable.

"Holy Mother," he said on nothing more than a breath.

"What?" What was wrong?

"You are so fucking beautiful."

She felt her brow rise into her hairline. "Down there?"

"All over. But especially down there. It's pink and plump and begging me to suck it." He didn't look up, but simply raised a finger, trailing it down her center. "And you're so wet." Lifting his gaze to hers, he sucked his index finger into his mouth and closed his eyes. "Jesus, you taste good."

Faith swallowed, then bit her lip. No one had ever spoken to her like this. No one had ever said anything like . . . that. She'd never met a man like Connor before. Her previous lovers just . . . did it. Sometimes they made noises of appreciation, but there was nothing like this. No one like Connor.

His head back, his nostrils flared, a slight smile on his lips, he breathed deeply. "I'm going to make you come fast and hard, then we can slow it all down, but I need that first." He opened his eyes. "Okay?"

She wore her jacket, her blouse was halfway undone but still tucked in, and her skirt rode her abdomen. She felt hot and decadent. Wanted. "Yes. Please," she whispered.

"Thank you, baby." Then he shoved his fingers under her hips, took her buttocks in his hands, and set his mouth to her.

Faith almost screamed. His lips were hot, wet. His tongue traced her labia, flicked just under her clitoris, down to her opening, and quickly back up. Then he teased the very center with the pointed tip. Faith was afraid to touch him in case he stopped. His tongue swirled around her one way, then the other. He sucked her hard, then let her go and swirled his tongue all over again. She couldn't stand it. Arching, she pushed herself harder against him. His fingers bit into her butt. She grabbed his head and held him right where she wanted him. Oh, oh, nothing had ever felt like this. He did something miraculous with his tongue and heat shot like a fireball up through her center. Faith cried out his name. Her ears were ringing when she floated back down from the place he'd blasted her to, and his fingers stroked and soothed along her thighs.

"I debauched your wedding outfit."

She covered her eyes. "Do you think anyone heard me?"

"I hope so. I want them to know I'm doing my job properly."

She raised her head. His lips glistened, and his hair was a spiky mess where she tried to pull it out by the roots.

"Was it good?" he asked with little-boy eagerness.

"You know it was."

"Then come here and give me my wedding kiss." He pulled her up by the arms, wrapped his across her back, and stopped, his mouth scant inches from hers.

The scent of hot sex was all over him, the aroma of musky male and female desire, and she lost herself in his magician's gaze. Then he closed the last microns between them and claimed her. It was like the kiss he'd taken that night in the garden, the mingling of flavors, his and hers, becoming one. His taste intoxicated her. His scent mesmerized her.

They'd said the words, signed the document, but the kiss sealed their future. "Make me a baby," she whispered.

Connor laid his wife back on the bed and undid the rest of her buttons. Reaching beneath her, he unzipped the skirt and pulled it over her hips. She had glossy red hair between her thighs with none of the blond streaks. She'd tasted like sweet aromatic wine. He wanted to bury himself in her now, without even removing his pants or his shoes. A swift, hard come shooting inside her, deep enough to take possession of her womb.

But he wanted to feel her naked skin against him. He petted the soft skin of her thighs, her belly, rising to the underside of her breasts. Her eyes followed him, but she said nothing.

He knew she was unsure of herself. If she had her way, she would have turned off the lights and covered herself to the chin with the bedclothes.

The mirrors in the bathroom had terrified her.

He bent to nip the smooth flesh of her hip, tunneling between her pussy lips for just a moment. She made a small sound, and heat and wet coated his finger. God, when she came into her own and let herself loose, she'd be dynamite in any man's hands. In his, she'd be incomparable.

Raising his head, he gazed up the length of her. She was naked from the waist down, but still wore her jacket, blouse, and bra, though everything had been undone and lay askew. Sexy, hot, rumpled, ready for so much more. "No fast, hard fuck for you, Mrs. Kingston." Jesus, he did like the sound of that. "It's going to take all night long."

He hauled her to her feet. "Let's get naked." He divested her of the remains of her wedding outfit, then put her hand on his belt. "Your turn. You know, you've said barely a word."

She arched one brow in a haughty manner so like the *ladies* at the country club. "I do believe I screamed your name," she said. "What more do you want?"

She was exactly the way he wanted her. Sure of herself for that moment. "That'll do for now. Undress me."

"Did you give me this many orders before we married?"

"Yes." He chucked her under the chin. "You did everything I told you to and loved it."

She tugged on the buckle and unzipped his pants, but instead of pushing them off, she pulled at his tie. He'd worn his plain blue interview suit. He'd worn his fucking interview suit to his wedding. Connor smiled. That said it all.

"What's so funny?" She unstrung the tie from his collar and threw it on top of her clothing. When he looked down at her, she pushed his chin back up. "Look straight ahead."

Which meant he was looking over her head, and he suddenly realized she felt uncomfortable in complete nakedness while he still had all his clothes on.

Only Faith was trying to hide it. Putting on a stoic face, so to speak. He was glad he'd asked for a room with mirrors in the bathroom, even if the clerk had looked at him strangely. He'd introduce Faith to her own glory in those mirrors.

"I was laughing that I got married looking like I was going to a job interview. I should have rented a tux."

She smiled at his throat as she finished undoing his buttons and pushed both jacket and shirt off his shoulders. Then she stopped, and her breath was audible in the quiet of the room.

"What?"

"You're beautiful." She played with the light swath of hair on his chest, tickled first one nipple, then the other.

"Suck it," he murmured.

He closed his eyes as he felt the brush of her skin against his abdomen, the lush sweep of her hair across his flesh. Then she took him in her mouth. He didn't know if it was how a woman felt when her nipples were sucked, but it was halfway between pleasure and pain. As if someone tickled you just a little too hard, and he felt the tug of it all the way down in his groin.

And suddenly his cock wanted her mouth's attention, badly.

"Toe off your shoes," she murmured, giving his nipple one last swipe that sent a shiver down to his gut.

He kicked his shoes aside while she pushed his pants and boxers down his legs. He sat on the edge of the bed, yanked everything off the rest of the way, and threw them.

"Should you treat your best suit that way?" She picked up the pants, held them in front of her, smoothing them and covering her own naked body. "You might need it again."

"I'm done interviewing. I got the job."

She moved around the room picking up the bits and pieces of clothing they'd discarded.

"Are you nervous, Faith?" he asked gently.

"Of course not. Don't be silly." She heaved a sigh he felt deep inside. "All right, a little."

He held out his hand. "Come here."

She did, with clothes covering the parts of her body he wanted to touch. He grabbed the whole mess and tossed it.

Taking her by the hips, he reeled her in and put a kiss to her belly. "You're beautiful," he whispered.

Her skin flushed with a pink glow. "We agreed you weren't going to give me a bunch of compliments that aren't true."

He tilted his head back and kissed the sweet bead of a nipple. "I said I wouldn't lie to you. You have gorgeous breasts." He slid over her abdomen to the abundant red hair, and finally inside the jewel between her legs. "And you have the most delicious pussy."

He fingered her clit slowly, lingering while her body softened for him. He eased up inside her, riding her gently, until she gasped and grabbed hold of his shoulders.

"You feel good, you taste good"—he rubbed her belly with his nose—"you smell good." He bit her lightly, then eased back from her opening to caress the sensitive flesh right before her ass. She was close, so close. He nudged between her lips with his tongue and tasted the nectar, stroked her clit until she began the slow, sweet grind of her pussy against his mouth.

Then he pushed her to the carpet and rose over her. Holding his cock in his hand, he grazed the tip up and down her slit. She was so wet, and his own come mingled with hers in a delicious slip-side of bodies. He rode her clit from the base to the tip of his cock and back again, then teased with just his crown.

"Do you like this?"

She nodded, dragged in a breath, then arched off the carpet.

"It's good, but it's not enough to make you come, is it?" It wasn't a question; he knew the answer, but he wanted her to beg for more.

"No, it's not enough."

Pushing the tip of his cock just inside her pussy, he held there with a light pulse of his hips.

"Connor, please." That was all she said.

"Please what?"

"Get inside me."

Ah, that's what he wanted. Her capitulation. Yet he still had so much more to show her before the big moment. "Weren't you afraid it wouldn't fit?"

"It'll fit." She wriggled her intention. "Please."

"No. I think we need to make sure." He pulled out, slid once more over the crest of her clit, then rose to his feet.

"What are you doing?" She didn't bother to cover herself. Good. Her desire was rising, her fears and inhibitions receding.

"I want to watch us. I want to see my cock slide inside you. Just to make sure it fits perfectly."

He grabbed the desk chair, carried it into the bathroom, and set it facing the full mirror along the wall. Then he sat, his gut screaming that he was pushing too hard too fast.

She'd rolled to her stomach, propped herself on her arms and stared through the doorway, first at the hard jut of his cock, then the chair, and finally the mirror.

"Let me show you how we're going to keep our marriage exciting, Faith."

He held out his hand and prayed she'd take it.

9

STANDING in the doorway, her legs were weak, her heart pattered loudly in her chest, and blood buzzed in her ears. The sexual hum hadn't evaporated, yet she'd come down from the high enough to feel self-conscious without her clothes.

"Come to bed," she said. It would be so much easier beneath the covers. She'd welcome anything he wanted to do to her then.

"I want you to watch us. We'll fit, Faith. I promise."

He was so magnificent, smooth, hard chest with a dusting of hair, muscles, firm abdomen, and that mouth-watering penis. It wasn't the fit she worried about. It was seeing herself in the mirror, knowing he saw exactly the same thing. All her flaws.

She did not want to step into that bathroom. Right now, she couldn't see herself, his body in direct line with the mirror.

"Haven't you ever made love with the lights on?" He raised one brow. She loved when he did that; he looked so wicked, and she liked him that way.

She didn't like the mirror. She knew there wasn't a woman on the face of the planet who was happy with the way her body looked. Trinity wanted Faith's breasts, and Faith wanted Trinity's trim waist. All women lusted after the perfect body, and no one quite agreed what that was. Faith did know hers wasn't it. She was Marilyn Monroe on a heavy bloat day.

She wanted to beg. *Please don't make me do this.* But revealing her insecurities aloud would give him too much power.

"Come on, baby."

She closed her eyes, loving the sound of that endearment on his lips. Then she felt his hands at her waist, lifting her, easily, as if she weren't . . . a bloated Marilyn Monroe.

"Wrap your legs around my waist," he urged.

His penis nudged her as she locked her feet behind him and clasped her arms around his neck. Then he carried her back to the chair. "I won't make you watch this time, but I'm going to love seeing every inch of my cock sliding inside you."

He sat once more, pulling her flush up against him as she touched the floor, balancing lightly on the balls of her feet.

His eyes were obsidian dark and devilishly hot. Pushing her back to slip a hand between them, he tested her folds.

"You're very wet. Perfect."

She swallowed, biting back a moan when he grazed her clitoris with the tip of his finger.

"Make noise if you want to, Faith. I like it."

"Someone might hear us."

"Fuck 'em." He grinned when her eyes widened. "I'm not a gentleman. I like the words *fuck*, *cock*, *pussy*." He fit a finger inside her, but didn't pump it, letting the warmth of his palm and the feeling of fullness inside her work their magic as he seduced her with dirty talk. "And I'm going to say them. As in, let me fuck you, baby. I want my cock deep inside your sweet, delicious, fuckable pussy. I want to fuck you until you scream."

She felt her breath stop halfway down her throat. "I like it when you talk like that."

He laughed and hitched her closer with an arm across her back.

"You're blushing." He pulled her bottom lip between his teeth and sucked lightly. "Fuck me, baby." He swept his tongue along the seam of her lips. "Let me watch my cock while you fuck the hell out of me."

In one fluid movement, he grabbed her butt and raised her over him. "Take me inside you."

Faith closed her hand around him one finger at a time. He was hot, steel hard, and wet with pre-come. Putting her feet on the bottom rungs of the chair to steady herself, she took him.

"Slowly," he murmured, his head bent, his hands holding her, guiding her. "Watch me take you, baby."

There was something wholly erotic, completely seductive about watching his body glide between her lips. Her clitoris was a hard, achy bead, her pussy plump, begging. And the feeling, all that heat, the friction, the sense of being filled. She dug her nails into his shoulders.

"I told you it was beautiful." Then he pulled her down sharply, to the hilt, her clit pushed against his pubic bone, and she almost screamed, almost came.

Her breath came in harsh gasps, and her body seemed to liquefy around him. "Oh God, that's good," she whispered.

"Ride me and it'll get better."

And Faith rode him. He held her close, his chin over her shoulder as he watched in the mirror. When he spread her cheeks, she knew he was exposing the slide of his cock in and out, covered with her moisture, his come. She hung on, let him guide her to a faster pace, the slap of her bottom against his thighs, the sound of slick bodies coming together, the harsh beat of his breath against her ear, and his constant litany of words.

"That's it, baby, fuck me hard, so good. Jesus, Faith, you are so fucking beautiful."

For long glorious moments, he pounded into her, then he slid his fingers into her hair and pulled her head back. "I want you to see this."

Her own reflection flickered in his dark eyes. "Please," she whispered. *Please don't make me* or *please let me*, she couldn't say. She wanted to turn and look in the mirror, yet terror of what she'd see made her clutch harder to his shoulders.

His gaze shifted across her face, then his lips slammed down on hers, sucked her tongue into his mouth. Fast, hard, then he stood. Plopping her on the bathroom counter, he pushed her chest. "Lean back and hold your legs wide."

She was exposed and out of control. And he took her higher than a man ever had. Curled at the waist, she could see every inch of his cock sweep in and out of her, feel the slap of his testicles on her butt. Her breasts bounced, and Connor reached out to pinch a nipple. Deep inside her, he started to pulse.

"Touch your clit, now."

He closed his eyes, bared his teeth, held her at the joining of her hips and thighs, and thrust home, faster, harder, deeper. Faith put her finger to her clitoris.

The room simply exploded into lights. She half screamed, half moaned and if he said anything, she couldn't hear it over the roar in her ears. Liquid heat filled her, pulsed inside her, then she felt him gather her into his arms and slide down the vanity until he was seated on the floor with her in his lap.

She heard his voice over the drumbeat of her heart. "Hold me inside, baby. As long as you can."

She fell asleep with his body buried deep within her.

SHIT. That was so damn good. He wished he'd stood her on her feet though, bent her over the countertop, and taken her from behind so they could both watch his cock in the mirrored wall.

He'd never seen anything lovelier than the sight of her ass in the reflection, his cock filling her, her pussy devouring him. Why could she not believe how absolutely gorgeous she was?

When she'd agreed to watch, he'd almost lost it right then, deep inside her. Christ. Her guard was down, and she'd wanted, badly. He'd flopped her down on the counter because he couldn't bear to pull out. Not right then. Tight and hot, her body milked the best damn orgasm from him that he'd had in years.

But his ass was falling asleep against the cold tile floor.

She had so much potential. He'd had her, and he wanted her again. He imagined all manner of things he could do to her. A little kink, a lot of hot action. He would please her, and she would please him. He wanted her to surpass him, surprise him, take control, and blow his mind. Yeah, he'd made a good choice.

Lust was so damn good when it wasn't all fucked up by the concept of love. He was well versed in that notion. After his mom died, his dad drank himself to death all because of the loss of *love*. It had taken only two years to accomplish that feat. Connor had had his own brush with the sometimes fatal emotion. She was in his last foster home. He'd loved her for almost a year that felt like a lifetime back then. They'd made momentous plans for the day he turned eighteen. Two weeks before, he found her in bed fucking their foster dad. If it had been molestation, he'd have understood, but she was older than Connor by six months, and she told him "Dad" was getting a divorce to marry her. He'd come out of it with an important lesson. Love sucked. It was just a word. It didn't mean a goddamn thing.

This, Faith sated in his arms, his body on the edge for more, *this* was so much better than love ever could be. When she opened herself completely to him, came into her sexual self-esteem, he'd have perfection in his grasp without fear of crossing the line from love to hate.

FAITH put her hands on her hips and surveyed the living room of their newly rented condo. She didn't mind it being furnished with someone else's seconds, but she did want some of her own things. The load, packed up from her father's house, consisted of her king-sized bed, the dressers, her vanity, a flat-panel TV, an easy chair, and her clothing.

All Connor brought with him were three boxes of clothes, shoes, papers, and his computer. Oh, and his toaster.

They'd gotten married Friday, honeymooned Friday night and Saturday morning up in the City, then in the afternoon, back to the condo for the delivery. Connor had wanted to spend the weekend in the City, but the hotel was much too expensive, and she'd used the furniture as an excuse to come home.

All right, that wasn't the whole truth. When she woke in the morning, she suddenly found the room . . . tiny. Confining. They hadn't an ounce of privacy. That didn't seem to bother Connor, but there were all the little intimate things she hadn't even thought of, something as simple as brushing her teeth before she encountered anyone, let alone exchanged a kiss. And all the other personal needs a woman wanted privacy to attend to.

It was actually easier having sex with him than using the bathroom in front of him. *That* was terrifying. At least in the condo, there were two bathrooms, one upstairs, one down, three small bedrooms on the second floor, and on the first, a combo living room and dining room, and a spacious kitchen.

Space. She could breathe and try to settle her nerves. And think about furniture and what kind of dishes and flatware she needed to buy instead of how she was suddenly living with a man she barely knew except in a carnal way.

Faith puffed out a breath. Three cheesy prints—a sailboat, a vase of flowers, and a forest scene with Bambi in the foreground—graced the living room walls, probably to hide a few holes. The bright, ultrafeminine flower-print sofa and love seat didn't suit Connor in any way, shape, or form.

"We could bring some furniture from your apartment, too."

Connor dismissed the idea with a grunt. "Hand-me-down crap from the Salvation Army. I'm getting rid of it all. If you don't like this sofa, we can buy something else."

"We don't need to spend the money."

He eyed her, shaking his head. "We don't have to watch every penny. I've got a perfectly respectable bank balance."

Except that he hadn't shown her the bank balance. Not that it was any of her business. Theirs wasn't a real marriage; it was a marriage of convenience, which meant they didn't share every single detail with each other.

"Buy what you want this week," he added.

She waited for more. Nothing came. "Don't you want to give me some sort of budget to work with?"

He took her arms, turning her toward him. "What's the big deal about the money?"

She looked down at her toes. Last night—and early this morning—had been wonderful. After she'd gotten over her initial nervousness. Now her stomach churned with all the day-to-day issues of being married to a man her father had bought for her like a prize bull off the auction block. God, why couldn't she get that thought completely out of her head? "I like the sofa. I just thought maybe you didn't."

"I'm fine with the furniture, but if you want something else, I can afford it."

Faith didn't really have a concept of money. She charged what she wanted, and Daddy paid for it. As a teacher, she made a pit-tance, and it was barely a drop in the bucket to what she spent. She thought nothing of plunking down three hundred for shoes, and that was pretty cheap compared to some of the stuff Trinity bought. She drove a Lexus her father paid cash for; she had her weekly facial and massage. Still, she wasn't extravagant compared to many of the people she knew. Really, paying over two thousand dollars for a dress was ridiculous.

But that wasn't the world Connor came from.

"I need a limit on how much I can spend," she whispered.

He tipped her chin to look at him, his eyes suddenly smoke before the fire. "What did I tell you about limits?"

She swallowed. "There are none."

They hadn't exercised any so far. Faith blushed thinking about the bedroom things he suggested they try. Doing it in front of the mirror was tame as far as Connor was concerned. She didn't know how a man was able to come four times in one night.

He popped the top button on her blouse. "You know, we don't need new stuff until we find our own house." He slipped his hand inside her bra. "There is, however, one thing you need to buy for the condo, and there's no limit on how much you can spend."

Her nipples burgeoned under his attention. How did he do that, talk about getting things for the condo while he played her breasts and rubbed his erection against her belly? She couldn't concentrate at all.

"What?" she managed to say.

With his other hand, he tugged up her skirt and slipped inside the elastic edge of her panties. "You need to get that vibrator." He slid across her clitoris just as he said the word, and she jerked, then clung to his arms.

She closed her eyes and rocked with the slow caress of his hand. "Why don't you get it and give it to me as a present?"

"A vibrator's too personal for someone else to buy." He tapped her chin. "Open your eyes."

She did, drowning in the heat of his gaze. She was so hot and wet, and his face was hazy in her vision.

"You have a parent-teacher day Monday, don't you?"

She nodded, sliding one leg up his to open herself more fully for him. God, the way he made her feel was . . . out of control. Willing to do anything. No limits.

"Buy it at lunch."

"Okay," she murmured, her head falling back. Her body bucked against his hand.

"Good girl. You deserve a reward." Then he picked her up, pulled her legs around his waist. Carrying her into the bedroom, he tossed her on the bed and climbed on top with a predatory, wholly carnal glint in his eyes.

Who cared about a sofa? All they needed was the damn bed. Faith pulled him down.

THE money might turn out to be an issue. If anything, Connor would have expected Faith to overspend, but the woman was reticent about every dime. As if she didn't trust him to take care of her without digging into Daddy's pockets. Or maybe she thought that without her father, he was incapable of supporting her. He'd been taking care of himself since he was eighteen.

He wouldn't let her fortune stick in his craw. It was enough that *he* knew he could take care of her adequately, even without Daddy's CEO job.

She snuggled against him, her ass cradling his cock, her breath heating the flesh along his arm. He'd come twice and still he wanted her again. Maybe it was because he hadn't dated in the six months he'd been at Green's. He'd been building his plans, and sex had taken a back seat, nor did he want any tales to make it around the country club circuit. Instead he'd taken care of things himself. But damn, there was nothing like the real thing. Nothing like a full-bodied, glorious woman.

Marrying her wasn't about the money. It was about a legacy, what you left behind, how people remembered you.

Maybe he should have solved the problem by letting her bring the furniture from his apartment. Except that it was a bit ratty, plus he wanted to leave it in the apartment. He said he'd never lie to her, and he hadn't. She just assumed he'd let the apartment go, but it was the last thing in his life that was his. Yes, he wanted Faith and he wanted her father's legacy, but he needed one thing that was his alone. A place he could retreat to if he wanted. It was about choice. He'd probably never set foot in it, but he wanted the option to do so.

She was soft, smooth, and warm against him. He traced the curve of her breast. Her nipple peaked, and she murmured in her sleep. Faith was hot-blooded even if she was shy. He had so many things to show her, so many things to teach her.

He delved between her pussy lips. She made small mewling noises as he stroked. Lifting her leg over his, he nudged the tip of his cock inside her. Flexing his butt muscles, he rocked in and out, slowly, gently. She moaned. Soon she'd wake up.

Oh yeah, he didn't mind how much she spent, but her first purchase better damn well be that vibrator. Staking claim to her own pleasure.

It would be one of many lessons, until his pupil surpassed her teacher.

CONNOR started his campaign to lure his wife to greater heights. He called her on his cell phone as he headed out to the plant on Monday.

She laughed when he said hello. "What, are you nervous on your first day at a new job?"

Her laughter made him hard. He couldn't say why, except that if she was laughing, she wasn't being shy with him. He didn't want to do things *to* his wife. He wanted them to do things to each other. Mutual.

"Yeah, I'm nervous about facing my new boss," he teased. "Tell me what you're wearing so I can get my mind off it."

"You saw me before you left," she said. "My jean skirt and a blouse."

The midcalf skirt pulled tight across her ass and had a slit up the back to just above her knees. Yeah, perfect. "What I want to know is what you're wearing underneath."

She was silent a moment, not even a hint of her earlier smile. "Underneath?"

"Panties or no panties? Bra or no bra?"

"I've got school. Of course I have on a bra and panties."

"You can keep the bra, but ditch the panties."

She gasped. "Connor, I'm going to *school*."

"You've got parent-teacher day. No kids on campus. I want to think of you without panties while all those fathers sit on the opposite side of your desk."

"It's mostly moms."

"Faith." He waited a long moment, then added, "Take off your panties. Because that's how I want to think of you today. All day. I just might have to go into the men's room and whack off because I'll be so damn hard thinking about it."

Her sexual esteem needed building up, and telling her things like that would go a long way. Especially since it was true.

"I'm hard already." He stroked his cock through his pants a couple of times. "Really hard."

"You're insatiable," she whispered, almost in awe. "You came just before we got up this morning."

"So did you. But you're wet again."

Her silence told the story.

"Take off your panties. I'll call you later to make sure."

He disconnected, smiling. She was a hot item under all those inhibitions.

Reaching the monument sign announcing his destination, Connor pulled into Castle Heavy Mining's parking lot. The board meeting, his introduction, was at eight thirty. He smiled to himself. It *was* a bit like a kid's first day at school, and tonight, he'd rush home to his wife to tell her all about it.

Damn. He hadn't realized until this moment how sweet a feeling that would be. Coming home to Faith. He'd make sure she was so damn hot by the time he walked in the door that she'd barely be able to say hello before she had her hand on his cock.

THE manufacturing plant was one long building designed for efficient materials and process flow, and next to it sat the two-story head office. Employees came and went, the lobby a beehive of activity. He caught a few glances and assumed word was out that the new CEO started today. Everyone wondered if it was him.

For his headquarters, Jarvis Castle had spared no expense, creating a world-class lobby of glass and chrome. A long black marble countertop offered coffee, tea, water, or juice, and a mounted TV tuned in to one of the cable financial news networks.

The receptionist was male, with politeness down to an art form as he directed Connor upstairs to the boardroom where his introductory meeting as CEO would be held in—he glanced at his watch—five minutes.

The board consisted of family members with varying percentages of ownership. Jarvis Castle's cousins. They weren't a close-knit bunch, Faith had revealed, and from snippets he'd gleaned from associates at Green Industries, Connor gathered that Jarvis was a bit of a tyrant.

It was all fine for Connor. He wanted to be the glue that brought the family corporation back where it should be. Even if he didn't have the blood relation.

Connor welcomed tough situations.

It was bedlam inside the lushly appointed boardroom. As with the lobby, no expense had been spared. The table was polished mahogany, the chairs leather, and the room outfitted with state-of-the-art video conferencing equipment. Brewing coffee emitted a rich, luxurious aroma. The board members didn't even notice him, and Connor used the time to take stock of them. Jarvis, in his old-fashioned three-piece suit, was the oldest. The three female board members were clearly outnumbered by the seven men. Though a privately held corporation and not governed by the same rules as publicly traded companies, Castle had done a bang-up job on its annual report, designed primarily for suppliers and customers, including all the requisite facts on its board. He recognized individuals from their pictures.

"You can't just drop a bomb like this on us without some discussion, Jarvis."

That would be Preston Tybrook. At 12 percent, his was the largest family holding next to Jarvis's 48 percent. Gray hair, early fifties, Preston was in gym-toned shape, but his face was far too florid at the moment for his own good. He looked like he might pop a blood vessel.

"Preston's right, Jarvis. This is unacceptable. You can't just foist the man on us like this."

That would be Tybrook's wife, Dora. Like Connor, she'd married into the company. Her hair was dyed jet-black, and she wore it long, which made her white face far too stark and showed the lines of middle age, though she probably thought it made her look younger than her true age of fifty. Upon the birth of their daughter Josie twenty-odd years ago, 3 percent of Preston's original 12 had gone to Dora and guaranteed her board seat.

Though crowded around Jarvis's end of the table, the rest of the assemblage didn't say much beyond a smattering of grumbles. There were the Plumleys, Thomas, Richard, and Alexis, siblings ranging in age from early to midfifties, 5 percent ownership each. Then the Finches, Branson, Gabriel, and Cyril, ages in the forties, 5 percent ownership. And finally, Nina Simon. She was gorgeous, Connor had to admit. Her hair caught his eye, Faith's color, reds and golds, but while Faith's was natural, Nina Simon's looked bottle-born. She stood back from the rest, arms folded beneath ample breasts, a slight curve to her ruby lips. Her short skirt showcased a decent pair of legs and around her ankles, silver bracelets with tiny bells. Close to his own age, she had the look of a man-eater about her, a seductive jut to her hips, her high-heeled shoe tapping on the plush carpet, the anklet bells tinkling. 5 percent holding like all the rest, but hers had come by way of her husband's death.

Faith rounded out the ownership with her 5 percent.

"And speak of the devil, here he is."

Jarvis damn near beamed at Connor. Elbowing his way through the combatants, he held out his hand for a good shake.

Connor smiled, pumping his father-in-law's hand. The old man had set him up. He'd set the board up, too. It was obvious Jarvis had sprung the news of Faith's nuptials and Connor's employment contract just before Connor walked in the door.

The board resented him before he'd even gotten started.

Jarvis clapped him on the back with a far firmer slap than Connor would have imagined. "My son-in-law, Connor Kingston."

Preston Tybrook was the next to take his hand. "Welcome to the family." His nostrils flared and something dark swirled in his gray eyes. "My wife, Dora."

Dora shook his hand, her grip firm, actually squeezing his fingers like a man trying to show superior strength. Her blue eyes would have been prettier without the ice chips in them.

Nina Simon was a different kettle of fish. She took his hand and didn't let go. "I can't believe Faith kept *you* a secret." She gave him a sexy, half-lidded once-over.

Oh yeah, his work was cut out for him. Cousin Nina just had an atypical approach from the rest of the family. Getting this group to buy into any cost-cutting measures would be a major challenge.

Earning his 5 percent share wasn't going to be a cakewalk, Connor knew, but the old man had just issued a challenge neither of them would back down from.

"WELL, guess that means Connor is ratified as our new CEO."

"Like it wasn't a forgone conclusion, Jarvis." That grumble came from Thomas Plumley. His bald head gleamed in the overhead lighting, and he slumped slightly in his cushy leather chair.

Thomas was right. Jarvis had it in the bag. He owned 48 percent, so technically, he could be outvoted, but he also had Faith's proxies for her 5 percent. Jarvis ruled.

"Let's give Connor a round of applause." Jarvis was tickled pink with himself. Even his eyes twinkled.

The round of applause was halfhearted. Connor's five-year CEO contract had been confirmed—though it was nullified if he broke the prenup terms—and earning his percentage share of the company upon meeting his cost objectives approved.

"Fifteen-minute break, people, then we've got other business." Jarvis rose, grabbed Connor's arm, and leaned in. "Didn't say I was going to make it easy."

"I have to hand it to you. You outsmarted me."

Jarvis had outsmarted himself, too. This portion of the meeting had lasted an hour and a half, and in that short space of time, Connor witnessed firsthand how Jarvis's family felt about him. He could almost hear their thoughts. *"What's the fucking point in voting on anything?"* It was Jarvis against them. Not a single member of that board voted with Jarvis on anything, even on the authorization to repave the parking lot. Jarvis was a micromanager of the worst order, and his board—his *family*—hated him. It was a wonder they still had a functioning business.

Jarvis walked him halfway down the hallway outside the boardroom. "Didn't you say you enjoyed a challenge?"

"Yes, I did say that somewhere along the way." A bigger challenge than he'd anticipated, but he *would* win in the end.

"Good. When are you going to provide me with those cost-cutting measures?"

"One month," Connor said. He hadn't even toured the plant yet, but Jarvis was push-push-push. He wouldn't let the old man get the better of him. "Now if you'll excuse me, I need to check in with your daughter."

Jarvis rubbed his hands together. "Ooh, she's got you on a tight leash."

He didn't mind giving Jarvis that impression. "Very tight."

Outside, he made his phone call. Faith didn't answer. Probably in with a parent. He left her a brief message. "How wet are you now? I'm so hard thinking about what I'm going to do to you tonight that it's embarrassing in front of your family."

He wanted her thinking about sex, sex, sex all day long. He wanted her wild when he got home to her.

Oddly, *she* was the reward for getting through today rather than the other way round. Connor didn't pause to ponder that thought as he returned to his father-in-law and the lion's den.

SHE'D been married a little over three weeks, but Faith feared she'd spontaneously combust right there in her tiny school office with her cell phone tucked against her ear.

"Are you hot?" Connor murmured.

"Yes," she whispered, as if someone would overhear. She'd closed her office door after her last meeting. There'd been no classes today, just a series of teacher meetings to discuss everything from sixth-grade graduation to summer school to who was bringing the potato salad for the potluck on the last day of the term. All day, Connor left her messages that made her a little insane. He'd told her to go into the bathroom and touch herself. Good Lord, she'd done it, too. Thank God no one had been in the teachers' lounge at the time. Not that she'd made any noise in there, but . . . it was the thought.

And there were so many more messages.

"I want to bend you over your classroom desk, lift your skirt, and slide my cock deep inside."

"I want to slam you up against the chalkboard and do you hard and fast until you beg."

"I need your lips on my cock right this goddamn minute."

With his final message, he'd told her to call him back. Her fingers had trembled punching in his speed-dial number. He'd been number one on speed-dial for three weeks, replacing Trinity.

"Are your nipples hard?" he murmured.

So hard. All morning, all afternoon. "Yes."

"Touch them through your blouse."

"Connor." She hesitated. God, she wanted to touch herself for him, here, now. Secluded in her work office, phone sex had an added thrill over how she'd felt alone in her bed with his voice in her ear. Yet . . . this was risky. "Where are you?"

"I'm in my new office. And right now, I'd like nothing more than for you to walk in, lock the door, spread yourself out on my desk, and beg me to go down on you."

She went up in smoke.

"Pinch your nipples and imagine it's me." He gave the briefest of pauses. "Do it now, Faith."

She did, undoing one button to reach inside her blouse. A tingle streaked down to her pussy. A little moan escaped.

"That's it, baby. You're so hot you could almost come without touching yourself, couldn't you?"

He was such a seducer. She loved how he made her feel—desirable, wanted. She adored the low cadence of his voice, his slightly harsh breath, his words laced with need. She loved it when he came on the phone with her, his rough growl in her ear, the deep groan of satisfaction, and her name on his lips. She wanted him to come now, with her, for her.

She was losing her mind.

After rebuttoning her blouse, she transferred the phone to her other ear. "Connor, we can't do this now."

Yet, he made her want to so badly. Common sense flew out the proverbial window when he talked to her like this.

"Baby." He purred the endearment. "You need to learn that a little risk adds a lot of spice. And really, with the door locked, how big is the risk?"

"It's just that we're both at work."

"That's why it's hot."

"Connor." Someone had to act like the responsible adult.

"You win. But you have to give me something else instead."

Sensation trickled down her spine. "What?"

"Buy the vibrator. Bring it home. You've been stalling me for three weeks. That's long enough."

His request made her feel as she had in front of the hotel room mirror on their brief honeymoon, exposed, vulnerable. Connor just didn't get that buying a vibrator was akin to laying out her sex life for a total stranger. Not to mention what *Connor* would make her do with it.

"What makes you think I didn't buy it at lunch like you told me to?" As he'd told her every day for the past three weeks. And every day, she had another excuse why she hadn't had time.

"Oh, Faith, baby, I know when you're lying. You can't hide anything from me."

It was scary. He was right. Her every emotion was written on her face or in her gaze. All Connor had to do was look, and he knew what she was thinking. Correct that, he didn't have to see. He knew it over the phone. Even her voice was transparent.

"You're a hot-blooded woman, Faith. Act like it." He lowered his voice. "Own it."

She bit her lip, then pursed them together. "Why is it so important to you?"

"Sex is important to me. I want it to be equally important to you. I want an active participant who fearlessly takes what she wants. Because I'm going to take what I want."

"Is this bondage?" Or was he telling her he'd find sex elsewhere if she didn't live up to her end of the bargain? Her sexual desire was rapidly circling the drain.

"No. It's being equals. It's pushing each other farther than we've ever been. That's what makes sex so fucking good."

He scared her. Not in a physical, life-threatening way. But where she preferred doing it in the dark under the covers, he would force her to do it in front of the mirror, though *force* wasn't the right word. He'd turn her inside out until she was begging to do whatever he wanted.

She was afraid she'd come to crave what he gave her, to the point where she couldn't live without it. That would give him all the power in the world.

10

CRAVING the delicious sexual things he did to her only gave him the power if she allowed him to have it. That fact, which should have been a no-brainer, took Faith an hour to figure out after pressing the end button on her cell phone. When it came to men and sex games, she was a slow learner.

Right now, Connor was in charge, telling her what to do, how to take care of her own needs, yadda yadda. Once *she* took charge, he wouldn't have any power at all.

She parked her car in a lot on the back side of Main Street and sat for a moment in the late afternoon sun. A young mother unloaded her baby from the car seat of her SUV, put the child in a stroller, and hooked a diaper bag over the handles.

Faith wanted a baby, and she didn't want Connor to cheat. She'd made an agreement with him, basically giving him sexual carte blanche. He didn't put the emotion into that, *she* did.

Maybe promising to buy the vibrator, then not doing so was a passive-aggressive attempt at gaining control. She didn't want to be under his thumb, needing him so badly she'd turn a blind eye to whatever he did.

To buy or not to buy, that was the question. Was it giving in to Connor or taking ownership of her sexuality? Come to think of it, was *not* buying the damn toy simply giving in to cowardice? Ooh, she hated all this overanalyzing.

Faith yanked the car door open and marched to Main Street as if she were on a mission. She knew the shop. At Halloween they'd displayed a gorgeous array of feather masks.

Inside, leather, vinyl, and lace abounded, hanging from the walls and racks set about the shop. An assortment of bronze, silver, gold, and black sparkly eye shadows and lip glosses glittered beneath the glass counter. Tittering in the corner, a group of teenage girls fingered through a rack of kilts.

The glimmer of gold caught Faith's eyes. A halter top fashioned of gleaming gold-colored coins dangled from a bust-shaped hanger. Faith ran her palm along the bottom, then gathered the coins in her hand. Heavy and cool to the touch, she imagined how it would feel against her breasts, the metal heating with skin contact. She wanted it, but . . . well . . .

There'd be way too much bare flesh showing below the halter. The thought of trying it on for Connor, then having him say it didn't suit her was demoralizing.

Besides, she was here for a toy, and that room was somewhere in the back. She waded through the rows of skimpy lace teddies, past the crotchless panty rack, and entered a narrow corridor lined along one wall with feather boas of every color imaginable. On the other wall, umm, penises. Gag penises. That didn't sound good, either. They were penis-shaped gag gifts. Penis suckers, penis lipsticks, pencil erasers, swizzle sticks, and highlighters. Next to that were the boobs. Beer mugs with boob handles. Straws with a boob on the top. There was even a child's sippy cup. Now that was in bad taste, no pun intended.

She slipped through the bead curtain at the end of the hall, a million tiny beads clattering to announce her arrival.

"Hi, sweetcheeks, what can we do you for?"

Who was the *we*? The back room was thankfully devoid of customers. Just one giant-sized sales clerk. Of the male variety. With short, spiked pink hair, eyeliner, mascara, and a pair of jeans that hugged his . . . package.

Oh gawd. A man was beyond the pale. Yet she smiled as sweetly as her cheeks would allow. "I'm just looking, thank you." *Please don't follow me. Please don't keep talking to me.*

He merely smiled. "Shout if you have a question."

Faith almost sagged with relief when he squeezed behind the counter and began leafing through . . . yes, it looked like a calculus textbook.

The room was as comparatively pint-sized as the man was giant-sized, but it was jam-packed with sexual accoutrements. Handcuffs, blindfolds, and chains draped one wall. Erotic videos and books filled glass shelves, the covers suggesting something more tasteful than a male porn movie. Stands of varying sizes took up the center floor, individual compartments overflowing with neon condoms, sexual gels, enhancers (for what, she wasn't quite sure), what looked like little plugs (no, she wasn't going to ask). So much . . . stuff. Something for every fetish.

And an entire wall filled with vibrators.

It was an amazing assortment. The John Holmes model was designed for a horse, not a woman. No, the legendary porn star couldn't have been *that* big. Next to "John" was "wet-n-wild," which was plain but more her size. The "pleasure wand," the "swan," the "woman eater." Who came up with these names?

"First time?"

She practically jumped out of her skin. Though, by his liberally applied cologne, she should have known Spike was in the near vicinity. It wasn't a bad smell, something expensive from the men's counter that reminded her of an ocean sail on a hot summer day, nor did it sting her eyes. It was just too *there*.

She knew what he was thinking. He had a pathetic, lonely female on his hands who'd succumbed to the desperate call of the vibrator. All right, that was the third reason she hadn't wanted to come here. Maybe the most important reason.

"Are you looking for hi-tech or low-tech?" he asked when she obviously didn't have a voice to answer with.

Faith shrugged, her mortification growing exponentially. Was it better to stay rooted to the spot or scoot like a mouse?

Pulling a model from the wall, he turned it over to read the back packaging. "This one's programmable." Glancing down at Faith, his blue eyes sparkled. "You can set the speed, the angle of rotation, the level of vibration, changing it all at intervals of thirty seconds. All you have to do is strap it on, then lay back and let it do everything for you."

She couldn't help herself; Faith laughed. "It sounds like one of those treadmills at the health club where you program in the hills and the speed changes."

He slipped it back on the hook. "You're right. Too much like a workout. Now here's a dandy model."

Pink, penis-shaped—obviously—with even a crown and an odd protuberance halfway down the shaft almost near the base.

"This," he said, holding it out for her inspection, "has a clitoral stimulator. And this"—he pointed to the protuberance, a bit like the stalk on a cactus—"works the outside."

Faith's cheeks flamed at the implications. She was talking to a . . . man about . . . vibrators and clitoral stimulators.

Yet he had such a sweet smile and a kind of little boy excitement that was almost infectious. What the heck, she was here, why not have a little fun, too?

She wrinkled her nose. "It's too big."

"Honey, nothing's too big when you're in the right mood, not even John over there." He flapped a dismissive hand at the monster vibrator. "But here's a little secret I tell all the girls," he went on, grabbing a simple "pleasure wand" in zebra stripes. "Nothing fancy, no frills, it just vibrates like the dickens. And the nice thing about it is your man can be doing manual or oral while he's got it inside you or he can be inside and use it for clitoral stimulation."

She should have been a puddle of mortified embarrassment at his feet, yet he'd naturally assumed she had a partner. A man. She wasn't just a pathetic loner.

He rolled his eyes. "With this other stuff, *things* get in the way, if you catch my drift."

It was the right size, simple, no gadgetry, and the zebra stripes would make Connor laugh. She hoped.

"I'll take that one."

"The right choice, sweetie." He tossed it in the air and caught it. "You want to try it out first?"

She felt as if her eyebrows topped out in her hairline. "Try it out?"

"Yeah. It's important to like the feel of it," he said over his shoulder as he headed to the sales counter. "Batteries not included, but I've got some back here."

She watched, terrified, as he popped the plastic packaging. Try it out? They had another back room where she could . . .

"Here we go." He strolled back, grabbed her hand, and plopped the vibrating zebra stripes in her palm. "Nice?" He gazed at her expectantly.

The thing sent vibrations all the way up her arm until she thought her teeth were chattering. Then she started to laugh, biting her lip to keep it in until she could find her voice. "Yes. It's nice."

He sighed belly deep with satisfaction. "You don't have to buy the most expensive to get the best. My S-O *adores* this one."

She had to think. S-O. Oh yeah, duh. Significant Other.

He shook it at her. "So if you and your man don't like it, you bring it back, okay?"

Again, her eyebrows shot to her hair. "If I've *used* it?"

"I can't take it back, but since you bought it on my recommendation, I'll exchange it and toss it." He beamed. "Happy customers are what we're all about." He nipped behind the counter and kachinged on his register. "Oh, and we've got a sale next week on handcuffs. Your man like to restrain you a bit?"

"I don't know. I'll have to ask him."

Connor would die when she told him about this.

It struck her this was the first time she'd thought of running home to tell Connor something, anything. As if he were her man, not just the man she'd married to get a child.

"WHAT the hell is that?" Jarvis stood stock still in the middle of the QC lab, pointing like the grim reaper.

Larry almost tripped over himself, as well he should. Another cousin. They proliferated the work site. This one belonged to Richard, or was it Alexis? One could never tell.

Larry merely stared goggle-eyed at the piece of test equipment sitting in the middle of the linoleum tiles. It was so new it lacked its asset tag and still wore its manufacturer's stickers. The little Asian girl bent over her station, her long, dark hair obscuring her face. Jarvis always forgot her name because she was so silent whenever he entered the lab that he almost forgot she was there. A male QC tech—all Jarvis could see was his white-coated back—rolled a computer cart to the far end of the lab, presumably out of shouting range.

"I didn't authorize this," Jarvis boomed. It was good to use a loud voice to let subordinates know you meant business.

"N-n-no, s-s-sir," Larry stammered. He'd never make it far in this world with that stammer. Hence his being QC supervisor at Castle. Castle was a refuge for family cast-offs.

"Then what the hell is it doing in this lab?"

"I authorized it," Kingston's voice carried into the lab.

"You don't have that much authority for signing CEAs," Jarvis snapped.

Capital expenditure authorizations were the way Jarvis controlled spending, with board approval over ten thousand dollars. And that damn tensile tester was over the mark.

Damn wastrel. Kingston overstepped his bounds left and right. He'd also impugned Jarvis's management skills. He'd actually suggested Jarvis shouldn't yell at his employees. Jarvis never yelled; he simply made his position known in no uncertain terms. In the three weeks since Kingston arrived at Castle, he'd thrown everything into turmoil.

"CEA signing authority for the CEO *is* ten thousand, Jarvis."

Jarvis wanted to snarl. Kingston was all cool, unruffled feathers. The man had no emotion. How could that be good for Faith? And dammit, he was right, too. The signing authority was set when Jarvis was CEO, and he'd forgotten to change the company procedure. Jarvis didn't want to admit he'd forgotten anything.

Connor went on in that calm voice. "We've been spending fifteen thousand a month on outsourcing the analysis." He leaned into Jarvis. "Cost savings, five K per month. That's half a percent toward my first goal."

Bastard. "Once we figure out the problem with the teeth, we won't need it." Recently, the teeth were busting off the shovel buckets when under high stress levels.

"Correction. We've learned it's a test we need to perform on the teeth all the time."

For a moment, Jarvis felt like an idiot. He had a stack of CEAs on his desk, but so much had been happening, he'd pushed that duty to the wayside. It wasn't like him. He almost hated Kingston for making him doubt himself.

"Fine. I approve the purchase. But I want the procedure on my desk to make the necessary change to the signing authorities."

"I'm already working on the procedure," Connor said. He was a smooth one, with that slick smile. "In my opinion, the levels are too low. VPs should have at least twenty-five K."

"They'll bankrupt us!"

Connor didn't say anything, and Jarvis was suddenly aware of the audience. The two QC techs, a receiving boy who'd just entered, and Larry. There was a whole lot of silence going on in that lab, and Jarvis didn't like it. "Don't your people have some testing to do, Larry?"

"Yes, sir." He waved his hand, and everyone pretended they were hard at work.

Jarvis was outmanned and outgunned. For the moment. "You need to check with me on any changes you want to institute."

Connor looked up, gauged the distance between themselves and the lab's occupants, and lowered his voice. "In our agreement, you gave me authority to institute changes and cost reductions."

"With approval." Jarvis felt himself fairly vibrating with tension. "It's my company, and I'm still chairman of the board."

He thought he saw Kingston's jaw flex. Good. The man needed to learn who was boss. Just because he'd married the chairman's daughter didn't mean he'd become king of *this* Castle.

CONNOR cracked his knuckles, poured a finger of scotch into a glass, and relaxed into the couch. Another long day. After three weeks, he was still getting to know the inner workings of Castle Mining. He'd run late tonight for a meeting with Masters, the head of program management. Instead of dashing home to Faith, he'd stopped by his apartment to unwind. And to think. He didn't think well around Faith. He simply wanted to jump her. He processed the day's events only after she was asleep. This evening, he needed to consider what to do about her father.

Jarvis had humiliated Larry Plumley in front of his work crew. It was an unforgivable thing to do to any subordinate. If you needed to ream them a new asshole, you did it in the privacy of your office, not in full earshot of their workers.

Jarvis Castle was a micromanaging control freak. If he wasn't careful, he'd lose his engineering VP, Don Biddle. And Biddle was too good an asset to lose. Dammit. Connor knew he'd have a fight on his hands, but this wasn't what he'd planned.

The worst was that Jarvis refused to deal with the quality on his purchased parts. Specifically, those from Green Industries. The scope of it had hit Connor the first week at Castle, yet it was still unclear whether the problem originated with Green or if it was something Castle was causing.

His cell rang. Faith. He'd given her a special ring tone.

"I'll be home soon," he said before she even spoke.

"Okay."

That was one of the things he liked about her. She wasn't a nagging wife. "Things ran late here," he explained. He wasn't a loner, but he was better at recharging his batteries alone. Faith, however, was better off with the inference that he was still at the office. "I'll head out in about ten minutes."

"I'll order Chinese. Should be here when you get here."

"Thanks, baby."

Married life was great. Now if only he could fix Castle. It was a challenge. But he thrived on challenge. He'd eventually get Jarvis to see the error in his management style.

Instead of ruminating on his Jarvis problems, though, his mind drifted to Faith. Sipping the last of his scotch, he contemplated all the ways he was going to make her come tonight.

FAITH surveyed the Chinese food bags on the counter. Maybe she should learn how to cook. Sure, she could heat spaghetti; she wasn't useless. But she'd never thought about the domestic thing when she'd agreed to marry Connor. She assumed they'd be living in her suite and eating in Daddy's dining room. Actually, she hadn't thought about it at all until Connor flatly refused to live in her father's house. Just as she hadn't thought about the lack of privacy, though she was starting to get used to it.

And what about the laundry? Or changing the sheets and cleaning the bathroom? To date, she'd borrowed Estelle six times, but she couldn't keep taking her father's household staff.

She hadn't realized she was such a priss. Or so pampered.

"Did you buy it?"

She almost jumped out of her shoes, then her heart stopped beating when she turned.

He was so magnificent. Connor stood in the kitchen doorway, arms akimbo, hands on his hips pushing his suit jacket open, white shirt, striped tie, all that long, lean male body, and a devilish smile on his handsome face.

He stole her breath. He made her legs weak. He heated the blood in her veins. He muddled her brain, and she forgot all about the funny story she'd wanted to tell him. Her marriage was starting to get frightening; or rather her emotions about her husband were getting dangerous.

She knew he wasn't talking about the Chinese food. "I bought it." She tipped her head and tried for saucy to hide the effect he had on her.

He jutted his head forward. "Where is it?"

"Up in my nightstand drawer where it belongs." She turned slightly and flourished her hand. "I've got din—oof—"

Connor had crossed the kitchen without her even seeing, doubled over, and put his shoulder to her stomach for the fireman's carry, his arm across her bottom holding her in place.

Faith squealed. "What are you doing?" She bobbed against his back as he climbed the stairs.

"Dinner can wait. My cock's so hard I could poke a goddamn fire with it. I want you naked now."

He wasn't roses and candlelight and soft music. He wasn't sweet nothings and poetry. But God, he made her insides liquefy.

Setting her on her feet in the bedroom, he took possession of her face with both hands and devoured her lips in a hard, bone-melting kiss. His tongue invaded and owned.

She was halfway to orgasm by the time he stopped. "You taste like . . ." Tipping her head, she considered. "Scotch?"

He grinned. "After five, business meetings go over better with a little alcohol to free the thinking." Stepping back, he tugged off his jacket, tossed it, then yanked his tie. "Take off your clothes," he ordered, a fire in his dark eyes.

Would he be disappointed with the vibrator? It was slim, no bells and whistles. But he could put it in her and use his fingers or his tongue. Or he could climb inside her himself and use the tip of the vibrator on her clitoris.

That's what Spike had recommended. Satisfaction guaranteed or she could bring it back.

"You're lollygagging, Faith."

She started with her shoes, then unbuttoned her blouse. Nervous butterflies fluttered in her stomach. She *still* didn't like undressing in front of him. He was gorgeous; she was . . . not. Naked from the waist up, his body had her salivating.

He tipped her chin with his finger. "You've got the most perfect breasts I've seen in my whole fucking life."

Oh God. He disarmed her with a statement straight from his gut. He didn't say she had the perfect body or that she was beautiful. He chose the one thing she was actually proud of about herself. Or two, as the case may be.

Connor fingered a nipple, his gaze focused, a flush on his cheeks. "Not yet," he whispered as if he were speaking to himself. "Later. I'll take these later."

Then he stepped back once more and unbuckled his belt. She couldn't take her eyes off the hard ridge of his penis bursting from his boxers. The tip glistened.

"It was embarrassing," he said. "I had to keep my suit jacket buttoned so no one saw the come stains. You made me wet all freaking day long."

God, he just *said* things. She'd never known anyone like him. "You were the one who kept calling me."

"You made me call you after you forced me to have sex a million times this weekend."

She laughed. That was another thing Connor did for her—he made sex fun. Some day, there would be one too many things Connor did for her, and she'd be lost in needing him.

"Now get the rest of those clothes off and lay on the bed." He pointed as he rounded the end and opened her bedside drawer. Closing her eyes, Faith dropped the blouse, popped the snaps on her skirt, and let it fall to the floor.

He was so comfortable in his nakedness, because he was so beautiful in his skin. She'd never feel that at ease.

"Faith, my darling, I know you can take something much larger than this."

She turned to find him shaking the vibrator at her. He'd ride right over her if she let him. He might not mean to, but they'd both lose sight of what he wanted versus what she wanted if she didn't draw the line, as hard as that was for her to do.

She shook her finger at him in imitation. "It's *my* vibrator, not yours. So I got what *I* wanted."

He kissed the tip of *her* instrument. "Ooh, baby, that makes me hot. I love it when you take charge."

He would, but only to a point, she feared. Then he'd slam her down. Except that he hadn't gotten annoyed with all her excuses for not buying the darn thing until today. He simply asked her the next day. She'd never actually seen Connor angry.

Faith climbed on the bed and flopped onto her back, trying to appear totally at ease. She fluffed a pillow beneath her head. "Now, surprise me."

"Baby," he whispered from afar, "you're the one who's going to surprise *me*."

Oh Lord. That sounded ominous.

The bed dipped beside her, the vibrator buzzed as he turned it on, and Faith rolled her head on the pillow in time to see him suck the tip. Then he touched it to her nipple. An electric charge shot to her clitoris.

"Do you like that?"

Nodding, she punctuated with a murmured "Mm, yes."

He switched it off and laid the toy between her breasts.

"Good, show me everything you like."

She widened her eyes, the momentary lassitude shooting out of her. "Aren't you going to do it for me?"

"No." He wiggled his eyebrows wickedly as he backed off the mattress to grab a chair and pull it to the foot of the bed. "I had it in mind that you'd perform for me."

She'd masturbated with him, but that was on the phone. He couldn't actually *see* her. He'd taken her in front of the mirror, but she'd never turned around and watched. "Why do I always have to be on display?"

She regretted the question the moment it was out of her mouth. She was supposed to test her limits, but letting him know when she'd a reached a limit gave him the control.

He crawled up the bed and leaned over her. "Spread your legs and fuck the hell out of her yourself with that vibrator." He ran his nose up the side of her cheek and put his lips to her ear. "Because I want to watch you." He licked around the shell. "Because I've been so fucking hard all day imagining it."

But, oh, he knew the right words to make her flush the idea of control down the drain. He took her to 90 percent humidity in less than a second.

"Do it, Faith." It wasn't a demand. It wasn't a plea. It was permission to let herself go; it was his desire to watch.

When she opened her eyes again, he was sitting in the chair, his legs negligently propped on the bed.

"Start with your nipples." He lightly stroked his full, hard cock.

She turned the base, giving it half speed, then rubbed it around her still glistening nipple. "It's not the same as when you do it." There wasn't a jolt, not even a spark.

"Then spread your legs and caress your pussy lips with it. But don't touch your clit yet. And Faith?" He paused until she glanced up. "Look at me while you're doing it."

It was his eyes on her. It was his hand on his cock, slowly pumping. It was his whisper. *Fuck the hell out of yourself with that vibrator because I want to watch you.* Faith couldn't resist him. She couldn't resist the lure of how he made her feel. Wet. Hot. Desired. As if he truly wanted her. *Her.* It was the most powerful aphrodisiac of all.

She turned the vibrator on high, spread her legs, and eased the tip down over her lips. She didn't touch it to her clitoris, yet the sensations hummed through all the nearby erogenous zones. She moaned, because it felt so good and because Connor watched with that intoxicating, hungry light in his eyes. Palming his crown, he smoothed droplets of come over himself.

Faith licked her lips and gave in to him completely.

"Does it feel good, baby?"

"Yes. So good." Her body jerked as she accidentally slid right over her clitoris. Oh, oh, more, but she kept the steady rhythm all around.

"You're so damn wet, I can hear it and it makes me wild." He pumped himself faster. "Touch your clit."

A jolt of lightening streaked through her and she cried out. The vibrations were incredible, setting off mini-explosions, not quite an orgasm, but a sweet prelude. She started to pant.

"That's it, baby. Love yourself with it. Make all the noise you want."

She moaned for him, long, low, then thrashed her head on the pillow. Her body shuddered with need, her breath came in gasps, but drinking in the sight of his hand fisted around his cock, she held off. She wasn't ready to let it end. Sounds rose up from her throat, and she squeezed her eyes shut for a moment, savoring the sensations and the beat of his hand against his own flesh.

"Now dip it inside."

Oh God, yes. With slow, delicious penetration, Faith did what he told her to. The sensations almost too much, she pushed her head back into the pillow as her pussy clenched around the vibrator.

"Fuck yourself with it, baby. Fast."

With his voice urging her on, she pumped in and out, the buzz streaking out to her extremities, along every nerve ending of her skin, and deep, deep inside. She couldn't keep her eyes open. She could only let the scent of sex, the sound of harsh male breath, and the slap of flesh seduce her, drive her higher.

"Pull it out slow this time, baby. And angle it high to hit your G-spot."

She could barely understand, but her body seemed to know. Arching, she dragged the humming toy over a spot that forced a wail from her lips.

Oh, oh, God, so good. So good.

"That's it, baby. You found it." Between her legs, the bed dipped, and he was there, big, hard male cock in his hand, hot, avid eyes taking in the sight of her gripping that vibrator.

"Don't stop, baby. We're almost there."

She panted, then Connor set his knee to the end of the vibrator, holding it deep inside her as he pumped himself fiercely in his hand. A groan rose from his belly, then he hit her clitoris hard with his orgasm, hot come pulsing against her.

And Faith screamed in endless ecstasy.

HOLY Hell. He cradled her damp body in his arms. Tears had leaked from her eyes at the end. She'd screamed his name, and she'd come so hard, he was sure she'd passed out for a moment. Her hair was a tangled mess. He kissed her forehead, then pushed the strands away from her eyes.

"That was beautiful, baby," he whispered in the moist locks.

She muttered, wriggled, then settled once more in his arms.

She had so much passion locked away inside her, it was an honor to help her set it free.

*   *   *

FAITH heard Connor muffling around in the kitchen as she padded downstairs in her robe.

"Hungry?" he said, holding out a fork as she leaned against the doorjamb to watch him.

He was too gorgeous for words, especially since her brain hadn't fully recovered from that orgasm. One unbelievable, stupendous orgasm the like of which she'd never experienced. Yet he hadn't even given it to her. She'd done it herself. Admittedly, it was his gaze on her that made her blow sky-high.

God. She was a closet exhibitionist.

"I'm starving," she said, which she supposed was appropriate after great sex.

Handing her the fork, he unloaded Chinese food containers from the bag. "Your father and I are going to South America next Monday."

It felt like he'd sunk a punch right in her midsection. She couldn't breathe for a moment.

"We'll be gone about two weeks."

Two whole *weeks*? "Why didn't you tell me before?"

He raised a brow. "This is the first chance we've had to talk."

"You could have told me when you walked in the door."

He cocked his head, like a dog that couldn't figure out where the strange noise was coming from. "I didn't feel like telling you then."

"So we had sex beforehand to mollify me." Oh my God, she sounded like . . . a wife.

He opened a container, eased back against the counter, and grabbed a fork. "We had sex before I told you because I've been so fucking hot for you all day, I couldn't wait."

Why did he have to say things like that and totally throw off her equilibrium? She grabbed her own fork and a container, this one full of lukewarm broccoli beef.

He finished his bite of lemon chicken. "It was a given I'd have to go down there sooner or later."

Of course. Her father went down quarterly. But lately, the trips had been wearing on him. He needed a younger man to take over. Why was she being such a bitch? Why did it . . . hurt?

Because, dammit, it felt like Connor was tired of her already, that he didn't even care if he was leaving her for two weeks. And she *hated* the whiny, naggy feeling eating her up inside. She hated sounding like a wife.

Faith squashed her rising emotions. "We shouldn't have wasted the sperm if you're going to be gone that long."

Setting his Chinese box on the counter, he grabbed her chin, held her, forced her to look at him. "It wasn't a waste. It was so goddamn hot, I almost passed out."

She was the one who'd almost passed out. But it was sweet of him to say. He didn't owe her any explanations about the South American trip. Of course he'd be going sometime. She needed to get hold of herself. This—what was it?—this *emotionalism* just wouldn't do. It wasn't part of their bargain.

"Well, you've got almost a week to impregnate me before you go," she quipped, ignoring the hollow feeling in her stomach.

He kissed the tip of her nose. "I'll make it my priority to fuck the hell out of you at least two times per day. And no more coming outside, only deep in your hot, sweet pussy."

God. Things like that just slid so easily off his tongue. And made her so incredibly hot. "Only two times?"

"Twice on weekdays, but weekends, it's four times a day."

Could people actually have *too* much sex?

He considered the horrified expression on her face, then spoke with the most serious of tones. "This baby-making thing is a lot of work, honey. You've got to be totally committed to it."

He was joking; she knew he was. Yet, his words speared straight up inside her. She was committed. She'd traded her father's company for him. She'd given her body over to him.

He was her husband. He was to be the father of her child.

She was suddenly so terrified, she could have thrown up on the floor right there in front of him.

Instead, she gathered plates from the cupboard. "You know, this would be a lot better if we heated it up."

He grabbed her once more, took her mouth, all sweet and zesty. "It would be a lot better," he murmured against her lips, "if we ate off each other's bodies upstairs in bed. I feel my little sperm working up a head of steam again."

Her heart turned over, yet she laughed. "You're voracious."

"There're so many things we haven't done yet."

"Well, we can't do them all tonight." She sounded horribly prim as she dished out the mu shu, rice, beef, and chicken.

"Will you use your vibrator while I'm gone?" He snatched a bit of chicken off the plate before she put it in the microwave.

She shrugged. "Maybe."

"Promise you will."

She shrugged the other shoulder. "How will you know?"

"I'll know. Now promise me."

"I'll think about it and give you my answer before you leave." Okay, that was good. Feisty and sassy.

He crowded her up against the counter and leaned down to whisper in her ear. "You're a hard woman, baby, but I'm a hard man." He punctuated with a roll of his hips. "So do it."

She pushed back. "You know, there's the possibility that I might start liking the vibrator better than you."

"Tease."

She tipped her head back, smiling at him. "That gives me an idea. We can save up your sperm and while you're gone, I'll use a turkey baster to impregnate myself." She let her mouth drop open and gave him an oh-so-innocent gaze. "In fact, with my vibrator and a turkey baster, I might not need you at all."

He pushed aside the boxes, turned her, grabbed her butt, and hoisted her onto the counter. Shoving his hard body between her legs, he growled low and swiped his tongue across her neck. "You need me, baby. Plastic will only go so far. Then you'll be begging me to ram my cock straight up inside you."

"You'll beg first." She shoved him back and put her nose to his. "Because you adore my hot, sweet pussy." She smiled, saucy, a woman totally in control of the banter, and raised one eyebrow. "Isn't that what you said? *Baby?*"

Before she had a chance to move, or even think, he tugged aside her robe and his, and took her sweet, hot pussy high and hard with his cock.

"Yeah, baby, something very close to that."

He rotated his hips. She almost came. Clutching his biceps, she spread her legs to take all of him.

"You've got the sweetest"—he breathed the words against her ear—"hottest"—he slipped a finger between their almost vacuum-packed bodies to caress her clitoris—"most delicious pussy"—then slid inside for dual finger-cock penetration—"and it's all fucking mine." He hammered home one last glorious time.

Faith screamed his name and came apart from the inside out.

Oh God. Her body *was* his.

If she wasn't careful, her heart would be, too.

11

A week later, on a different continent with a long plane ride and a four-hour time change between them, Connor was still amused by her turkey baster comment. Faith had fire. Trinity had portrayed her as sweet but a bit milquetoast, which had been fine with Connor.

Faith was so much more. And no way in hell was she getting herself pregnant off a goddamn turkey baster. Not that he believed she actually could. That was just a myth.

They would make fine children together. She needed him for that at least. Needed him badly.

Didn't she?

He felt the smallest edge of . . . something. He didn't want Faith to *need* him, and he didn't *need* her. The word *need* connoted emotion. This wasn't about emotion; it was about . . . obligation, tit for tat. He got saddled with Jarvis, and she got a baby.

Christ. He had to laugh. In this bargain, she was making out a lot better than he was. The old man was a pain in the ass.

"This damn meeting is a travesty and you're smiling?" Jarvis lowered his voice to a gravel pitch, as if he feared the CEO of Venezuela International Mining had a stoolie standing outside the conference door to eavesdrop on their conversation.

Connor filled a glass with spring water from the carafe and handed it to Jarvis. The meeting in VIM's boardroom at its Caracas headquarters had dispersed for a brief bio break. The room was excellently appointed with comfortable cloth chairs and lateral blinds to shut out the sun as it streamed across the solid wood table. Upon arriving, the Castle delegation had been plied with coffee, tea, bottled water, and light sandwiches.

VIM's accommodations weren't the problem. Jarvis was.

"Our group is handling the presentation well," Connor said.

"Handling it? What the hell does Biddle think he's doing?" Jarvis was close to sputtering, but though they were alone in the room for the moment, he kept his voice low for propriety's sake.

Connor wouldn't be surprised if Biddle was out looking for a new job the minute he got back to the States. Jarvis had a way of making an extremely capable vice president look like an ass.

They'd arrived in Caracas, Venezuela, late Monday night. In addition to Preston Tybrook, the entourage included Dressert from Sales, Biddle from Engineering, Lukbar from Quality, and Preston's daughter, Josie. She was a pretty little thing but a bit on the butch side. Or maybe her manly attire, consisting of a tailored suit complete with dress shirt and tie, cropped dark hair, and no makeup, was her way of holding her own in a man's world. Josie Tybrook was program manager on several of their South American projects, including two ongoing with Venezuelan International Mining.

The full travel group was rounded out by Dora Tybrook and Nina Simon. Unlike Josie, those two ladies had declined attendance at today's meeting in favor of shopping.

"Jarvis, what the hell are you doing?" Preston, upon reentering the room, headed for the water bar. He'd removed his jacket in deference to the humidity. His shirt sported underarm rings, and his face was too florid for good health.

Jarvis jutted his chin. "Stepping in where your boy can't get his finger out of his butt."

"*My* boy? I might have brought Biddle in for the first interview but you approved his contract as Engineering VP."

"Only because he falsified his history and said he was a graduate of Cal Tech when obviously he got his degree off the Internet in two weeks."

They were like squirrels chasing each other. They darted this way, then the chasee turned on a dime and became the chaser. Back and forth, an irritated high-pitched natter, like squirrels outside the window at five in the morning.

Connor stepped into the fray. "Excuse me, gentleman, but the point you're both missing is that Biddle is covering our collective asses by not admitting to our customer that we don't have a clue as to why the shovel teeth keep snapping."

Biddle had actually executed quite good foot play. It would have gone off a lot better if Jarvis hadn't interrupted the man's presentation, breaking the cardinal rule: Don't ream your own player a new asshole in front of the other team; wait till later.

VIM's delegation began to return in dribs and drabs. They'd dressed for the humidity in light cotton. Preston still steamed under his shirt; Jarvis muttered and narrowed his eyes.

Connor took clear stock of the fact that Jarvis Castle needed to step out of his own way.

IT had been an excruciating day. Jarvis had undercut his team no less than four times that Connor observed. It wasn't just his board that Jarvis dictated to; he was in serious danger of alienating his entire management team.

"You meeting us for dinner, Connor?"

Josie smiled at him. She had an eager smile of youthful enthusiasm. A good project manager, she'd be a true asset to the company when she fully matured. He got the impression she and Faith didn't know each other well despite being cousins. The family animosity between Jarvis and his board had affected Faith's relationships, too. That was something he could help with. Faith needed her family. They'd be the most important thing in the world when she got pregnant.

The members of their party had piled into two cabs back to the hotel. Having gotten the riskier cab driver, Jarvis and Preston were already going at it in the bar, and in two hours, VIM's executive group had set up a dinner at a restaurant just down the street. Authentic Venezuelan food.

"Wouldn't miss it." He returned Josie's smile. "I just want to check in with my wife first."

Shit. What was up with that? It made him ridiculously giddy to say it. Maybe it was the word *my*. Connor hadn't been able to say *my* father, mother, brother, sister, family, or whatever since he was nine. He liked the proprietary feeling it gave him. And the sense of belonging.

He punched the elevator button. The hotel was a behemoth. Watching the movies, one got the impression that South America was quaint adobe settings with courtyards, trees, and curlicue railings. The Empress was a modern high-rise with valet parking, luxurious rooms, and secure interior corridors. His suite—with living room, balcony overlooking the Caracas skyline, minibar, and a Jacuzzi tub in the bathroom—was on the eighteenth floor.

Travel would undoubtedly be his next cost-cutting measure. They'd flown first class when business class was adequate, and a room rather than a suite was all one person needed if they weren't entertaining. Which, on this trip, he wasn't.

His door wasn't latched.

There was a trace of perfume, one he recognized, having sat next to it during yesterday's air excursion.

The balcony door was open, and a gentle breeze billowed the see-through drapes. He hadn't ordered it, and it wasn't there this morning when he left, but now a cloth-draped trolley sat in his living room topped with a bottle of Veuve Clicquot in an ice bucket, two brimming glasses, and a tray of chocolate-covered strawberries.

Stepping through the fluttering balcony curtains, Nina Simon snagged a glass and held it out to him, a feline smile on her ruby lips. The shade matched her nail polish.

Connor took the champagne. Hell, he figured it was charged to his room bill, so he might as well indulge.

Yeah, he'd really have to take expense reports in hand, starting with the board of directors.

She tapped her glass to his, then sipped, keeping her eyes on his, lids lowered seductively. Her anklet bells jingled lightly. A droplet of condensation fell from the stem, landing square in her cleavage and sliding down, down, down to disappear between her breasts.

It was too damn perfect to be unplanned.

She had voluptuous breasts on par with Faith's, but less hip. Though her hair was red gold, it lacked the glorious, natural sheen of Faith's.

"I hope the bribe you paid someone to let you into my room doesn't appear on your expense report when we get back."

She smiled. "Would I try to screw the company like that?"

The answer was yes. She'd also try to screw *him*. One way or another. That had been clear the moment she took the first-class seat beside him. She was an expert conversationalist, leaving most men wondering if she'd just made a sexual innuendo, or questioning if he had a dirty mind.

Connor knew he had a genuinely dirty mind. He also knew she was making innuendos.

"To what do I owe the pleasure?" He smiled, sipping. Two could play her game. Maybe it would have been smarter to kick her out on her ass, but he wanted to know if this was a board-ratified setup or if she'd planned it on her own. It was also possible that Jarvis himself had put her up to it.

"I know how those all-day meetings can be. I thought a toast to surviving your first was in order." She'd moved infinitesimally closer, stretching one high-heel–clad foot out so that her toe touched his. She now appeared a tad shorter, her cleavage a tad deeper. Her bells tinkled. She rolled the stem of her glass between her breasts absently, though he was sure Nina never did anything absently. There was always intention.

It was no wonder Faith never wanted a thing to do with the company. She'd have been the baby bunny in the midst of a pack of hyenas. How had she remained fresh and untouched by the decadent, amoral world she'd grown up in? Even Trinity, as sweetly ditzy as she appeared, was more savvy.

"A shame to waste the bottle on just two of us. Why don't I call Jarvis and Preston?" he suggested. "They're in the bar."

She licked her lips, leaving a glistening trail. She was so damn overtly seductive it was off-putting. He preferred Faith's shyness. He wanted his wife—hell, yeah, he really enjoyed saying that—to be assertive with her needs, but Nina was beyond assertive. She was into the realm of uninteresting.

He smiled. And wasn't that the kiss of death to a woman, to be merely uninteresting.

"I think we should keep it a duo." She punctuated with a little moue.

Ungentlemanly of him, but he wanted to laugh. She'd watched too much film noir and taken the role of femme fatale. Sidling closer, she brushed her hip to his. "Would you like a treat?" she said, fluttering a hand toward the tray of fruit. "Or shall we wait until the main course?"

She sure as hell wasn't talking about food. Connor realized he wasn't going to get a clue one way or another as to whether she and Dora had cooked up this little scheme when they'd made last-minute plans to tag along on the trip or if the scheme was all her own. He truly did have a suspicious mind. Maybe she just wanted to get fucked, and he was the moment's choice.

Gold pants hugged her legs, and the plunging neckline of her jacket didn't appear to harbor anything close to a blouse beneath it. It wasn't shopping expedition attire. It was fuck-me wear.

He wanted to change at least his shirt before dinner. "We're meeting VIM in an hour and a half. I'd like to get a call into Faith before then." Hint, hint. He'd prefer not to make an enemy of her by flatly refusing her offer.

She let the glass stem sway in her hand. "Ah, darling Faith. You know, she really is the smartest of us all, having Daddy buy her such a gorgeous little plaything." She trailed a fingernail down his arm. "Tell me, is she strictly missionary?"

Godammit. It pissed him off that everyone assumed Faith couldn't get a man without Daddy bribing one. He admitted the prenup—which the board knew about due to having ratified his future ownership in the company—didn't help the situation, but the fact was if it weren't for her own fears and insecurities, Faith would have been snapped up a long time ago by a man who was after more than just her father's legacy. Connor didn't like that she was so underrated, especially by her own family.

Suddenly, he didn't give a fuck about making an enemy. Besides, if Nina wasn't before, she would be the minute he disallowed her expense report at the conclusion of this trip. He had her pegged. She'd attend one meeting during the two-week trip, then ask for all her expenses to be reimbursed. *No such luck, sweetheart.*

She didn't give a damn about her position on the board, and the company itself didn't mean a thing to her.

"Are my wife's sexual preferences important at the moment?"

She shook her head slowly, a seductive smile spreading across her lips. "No. Not at all."

"Then I suggest you just blow me. That's all I feel like doing right now. That way we won't have to worry about ruining your delightful outfit. No fuss, no muss."

He'd expected shock, maybe indignation, or even a healthy fit of hysterics. Nina merely lifted one eyebrow in exactly the same manner as Jarvis, despite being related to him only by marriage. "What about *my* orgasm, darling?"

He smiled with equal pleasantry. "I don't care about your orgasm."

It was enough to make her take a step back. The bells on her anklets jangled harshly. "How does Faith deal with that?"

"Her pleasure I care about. Yours, I don't."

There wasn't a woman in the world who would drop to her knees and suck a man's cock after hearing that.

Yet Nina stepped forward and put her hand on his pants, then smiled as if she thought she had him. Ah. So it was a scheme, not just a quick fuck on a business trip.

He put his hand over hers and pulled her fingers back. "I've changed my mind. I'll take care of myself later."

Her nostrils flared. "It's not very nice to tease a lady."

"You're correct. That's why I don't tease *ladies*."

Ice chips gathered in her irises. She was in no doubt as to his meaning. "I don't think you're very nice, Mr. Kingston."

"I'm an asshole. And you don't have to like me any more than I like you."

"Asshole," she mused, her eyes narrowed. "It fits you like a glove."

"One more thing: don't disparage Faith. I don't like it."

"Ooh. You sound so sincere." She tossed her hair, laughed, playing the femme fatale again—badly. "But like all men, you have an Achilles' heel." She smiled and dropped her voice to a seductive pitch. "And I will find it."

"And do what with it?" He raised one brow in query.

Nina merely smiled.

He'd been conciliatory with Preston, complimentary to the man's wife, friendly and nonjudgmental with the other board members, Jarvis's so-called family. He'd kissed ass.

Now he realized he wasn't going to be able to ride the fence, play the diplomat, and make friends, not enemies. It was Jarvis against the rest of the board. If Connor didn't want to be caught in the cross fire, he was going to have to take sides. He'd seen that plainly enough over the past weeks, felt it in his gut during today's meeting. Now, it was a shot between the eyes that couldn't miss. The board would try to bring him down if they could. His best bet was to solidly join forces with Jarvis.

"By the way, before you leave"—he held out his hand—"I'd like the card key you used to get in."

She drew the key from her inside jacket pocket, revealing a great deal of flesh at the same time, and held the slim card out before dropping it to the carpet. After another sip of champagne, the wine glimmering on her lips, she set the glass on the trolley. "Watch your back, Connor," she murmured. "You're not going to know who's holding the knife."

Then she sauntered to the suite door.

Giving her his back, he refilled his glass and sipped champagne, waiting for the slam of the door. Her grand exit.

It never came. Connor turned.

Jarvis stood in the open doorway. Over his shoulder, Nina smiled and waved her hand.

Busted with a beautiful woman in his room. If there'd been lipstick on his collar, he'd have been a dead man.

JARVIS raised one eyebrow at his son-in-law.

"Do you really think I'd be that stupid, Jarvis?"

Actually, Jarvis didn't. Kingston was smooth, charming, manipulative, and sneaky. But not stupid. Nina, however, was.

If she wanted to trap him, she should have used a little more discretion. Jarvis was sure Kingston could be had for the right inducement. If he thought he could get away with it.

"I'm watching you," Jarvis warned.

Kingston smiled. He had one of those supercilious smiles with a hint of sarcasm that said he was doing nothing more than laughing at an old man. "You won't find anything."

That's what Jarvis was afraid of, that he wouldn't see it until Faith had been hurt. "I love Faith, you know." He couldn't remember actually mentioning that to Kingston.

The young man smiled again. "Yeah. I know." There was something about that smile beyond the usual. The sardonic curve of his eyebrow faded, and his eyes . . . softened. It was almost damn frightening how genuine that tender smile appeared.

Jarvis couldn't afford to contemplate that Kingston might come to care for Faith. If he let his guard down for a second, Faith would pay the price, so he wouldn't believe in the sincerity of that smile. He'd watch the manipulator like a hawk.

But that wouldn't stop him from enjoying it when Kingston brought down the hammer on the board.

"I want sex, and I want it now, so get your cock ready for me." Though she was giddy with her own daring, Faith blushed.

Connor was two thousand miles away in a time zone four hours ahead, but she blushed anyway. She didn't know if she said it for him, because he wanted her assertiveness, or herself, because she craved the feeling of him inside her. He'd only been gone thirty-six hours, but she missed him.

"Now what if your father answered my cell phone for me while I was in heavy negotiations with a customer?"

She loved Connor's voice over the phone, even laced with humor rather than desire. "You wouldn't leave your cell phone lying around for him to answer."

"True. My cock's out, and I'm stroking it."

"Are you in your room?"

"I'm on my balcony. The night is sultry and warm and I can almost feel your mouth sucking the crown of my cock."

She'd been living in a fantasy world for a week. They'd had so much sex, she'd lost six pounds from the workout. She felt deliciously creamy on the inside. After the last student left at the end of the day, she'd stretch languidly, and her nipples would burgeon thinking about Connor. Driving home, she'd catch herself with a ridiculous smile on her face. Last night on the phone, his voice in her ear, she'd come three times. She loved the sound of his deep groan when he climaxed, the hum of her name, like chocolate sauce drizzled over ice cream.

"Spread your legs and shove your vibrator all the way in. Because that's how I'd do you if I were there. Hard and high, no foreplay, just a sweet, fast fuck, baby."

She almost creamed herself right then. God, how she adored his dirty talk. The vibrator slid deep in all her juices.

His voice whispered over the airwaves. "Fuck me, Faith."

It was almost as if he'd asked her to make love to him.

HE'D left the balcony door and the drapes open. The night breeze felt like Faith's fingers on his skin. He stacked his hands beneath his head on the pillow and stared at the ceiling.

Fuck. She was so good. All he had to do was get her to let loose like that when they were together. Recalling her opening demand had him all horny again. Connor figured he'd been ignoring his libido over the six months. It could be the only explanation for this insatiable . . . lust. He meant every word he'd told Faith about feeding lust with all manner of acts new and exciting, but he hadn't anticipated getting caught up in teaching her. He stroked himself idly, feeling the build in his balls, the quickening of his pulse, the blood rush to his cock.

There'd been nights he'd had her three, four, and once even five times. Yet he wanted her to have *him*. To take *him*. It was nothing so simple as submission versus dominance. It was a need to drive her beyond any place she'd ever dared go. To excite her until her barriers fell, and she'd do anything he wanted. And come up with some things he'd never even dreamed of.

Why did he want these things from her so badly?

She had such a naïveté; perhaps he was simply the type who needed to corrupt. His cock fully hard in his hand, he groaned. He was so fucking lucky compared to the suckers who'd passed her by in search of skinny, vain, high-maintenance beauty queens.

Hell, why ask why? He had Faith. She was all a man needed. Because he knew for sure that one day he'd get her to drop every barrier to her sexuality and send him to the moon.

12

FAITH tried not to be so excited that Connor was coming home in two days. Last week, she'd given her class their summer send-off. Next year, they'd be first graders. How time flew. How her heart had ached watching them. She wanted to watch her own child graduate from kindergarten. While Connor had been away, her fertile time had come and gone, and really, that was why she wanted him home. Honest. Oh God, what a lie—she'd missed him, not just his seed. Badly.

She didn't want to be needy, yet her mind was a jumble of thoughts, her body a riot of emotions. With school out, she didn't have a thing to occupy her mind except Connor. She should have signed on to do summer school. She needed something or she'd go crazy every day waiting for him to come home.

What was that manila envelope stuffed under the front mat? It hadn't been there when she left to have her nails done.

The moment she picked it up, a chill passed over her arms, raising the little hairs. No address or postage, just her name, her new name, *Faith Kingston*, scrawled across the front. She wasn't used to it yet, especially when one of the children actually called her

Mrs. Kingston. Seeing it now in block letters on the envelope, her heart tripped all over itself.

Whatever it was, it wasn't good.

Inside, the sun shining through the long bank of windows overlooking the back porch had heated the condo. Faith closed the curtains, not so much to keep out the heat of the June afternoon, but because she felt almost as if someone might be watching her.

The envelope hadn't been sealed except for the metal clasp, which she undid, then pulled out a sheaf of photos. On the top, a note had been clipped on.

What your husband is UP to while he's away.

Faith closed her eyes. The note didn't completely cover the contents of the first picture. A black-and-white. A man standing; a woman on her knees. Her hand wrapped around his penis, the crown slipping between her lips.

Even closing her eyes didn't shut it out.

Connor wouldn't cheat. He promised.

Her blood pounded against her ears. Dizziness swamped her, and the pictures fell to the floor, the note and clip pulling loose, and the photos scattering all over the carpet.

She didn't want to look, but she had to. Sex, so much sex. The woman's lips drawing the nectar from his erection. Her gorgeous body, toned curves, the outline of a voluptuous breast. She was everything Faith wasn't but yearned to be.

She stood there a moment until she realized her body was shaking and the backs of her eyes ached, holding tears at bay.

Her vision swam in the moisture but she could still see those pictures in her mind's eye.

The woman's body, his hands threaded through her long hair, his . . . Faith realized his face never made it into the pictures. She hunkered down and shuffled through the photos. Glossies from a photo printer, all were of him from the neck down. In fact, Faith wouldn't be able to pick out the woman in a room full of long, dark-haired ladies, either. The angle of the camera didn't show her clearly. It looked almost as if the man held the camera himself, up high, and shot pictures of the action.

This didn't *have* to be Connor. It could be . . . anyone.

It could be some nasty prank someone wanted to play on her. Or a malicious lie someone was spreading about Connor.

But who? Faith snorted. Any number of people, from Cousin Preston, who hated Connor taking over, to Lance, who seemed to think he'd been robbed of something, too. Even her own father could have engineered this. Not that Daddy would ever stoop this low. Besides, why sabotage things *after* they'd gotten married?

Faith ripped each photo into pieces, then walked them to the outside trash. She didn't want a single shred in her house.

"It wasn't him," she whispered aloud. And really, she believed what she was saying. That's why she had absolutely no intention of telling Connor about it. She wouldn't let him think she didn't trust him.

FAITH stared at herself in the full-length bedroom mirror. She wasn't sure she liked the dress Connor had bought her in South America. The neckline plunged—if she bent over, the other country club guests would see her nipples—and a slit rode high, revealing the lace band of the silk stockings he'd purchased.

Stepping up behind her, he put his hands on her shoulders, leaned down, and nibbled her ear. "You look gorgeous."

She didn't. She looked . . . well, okay, not frumpy, but the thigh-highs made her thighs feel chunky. In his new tux, he looked . . . edible. Completely. Totally.

Every person at the country club tonight would be doing the compare-and-contrast routine. They'd all be saying that Daddy bought her a husband, and what a fine specimen, too. There'd be bets on how long it would take Connor to cheat and with whom. She so did not want to attend tonight's party. But try as she might, she couldn't tell Connor that. He wanted to "show her off," as he called it, and she just could not admit to him how terrified she was.

They lived together, had sex like rabbits, but she couldn't lay out all her fears for him to dissect.

Looking at their reflections in the mirror, it scared her how much she'd missed him when he was gone. He smelled so good, a subtle cologne mixed with his own unique male scent. Her heart hurt looking at how beautiful he was, but, as Connor said, this was lust, giddy and overpowering. That ohmygod-I-have-to-hear-his-voice-or-I'll-die feeling would fade. It was the newness.

He caressed her bare throat. "I have a present for you. For our one-month anniversary."

God. He'd bought her jewelry like a real husband. She wouldn't dare ask him how much he'd spent.

The box he set on the counter was bigger than a jewelry box. Tissue paper frothed out when she opened it, and Faith poked around until she found black lace panties.

All right, so Connor wasn't the typical husband. On a business trip he'd brought back a sexy evening dress and thigh-high stockings, now this.

"Put them on," he urged.

They were . . . heavy. She peered at the crotch. "What *is* this?" In the center lay a silver cylinder shaped like a bullet but several times larger.

"Loaded panties, and I want you to wear them tonight."

She laughed and gasped at the same time as the thing started to buzz in her hand. Okay, so Connor was the furthest thing from a normal husband. "It's a vibrator."

He held up a flat device in his palm. "The remote."

"You're going to buzz me while we're at the party?"

"If I see you looking bored or giving some hotshot the eye, I'll give you a little warning."

He made her laugh as easily as he got her wet. "You're crazy. And I cannot go to the country club with a vibrator stuck up my—" She stopped. "What if someone hears it?"

"Put it in and we'll check it out."

"Connor." She wasn't so sure about this.

"Faith." He wasn't going to back down.

She sighed, as if there weren't a distinct thrill shooting straight to the heart of her clitoris. "All right, fine." She shimmied the dress high enough to grab the elastic edge of her panties and rolled them down her legs.

Connor held the vibrating panties out for her to step into, and she steadied herself with a hand on his shoulder. Sliding them into place, he dipped inside the panty, slipping over her slick clitoris before he tipped the little bullet vibrator up into her pussy. His palm was warm, the metal cold, the sensations absolutely shivery.

Then he removed his hand, the panty holding the vibrator snugly in place, and pressed the remote. Faith dug her fingers into his shoulder.

"How's it feel?"

It felt like a tongue lapping at her on the inside. Hot, but not enough to make her come. "Nice," she whispered.

"I can't hear a thing. We're safe, sweetheart." He kissed the tip of her nose. "I'll just buzz you when I want you."

"I can't believe you're actually going to do this."

"I told you I like a little excitement."

"This is kinky."

"Believe me, baby, you ain't seen nothing yet." He shoved the remote in his jacket pocket. "We don't want to be late." Raising her hand to his lips, he sucked one finger into his mouth, his gaze steady on her, then he whispered, "Let's see how many times I can make you come without anyone knowing a thing."

He made her crazy, scared, and wet.

But at least for the moment, he made her forget her nervousness about tonight's country club gala.

FUCK. She was hot in the tight dress. It defined her gorgeous curves, her sweet breasts, the roundness of her belly, and the softness of her thighs. The skirt flared at the bottom, accentuating calves toned from her daily lunchtime walks at school. The slit up her thigh made him hard, but her unbound hair flowing over her shoulders and back was the crowning glory. He wanted nothing more than to bury his face between her legs and lick her to a screaming orgasm.

Ah, but he'd have to wait. The club ballroom overflowed with crepe paper decorations in honor of the July fourth holiday and party dresses, anything from short-short to full length, most in red, white, or blue, a few in black like his wife. The women strutted their bright plumage like peacocks. He wondered how much had been spent on face-lifts this past year. Male attire was either black tux or dark three-piece suit. The scents of mouthwatering appetizers overlaid the application of expensive perfume. Laughter and voices drowned out the piped-in music. There'd be fireworks at nine, then dancing.

Faith had gone immediately to say hello to Trinity and her father. Connor's portly former employer reigned over a small table close to the food and the bar. Herman liked his appetizers and his alcohol. Trinity played queen to her father and an impeccably handsome man with roman numerals after his name. Harper Harrington the *Third*. She'd finally found a live one, even if he did look like a cold fish. Good for old Trinity.

Jarvis had joined them eventually, and Connor had done the obligatory glad-handing, bought a round of drinks, then left to make a brief scouting trip for the perfect spot to cop a feel off his wife later. Instead of returning to her side, he'd slipped into an alcove to watch her. She was a mixture of contrasts, shy and hesitant, but with a friend, bubbly and full of laughter.

She'd been nervous about tonight. The party was their debut as a married couple. Connor didn't want the country club circuit espousing the story that he'd married Faith for her money. Faith was a sensitive creature, and the more it was bandied about that he'd hunted her fortune, the less comfortable she'd feel. He wanted

Faith . . . comfortable. Willing. He wanted her stepping out of her shell. Just as she'd done every night he was away.

Hence, the micro-vibrator strapped to her panties. He was fucking brilliant with that one. He buzzed her now, just for good measure. Across the room, he saw the slight sexual roll of her shoulders. She turned slowly, jutted her hip, put a hand there, and cocked her head, searching for him in the crowded room. The slit of the dress showcased her luscious thigh in the lacy stocking he'd given her. Connor surveyed her immediate vicinity.

Behind the counter, the bartender sopped up a splotch of fine whiskey he'd accidentally slopped over the side of a glass. He couldn't take his eyes off her, and he wasn't the only one. Several covert glances slid her way. A silver-haired gentleman tapped his male companion's arm, and they exchanged appreciative glances. *Oh, baby, you don't even have a clue, do you?*

Faith noticed the slurs, not the compliments. One day he'd get her to pick up on the latter and ignore the bullshit.

"She's looking for him." The female voice came from beyond the monstrous potted plant outside his little alcove.

"Where'd he go?" Also female. He didn't recognize either.

"He's hiding from her. Wouldn't you if you were him?"

"That's catty." Yet they tittered together.

Connor got a twinge in his gut.

"I heard her father made him CEO to get him to marry her."

Bitches. He glanced at Faith. She put her fingers to her lips, smiled damned seductively, then turned back to pretend attentiveness to Trinity's father.

She knew he was watching her. He liked that she didn't have a doubt about it even if she couldn't see where he was.

Now to deal with the bitchiness outside his alcove.

"I'll bet you a deep tissue massage at Casio's that he's cheating on her by . . . the end of July."

"What makes you think he isn't already?"

Gasp. "With who?"

"Well, he was doing Trinity Green before. A little bird told me he still is."

He was going to murder Trinity Green.

Except . . . he'd swear Trinity actually cared about Faith. She could sometimes be a flighty ditz, but she wasn't a backstabber. More valuable than a deep tissue massage, he'd stake his life on it. Trinity wasn't the one.

He had, however, seen Nina Simon skulking around tonight. When he'd slammed her down in Caracas, he'd known he was making an enemy. Perhaps she was retaliating. Though he didn't quite get the woman. For the remainder of the trip, she'd continued her little flirt, as if she didn't hold the rejection against him. That added to his expectation that she'd bring the hammer down in another, more devious manner.

Right now, he had more immediate things to deal with. Ready to step out and confront Ms. Cunt One and Ms. Cunt Two, Connor counted to ten. It wouldn't stop the rumors. It would only make them fly. The tale would get around that he was afraid he'd get caught cheating. Making a shitty scene would only hurt Faith.

Besides, actions spoke a lot louder than words. Wasn't that the old saying? He had a better plan than open confrontation.

"ISN'T that right, honey?"

She was hot. And it wasn't the crush of the party crowd. How could Connor expect her to answer, much less pay attention to the conversation, when his touch, even the stroke of one finger along her nape, threatened to send her into orgasmic nirvana? Not to mention the vibrator in her panties. "Yes, dear."

Okay, she had been listening. With half an ear. Connor told Mr. and Mrs. Biddle the story about the Weederman boy verbatim. Just as she'd told it to him at dinner *before* he went to South America. He'd actually listened.

So did the Biddles. Mr. Biddle was tall, angular, and completely bald, yet a five o'clock shadow showed where the fringe of hair used to be. He probably should have left it since his head was shaped rather like an egg.

Connor kissed the tip of Faith's nose. "She'll make the best mom, won't you, sweetheart?"

She wanted to suck his tongue into her mouth.

"Oh goodness, you're pregnant." Mrs. Biddle beamed. Older than her husband by a few years, when she smiled like that she suddenly seemed like a delighted child.

Yet Faith's orgasmic nirvana receded. She felt a jab right up under her rib cage. "Not yet," she murmured, looking at Mrs. Biddle's shoulder instead of meeting her eyes.

"But we're giving it the good old college try." Connor tipped her chin up and made her look at him. "One hundred and fifty percent effort, right, honey?"

He had that devilish glint in his eye, plying her with pet names and a feast of touches. It was sort of scary how he'd made her the center of his attention. He touched her constantly as they talked to people, a kiss on her ear, a squeeze at her waist, a thumb skirting the underside of her breast. Or he'd slide his hand in his pocket, and she'd salivate with anticipation as his mouth creased in a knowing smile just before he buzzed her.

Through it all, he'd introduced her to a number of his new work associates. She'd met most at Daddy's Christmas parties for his employees, but she'd never spent so much time talking to them. She'd moved on the periphery of social events, but Connor dragged her smack-dab into the middle. He complimented her, always included her, actually asked her opinion.

For the first time, she didn't feel like the drab mouse amongst all the beautiful people. God. The things he did. The emotions he evoked. She could almost believe . . . but believing was a slippery slope.

The Biddles moved on. Alone in the crowd, Connor snuggled her closer and put his lips to her ear. "I need a bio break, baby. Will you be okay for a few minutes?"

"I've been coming to these things alone for years."

He reeled her in, wrapping both arms around her. "On second thought, come with me and let me do you in the bathroom stall."

She laughed against his shirtfront. "You are so bad." And she loved it.

"But you're hot. I know you are." He nibbled at her earlobe. "Your nipples are damn near poking my eye out and"—he breathed deeply—"your hot, sweet, juicy scent is driving me wild." For good measure, he shifted ever so slightly against her, rubbing her with the hard ridge of his erection.

She wanted to rise on her toes, hug him close with both arms around his neck, and stroke her cleft against his cock.

God, she was even thinking like him and close to letting him drag her into a men's room stall. "Connor, behave." She should give the message to herself.

Sliding a hand down her back, he caressed the base of her spine in slow circles. "Tell me the truth. One more buzz and you'd come."

She pushed him away with the tips of her fingers on his chest. She wanted that buzz more than anything. But they were in the middle of a crowded ballroom and orgasming right here, right now, would be embarrassing. "Bio break," she said. "Go. I'm fine on my own."

"Don't flirt with anyone while I'm gone."

Yeah, right. She didn't say that, instead giving him a tap on the shoulder to head him in the right direction. Why was he so good to her? She could swear he hadn't once returned any of those longing glances that followed him everywhere he went, even now, as he headed out the double doors.

"I see he's playing his part to the hilt."

She jumped at the touch of a breath against her ear. And turned. "Lance." She backed away, one step.

His gaze pierced Connor's departing back. "He's laying it on a bit thick, though, don't you think?"

"What do you mean?" She regretted the question the moment it was out of her mouth. She *knew* what he meant.

"He's trying too hard to convince everyone this is a great romance when we all know he married you to get Daddy's company."

She swallowed hard and closed her eyes. Long enough to grab some semblance of composure.

Connor had been sweet, and kinky, with the vibrating panties. What more could she want from him? He didn't shame her. He made her laugh. He made her hot, wet, and excited.

He was acting perfectly for her.

She opened her eyes. "Lance." Glancing around, she lowered her voice. "I'll only say this once. I chose him. He chose me. The reason doesn't matter anymore." She leaned forward, tilted her chin. "So butt out. Your comments aren't appreciated."

He backed off, quirking one corner of his mouth. "A bit sensitive, aren't we?"

If he wasn't Trinity's brother, she wouldn't even be talking to him. Then again, he just made her plain mad. Aware of avaricious ears straining to overhear, she didn't care. "I've found a little backbone." *After all these years.* "Stop trying to push me around or make me think bad things about Connor."

Holding up his hands in surrender, he gave her a sad, woebegone smile. "I cared about you, Faith. I tried to help. But if you want to stick your head in the sand, so be it." Then he put a hand on her bare arm. "But when you need a friend, you can still come to me."

He'd never offered her anything that didn't gain him far more in return. She stepped back, his hand falling away. "I won't need it."

She walked away. Dammit. Lance ruined her buzz. She covered her mouth to hide a bubble of laughter. It was Connor's buzz. He'd been buzzing her all night. But Lance's words had been ice cubes down her back. She melted and not in a good way.

Why had Connor disappeared so many times tonight? The men's room, to get her a drink, to say hello to someone. He always came back, sweet and attentive, but really, where did he go?

She was letting Lance's meanness steal the high she'd been on. Suddenly, the voices were too loud, the laughter around her too shrill, her skin cool and damp, and the thigh-high stockings made her legs feel chubby. Where was Connor, dammit?

Her body started to vibrate. Her clitoris hummed. She put a hand to her stomach and looked up. She couldn't see him, but Connor was playing her on and off with the remote in his pocket.

Putting a hand on the nearby table, she steadied herself. Oh. She tugged her lip between her teeth and breathed deeply. Ooh. When she closed her eyes, the purr of the vibrator, enhanced by the incessant pulse of the on-off switch, felt like flesh throbbing inside her. Her body had warmed the metal bullet, and its sweet little buzz fanned out from her pussy to her clitoris to uncharted territory beyond.

He was here in the room. She scanned the faces, looked for his head above the rest. Her nipples peaked against her bodice.

A hand touched her arm, and a voice broke her husband's spell. "Are you all right?"

Gray eyes, dark hair, and tall. Really tall and handsome in a Harrison Ford kind of way. Where did she know the man from? Oh my God, he was the bartender, out and about gathering dirty glasses. She must look like she was going to faint.

"I'm fine. I was just looking for my husband." Damn. That sounded pathetic, as if she'd been ditched.

The man eyed her, his gaze coming to rest on her chest. Her breasts rose and fell with her agitated breathing. She was afraid to look down because she was sure he could see her hard nipples just below the neckline.

What must the poor man think of her?

"You're flushed. Shall I take you out for some air?"

Well, duh, he thought she'd had too much to drink. "No. Thanks." She fluttered a hand. "I'll just go find my husband."

Then she winced. He was probably going to say he'd seen Connor stepping out onto the dark veranda with some other woman.

A jolt shot straight to her clitoris. Almost as if Connor knew exactly what she'd been thinking. "Yeah," she murmured, stepping back, "I really better look for my husband." With another blast, she almost moaned. Her fingers curled into a fist. "Thanks for your concern, though." She backed up, straight into a broad chest and a pair of strong arms.

"There you are, sweetheart. I lost you in the crush."

She tilted her head back. Connor stared the bartender down, who smiled slightly, picked up a dirty glass, saluted with it, then sauntered back over to the bar.

Connor leaned down and nipped her neck. "He wanted to fuck you, sweetheart."

He was fully aroused, his erection nestled along her spine.

She barely held back rubbing against him. "He did not."

"I watched him. He saw you alone, signaled for a replacement, then came after you." He licked the shell of her ear. "Aren't you glad I rescued you before he dragged you out into the dark and had his way with you?"

She twisted in his arms and steadied herself with both hands on his jacket lapels. Lacing his fingers behind her back, he held her close. She was aware of people around them, the crowd moving out to the lawn for the impending fireworks. Amid the clink of glasses and plates, the musicians began setting up, and the staff cleared the dance floor of tables. Yet there was only Connor's heat and the sweet wetness between her legs.

She didn't care about Lance. Or the bartender. Or what anyone thought. They could say he married her for her money, her father's company. She didn't give a damn, because Connor wanted her. Everything he'd done and said tonight was for her.

"Let's go home," she whispered.

"Let's take a walk," he countered.

"But—"

With a finger to her lips, he cut her off. "I found a place I want to show you." Sliding his fingers down her arm, he took her hand, pulled away, and turned her with him.

In that moment, she'd go anywhere with him. And she knew she was lost.

CONNOR had slipped out of the ballroom several times tonight looking for the perfect spot to take her. He wanted her here, right under their noses, the crowd she was a part of yet the world of people who made her feel less than she truly was. He was hot and hard contemplating it.

They passed a couple of teenagers in the corridor, then the crowd faded out as they entered a new wing of the country club which hadn't officially opened yet.

"Where are we going?"

Her hand was small and warm in his, her head barely topped his shoulder. He adored that she was petite. It made him feel protective. He'd never felt protective of anyone. It was a nice feeling, an appropriate emotion to feel about his wife.

He didn't want to control or dominate her. He simply wanted her to rise to her potential. He wanted her to hold her head high amongst her peers and feel beautiful and powerful no matter what they thought or said.

He squeezed her hand, drew her through a set of heavy wood doors, and pulled them closed behind them.

"Wow." Faith leaned back against the wood. "I didn't even know this was here."

"They'll be opening the piano lounge in a couple of weeks."

The only illumination in the room came from a row of lights along the bar top. The shelves behind the bar were empty but boxes were piled three deep with liquor and glassware. The floor was bare concrete, except for the raised dais on which a grand piano sat and the parquet dance floor in front of it. Black-lacquered tables had been stacked top to top in the corner. The socket in the ceiling over the dance floor, where presumably a chandelier would be hung, was bare wires. Beyond the floor-to-ceiling windows, partygoers gathered on the lawn for the fireworks, but behind the smoked glass, Connor and Faith were virtually invisible.

Dipping forward, he tried to see her face. "Would you like to come for a little dancing once the place is open?"

She stared at the dance floor, and the luscious sexual creature he'd held against his cock in the ballroom vanished. "Connor, you don't have to seduce me. We're married. You've got the job. You don't have to push anymore. All I want is a baby."

She thought as the rest of them did. Once he'd gotten what he wanted, she'd be nothing more than a pussy to stick his dick in and get off. *Just close your eyes, fuck her, and pretend she's someone else.* He'd heard the sentiment in men's locker rooms. He just didn't want Faith to think it.

"I want more than a baby. I want you to blow my mind and rock my world. What's wrong with that?" He tugged her against him, wrapping his arm across her back so she couldn't pull away. "Lust is so hot, Faith. Lust is dreaming about sex at work. It's coming home hard as a fire hydrant, whomping your woman down on the sofa, and doing her hard and fast before you get to dinner, then slow and sweet after dessert."

He could actually hear her swallow. Then she shook her head. "But it's not real. And it doesn't last."

"Fuck real," he whispered. "It's mind over matter. It'll last as long as we make it last." He'd made his decision the minute she said no infidelity, and he wasn't turning back. "If you don't want me to have a mistress, then *you're* my mistress."

She stilled in his arms, her wriggling ceased. He could feel her mind working in the air around them. The soft strains of music drifted beneath the door, and moonlight streaming through the wall of windows stretched its fingers across the concrete floor as far as the bar.

"I'm not the mistress type," she murmured, her gaze fixed on the pleats of his dress shirt.

He chanced letting go long enough to reach inside his pocket for the remote. In the relative quiet of the room, his ear picked up the light buzz only because he knew what it was. She sagged against him, and her heart beat erratically. Her nipples were hard nubs. She reached up, dug her fingers into the shoulders of his jacket, and arched into his cock.

"You're mistress material. Hot, sweet, and tasty, baby."

Backing off, he took her hand in his and pulled her up on the dais. He'd wanted her to take the initiative, to take *him*. It was a slow simmering need in his gut for which he had no explanation. Screw *why* he wanted that so badly; he just did. For now, however, he'd be satisfied with her participation.

Tugging her snug up against him back to front, he gazed down into her magnificent cleavage, and his hands begged to touch and caress. He slid straight down to cup her breast in his palm.

"Connor." She gasped when he flicked her nipple.

"Faith," he mimicked her shocked tone. Finding her sensitive spot, he licked the ridge of her ear, her shiver traveling the length of his body to lodge in the tip of his cock.

She flapped a hand at the wall of windows looking out on the golf course and gardens. "They'll see us," she whispered.

"They'll be watching the fireworks out there, not the ones in here." He covered her eyes. "Let's pretend."

She didn't speak, but neither did she tug his hand away.

He set about seducing her with his voice and his touch. "Let's pretend there's a crowd, and we're the floor show." He circled her tight nipple. "They've come to watch us"—he sucked her earlobe into his mouth, then let it slide slowly away—"fuck," he added on just a breath of air, almost without sound.

She trembled, then squirmed against his cock.

"Yeah, baby, they want to see me bend you over the piano bench and take you from behind." He hated to leave her breasts, but it took both hands to slowly inch up the tight dress. "Pinch your nipples for me."

She caressed herself with her fingernails, then pinched each nipple in tandem. And moaned. He wanted to sink his cock deep inside her so badly his erection surged hot and heavy.

With her dress now to her waist, he slipped a hand down between her legs. "You're drenched, baby. You're so fucking wet, I could drink you."

He wanted her to talk to him, to tell him what she wanted, the way she did on the phone, yet he wasn't sure at what point she'd balk. Cupping her mound, he reached in his pocket for one last buzz, the vibrations passing from her to his palm. She soaked him. Clasping his arm around her waist to steady her, he slipped inside the panty to delve along her slit. While the vibrator worked its magic on the inside, her fondled her clit.

"They want to see you come, baby. Make it a good one."

She moaned and shivered, rolled her head against his shoulder, and undulated with the rhythm of his stroke.

"Please don't stop, please don't stop." She put her hand over his and rocked with him, her legs tightly together, giving him enough room to slide back and forth while her body held the vibrator hard and fast.

"Come for the audience. Christ, you should see them. They're going crazy, they want to see you come so bad." He wanted to feel her detonate in his arms.

She bucked and heaved, and he felt her shudder start from the inside, and just when she opened her mouth to scream out her pleasure, he pulled her head back, took her lips, and swallowed the sound. She moaned as she rode the wave of orgasm.

And before she could come down enough to think, he tore her panties down her legs, rescued the vibrator, then pushed her hands to the piano bench. "Hang on, baby, hang on hard."

His cock was out of his slacks in mere seconds, and he almost came the moment he slid into her sweet depths.

"Oh God, Connor." She arched, her hair sliding down her back and off her shoulders. "You feel so good."

He rolled down over her, chest to back, held her, his cock buried to the hilt. "I want to fuck you so bad." He touched her clit, and her body jerked. "Tell me you want it. Here and now."

"Please, Connor, yes, I want it."

"Put your knee on the bench. I want you wide open for me."

She trembled and panted, but she did what he told her to.

With one last lick to her ear, he whispered a final inducement. "I want them all to see my cock sliding inside you. Remember, baby, they can see everything. It makes them fucking crazy to watch." It would make *him* fucking crazy to see the beauty of his cock riding her.

He straightened, braced her at the waist, and pulled out slowly until only his crown remained. His cock pulsed and felt close to bursting. He punched with short, fast strokes, just the tip, her pussy milking the sensitive ridge. Holy hell, it was too much. He held still a moment, caught his breath, then slowly entered her again, relishing the sight as her body swallowed him. He wanted her to see it. Someday he'd find a way to show her the beauty. "Gorgeous," he murmured.

In, out, he picked up the pace, increased the friction until he almost lost sight of where they were, a dark lounge, the moonlight across the floor like a still pond. All that existed was her sweet pussy, his cock claiming her body for his own.

"Stroke your clit, baby." He wanted her to come when his seed filled her.

She pounded back against him, taking him as much as he took her. Mutual fucking satisfaction. He closed his eyes, the throb building in his balls, yanking them up, squeezing. Outside, the fireworks burst in the air and everything inside him exploded as he lost himself in her completely.

13

OUTSIDE, the fireworks exploded in a crescendo. For a moment there, in the throes of orgasm, she'd thought *they'd* created the fireworks. Actually, they had.

"Jesus." His exclamation was a mere puff of air at her ear. "That was too fucking hot for words," he murmured.

His heart raced against her ear as she lay across his chest. Arms clasped around her, he leaned against a piano leg. Somehow, he'd pulled her dress back down over her hips, tucked his penis back inside his pants, and zipped up.

"Your tux is a mess," she said.

With his finger under her chin, he tipped her head to drop a quick kiss on her nose. "I say that was hot sex, and you worry about my tux?" He nuzzled her hair and lowered his voice to a seductive pitch she felt deep inside. "Screw the tux. Screw the mess. That was the fucking best. Admit it, baby."

It was, and she was fast becoming addicted. To the sex, his arms around her, everything he made her feel. Addicted to *him*. More than lust, her emotions were getting all tied up in him.

"It was good." She could at least give him that without giving away the rest.

He laughed, sucked her bottom lip into his mouth, then finally took her with his tongue, devouring whatever lipstick remained. "Screw good. It was perfect, and you know it."

The boom of the fireworks sounded as if they were in her head. A stab of fear, maybe even terror went through her heart. Why did he insist on that word? Why did he want her to say it?

Please don't lull me into thinking we're perfect, then pull the rug out from under my feet.

Instead of becoming more assured in their marriage, she was less secure than the day she'd agreed to marry him. She pulled away, leaning on her hip, feet tucked beneath her, and tried to re-store order to her hair. "It was better than mere *good*." She smiled to lull him into thinking she was teasing.

More than perfect, it was how she'd dreamed of feeling when her knight in shining armor finally came along and rescued her.

"You"—he tapped her nose—"are one hard-edged woman."

Let him think she was hard to get. It kept her safe. "And an-other thing. You can't say that word all the time. It'll steal into my vocabulary until one day it pops out at school."

He raised a brow. "What word?"

She shot him a stern look. The banter restored her equilibrium. "*That* word."

"*Fuck?*"

He was as mischievous as one of her students. "Yes."

"*Fuck* is a great word." He got right up in her face, his nose to her hair. "As in, that was the best *fuck* I've ever had." He raised his head like a dog and drew in a breath. Eyes closed, a slow groan rose up from his belly as he exhaled, then he impaled her with his dark gaze. "As in, your pussy is so *fucking* hot and juicy that I need to *fuck* you all over again." He pulled back. "See, it's an adjective, a verb, *and* a noun. That's a good lesson for your students."

He was so appealing. She hadn't bargained for this. She didn't want to feel anything, yet she couldn't resist him.

Please don't let me fall in love with him.

But oh, he made her feel wonderful. Never had she felt like this in her life. "No more exhibition sex," she whispered.

"Spoilsport," he murmured.

"I'm a good girl."

He nodded his head slowly. "Oh yeah. You are so fuc—"

She slapped her fingers lightly against his lips. "No more saying that naughty word."

"How about I only say it in the privacy of our own home?" he said against her fingers.

She felt a kernel of fear burgeon inside her. Felt it grow, hot and heavy under her rib cage.

"Or on the phone when we can't be overheard," he went on.

He could hurt her so. He could make her need what he gave her, then take it all away in the blink of an eye when he got tired of her. Despite what he claimed about keeping lust alive, it would evaporate like water in the hot sun.

"Faith."

She blinked. "What?"

"You're thinking, and it's not good things."

He could read her like a book, she was so pathetically obvious and open. And she was going to ruin the best thing that had ever happened to her just by thinking too hard.

"I don't think you do know," she countered.

He tipped his head in a "try-me" gesture.

"I was thinking that when I get you home, I'm going to . . ." She trailed off and fluttered her eyelashes. "No, I think I'll keep that a surprise."

He grabbed her hand and pulled her to her feet. "Then I better get you home right away."

"Patience. You'll have to wait. I want to see the rest of the fireworks." She stepped off the dais and wiggled her butt as she headed to the door.

She'd enjoy what he did for her. She'd take full advantage of the moment instead of worrying about when it would end. She'd relish the pleasant buzz zipping through her body instead of destroying it with a bunch of what-ifs.

Flapping a hand over her shoulder, she added, "Don't forget my panties and the vibrator, dear."

Behind her, he laughed. "Yes, dear."

Then she gasped and stopped and . . . oh my God. "That chair wasn't there when we came in."

He stopped behind her, his body warmth caressing her. "I didn't notice."

"It *wasn't* there." She remembered the stacked folding chairs along the wall when they first walked in. She might have been filled with Connor's irresistible scent and surrounded by his aura, but she'd noticed. And that chair hadn't been next to the door like that. As if someone had unfolded it, set it against the wall, and . . . "Someone was watching us."

"Baby, you're imagining things."

She tipped her head back to look at him. "No. I'm not."

In the dark, a smile grew slowly on his face. His signature devilish grin. "Cool."

"You're bad," she said. She should have been horrified. She *was* horrified.

"Yeah. And you like me that way."

They could have been arrested for . . . indecent exposure, lewd behavior, something. At the very least, they could have been the gossip of the country club. Her father would have had a heart attack. But somehow, Connor turned everything into a sexual fantasy for her. Her heart actually picked up its tempo.

He was so right. She did like him that way. Instead of horror twisting her insides, the most delicious thrill shot straight down to her clitoris at the thought that someone sat in that chair and watched their performance.

Good Lord, she was becoming kinky. Now, if she just kept her emotions in check, she'd be . . . perfect.

CONNOR smiled, totally pleased with himself and his wife. Hell, she hadn't freaked when they realized they'd been seen. Instead, her nipples peaked. And they said women got even hornier when they were pregnant. He'd be in seventh heaven.

He was in fucking seventh heaven now.

"A champagne cocktail, please."

The bartender, the one who'd eyed Connor's *wife*, jumped to do his bidding. The fireworks had ended, and everyone was in line for a refresher. Connor had made it before the rush.

Faith had made a sojourn to the ladies' room to make sure her dress and makeup were properly repaired while Connor returned to the ballroom to order her a drink. He wanted to show Faith off some more in that dress.

"Where's the wife, darling? Gotten rid of her already?"

Nina wore a red and white top cut low enough to reveal a touch of aureole and silver satin shorts that didn't quite conceal her butt cheeks. She'd switched out the ankle bracelets for a pair of knee-high black boots. He had to admit she looked good in the getup, which couldn't be said of a number of women in their midthirties.

He fished a bill from his wallet and laid it down. "She's powdering her nose," he supplied.

She pursed her lips, smacking them. "Did she miss you while you were gone in South America?"

He grinned. "I missed her more."

"You know, you've got a pretty good act going there. I bet some people actually believe it." She leaned on the bar, swaying her backside and affording him a full view of her nipples. "I think I'm actually starting to like you."

"Thank you."

On the trip, she'd enjoyed baiting him. Sidling up close when Jarvis was in clear view and playing games. It had begun to amuse him. Obviously it amused her, too.

She batted her eyelashes. "Did you sign my expense report?"

"Since you only went to one meeting in the eleven days we were there, I signed off on a ten percent payout."

She tilted her chin and ran a finger from the hollow of her throat to her blouse's neckline. "How about you sign off on all of it and I promise not to tell your wife I was in your suite?"

"How about next time you go to all the meetings and then I'll consider giving you full reimbursement?"

She smiled like Helen of Troy, then pushed away from the bar. "I might have a growing soft spot for you, Connor, but I will make you pay for being such an asshole."

"I'm sure you will, Nina. And I'll enjoy figuring out ways to show you your real place."

She blew him a kiss, whispered "asshole," then turned and wriggled her way back into the crowd.

Connor had thought he had her figured out that first night in Caracas, a man-eater with whom he'd have to watch every step. She'd surprised him. She enjoyed playing men, teasing them, putting them in the one-down position. Even more, she relished the game. She wanted him, mostly because he'd turned her down, and she'd escalate the play until she got what she wanted.

Except in this case. Truthfully, she held no appeal whatsoever. He'd tasted Faith, and she was infinitely a sweeter vintage than Nina Simon could ever be.

"Your drink, sir." The bartender palmed the cash and left the change in one-dollar bills. "There's your lady." He tipped his chin, pointing over Connor's shoulder. "You're a lucky man."

"Yes, I am." He left the bills on the bar and turned to find his

lady, sexy Faith in the black dress. *Christ*. She wasn't wearing panties. They were safely tucked in his jacket pocket. He felt a swell
beneath his tux.

He wondered if Nina would follow through on her threat. He
wondered what Faith would believe. He wasn't completely sure of
either of them. And hell if that didn't make life interesting.

IT was all she could do to hold her chin up. The way Nina looked
at him. The way he looked at her.

There was a horrible intimacy between them. A hand squeezed
her heart. Was it Nina in the piano lounge? Had Connor told her to
be there? Was this some sort of game they were playing?

Panic seized her throat, and she almost tripped over an infini-
tesimal bump in the ballroom carpet. The woman in the photos
could have been Nina. The man could have been Connor.

Related only by her marriage to Cousin Lionel, Faith had always felt as though the woman were secretly laughing at her. *Please
don't let Connor be doing her.*

They hadn't seen her. She could walk away and pretend she
hadn't witnessed their exchange. She could pretend—

"They're married a week, and can you believe it, he leaves on a
two-week *business* trip, and *now* he's having nookie at the country
club with someone else. Don't you think that's *bold*?"

She almost stopped dead in her tracks. Did they think she was
deaf *and* stupid? Only pride kept her moving. It was shades of
hearing about Lisa and her cheating husband in the ladies' room
that first night she met Connor. Only this time they were talking
about Faith. She wanted to throw up.

Nina blew her husband a kiss and melted into the crowd on the
other side of the bar.

"I mean, really, he was doing her right in the new piano lounge.
You'd think he'd have a little more common sense. Of course,
someone was going to see him."

This time, Faith did stop, her heart pounding. *I was with him in the piano lounge.* Yet it was as if they couldn't even consider it a possibility that Connor had been doing *her*.

"Oops, God, you don't think she heard us, do you?"

"No way. But I feel kind of sorry for her. She doesn't look like she has a clue."

The bartender slid a champagne flute across the bar to Connor and tipped his chin in her direction. For just a moment, she locked eyes with him. She saw . . . something in the man's gaze. A flicker of interest maybe. Then Connor turned. He smiled, and her heart stopped. He held out his hand, and her bones melted.

She didn't look at her tormentors—she didn't want to know who they were, or to tell them they didn't have to pity her. At least not about the woman with Connor in the piano lounge.

God. She needed a psychiatrist, and maybe some drugs for manic depression. Her emotions had never bounced all over the map before she met Connor, especially not in the space of ten seconds. The elation she felt was the polar opposite of the despair gripping her insides when she'd seen him with Nina.

Maybe she was pregnant, which would explain her mood swings. She closed her eyes and touched her belly. *God, please let there be a baby soon.* She could survive anything if there was a baby.

When she came back to the room once more, he was giving her such a look. If she'd still been wearing the vibrator, she was sure he would have buzzed her.

That look was all she had to hang on to, so she walked to him, took the champagne, and let him fold her beneath his arm.

He nuzzled her ear. "What's wrong?"

"Nothing." God, it was so typically . . . wifely. *I'm fine honey. Which means I'm not fine at all.* Faith didn't want to sound like that. She lowered her voice to a hopefully husky note. "I'm merely in recovery over what you just did to me."

He chuckled. "Don't recover. I want to plow into you the minute we get home, so you better stay wet."

She was aware of eyes on them. Curious, avid gazes. How could she tell him everyone thought he'd been doing someone else? Secretly, she wanted everyone to *know* he'd been with her.

"Drink up," he urged. "We should get out of here soon. Because something's come up. Again."

Trinity—wherever she'd come from because Faith certainly hadn't seen her—put her arms around them both. "Sweetie, can I borrow your husband for a quick dance?"

She glanced at Connor, who raised his shoulders slightly.

Trinity didn't even wait for a yes. "And I want you to go over there and talk to Harper because I absolutely have to know your honest opinion of him. You're the only one I trust, so"—she gave Faith's shoulder a little push—"tell me if he's divine or it's only my imagination because I think I'm totally in love."

Tonight was the first Faith had even heard of Harper Harrington the Third. Connor raised a brow, smiling first at her, then at Trinity, and allowed himself to be dragged away.

Faith wouldn't think about how good they looked on the dance floor. She wouldn't wonder what caused that intense look on Trinity's usually sweet, smiling face. She wouldn't let all sorts of thoughts into her head about what they could possibly be discussing with such concentration. She wouldn't . . .

Oh my God. She was jealous of her best friend. Her emotions about Connor had gone far beyond lust.

DESPITE the slow, seductive tune, Trinity Green danced like a stiff board, holding herself several inches from him and pinching the shoulder of his tux as though that was all she could bear to touch. A pucker marred her forehead. She'd need a shot of Botox to get rid of it if she didn't watch out.

"You are *such* an *ass*hole," she hissed. "I'll murder you."

Interesting. He didn't think Trinity knew the word *asshole.* "I wondered when you'd congratulate Faith and I on our marriage."

She looked as if she could spit pea soup. "Who was she?"

"Who?"

"The woman in the new piano lounge." She raised her hand as if she would dearly love to hit him. "*Everyone* knows. *Everyone*. You humiliated Faith. And I trusted you. I introduced you to her. Like giving a bunny rabbit to a wolf. She told me you promised, but the first chance you get, you—"

"Trinity."

She stopped as if he'd actually put his hand over her mouth.

"I wasn't with another woman in the piano lounge. So who told you I was?" Godammit. A little innocent fun. All right, not so innocent. Hot as hell, in fact. But he hadn't intended *this*, for the club circuit to assume he was with someone else.

"No one had to tell me. It's buzzing in every corner." Trinity groaned and seemed to sag a little in his arms. "This is *all* my fault. I should have *known* you'd cheat on her."

For God's sake. Did no one think he had any integrity? Not one person? Even for Faith, he'd had to sign a prenuptial agreement stating that he got nothing if he committed adultery. Nina finagled her way into his hotel room and was shocked, dammit, *shocked* he didn't take her up on her offer. Jarvis believed he hadn't only because he didn't think Connor was that stupid. And now Trinity, who'd always seemed to see him in a slightly better light than anyone else did, except Faith.

He almost shook her. "I did not cheat." He leaned down and spoke right in her face so she'd *get* it. "And I'm not going to."

"But—"

He gave her a threatening look that quelled insubordination. But what was he supposed to say? Tell her he'd been with Faith?

The song ended, another began. Connor tipped his head. Possibilities started to abound. Ideas clicked on like the proverbial lightbulb. Yeah. He needed something to stop the talk. Something to show the holier-than-thou, jet-setting, hypocritical crowd that

Connor Kingston wasn't a cheat and a liar, and that Faith was more woman than they'd ever suspected.

"I *don't* like that look, Connor," Trinity said in her best stern imitation of Faith.

"What happened isn't what you think. Do you believe me?"

She examined his eyes, her feet barely moving to the music. "This time," she murmured. "But if you *ever* hurt Faith, I *will* rip out your innards and hang them from the Golden Gate for the seagulls to peck at."

"I never knew you had such a vicious streak."

"She's my friend."

He'd always thought she was a flighty, vain creature. Maybe Trinity was, but she was also a loyal friend, and for that, he admired her. "And she's my wife. So you just follow along with everything I say."

"Uhh . . . okay."

He could tell she wasn't too sure about it. He didn't care. Steering her off the dance floor, he headed toward the group knotted around Trinity's new "flame." Faith stood at the edge of the small crowd looking lost. She'd heard the nasty rumors.

As he wrapped his arm around her, she gave the slightest cringe, an almost imperceptible tightening of her body.

"So, baby, what did you think of the new piano lounge?" he said, his voice overloud and attention-grabbing.

Conversation stopped, heads turned. Trinity gaped. She would have hated that look if she could see it in a mirror.

Faith doe-eyed him. The deer, the Mack truck headlights, the whole thing. She was so adorable with that I-can't-believe-you're-bringing-that-up-now expression, he kissed her nose.

"The piano lounge?" she said, her voice barely a squeak.

"Yeah. Great for dancing"—he smiled—"and other things."

Trinity damn near spat out her sip of champagne.

Connor snugged Faith closer and spoke to the crowd around them. Which had grown in size in the past minute. "Faith and

I thought we'd check out the new digs. Quite a nice setup." He chucked his wife under the chin. She gazed up in . . . utter shock. "We'll certainly be going back there, won't we, baby?"

Trinity finally found her voice. "*You* were with Connor?"

Except for the ensemble music and the clink of glasses at the bar, there wasn't a single other sound.

Faith locked gazes with him for the longest damn five seconds, and he couldn't read a thing in her eyes. She was usually so transparent. But not now.

Finally, she relaxed, smoothed her hand along his lapel, and turned to Trinity. "Of course Connor showed me the lounge." She tipped her head back to look at him. "We got a very close-up view of it, and it's got the most gorgeous grand piano I've ever seen. Right, honey bunch?"

He wanted to kiss her. Long and deep. "Absolutely the most gorgeous thing I've ever seen."

A man coughed. A woman gasped. Another snickered. Then whispers filled the air like locusts swarming a fat wheat field.

Faith's heart pounded. "I can't believe you said that," she muttered under cover of the drone around them.

"And let them think I was with someone else?" Connor asked.

She didn't hesitate. "No." Then she bit her lip. "But they all know what we were doing in there."

"Are you embarrassed?" Connor slid a hand beneath the hair at her nape.

"Horrified." At least she *should* have been horrified. Yet she wasn't. Instead she felt warm inside and out.

He smiled that lovely, wicked smile she adored. "You'll get over it."

"Yes, I do believe I will." Then she pursed her lips primly. "But we can't ever do anything like that again."

With both arms around her, Connor pulled her tight against him, his erection hitting her abdomen. "Now that's a promise I have no intention of keeping."

What if the tale got back to her father? Her membership could be revoked. They'd practiced indecent behavior in a public place. So what if they *thought* they were alone. They obviously hadn't been. Instead, they'd created a veritable scandal.

Faith didn't care. Connor had told everyone the woman he wanted was his wife. Looking up into his handsome face, Faith Kingston fell irrevocably in love with her husband.

She loved him. He lusted after her. It was enough, more than she'd ever hoped for.

14

"YOU want to go to *Egypt*?" Faith couldn't keep the utter incredulity out of her voice.

Trinity grabbed her arm and pulled her to the next mummy exhibit for a front-row view. Monday morning at the museum wasn't what one could call busy, and after the busload of summer school students moved on, she and Trinity were alone.

"Harper adores everything Egyptian," Trinity told Faith for the umpteenth time. "He dreams about being the first person to walk into King Tut's tomb."

"Someone walked into King Tut's tomb a hundred years ago."

Trinity flapped her hand. "You *know* what I mean."

Faith didn't. Saturday night at the country club was the first time Faith had even heard of Harper Harrington. Then Trinity had called her at eight this morning and told her they simply *must* go to the museum in San Jose because they had *the* most *marvelous* Egyptian mummies. Faith drove—heavy city traffic scared the heck out of Trinity—to a litany of Harper Harrington the Third's *absolutely magnificent* qualities.

"You know"—Trinity pondered the shriveled unwrapped mummy—"I don't get it. They've got Eva Peron's body mummified under glass down in Argentina. But if that's how she looks"—she fluttered a hand at the almost-unrecognizable-as-a-human remains—"why would she bother?" Trinity made a face. "I mean, *eewwe.*"

Faith laughed. "I don't think it's been on display for years and years. And if I recall, she wasn't mummified either." Maybe she should Google Eva's corpse. "How did you meet Harper?"

Trinity grabbed Faith's arm and looked positively . . . dreamy. "It was at the salon. My manicurist got his manicure slot mixed up with mine, and"—she melted into a sigh—"he let me have it and waited right there talking to me the whole time." She held out her fingers. "He even picked out the polish. Asian orange."

It sounded like something dropped on helpless people during a war. Looked a bit like it, too. Trinity's nails . . . glowed.

"What color did *he* get?"

Trinity laughed. "Don't be silly. He got clear. Then he asked me to lunch afterwards. Come on, I want to see the jewelry." Trinity pulled Faith to the next room.

A couple of tourists strolled through, their reverent whispers rising to the vaulted ceilings with a hiss.

"What does he do for a living?"

"He's an entrepreneur." Leaning just her palms on the metal edge of a glass case, Trinity surveyed the contents. "Hmm, that's pretty unimpressive."

Small trinkets of beaten gold lay on velvet trays. A pendant with a mosaic of tiny intricate pieces forming a woman's face was astounding, but Trinity was into more modern fashions.

"What does an entrepreneur do?" Faith asked.

"You sound like Daddy." Trinity bumped hips with Faith.

She bumped back. "Sorry. I've just never seen you quite so . . ." She couldn't say "bubbly" because Trinity was always bubbly. "You've never gone to a museum for a man before. Not to mention considering a trip to Egypt, where it's dusty and dirty and hot and you'll get all sweaty and your pores will clog."

Trinity laughed. "Don't worry, I'll bring my salon girl with me. And if we start thinking marriage, Daddy will order a background check." She tapped her fingernails on the glass. "Did your father get a background check on Connor?"

As if someone had flipped on a spotlight, Faith saw the real reason for this excursion. "No." She paused. "Do you think I'd have learned something that would have changed my mind?"

Trinity shrugged, her straight blond hair falling over her shoulder. "No. Let's move on. Mummies and their jewelry aren't quite what I'd expected. We should have gone up to the Legion of Honor in San Francisco. They've got a Van Goff."

"You know it's Van *Gogh*," Faith admonished. Trinity had loved art history in school. Faith had never been sure why Trinity felt she had to dumb herself down like that.

Heels clacking on the hardwood floor, Trinity studied her map. "Let's go see the cat mummies down there." She pointed and sidestepped a tour group milling about in the main hall. "What if I did know something? Would you want to hear it?"

Faith's heart plunged to the toes of her sensible walking shoes. "About Connor, you mean?"

"Yes, about Connor." Engrossed in the map, Trinity missed the arrow on the wall indicating the mummified pet exhibit.

Faith didn't point her in the right direction. "That depends on whether it's fact or rumor."

"A bit of both, I guess." Trinity stuffed the map into her bag. After long seconds of looking at everything *but* Faith, she finally met her gaze. "*Was* it you in the lounge with him?"

Trying to wipe all expression off her face, Faith didn't say how much that hurt. "You think I lied to hide my humiliation?"

"I don't know. But doing . . . *that* . . . in a public place . . ." Trinity waved her hands in the air as if that would conjure the right words. "It's just not like you."

Connor gave her the freedom to do things that weren't like her. "It's not like me to lie? Or it's not like me to have a man desperate to make love to me?" Her heart ached merely asking the question.

"I just meant that you've always been so . . . *shy* about stuff like that." Trinity stared at her with limpid blue eyes and blinked back what might have been tears. "Sometimes I don't think I know you, Faith. Especially since Connor."

"We discussed this. I trust him." Even if Daddy had bought him for her. She closed her eyes a fraction of a second.

"But isn't it possible you only trust him because of the agreement he signed?"

She trusted him because she loved him, but she couldn't tell Trinity that. Even Trinity would call her a fool, and her feelings were too new, too tender and uncertain to tell anyone. "It isn't just because of a legal paper. It's the way he treats me, Trin. With respect and caring. It might be a marriage of convenience, but that doesn't mean he thinks I'm a skag."

Trinity yanked her to an unoccupied bench by the wall. "Don't you *ever* say that about yourself." She took a deep breath. "But not all men can play the monogamy game, even when they've got a lot to lose if anyone finds out."

"Just tell me what it is you know. I'm tired of the games."

Trinity bit her lips, heaved a great sigh, then perused her fingernails. Asian orange really wasn't her color. "He had a woman in his room down in South America."

The pictures popped into her mind. *It wasn't him.* And it wasn't Nina. Or at least it wasn't Connor *with* Nina. Except that Trinity wasn't talking about pictures. "Who told you?"

Trinity just came out with it. "Lance."

That sneaky snake. "How would he know? He wasn't there."

"Green talks to Castle and vice versa, and he *heard*."

A child dropped the ice cream off his cone onto the lobby floor and started to wail. Faith felt like wailing with him.

It was those damn photos and that damn agreement making her

doubt Connor. The prenuptial was a thorn in her side. She couldn't know for sure he wouldn't stray without it in place.

A fact that hadn't mattered before Saturday night. Before she fell in love with him.

"Why didn't Lance say something on Saturday?"

"He said he couldn't bear to hurt you that way."

That was so much crap. "So he sent you to do it?"

Trinity stroked Faith's arm. "I'm not trying to hurt you, sweetie. I just feel responsible. I don't *want* to believe any of these things I hear, but I can't *not* tell you."

"Why not?" She took Trinity's hand, squeezed it. "Why not just *not* tell me?"

"But Faith—"

"Think about it, Trinity. If it was you, would you want your friends telling you every nasty rumor flying about the man you"— she managed to pull back at the last moment—"married?"

Trinity stared at their clasped hands. "I don't know."

"Wouldn't it put a strain on your marriage if you ran to him every time you heard another story being passed around?"

"But where there's smoke, there's fire."

"Maybe there's people who don't like your husband, who don't like that he took over your father's company. People who have a vested interest in making you believe he's a cheat and a liar."

Trinity gasped. "Lance?"

"Anyone. Who started the rumor about Connor being with another woman in the piano lounge?"

"Well, that wasn't—" Trinity studied her hands sheepishly. "Okay, I heard it in the ladies' room."

Jeez, that was where all the gossip started. She and Connor had an agreement. He wouldn't break it, not when she'd done every kinky, delicious thing he'd told her to. Hadn't she?

Faith resisted rubbing the headache away from her temples.

"You're right, Faith. I'm sorry."

Now Trinity changed her tune?

"That's okay." But was it? A knot of anger lodged in her chest, and she wanted to take it out on her best friend.

"Connor wasn't very happy when I asked him about it."

Faith let her mouth drop open. "You asked Connor?"

Trinity tipped her chin defiantly. For the first time in their relationship, Faith actually felt in the one-up position.

"I told him that if he ever hurt you, I'd hang his guts from the Golden Gate Bridge for the seagulls to eat."

She couldn't help herself—Faith laughed. As usual, heads turned, but this time she didn't feel self-conscious. Connor liked her laugh. "And what did he say to that?"

"That's when he dragged me off the dance floor and told everyone within earshot that he'd *shown* you the piano lounge."

Faith's heart beat furiously all over again, just as it had in the ballroom. He'd done it to protect her from the malicious gossipmongers. The ones Trinity had believed.

"Here's the deal, Trin. Unless you personally see Connor doing something he shouldn't be doing, I don't want to hear it."

"But if I *personally* see it, you want to know. Right?"

It took her forever to think about that. "No." Connor wouldn't break their agreement. But what if there wasn't an agreement between them? Then what would happen?

Trinity let out a long sigh and sagged back against the bench. "Oh, thank you. I so don't want to have to go through the last few days again." She waved her hands. "Should I, shouldn't I? You can't imagine what it's been like." She held Faith's gaze, her blue eyes misty. "Do you still love me, Faith?"

"Yes, Trinity, I still love you."

"Will you be my maid of honor?"

Faith grabbed her hand. "Harper asked you to marry him?"

"Not yet. But he will. So I want to make sure I have all my ducks in a row."

"Are you in love with him?"

"I will be by the time he asks."

"Oh, Trinity. I can't be your maid of honor"—Trinity's lip quivered at Faith's words—"but I can be your matron of honor."

And Trinity beamed.

Forgiveness was that easy. If only she could forget about that damn prenuptial agreement just as readily.

FAITH blinked, and the mascara she'd just applied smudged beneath her eyes. Dammit. She wanted her makeup on before Connor left for work, so she could kiss him good-bye without looking a total fright.

All week, Trinity's questions at the museum had haunted her. Yesterday, Thursday, Faith had gone down to a real estate agent to get the ball rolling on finding their own house. She wanted to be settled in before school started again in the fall, but in addition, she needed to do something, anything, to occupy herself while Connor was gone all day.

When she'd arrived home, another manila envelope had been tucked under the front mat. This time, there was simply a question mark on the outside, and the photos were of a man and woman doing it doggie style on a bed. The camera must have been mounted on a tripod. The pictures were color, the woman had red hair, and once again, the man's head wasn't in the frame.

Nina had red hair, and Connor loved that position. It was the way he'd taken Faith in the piano lounge.

No, no, no. That was not Connor in those pictures. Someone was trying to sabotage their marriage. In her office—she and Connor had each taken a spare bedroom—she'd hidden the envelope at the back of the drawer of her new IKEA desk, buried beneath a couple of grade books. Maybe she'd been rash in destroying the first set. She didn't know how she'd prove anything right now, but she was saving these for future evidence. That was the only reason she was keeping them. Really.

She trusted Connor. She did. But that damn prenuptial indicated the exact opposite. How could Connor truly come to care for her with that agreement in the way?

All her doubts had been circling like buzzards around her head since her Monday date with Trinity. Connor was right. Lust *was* better than love. She'd been absolutely miserable after she'd fallen in love with him.

She dabbed at the mascara she'd messed up.

She wanted him to care for her. Only he couldn't care for her with the prenuptial like a flashing sign saying, "I trust you only if you've signed on the dotted line and you stand to lose everything if I decide I don't feel like trusting you anymore."

If she told anyone, certainly Trinity, and especially her father, they'd tell her how backwards that logic was, that Connor only toed the line *because* he'd signed away everything.

She was doing it again, her mind going round and round, like water circling the drain. But the question remained: Without the agreement, could their marriage grow to a new level?

"I'm leaving," her husband called.

Faith bounded down the stairs and threw herself at him from the third step.

"What's this in honor of?"

God. That was stupid. He might think she was starting to get all possessive. "Because that *thing* you did in the middle of the night was so good, you deserve an extra hug this morning."

He grinned. "What *thing*?"

"You know, where you had your tongue *there*, then you put your finger back *there*."

"And you went off like a freaking rocket. Now I remember that *thing*." He rubbed her bottom. "What are you going to do today while I'm gone?"

He smelled so good, some manly aftershave and her shampoo because his bottle had run out. She loved smelling her scent on him. *Be bold; ask for what you want.* "I thought I'd drop by and have lunch with you today."

He stroked her arms up beneath the robe sleeves. "I've got a board meeting at one thirty."

Her skin tingled with the glide of his fingers. She was naked and moist beneath the terry cloth. "That's fine. We'll have lunch, and I'll go to the board meeting with you."

"Why the hell would you want to attend a board meeting?"

She felt a tiny pinprick in her bubble. Didn't he want her to go? Maybe he had lunch plans with . . . Nina. "I own shares even if I don't vote them. So I'd like to go."

He wrapped his arms around her, sliding down to cup her butt once more. "It'll be boring, but that's your choice. How about we invite Josie for lunch, too?"

"Josie?"

He interpreted her look and shot an astonished question at her. "Josie Tybrook? Your cousin?"

"Oh." That Josie. "I don't really know her all that well."

"Then maybe it's time you get to know her." He squeezed her bottom lightly. "Family is important. And just because your father doesn't get along with his cousin doesn't mean you won't like Josie. She's nice. Give it a chance."

She felt lots of tingles now, and they weren't a good kind. "Today is special, our first lunch date since you got back from South America. I'll do lunch with Josie another time, okay?"

He nuzzled her robe apart and dropped a kiss on her collarbone. "Fine. Think of somewhere special you'd like to go." He pecked her cheek, grabbed his briefcase, and headed out.

Faith was left staring at the door. *Josie?*

It wasn't Josie in the pictures. Was it? No. Josie had very short hair, at least she did the last time Faith saw her, which was at the company Christmas party.

It wasn't Connor, either. The two people in those photos could have been *anyone*. She was going to stop making herself miserable over everybody else's what-if scenarios about Connor cheating. They weren't even *her* doubts.

She loved him. She trusted him. She wanted to give him proof of that trust. And there really was only one way.

Gathering her robe in her hands, she ran barefoot up the stairs. She had so many things to do before lunch. A new outfit. A trip to Daddy's lawyer. She had to do it today, Friday. When she had the agreement annulled, or whatever it was you did with prenuptials, he'd *know* she trusted him.

They could start being a real wife and husband.

"JOSIE will make a great program manager on this project."

Connor's father-in-law didn't even look up from his *Economist* magazine. "She hasn't the experience for a job the magnitude of the Dominican project."

Connor countered. "How is she supposed to get major project experience if you don't give her the chance?" He was fighting a losing battle. Jarvis had his head stuck in the sand.

Jarvis finally looked up, his eyes narrowed. "Why are you so interested in her anyway?"

"She's a company asset. And as with all assets, if you don't maintain them properly, they stop functioning at the highest capacity." Josie was also the only family member who didn't seem to have an agenda about how and when she could sell shares and get the hell out. She actually cared about the company and about her job.

Jarvis had alienated everyone else.

"The answer is still no. She's not ready."

Connor tapped his fingers on the arm of his chair. He was married to the man's daughter, but he was still on the outside looking in, sitting opposite Jarvis with that huge desk between them while Jarvis threw out edicts. He'd come up with several plans for cost improvement. They all required Jarvis's approval, and the man gave far too many of them a thumbs-down.

"Effectively, you're saying I don't have the authority to implement any of my proposals without your approval."

Jarvis smiled. "I agreed to the new travel policy."

Right, because the new policy stuck it to his family. The fact remained that Connor was merely a figurehead. Jarvis had hosed him. He'd let Connor marry his daughter, but he wasn't about to let him have the company. Maybe he was hoping Connor would just fade away. After he impregnated Faith, of course.

Shit, he couldn't even get that job done, either.

Since when the hell had he been so defeatist? He squashed the thought like a bug under his Italian leather shoe.

"Jarvis, you're making a mistake." He micromanaged his entire staff and drove them crazy with it, but Connor wouldn't even get into that. "Josie will do well for us."

"I still want to know why you're so interested in her."

"Because she loves this company." Connor stopped, realizing he was only digging himself a hole. His father-in-law would soon be asking if Connor was having an affair with the girl. "Fine. Who do you want on the project?"

"Masters."

Masters was the worst choice. Connor looked at his track record when he was making his own list of candidates. The man hadn't come in on budget since 2006. Why Jarvis hadn't fired or demoted him, Connor didn't have a clue. Jarvis was the sole decision maker in the company, and he played favorites. Maybe his choice of favorite had to do with history. Masters had been around a long time, and his performance had been better than par until the last couple of years. Maybe it was loyalty as it was with Herman Green. Herman, and by extension Green Industries, could do no wrong despite evidence to the contrary.

Jarvis Castle was an enabler, yet his loyalty didn't extend to his family, except for Faith. The old man had probably been at loggerheads with the rest of his clan since he took over the company from his father thirty-five years ago.

The question was, how to fight Jarvis. Or rather, how to get him to see things Connor's way.

"That might be overloading Masters. He's got Republic going, and they're a tad overbudget. How about Ronson?"

Jarvis seesawed his head side to side. "He might do." He puffed out his cheeks, looked into space a moment, then nodded. "He'll do."

Connor would assign Josie as Ronson's second-in-command. She needed experience, and she'd get it on the Dominican job. "Good." He checked that task off on his day planner. "Now let's talk about the Republic contract." Connor flipped open the file he'd laid on Jarvis's desk. "I've got a few ideas on how to alleviate the cost overruns."

For the next half hour, they dickered back and forth. Jarvis was mostly take and no give, but Connor counted two scores in his own favor.

Yeah, it was a matter of managing Jarvis. But by the time the meeting was over, his temples throbbed. In his office, he downed a couple of ibuprofen. Faith would be here soon.

At least marriage was going in his favor. Every time they came together, he pushed her a little harder, got her to drop one more barrier between her inhibitions and ultimate pleasure.

Last night had been another triumph. But this morning . . .

At the soft shush of shoes on his carpet, he glanced up. She stood in his office doorway. And Christ if she didn't take his breath away for a moment.

Connor couldn't pinpoint what was different about her. Maybe it was when she'd thrown herself in his arms this morning. It was . . . odd. A tad nerve-racking. Faith wasn't demonstrative unless he had her so hot, she lost control. Certainly the new outfit was a change.

What was the neckline called? A cowl, he was pretty sure. Women wore the most amazing fashions. As she leaned forward slightly, bracing herself on the doorjamb, he could see straight down to the lacy half cups of her bra and the dusky outline of her nipples. The filmy skirt was tight across her hips, then flared into a flirty hem that begged him to raise it to the level of her pussy and drink in her hot scent.

Yet it was so much more. It was the way she moved, giving her ass an enticing wriggle, her breasts out, her chin tipped, a sultry cast of her eyelashes. And all so very understated. A slight adjustment in attitude he wasn't sure anyone else would notice. But he noted every subtle nuance.

"Have you picked out a place to eat?" He grabbed his suit jacket off the rack.

Faith leaned against his office door, and he heard a decisive click of the lock.

"Oh yes, I know exactly where we're going to eat." She sauntered forward. "And what we're going to eat."

He noted the sexy sandals laced up to just above her ankles. For whatever reason, the new footwear made him hard as a hammer. "And where would that be?" He put his jacket back on the rack.

"Right"—she traced a finger along the edge of his desk, round the corner, to his side, stopping next to his chair, her finger in the center of his blotter—"here." She twirled his leather chair, stopping it when it faced him. "Sit, boy."

Holy hell. This was exactly how he wanted her. Demanding laced with a touch of fun.

He sat, faced her, spreading his legs to encompass hers. "So I'm your pet now?"

She smiled, sultry, sexy, her lashes at half mast. Reaching behind, she undid the mass of her hair from its mooring. Her breasts lifted, the jersey material stretching to reveal her peaked nipples.

"Yes, you're my pet. And if you want your reward, you're going to have to perform exactly the way I tell you."

She hoisted herself up on his desk, shoved aside his computer, some paperwork, and his PDA.

"I'm ready to obey any order," he murmured, his fingers itching to ride up her bare legs and under the hem of her skirt.

Putting her sexy sandals on the arms of his chair, she leaned back on her hands and drew him in. Her scent washed over him, hot, wet woman.

Cupping her calf, he kissed her knee. "Love the sandals."

She twisted her foot. "I liked them, too." Then she slid her feet back to the very edge of the armrests, her knees rising until he got a shot of her luscious pussy.

"Bad girl," he whispered. "Where are your panties?"

"In my purse. I'll put them on later. After you're done."

He raised his gaze to hers. "Done with what?"

"Having me for lunch." She smiled, sexy, confident. It was such a goddamn turn-on, he wanted to drive into her right now.

Instead he watched as she pulled her skirt up her thighs, let her knees fall apart and gave him the most gorgeous view of her flaming red bush, the color matching her hair. Her lips were plump and needy, her clitoris already burgeoning.

"Have you been thinking about this all morning?"

"Uh-huh." She punctuated with a nod. "Eat me, baby. Now."

His body damn near went up in smoke. The sultry tone of her demand, the wanton pose as she leaned back on her elbows, her body spread out like a feast on his desk. He slipped his hands under her butt and pulled her to the edge.

She tasted like ambrosia. Running his tongue up her slit, he circled her clit. Yeah, she was hard. And wet. He sucked her, played her, then slid a finger inside to caress the little sweet spot there. She arched, moaned, then squeezed her thighs against his ears.

He worked her inside and out to a litany of soft, sexy sounds that made his balls tighten in his pants. Easing her legs apart, he raised his head to look at her.

She pinched a nipple between her thumb and forefinger, then stared down at him. "Don't stop."

"I won't." But neither was he going to let it be over too soon. Smoothing his hands across her thighs, he pushed her legs as wide as they'd go. He traced a finger down, slipping inside. "You're so wet."

"Lick it up," she urged.

He gathered all her moisture, then slid back up to smear her clitoris with it. "Tell me exactly what you want."

He wanted to hear her say it. He wanted to know what turned her on in her own precise words. He wanted to know what took her to orgasm the fastest.

"Use the tip of your tongue and jab my clitoris."

He did. She arched, fell back, and writhed against the desk top. "Now take it in your mouth and suck, but not too hard."

Her hot arousal burst on his tongue. She tangled her fingers in his hair, directing. Then she pushed up against his mouth, and he knew she wanted it hard.

She groaned when he backed off.

He blew on her. "Tell me how you want it now."

"Your tongue." She gasped as he gave it to her. "All around, really fast."

He circled and plunged, around, over, and under.

"Oh God, yes, baby, yes, just like that." She panted between each word. "Connor, Connor, oh my God."

Her hips rose. She ground against his face.

Then he hit her with his best shot. Thrusting two fingers in her at once, he stabbed his tongue at a spot just below her clitoris. She went off like last Saturday's fireworks, her body contracting around his fingers, squeezing, her pussy flooding his mouth. She rocked and flowed against him. But this time she didn't make a sound. Not a single sound, as if she knew one sound would lead to a scream that would raise the roof.

He didn't give her time to come down off the high. Instead, he yanked out his massively hard cock and drove deep. Ah God. He almost came the moment her soft, warm depths took him.

Curling his body over hers, he inhaled her, steeped himself in her scent, then moved in her. Gentle strokes at first, but his cock couldn't take that for long. With a mind of its own, it demanded. Harder, higher. She wrapped her legs around him, locking her feet at his back, and he fucked her until he couldn't remember who he was and didn't care where they were.

When he came, he filled her. He buried his hands in her hair and took her mouth, staked his claim as her body convulsed around him and tossed him into the sky.

What seemed like hours later, he stirred to look down the length of her body to where they were still joined. Her skin was damp, the cowl neck of her shirt revealing one pink-tipped breast. He licked the nipple, and she jerked against him. Sliding her fingers through his hair, she lifted his head.

"I didn't say you could fuck me. I only said you could eat me. You were a very *bad* boy."

He wanted to laugh. He wanted to shout for . . . something. Joy, maybe. He couldn't be sure.

"You loved it," he whispered. He loved the dirty words on her seemingly innocent lips.

It was the first time she'd used them.

Yet another thing different about her.

A twinge started in his gut. Why had she changed? He wanted her to, but . . .

Connor pulled out slowly. His come filled her, dripped out of her. Fuck, it was so hot. He pulled a box of tissues from the desk drawer and started to clean her.

"I can do that," she said, holding out her hand.

"I'll do it." He dabbed at his semen. He wanted her to dip her fingers in it and taste him, yet there was something so intimate about cleaning her.

The twinge didn't abate. It got worse. She was different. When she looked at him, her eyes were soft, her smile gentle.

As if she were falling in love with him.

He wanted her abandoned in her sexuality, eager to demand whatever she wanted or needed to please her. Falling in love wasn't part of the plan. That could ruin everything. Love was a messy emotion that turned people into jealous, possessive idiots. Faith knew the rules. She wasn't about to . . .

He wondered if *he* was following his own damn rules. Because he liked everything she did. Hell, he *loved* it. The word itself was enough to strike terror into his heart. The truth was he could count a number of times he used it in reference to something Faith said or did, something he did to her.

Ah hell. He didn't want love to screw with his perfect marriage to his wife. So he wouldn't let it.

15

HER body floating in orgasmic aftermath, Faith could barely pay attention. She wanted to tuck her legs beneath her and fold up into the cushy leather chair. Mmm, she could go to sleep.

Oh, that had been so marvelously, wonderfully . . . perfect.

"Why are you smiling?" Across the table, Nina frowned at her. It puckered her forehead in a most unattractive manner.

Faith almost giggled. Could one get drunk on great sex?

"We had a big lunch," Connor supplied. He touched her hand. "Eating always makes a person tired afterwards."

God. She couldn't believe he'd said that. He was *so* bad. She couldn't help smiling. It might have been Nina in those pictures, but it *wasn't* Connor. "You're absolutely right, honey. Lunch must have made you tired, too. You ate more than I did."

She couldn't believe *she'd* said *that*.

Connor's mouth quivered on the verge of a total guffaw, but he managed to contain himself. Instead, he lightly pinched her arm. She'd pay for her teasing later. Faith really looked forward to the payback.

Preston Tybrook stretched out his arm, pulling back his cuff, and looked at his watch. "Can we get on with it? I've got important things to do."

"What's more important than a board meeting for Castle?" Faith's father glared.

There was so much tension, far beyond what she'd noticed in the past. Her father wasn't fond of Preston, but this was downright antagonistic.

Preston replied to her father's dig with a mutter under his breath. Dora moved her hand under the table and silenced him.

Daddy tapped the table. "Faith, will you vote your shares today since you're here?"

"No, I'm fine with you voting them, Daddy." She wouldn't have any idea how to vote anyway.

Her father smiled and shot Preston a snarky glance. It couldn't be called anything else.

The board members opened their folders containing the agenda and backup. Faith leaned closer to Connor, and he tipped the page so she could see.

And they droned on. Nina Simon studied her fingernails. Cousin Branson Finch slumped in his chair, his hands clasped over his belly, and she could swear he was sleeping with his eyes open. Preston said something about a new venture. Her father snorted and voted it down. Thomas Plumley wanted to appropriate ten thousand dollars for a philanthropic project to save a beetle indigenous to the Santa Cruz mountains. Her father didn't even bother with a snort when he voted no.

Connor didn't get a vote. He was a mere officer.

Then Mr. Biddle was brought in. Technical-schmechnical, his dissertation had to do with Green Industries. Trinity's father provided some of Castle's raw parts, and quality had taken a complete nosedive.

The tension in the room broke loose. "That's bullshit," her father snarled. "We've been using Green for years and never had a single quality problem."

Mr. Biddle scratched the back of his bald egghead as if considering his words. "I realize that, sir, but we've narrowed the issue down to—"

"Your people need to go back to the drawing board."

"Jarvis, at least listen to the man." Connor was the voice of reason in the turmoil her father's outburst created.

Daddy threw out his arm. "He brought this up in South America, in front of our *customer* no less. And who the hell authorized this study?"

"I did," Connor said. "We've got a problem here, Jarvis."

"How *dare* you go behind my back with this, Kingston."

"Let's hear Biddle out." Branson's brother Gabriel pursed his fleshy lips. And waited. Her father simply ignored him.

Mr. Biddle went on to plead his case. "Sir, if you'd just read the report—"

"I don't have to read the report. It's wrong."

Connor held out his hand. "Leave it, Don," he said to Biddle, his hand extended. "We'll go over it."

Mr. Biddle glared at her father as he slid the report across the big table. The door closed behind him with an extra quiet *whoosh* as if he'd tried hard not to slam it.

Connor slipped the report beneath his board folder. "We've got quality issues, and we need to look at every avenue, whether you think it's the right one or not."

"Here-here," someone said under their breath.

For a moment her father looked ready to jump across the table and grab Connor's throat. What on earth was going on? There was serious stress she simply didn't understand.

If she didn't know better, she'd say the board members, his *family*, hated her father. No, that couldn't be, but one thing was for sure: she'd been wrong to ignore this. Connor had a point. She needed to be more involved with her family, and maybe she could bring them closer together. Or at least keep them from tearing one another's throats out.

Instead of continuing the argument, though, her father simply narrowed his eyes. "Fine, we'll bring Herman in on this. Next item on the agenda?" Then he smiled.

It was chilling, like the way a cobra puffed up just before it struck. Faith's heart sank.

"Ah, I see Connor has another excellent expense reduction proposal," he added. "Let's hear it, Mr. CEO."

She couldn't believe her father's tone. Denigrating. And it wasn't just Connor. He spoke that way to everyone. She wished she'd never come to the meeting. She didn't want to know this side of him.

"If you'll turn to exhibit A in the packet," Connor advised, "you'll see a twelve-month analysis of employee expenses."

Papers shuffled.

"Sonuvabitch," Preston muttered.

"Our travel expenses are exorbitant, thirty-two thousand in airfare for that South American trip alone."

"You expect us to travel economy?" Cyril glared. "On these long trips, we'd be basket cases by the time we got to our destination and lose a whole day recovering."

"I suggest business over first class on foreign travel and economy on domestic," Connor said rationally, despite the outburst. "And only one suite per trip. I understand the need for entertaining, but we can restrict a suite to the highest-ranking member of the party." Then he looked from Dora to Nina. "And the business purpose for the trip needs to be approved in advance or the trip isn't reimbursable."

"What are we?" Cousin Richard groused, scratching behind his ear. "Children who have to have our butts wiped?"

"Yes," her father cut in with a certain amount of glee. "If I'd known those airfares were thirty-two K, I never would have approved so many of us making that trip."

"Right. So *you're* going to travel economy, Jarvis," Preston scoffed. "Give me a fat fucking break."

"Watch your language, Preston. This is a business meeting, and there are ladies present." Her father seemed to enjoy the reprimand a little too much. A light danced in his eyes. "I'm voting yes on Connor's proposal."

Preston grumbled and voted no. Dora did the same, without the grumble, but there were extra wrinkles around her lips. Nina, on the other hand, smiled at Connor when she voted no, as if to say he'd taken this round, but the fight wasn't over.

After the exchange she'd witnessed at the club, Faith was a little relieved on that one.

"Then we put it into policy," her father quipped at the end of the vote, which of course, he won because no one else had the votes to counter, not when he voted Faith's 5 percent as well.

She could almost see him rubbing his hands like Scrooge.

"Any other business before we adjourn?"

The strain in the air was thick, oppressive, something she breathed with every inhale. She meant to tell Connor and her father privately about what she'd done this morning, yet when she married, she'd given Connor the company right out from under the noses of her family. Her marriage—and thus the prenuptial agreement— affected everyone in this room. They had as much right as her father to know what she'd done. Didn't they?

"I have something to announce."

Connor tipped his head to regard her.

"I saw Daddy's lawyer this morning." She slid her gaze around the room, landing on her father. His nostrils flared, and his eyes looked almost black as if his pupils had dilated his irises out of existence. Then she came back to Connor. "I had the lawyer tear up our prenuptial agreement."

For a long moment, Connor simply stared at her. Something flickered in his eyes, and she hated that she couldn't always read him. Was he glad? Triumphant? Couldn't care less? *What?*

Then, finally, he took her hand in his and squeezed tightly, a smile on his lips.

She didn't have any idea what the smile meant.

THAT was the last thing he'd expected from Faith.

He wanted to take her in his arms and kiss the soft, fragrant skin at her throat. He wanted to thank her for the trust, though he wasn't sure he'd earned it yet. He wanted to rock his body inside her until she cried out his name.

And he wanted to know why she'd done it. What did Faith want in return? Everything had a price. What was his wife's?

He was semilost in thought, pondering the ramifications, while Faith's family rose and gathered round as if she'd announced their impending marriage rather than the dissolution of the prenuptial agreement.

"How sweet, Faith. I know you two will be terribly happy." Nina air-kissed Faith's cheek, then leaned down to Connor's ear. "She's a gullible fool tearing up that prenuptial." Retreating several hairsbreadths, she raised her voice and imbued it with syrup. "You are such a *lucky* man." Nina patted his back, lingering too long in the action.

Connor stood to accept the Finch and Plumley obligatory back slaps. Dora Tybrook gave Faith a hug. He wanted them all to get out so he could put his finger on what bothered him.

Finally, he was alone with Faith. And his father-in-law.

"Are you an idiot, Faith?"

A phantom chill rode up the back of his neck. "Don't talk to her like that, Jarvis."

"Butt out, Kingston. This is between my daughter and me."

"Then make it civil." He'd like to smack the old man. But for Faith standing there, he might have. But for Faith, he might have gone for Jarvis's jugular over the whole Green issue. Herman was going to be the downfall of this company if Jarvis didn't get his head out of his ass. But no matter his business differences with Jarvis, he wasn't going to let the old man treat Faith as if she were one of his subordinates.

"It's okay," Faith said, a soft smile gracing her lips.

He wanted to shout at her that it wasn't *okay*. But there were some things she had to figure out for herself. He could help her perceive her sexual beauty, but he couldn't show her that her father had no right to talk to her that way.

She touched her father's arm in appeasement. "Daddy, I—"

But Jarvis was ready to rage. "It wasn't only *your* agreement to dissolve, Faith."

"It was about *my* marriage, and I don't want that agreement. Once I'm pregnant, I don't want that thing hanging over our heads. Connor will be the father of my children."

Connor's insides twisted. Her words humbled him. As much as he wanted to give her, it was nothing compared to the trust she'd just given him.

"Well, you're not pregnant yet." Her father narrowed his eyes to a laser point. "Are you?"

She bowed her head a long moment. Connor's heart suddenly jumped to his throat. *Holy hell*. Was that why she seemed so different? The rush of baby hormones?

He couldn't breathe. Of course, he'd contemplated it, but in an almost clinical manner. Get married, get the company, get her pregnant, create a Kingston dynasty.

He hadn't thought about how it would feel. Like a sucker punch to the kidneys, sudden inexplicable fear gripped him. He hadn't been afraid of anything since he was a teenager. Now he suddenly saw himself holding his tiny newborn in his hands . . . and his guts tensed up. What if he did something wrong? What kind of father would he make? Would they have a son? Or a daughter?

"No, Daddy, I'm not pregnant yet."

Connor's stomach dropped straight to the floor. Down, down,

down so fast he almost fell with it. No baby with delicate toes and tiny fingernails and Faith's red hair.

He held on to her hand because it was the only thing that kept him on his feet. *Jesus.* For the space of five seconds, he'd wanted that child more than anything, ever. He'd been scared shitless, but he'd *wanted*.

The old man didn't seem to give a shit. "That damn agreement was about *my* company, too. What he"—Jarvis stabbed a finger in Connor's direction—"has to do to earn it. Cost measurements." He started ticking them off on his fingers. "Goals, forecasts. And getting me a grandson, by God."

Jarvis hadn't even acknowledged her pain that a child wasn't already filling her womb. Connor felt it deep in his gut with her. She was dying for her father's hug, for his approval, his commiseration that she didn't yet have the one thing that would make her world complete. Connor badly needed to knock him upside the head to get him to see. *Look at her,* he wanted to shout.

Jarvis loved her, but Connor didn't believe he'd truly looked at his daughter in years. He didn't even know who she was or understand what she needed.

"The baby will happen in its own time, Daddy."

Connor prayed it had happened today, in his office when he'd shot his seed deep inside her.

Jarvis didn't hear the despair in her voice. "He hasn't done anything he promised, Faith. You've ruined everything. I gave you what *you* wanted, and this is how you repay me."

"I'm sorry." Her hand was limp in Connor's grasp.

Screw that. She didn't have a thing to be sorry about. "*I've* been called an asshole several times over the last weeks, but you, Jarvis, take the cake. You owe Faith an apology."

His father-in-law merely glared at him. "Like hell, I do."

He felt Faith's flinch despite the fact that the only part of her he touched was her hand.

Silence filled the boardroom for several ticks of the clock.

Finally, the old man actually looked at her without wrath blazing in his eyes. A wave of misery washed down his face, pulling his mouth into a grimace. He swallowed hard, as though a lump stuck in his throat. "I'm sorry, sweetheart. I was a little upset and forgot myself. That was no way to speak to you." He held out his arms. "Forgive me?"

She hugged him hard.

But where Faith could forgive, Connor wouldn't forget. Jarvis Castle had crossed a line he couldn't easily brush aside. Working side by side with the old man wasn't going to get any easier. But there was one thing Connor did need. He squeezed Faith's hand. "Baby, I'm taking the rest of the afternoon off, and we'll go for a drive in the mountains. Go powder your nose, and I'll meet you in the lobby."

She left, though by the look she slid over him, knew full well he had a few things to say to his father-in-law before he took her for that drive.

"Draw up another agreement, Jarvis. I'll still abide by my cost objectives and due dates and all the rules we set forth concerning the business."

"I'll have it on your desk tomorrow," Jarvis said, his glare all maniacally serial killer again.

Without the terms of the prenuptial agreement, Jarvis couldn't easily get rid of him, at least not for the five-year term in his CEO employment contract. But without that agreement, Connor didn't get his five percent share. It wasn't Faith's fault that he'd lost that guarantee when she dissolved the prenuptial. He'd fucked up by not telling her it was there in the first place. He was pretty damn sure Jarvis hadn't, either. She hadn't read everything completely, and she'd signed because she'd trusted her father to take care of her. She'd thrown out the piece of paper because she now trusted Connor.

Yet Connor needed an agreement in place as much as Jarvis did. He didn't trust his father-in-law to give him what he earned. And he would earn every percent despite the roadblocks Jarvis threw in his way.

He wasn't, however, going to let Jarvis disrespect his own daughter in the bargain. That thought brought him full circle to the moment she revealed what she'd done.

What price would Faith try to extract from him? If it was love she wanted, he couldn't pay. But if it was his child she craved? *His* child. God. It hit him all over again. That moment he'd thought his baby grew inside her. *I want that,* his mind whispered.

With or without a physical piece of paper between them, he wanted her body, he wanted to fill her with his cock and his seed. He wanted his child in her belly.

He couldn't give her love, but maybe she'd realize that what he could give her was enough.

THE road Connor chose wound up into the mountains. Faith slouched in her seat, the sun streaming through the side window. Dreamy and warm, she watched Connor's hands on the wheel. He had gorgeous hands, long fingers, large palms. When he touched her, he moved her to ecstasy. When he held her hand and told her father to apologize, he'd chosen her over the company.

She shifted and raised her gaze to his profile, hiding her perusal beneath lowered lashes. Could he be falling in love with her? Why else would he care when her father had gotten so angry?

She shouldn't give herself hopes like that. Not yet.

He'd removed his suit jacket, thrown it across the back seat, then rolled up his shirtsleeves. A dark dusting of hair covered his forearms. With every turn of the wheel, muscles flexed. His scent filled the car, a woodsy aftershave and his unique male aroma. Her body melted on the inside like hot fudge.

He steered the car into another turn, and she allowed the motion to rock her closer, close enough to reach out and touch. Her fingers twitched in her lap.

"You look like Little Red Riding Hood getting ready to eat the Big Bad Wolf." Though relaxed in his seat, seemingly concentrating on his driving, he'd been aware of her scrutiny.

Faith liked that awareness. And she did want to eat the Big Bad Wolf. She'd taken the initiative in his office, and he'd loved it. He seemed to adore having her tell him what she wanted, how fast to lick, how hard, where.

He liked her dirty talk.

"I like your cock." She breathed deeply. "I liked it"—she exhaled, her breath brushing his arm—"when you fucked me on your desk."

He glanced over, not a flicker of movement on his face and his eyes hidden behind dark glasses. Then he shoved his fingers through her hair, caressing her scalp for long sensuous seconds before he pulled her head down to his lap.

"Then fuck me right now with your mouth," he whispered, "because I'm so damn hard, it hurts." The words were Connor's version of sweet nothings.

She unzipped and drew his erection from his shorts. Droplets of semen beckoned. Faith lapped them up. "You taste good," she murmured.

He shifted slightly in his seat, giving her a better fit before the wheel. "I want to be inside you."

She took him inside. Her mouth ringing his crown, she circled the sensitive ridge the way he liked.

"Christ, baby, you make me crazy." He stroked her hair.

Come dripped from the head of his cock, coating her tongue. She thrived on the deep groan that rose up from his belly.

Outside, she heard a car pass on the macadam, the shush of tires and air rushing between the vehicles.

Connor pulled up her skirt and caressed her butt, sliding along the edge of her daring thong panty. She gushed moisture and need and took him as deep as he would go, her lips brushing her fisted hand as she worked him with her tongue and mouth.

A litany of dirty words fell from his mouth. She cupped his

balls. They were tight and hard in her palm. Squeezing, she milked him to a stupendous erection.

"Shit, Faith." Over her head, she felt him yank the wheel, step on the brakes, and the car rolled to a stop. Both hands free now, he held her head, guided her with words and motions. "Fuck me, baby, please fuck me. Make me come."

He was close, throbbing in her mouth, and suddenly it wasn't enough just to taste him or swallow him. She wanted all of him.

She let his cock fall from her lips and looked up. Need etched lines into his face.

"I want inside you," he whispered. "Now."

She wanted it just as badly. Pushing him back against the seat, she climbed over him, spread her legs, wedging her body down between his belly and the steering wheel. His cock was hard and heavy against her aching clitoris, and she yanked the edge of her thong aside to slide along the full length of him.

"Jesus, baby." That was all he said, holding her by the arms, arching his cock against her.

Power flowed through her. "Do you want to fuck me, Connor?"

"Jesus, please."

He'd pulled the car to the side on a deep curve, facing the up-hill, a long stretch of road bearing down on them. Anyone driving down would see them. So would anyone coming up the hill.

"Right here, Connor? Where anyone can see us?"

"Yes, Jesus, God, Faith, I wanna fuck you here and now."

She plunged down on him hard and almost screamed it was so good. He rammed up to meet her, the friction incredible, unbearable. Then they simply pounded at each other. She couldn't think, only feel, the hard glide of flesh inside her, the bite of his fingers on her upper arms.

She panted and ground and wanted and took as if he were her prisoner. Hers. Sensation built and rocketed to her nerve endings, her body just short of orgasmic contraction. Then a horn honked, and she opened her eyes to a truck headed straight for them, a face, male, through the windshield, and she screamed, long, loud, unstoppable. As unstoppable as the orgasm that rolled through and dragged her under like an ocean wave.

SHE was pregnant. He goddamn knew it. He'd blown so high and so hard, his sperm couldn't help but reach their destination this time. Connor wanted to reach out and touch her stomach, caress the new life that had to be growing inside.

The idea of *his* child inside her didn't scare him the way it had in the boardroom, and this new emotion inside him had nothing to do with falling in love with his wife. Love wasn't something he was capable of. But damn, he would give Faith this, his total commitment to fatherhood.

"Do you think he knew what we were doing?" Faith was safely back in her seat and his cock tucked inside his trousers. He didn't hear any sirens on the road behind them.

Connor laughed. "Hell yes, the guy knew. He was probably unzipping his pants to whack off as he rounded the corner."

They'd been in plain view. He hadn't intended to take her there. He just didn't want to cause an accident when he blew to kingdom come in her mouth.

Je-sus. Somehow, since Saturday night, she'd given herself over to him. Anything he wanted. Anything *she* wanted. She ordered him to go down on her in his office. She blew him while he was driving in broad daylight, then fucked the hell out of him in direct line of sight of oncoming traffic.

Thank God it hadn't been a mom and her underage kids. The truck driver, on the other hand, had given Connor the high five.

She curled up in the passenger seat, sliding her feet beneath her, and smiled at him. "That was very naughty," she said. "Don't do it again."

He had so many things he wanted to do to her. Her willingness to drop her barriers humbled him. Her trust moved him. As if the prenuptial agreement itself were a barrier, once it was gone, she'd released her remaining inhibitions with it.

He wouldn't hurt her. He might not be able to love her, but he would never hurt her. He needed to give her something to seal that unspoken promise, something just for her.

Connor smiled to himself. He knew the perfect thing.

16

FAITH had taken to heart Connor's belief that she should have more of a "relationship" with her relatives. Thus, on Friday, only a week later, here she was at the Bell Tower Café having lunch with Josie *and* Dora. The restaurant was in an old renovated church. One had to reserve a week in advance to dine in the bell tower itself, so instead, they sat in the courtyard beneath some shady trees. Great, except for little seeds (or something—*eewwe*), which kept dropping into her Chinese chicken salad. Faith picked out yet another . . . thing.

"So you like being a project manager at Castle?" Despite having to make small talk every day with parents, teachers, yadda yadda, Faith had never been comfortable with chitchat. The discomfort grew even worse because Josie was her *blood* relative.

"I love it." Josie speared a piece of tomato on her Gorgonzola salad, picked off one of those damn seeds, and glared at her fork. "Maybe we should ask to be moved inside."

"They come off trees and are therefore natural, so they have to be good for you," Dora said. "So just eat them."

They groused more like sisters than mother and daughter. Josie was a year younger than Faith, but with her pixie haircut and boyish figure, she looked barely out of her teens.

"And Connor wants to put me in charge of one of the big projects, like the Dominican job." She rolled her vibrant green eyes beneath long, lush lashes Faith envied. "Except for your dad. He's trying to nix the deal, thinks I can't do it."

Why *was* Connor so interested? First he wanted Faith to be friends with her, now he advocated putting her in charge of a project Faith's father didn't think she was capable of doing.

"I'm sorry." Faith really didn't know what else to say.

Josie flapped a hand. "Connor'll fix it eventually."

He had one ally at Castle, but Faith felt a twinge.

"How's everything, ladies?" Their waiter tucked a tray beneath his arm.

"These trees suck." Josie beamed at him with a sweet smile.

The man, at least ten years older than her yet obviously captivated, gave a goofy, apologetic grin. "Sorry. I'll put out the umbrella."

He dragged a green canvas sunshade to the side of the table, tilted it on its wood stand, and sheltered them from the trees.

"You're a total doll. Thank you." Josie gave him another of those sunbeam smiles, and he wandered off bemused.

"If you turn some of that charm on Jarvis, he'd let you have the Dominican job." Dora dipped a chicken bite into a side dish of lime juice. That's all she had, greens, grilled chicken, and lime dressing. Her eating habits were more outlandish than Trinity's. "Though why you'd want to travel to godforsaken places to see *gravel trucks*," she went on, "I'll never know."

"Mom, they're not gravel trucks. They're earthmovers and all this really cool stuff."

"But the mines are in the middle of nowhere without modern conveniences."

"They have flush toilets, Mom."

While the headquarters of the companies her father dealt with were in major cities, the mines themselves were often out in the boonies. It *was* kind of cool that Josie got to go to them.

"I think I'm jealous," Faith said, a smile on her lips to let her cousin know it was a good envy. "You get to see so much more than the normal tourist would see."

"But Faith." Dora lowered her voice. "There's *no* shopping. Zippo. Zilch." She added a throat-slashing gesture in case they didn't get the immensity of the issue.

Josie wore blue jeans and a T-shirt emblazoned with "Your village lost their idiot. Shall I let them know we found you?" Faith didn't think Josie cared much about shopping.

Josie leaned forward and studied Faith with a steady gaze. "Faith, this is a very important question. Do you love to shop?"

"Umm." She looked from Dora's sleeveless designer knit to Josie's T-shirt. Was there a right answer? Then she saw the twinkle in Josie's eye. "I'd have to say I hate shopping."

Dora gasped. "You two received the wrong chromosomes. Faith, I was hoping you would be a *good* influence on Josie."

Josie had the eye roll down to an art. "Really, she loves me just the way I am. Don't ya, Mom?"

Dora merely propped her chin on her hand and changed the subject completely. "Did you like the dress Connor brought home for you from our trip?"

"Yes, it was lovely." And totally debauched. Faith couldn't wait to wear it again and relive the memories it evoked.

"I picked it out," Dora announced.

Josie almost snorted her milk out her nose. "You did not, Mom. You just seconded his opinion. And even if you said you hated it, Connor would have bought it anyway. He'd already made up his mind." She tipped her head to Faith. "I have a feeling that man doesn't change his mind easily once it's made up."

Faith couldn't say for sure. She'd only been married to him two months. Josie seemed to know him better than she did.

That fact grated along Faith's nerves.

"Honey, you don't know the man as well as you think you do."
Dora snapped her chin up haughtily, and for the first time, all the
banter between mother and daughter didn't seem so sweet.

"What's *that* supposed to mean, Mom?"

Yeah, Faith wanted to add, *what does that mean?*

Dora merely zipped her lip, glancing at Faith as she did so.
"Nothing. I've said enough."

"No, Mother, you need to finish what you were going to say."

Faith couldn't stand the arguing anymore. "Really, Dora, if
you've got something to say about Connor, then say it."

She asked for it, yet her heart was beating far too fast, just as
it had when she'd told Trinity to speak up. Trinity had left several
messages over the past few days, but Faith kept missing her on
the return calls. Maybe that wasn't bad. She hadn't wanted her
friend guessing her change in feelings about Connor. A lot of good
it did to avoid it with Trinity when she'd somehow fallen into *this*
discussion.

Dora put her hand over Faith's. The gesture didn't comfort
her. "You shouldn't have gotten rid of the prenuptial. A woman
needs protection. Some men"—she punctuated with a meaningful
shrug—"have that wandering eye."

"I don't think Connor does." Faith wanted to believe that with
all her heart. "Besides, I can still divorce him if I catch him doing
something he shouldn't."

"Yes, but California is a community-property state, and he'll
still get half of *your* five percent share in the company."

Faith hadn't thought of that. "He knows it doesn't belong to
him."

"I hate to bring it home, honey, but that's why he married you.
And it will upset the whole balance of power at Castle."

Josie's jaw tensed. "Mom, just drop it, okay?"

Faith couldn't let it go. "Connor's not going to cheat on me. I'll
get pregnant, and everything's going to be fine."

Dora gave her such a look, emphasized by a slow, sad shake of her head. *You poor deluded child.* "Faith, if you hadn't dissolved the agreement, I wouldn't *dream* of telling you this."

"Mom, I said stop it."

Dora didn't listen to Josie. "Faith, honey, he had a woman in his room when we were down in South America."

Her stomach burned all the way up into her throat. Trinity had said the same thing.

Josie slapped down her glass, splashing milk over the table. "That is bullshit. You're just spreading rumors."

Dora gave Josie the same sad look. "I saw it, sweets. It was the *wrong* kind of business, if you know what I mean."

This time Josie grabbed Faith's hand and squeezed. She felt as if she were being sucked into a meat grinder.

"Don't you believe it, Faith. Whatever was going on, it wasn't what Mother thinks. At the end of every meeting, he *always* had to rush out to call you. He's not cheating."

Her hands felt numb, her heart seemed heavy in her chest, and she had a piercing pain right above her left eye. Maybe she had an aneurysm that was ready to burst. Why did Josie want to defend Connor? Why did Connor want to promote Josie? Why, why, why? Who was in those goddamn pictures someone kept putting on her doorstep? And what about the times he came home with whiskey on his breath and said he'd been out to drinks with an associate?

All she had to do was ask him, yet she was terrified to. She'd fallen in love and become so insecure about her marriage that she couldn't ask her husband. She could fuck him, but she couldn't talk to him. God. What was she supposed to believe?

Faith didn't realize she'd closed her eyes until she opened them again. That really wasn't the question. What did she truly believe in her heart if she stopped listening to other people's slurs? She thought of him demanding her father's apology on her behalf, his announcement at the club that *she* was a woman worthy of taking in the piano lounge. Connor himself hadn't said or done a single thing to give her doubts about him.

"I believe in Connor."

"But, Faith honey—"

"I'm not saying you're lying, Dora, but you're wrong about what you saw."

Josie beamed that high-wattage smile again. "You're making the right choice, Faith. He's going to be good for Castle, just you wait and see."

"Do you want me to talk to him about making sure you're in charge of that big project?" Faith couldn't remember the name.

Josie blushed. "That's not why I'm standing behind him."

"I know." Faith was going to believe in Connor, and part of that was knowing his comments about Josie were because he admired her abilities, nothing more. "I'll lend my support in any way I can." She pressed Josie's hand, then turned to Dora. "Thanks for caring enough to tell me what you thought I should know."

"Faith, I don't want to hurt you."

"I know that, too. And I'm not going to be hurt."

Instead, she was going to believe in her husband. How could she get hurt if she did that?

DAMMIT, he was grinding his teeth to the dentin. Jarvis breathed deeply. His doctor said he needed to avoid stress. With Kingston in his life, he was anything but stress-free.

Jarvis snapped his wrist out despite the crack in his joint and flipped over his watch. Where the hell was the man? One fifty-five PM. Five more minutes, and he'd officially be late.

The dining room was clearing out. Jarvis had specifically chosen a late lunch so they wouldn't be surrounded.

Faith. How could she do that without telling him first? She always consulted him—until Kingston came into their lives. Everything was topsy-turvy. Why, Jarvis yelled at her yesterday. Called her an idiot. It was unforgivable, but he'd done it. That's the havoc Kingston wreaked. Coming between Jarvis and his daughter. But even if he was wrong, how dare Kingston demand an apology? He would pay for that humiliation.

At last Kingston sauntered in and sat in the opposite chair. Their waiter snapped the napkin and handed it to him.

"I've been waiting for fifteen minutes," Jarvis groused.

"Then you shouldn't have gotten here twenty minutes early."

They ordered, Kingston barely looking at the menu and choosing only a turkey sandwich where Jarvis wanted the filet mignon. Well, dammit, he wasn't going to help the whippersnapper make his cost-reduction goals by cutting down on his lunch expenses. He ordered the filet *and* a side of broccoli, which his doctor would love.

"It's damn lucky I did arrive early," Jarvis went on as if their conversation hadn't been sidetracked for several minutes.

Kingston arched one eyebrow. He really was quite a handsome man. It was no wonder Faith fell for his line of bullshit. Women were so easily taken in by a pretty face. Jarvis almost snorted aloud. So were men. "I've heard a lot about you."

"What," Kingston mocked, "have you taken to skulking in the lobby now?"

Jarvis ignored the insult. "Seems you've been dipping your wick in the wrong places."

"Dipping my wick." The young man sipped his water. "I like that. It's a nice, old-fashioned euphemism. My wick, however, has only burned on the proper occasions with the appropriate"—he smiled broadly—"candleholder in attendance."

Jarvis didn't like the reference. It was unseemly to discuss Faith and . . . wicks. "Davis told me you'd been *seen*."

Davis was his lawyer. The man claimed he tried to talk Faith out of tearing up the agreement, otherwise Jarvis would have fired him. Davis Sr., however, would have called Jarvis first, but he'd give Davis Jr. one more chance for loyalty's sake. Besides, it would be a pain in the ass to change attorneys.

"And Davis actually saw me?"

"He heard it from an acquaintance."

Kingston's eyes darkened to obsidian and the hardness of diamonds. "Who was the acquaintance?"

Jarvis shrugged. "How the hell should I know?"

"I'm not cheating on her." Kingston leaned in. "I will never cheat on her."

Jarvis let his breath hiss through his teeth. "If you do, you're out." He reached to his inner pocket, pulled out the reason for this friendly lunch, and tossed it on the table.

The *new* agreement. Jarvis was so looking forward to this.

Kingston let it lay there as their meals arrived.

"It guarantees your percentages if you meet your objectives, as we agreed the first time," Jarvis offered, waiting until the boy grabbed for it. Yet he didn't.

"What's the catch this time, Jarvis?"

"What do you mean?"

"You're too pleased with yourself for there not to be a catch." Kingston bit into his sandwich and chewed as if he were unconcerned.

He damn well better be concerned. Since he wasn't going for the bait, Jarvis would have to tell him. "I've thought it over."

"The cost objectives?"

"The agreement. I don't think we need one anymore."

Kingston's jaw tensed. Ah, good, a reaction now. "Why not?" he asked in the same calm tone belied by that muscle tick.

"Because I've decided there's no reason you should have a share in Castle."

His nostrils widened as he let out a breath. He was getting the picture. "Should I remind you that if Faith and I divorce, I get half her shares? Community-property laws and all."

That was all Kingston wanted from the beginning, but Jarvis had a delightful surprise for the man. "You've miscalculated. Faith's shares are in a trust that *isn't* subject to those laws."

The man's obsidian-dark eyes flared with rage, and his cheek muscles rippled. Otherwise, Kingston was perfectly calm. "Touché, Jarvis. Do you expect my resignation now?"

"It would be nice."

"Sorry. I'll be at work tomorrow as usual. We still have Herman Green to discuss."

Jarvis felt his own flare of anger. "I could fire you."

His son-in-law smiled. For some reason, it chilled Jarvis's bones. "Under the terms of my employment contract, you can only get rid of me for embezzlement, fraud, or negligence."

Jarvis grinned. "Yes. And isn't it the board that defines negligence?" There was an air of legitimacy about that, but they both knew who controlled the board. "Not to worry, you're married to my daughter, and I wouldn't want you unemployed."

He was going to enjoy making the boy's life a living hell. He picked up the agreement and stuffed it back in his pocket.

"This has nothing to do with how I treat Faith, whether I cheat on her or I don't. You simply don't like that I disagree with your management style."

With sudden, inexplicable anger, Jarvis wanted to pound his fist on the table. "My *style* has worked for thirty-five years."

"That's the problem. It's an anachronism."

Asshole. But Jarvis wasn't going to lower himself with insults. "You're free to bring any proposals for cost reduction or productivity improvement to the board for approval." He gave Kingston a beatific smile. "If we deem them worthy, I'm sure you'll get the necessary votes."

"Thank you for your support, Jarvis."

Jarvis studied his fingernails. "It's easy, you know. Make me like you, and perhaps I'll support everything you want to do."

Kingston picked up his sandwich again, but spoke before he took a bite. "If you don't support the things I want to do, Jarvis, your company is going down. It's only a matter of time."

"Is that a threat?"

"No. It's merely a fact. Green Industries and project cost overruns will destroy you. You're already drowning, Jarvis; you just don't know it yet."

Jarvis realized he hadn't touched a bite of his filet, and Kingston was almost done with his lunch. Dammit, the boy had put him off his meal while Jarvis had planned for the whole thing to be the other way round.

PRESTON sipped his neat whiskey and leaned back in his comfy chair, the view of his table obscured by a row of potted plants. Jarvis hadn't even known he was in the dining room. Preston slipped his wallet back in his pocket.

Some waiters were only too happy to report back on interesting conversations, especially when the price was right.

Well, well, well. That was an outstanding bit of drama between the son-in-law and darling daddy.

Preston was sure he could use it to his advantage. Dora, sweetheart that she was, wanted Connor out because he was going to crush poor Faith's heart. Dora also preferred the devil she knew to the devil she didn't. Connor had refused to authorize payment for her spa days, salon trips, and wardrobe costs, which she claimed she needed to maintain the perfect director image.

On the other hand, Preston saw an opportunity. Connor struck him as the take-the-money-and-run type. With him on their side, they might be able to oust Jarvis and sell the company right out from under the old bastard.

Preston would like nothing more than to be rid of his blasted cousin. If Jarvis was a reasonable man, well, things might have been different. Jarvis, however, hadn't seen reason since his wife died over twenty years ago.

Preston smiled. Yes. Very, very interesting possibilities were laid out before him like a feast. All it would take was for Connor to convince his wife to let him vote her shares.

* * *

WHO was spreading the talk, dammit? Someone who wanted Connor out of the way? Problem was too many people wanted him gone. Dora Tybrook had gone ballistic when he wouldn't sign her expense voucher for the day spa, though Dora's version of ballistic was silence for five seconds, narrowed eyes, a huffed breath, then the phrase "You'll be sorry." There was Nina, the rest of the board, Lance, Herman Green, even Trinity, if she still believed he'd hurt Faith.

Last but not least, there was Jarvis himself. At lunch today, the old man had screwed him but good. Since there was no longer an agreement, Connor could be fired at any time for negligence, as defined by Jarvis, and he wouldn't be awarded his 5 percent share for any cost reduction goals he met. Connor hadn't seen that one coming; why, he couldn't say. He should have known Jarvis was close to the edge. Faith's dissolution of their agreement had pushed him over. Or maybe it was the business with Green Industries. Connor had plans for correcting that problem he knew damn well and good Jarvis wouldn't approve.

Truth of the matter was he had one real chance against Jarvis now: Faith's proxy votes. He could probably get the rest of the board to go along with his new proposals, but he couldn't beat out Jarvis. The old man was determined to make his life suck even if it meant ignoring problems. Whatever the hell was going on with Green's product, quality was in the crapper, and Castle was sinking under the weight of cost overruns on the major projects. Jarvis had hosed him for sure, but the old man also stood to hose the whole damn company as well.

Unless Connor convinced Faith to let him vote her shares instead of her father. He could turn things around; he *knew* it. Castle would one day belong to his children, and he wasn't going to let Jarvis screw it up for them.

Tonight, however, he wouldn't worry about the company, about her shares, or about Jarvis. Faith was a totally separate issue from Castle Mining. And tonight, he was all hers.

He'd iced the champagne in the bucket that room service provided and chilled the two glasses. When Faith needed sustenance, a plate of fruit and cheese sat on the table beside it. He could have seduced her at home, but he wanted something special. The Fairmont in San Jose was a short drive and presented the elegance he required.

She would arrive in a few minutes.

He laid the video camera in the center of the comforter where she couldn't miss it. Connor wondered how she'd handle it.

17

"WE'RE going to make a movie."

Faith stared at the bed—and the video camera in the middle of it. "What kind of movie?"

He tipped her chin with his index finger. "Of us."

"Oh." She felt queasy. Nerves. Excitement. The need to jump his bones right this minute. But without the camera showing all her flaws.

He'd called her midafternoon and told her to meet him at the Fairmont at seven. When she'd asked what she should wear, he'd simply told her, "Something hot."

Faith took that to mean low-cut and no panties. Choosing a clingy top that showed her pert nipples and a long black skirt, she'd paired demure with brazen. When she didn't see him in the hotel lobby, she'd called his cell phone, and he gave her a room number. She started to pulse deep inside before she even made it on the elevator. He was always coming up with surprises.

But a camera. It made her think too much about the photos on the doorstep. Faith closed her eyes and shoved the thought away. She trusted him. Completely.

"Do you have a script?" she asked.

A lecherous half smile spread across his mouth. Tapping his temple, he said, "It's up here."

Faith badly wanted to take the lead, because she knew that's what Connor loved, but once again, he had her off balance. "And how does it start?"

"You turn around and let me see your outfit."

Closing her eyes, she turned slowly on boots with a four-inch heel. They'd made her hot the day she tried them on in the shoe store, and she'd saved them for just such an occasion.

Stopping, she cocked a hip, resting her hand on it, her head tipped to the side. A marvelous idea came to her. "You were lucky you called when you did. Because there was a man down in the lobby who couldn't take his eyes off my breasts." She cupped herself, then flitted a finger over one tightly beaded nipple.

"Faith, honey, most men can't take their eyes off your breasts." He reached out to caress the other nipple.

It was such a curiously erotic sensation, the two of them touching her at once.

"Most men"—he stepped closer still until his body heated her even through his suit jacket—"want to lay you down on the carpet and ravage you the moment they lay eyes on you."

A flash of worry nailed her insides. How far would he take this whole kinkiness thing? As far as having her sleep with other men? No. He'd promised right in the beginning that it would be only them. This was fantasy, exciting if she let go of all her worries. "Would you want to watch?" she murmured.

He wagged a finger. "Only *I* get to do you." Then he leaned in for a husky whisper. "But they can watch."

He knew exactly what to say, fueling kinky fantasies yet making her feel that she was the only one he wanted. Her breasts ached for his mouth, and she rubbed against him. The scent of aftershave and seductive male hormones rose to tantalize her.

"Strip," he breathed against her ear.

She was oh-so-willing. Until Connor backed off and reached for the camera.

She shook her head. "Not yet."

He pouted like a child. "Why, baby?"

Oh my God, she was really getting to like that little endearment. "Because . . ." She couldn't think of an excuse for almost a second. "Because I want to be naked and spread out on the bed when you turn it on."

He slid an arm across her back and hauled her against him. "Jesus, Faith, you make me crazy saying things like that."

She made herself crazy, too. She wasn't quite sure she could pull it off. "Pour me some champagne while I undress."

There was an art to stripping Faith didn't have, yet Connor was transfixed as she propped a foot on the bed and slid the skirt to her knee to unzip the boot. "Don't spill," she teased.

Connor licked a drop from the flute.

The skirt was a sensuous slide as she raised it a second time to remove the other boot. They both landed with a *thunk* at his feet where she tossed them. Hmm, now what? She wasn't wearing panties, but she was wearing a bra. Turning her back, she tugged the zipper down until warm air brushed her backside.

She hadn't heard him move, but he was suddenly up against her, reaching round to put the glass to her lips. "Drink."

It was fresh and tasted faintly of almonds. He gave her another sip before he backed off. Knowing he watched, she wriggled her hips, then let the skirt glide down her thighs to pool on the carpet.

"You're not wearing panties."

She looked over her shoulder and fluttered her eyelashes. "I don't like panties anymore. I threw all of mine out."

When he got hot, his eyes went dark and his lids lowered. He was burning up now, his slacks stretching over his erection. Faith bent over the bed, lifted one leg, then the other, climbing atop on all fours. Before she had a chance to stop him, he dribbled champagne down her butt cheeks, then swooped in to suck it off, sneaking one finger along her pussy.

"Christ, you're wet."

She could come just from that note of awe in his voice.

Rising fully to her knees, she swiped her top over her head and threw it behind her. Connor laughed. She so wanted to turn around and look at him, but she was putting on a show.

What would turn him on the most? What would make him lose control? She could do anything if she kept that goal in mind, driving Connor mad. She just didn't know how she'd feel when he finally turned the camera on.

Undoing the front clasp of her bra, she held the cups apart. "My breasts are so sensitive," she said as if she were talking to herself. Moving her hands, she traced the aureoles. And moaned. Then she flipped the bra off her shoulders and let it fall. She felt the material drift across her calves as Connor grabbed it.

"Oh, I'm so hot," she whispered, and did exactly what she would have done if she were alone. Sliding both hands down over her abdomen, she reached a finger inside the curls at her apex and stroked herself, arching into her own touch. "Oh yeah."

Then she went down on all fours once again, spread her legs slightly, and reached back to slide a finger inside. In this position, Connor could see everything.

"You're beautiful, baby."

Faith knew she was. "You can turn the camera on, honey."

"Sweetheart, it's already on."

"I knew that." *Not.* She glanced over her shoulder to find him studying the viewfinder. Her heart stuttered in her chest. "Are we going to watch this movie later?"

He gave her such a look, head down, only his eyes rolling up to gaze at her. "What do you think?"

God. Didn't they say the camera added ten pounds? She could do it. She had to since she'd promised him she'd push her limits. Still, her stomach quaked to think about watching her own body. "It can't all be me; you have to be in it, too." She flapped her hand. "Come on. Give me that thing, then strip."

"You're a demanding bitch."

For a moment, the word shocked her, like the first time he talked dirty. He raised that devilish eyebrow, and a smile hovered on his lips. She couldn't resist him. "You love it when I'm demanding," she answered. "You're a closet submissive."

"And you're a closet dominatrix." He gave her the camera and proceeded to strip, just as she told him to.

Her mouth dried up with each layer of clothing he tossed aside until the bare skin of his chest mesmerized her.

"You're not watching the camera, sweetheart. You're probably taking a picture of my navel."

"I like your navel." She centered on his chest, then moved down to his slacks as he unzipped. It was the oddest sensation, like looking at him from afar. "Your cock looks so small."

"Hey, I resent that."

"Don't worry, honey, it still works okay." The enormity of the moment hit her. She was teasing and taking pictures of her naked husband, and she wasn't the least bit self-conscious. It was yet another wonderful thing Connor had done for her.

Yet he was such a magnificent male specimen, she didn't want to think what she'd look like next to him on camera.

Connor grabbed her foot and pulled her to the end of the bed, messing up the covers.

Faith squealed and laughed, and the camera lens went all over the place. "What are you doing?"

"Give me that thing." With him being so much taller, she couldn't hold the camera out of his reach. Stepping between her legs, he aimed straight down. "Now *that* is a beautiful thing. All pink and pretty and wet."

Her face flamed. It was the compliments, not the embarrassment. He always said the most astonishing things.

Parting her, he stroked up, down, and around her clitoris, then dipped inside. Her body filled with moisture, and her hips seemed to move on their own. Watching through the viewfinder, he smiled. "Ah hell, you just flooded my fingers, baby."

"You can't take close-ups of my . . ." She hesitated, searching for a word that made her feel the least uncomfortable.

"Your pussy? Vagina? Honeypot? Sweet little cunt?"

With each word he said, he hit a sensitive spot deep inside. Faith bit her lip to keep from moaning. "Not the last one."

He glanced at her. "There's nothing wrong with calling your beautiful honeypot a cunt. You have the most gorgeous cunt."

"*Eewwe.*" But she writhed on the bed as he adored her *gorgeous cunt*.

"Then pick something you do like," he urged.

Vagina was too clinical, *honeypot* too ridiculous. "*Pussy* works for me." The sentence started on a moan and ended on a gasp as he pushed two fingers inside her.

"I adore your pussy," he whispered to the camera. Pulling his finger back out, he slid along her lips, holding her open, exposing the hard nub of her clitoris. "Touch yourself."

God, she couldn't help doing what he said. She wanted someone's finger right *there*, even if it was her own. They worked her together, Connor dipping inside to gather her juices and caress her pussy lips, her own finger working the bead of her clit. She was wet and hot, her hips rising. Tossing her head back and forth on the bed, she needed to come. Badly.

"Connor, eat me now, please." She bucked and rose against the combined touch. Yet before he could even move, she shot high into orgasm, screaming and clawing her way through it.

When she could open her eyes, he'd set up a tripod and angled the camera to take in the bed. Faith held out a hand. "Give it to me. I want to watch." Just because she came once, didn't mean he got out of making her come with his tongue.

Something deep and blazing flamed in his eyes.

Dragging her down to the end of the bed, he knelt, pushing her thighs wide to accommodate him, then raised her legs to his shoulders. He blew on her and she could barely keep the camera trained on his dark head.

"Suck me, Connor. Hard. Lick every inch of my pussy and make me come." The words were for him, the camera, herself. The dirty talk sent another surge of heat and moisture to her center.

For the camera, he gave a big, white-toothed smile. "Keep talking, baby." Then he spread her with his fingers and sucked her clitoris, tonguing her hard. She almost shot off the bed.

"Oh yeah," she murmured. "Lick me just like that. Right in the center." Telling him what to do was so damn exciting, far beyond merely letting him do it. Words could hold such power.

He cupped her butt and lifted her to his mouth. On the screen, his head bobbed and her body undulated. Powerfully erotic, the physical sensation combined with the sight made her pant and climb to orgasm faster than ever. He opened his eyes to stare in the camera, and it was the oddest feeling, detached, yet as if he were deep inside her with every fiber of his being.

She rose and fell, and finally, when she couldn't stand it anymore, she pushed her head back into the mattress and screamed through her orgasm. The contractions went on and on, mastering her completely, until she came down and realized his fingers were deep inside, her body milking them in the last throes.

And the camera was now in his hands.

"That was good, baby."

God yes. So good she couldn't even manage to speak.

"I wanna watch my cock slide inside you." He stood and pulled her legs to his waist. "Lock your feet behind my back."

Following instructions was the most she could do right now.

The camera in one hand, he stroked his cock up and down her slit, coating himself with all her moisture. Then he guided himself into her tender, sensitive pussy. Slowly.

"Christ," he murmured, "that looks so fucking good. As if you're swallowing me whole."

His cock filling her, his words stroking her mind, she almost hit her orgasm right then. Yet he pulled out as slowly as he'd entered until only the tip of his crown breached her, their only connection. "Jesus, Faith, it's so fucking beautiful."

He pulled out, then worked his cock in his hand until a bead of come coated his tip. He rubbed it over his crown. Faith's mouth watered. She reached, but instead of allowing her to touch, he started that slow, inexorable penetration all over again.

"Later," he murmured. "Right now, I want this."

The last millimeter, he slammed home, the camera bobbing. Faith moaned and arched, rubbing herself against his pubic ridge. He repeated the act over and over until she thought she'd gone mad and tears of need leaked from the corners of her eyes.

"Fuck me hard, Connor. I need it. Fast and hard and deep. Please, baby, please."

After planting the camera on the tripod, he pushed her higher on the bed, angling her for the right view through the lens, and finally, finally climbed on top to take her just the way she wanted. Already close, she flew off into outer space, screaming her orgasm against his mouth. She didn't know when he came, all she felt was the pound of his body straight up to her heart, the clean, sweaty smell of maleness, and his voice at her ear driving her over the edge again.

THAT was so fucking perfect, Connor had trouble moving a muscle for long minutes. Faith lay motionless against the comforter, her arms outstretched, her hair fanned about her head, and her eyes closed.

He stroked a few stray strands of her gorgeous red locks back off her forehead, then nuzzled her ear with his nose. "Died and gone to heaven?" he whispered.

"Mmm." She purred in her throat for him, but didn't move.

As he untangled their limbs and climbed off the bed, she whimpered. "Where are you going?"

"I'm plugging the camera in. I want to watch."

That got her undivided attention. Naked and glorious, she rolled onto one elbow, her breasts plump and enticing. Christ, he should have fucked her that way and come all over her throat. She had the perfect breasts for it. Ah, but they had all night.

"We're going to watch it on the TV?"

He almost smiled. She had that squirrel-about-to-be-squashed-by-a-Mack look. "Yeah, baby, we're going to watch on the TV because the viewfinder is too small."

"Oh. Of course." Though she didn't look convinced that it *had* to be done that way.

"Besides, I want to play with you while we watch."

"You mean while you watch yourself go down on me."

He grinned as he plugged in the connector. "Now you've got it. The next orgasm will be even better than the last one."

She made a noise.

"What'd you say, honey?" The endearment amused him. It was so ordinary, as if they'd been married years instead of weeks.

"I said I don't think it could get much better."

He didn't believe that's what she said at all, but glancing up from the TV, he smiled, slow and lecherous. "Wait and see."

By the time he was done, she'd snuggled under the covers. He crawled in, wrapped her in his arms, then pointed the remote.

His dick came to immediate attention during the opening credits, Faith on her hands and knees fingering herself. Hot didn't begin to describe it. He had the sudden urge to roll on top of her and pound her into the mattress all over again.

She laughed during his striptease.

"I'm offended." He clutched his chest in mock affront.

"We could send you out for lessons."

Beneath the covers her nipples rose to hardened peaks as they watched him playing with her sweet pussy. God she'd been wet, so fucking wet. When, on-screen, they both started playing her, he slid a hand down between her legs and tested.

"You're wet, baby." He gently nipped her earlobe. "You love watching yourself play with that hot little cunt of yours."

"Pussy," she whispered.

He stroked her lightly. She opened her legs for him and settled deep against the pillows.

When she came on-screen, he'd raised the camera to her face.

"Look at yourself."

It was the most beautiful thing he'd ever seen, her lips parted, the delicious sound of her orgasm rolling off her tongue. Her skin flushed, her breasts jiggled. He reached up to cup her now, squeezing one nipple.

She gasped and pushed down into the mattress, her fingers crawling between her legs. He toed back the covers to watch. On the TV, she begged him to eat her and took control of the camera.

Holy hell, he'd almost lost it then, but he'd wanted her taste on his tongue more than anything in the world.

He leaned down to lick a nipple just as his face came down between her legs. "Can you feel it all over again, baby?"

Her hips wriggled, her fingers flew. The need to take over simmered, but more, he wanted to watch her excitement rise all over again. On the TV, his head bobbed between her legs.

"Fuck, that's hot." He nuzzled her ear. "Do yourself, baby, fuck yourself. I wanna see you come."

She moaned and writhed, both on-screen and off. Her body undulated, and he could still taste her in his mouth. Whispering in her ear, playing with her nipples, he had a hard-on fit for twenty women. She was so fucking into herself, into watching, into replaying exactly how his tongue felt on her.

She jolted, screamed, and came to the combined sound of her voice on the TV and the real thing filling the room. This was how he wanted her, needed her. Turned on out of her mind.

He held her in his arms as her shudders fell away.

"Oh, Connor, you were right. That was just as good the second time."

"Told you, baby. But damn, I forgot to get you on camera sucking my cock."

"Next time," she murmured, snuggling close as their next scene began.

SHE was so far from finished. Her body was on fire. Connor had barely touched her. She'd done all that herself.

"That felt so . . ." She glanced up at him and let herself go. "So fucking good."

He kissed her hard, taking her mouth as if he were conquering her. Oh Lord, how he made her melt.

"You're a naughty girl." He licked her throat, then rolled to his back. "We're missing the movie. I'll have to rewind."

She put her hand on his arm as he pointed the remote. "No. I want to see this part."

"But I want you to see the way your body sucks my cock inside." He gave her a crooked smile. "And very, very slowly."

She couldn't define how watching made her feel. It was like being a voyeur and an exhibitionist at the same time. It made her so hot, she didn't have time to be self-conscious. When he put his tongue to her clitoris on-screen, she *felt* it.

Connor was right. Their movie was beautiful. Though she'd never believed it before in her life, *she* was beautiful.

Oh God. For a moment, she loved him so damn much for giving this to her that it *hurt*.

"Is that what I really look like?"

Powerful, elemental, his magnificent penis slid slowly inside, stretched her. She was pink, her clitoris hard, her lips plump and full, taking him, all of him.

"That's exactly what you look like." He gathered her close, then wrapped her fingers around his cock, and together they idly stroked him to greater hardness. A bead of come pearled on the tip; he used it to wet the whole length.

He kissed her temple. "That's it, baby."

On-screen, they'd flipped from him standing between her legs to the tripod-mounted shot centered on the bed. She'd been so damn hot, she barely remembered this part.

Her eyes glazed almost the moment he entered her. She started to pant and moan, and her fingers dug firmly into his arms. Hooking a hand under her butt, he angled her and hit deep. She was sure that was the moment she'd started to come.

Connor squeezed her hand around his cock and quickened the pace. "God, baby, you were high then."

She was. High on his voice, his touch, his possession.

"Come on, baby," she could hear him whisper on-screen. "I love it when you come. You do it so good." His hands traveled the length of her, caressing, even as his cock pounded into her. "Come on, baby, hard, do it for me hard. Take me all the way." As if he were crooning a love song to her, he kept up a litany of words. She hadn't heard each individual syllable, but she'd felt the essence deep inside. "Yeah, baby, God, baby, please, baby."

When she cried out, he took her mouth, kissing her into oblivion. When he started his own come, he took her face in his hands and held her, his body pounding into hers, his gaze claiming her. And his words.

"God, Faith, please, Faith." Then her name over and over as he filled her. She could almost feel the throb of his cock in her pussy, the pulse of his semen shooting into her womb.

She hadn't understood it when he took her, but she recognized it now on the TV.

Connor had made love to her. In living color.

Faith slid down his body and took him in her mouth, sucking him, tasting him. He was hers. He thrust up against her, held her head down, begged her with his body to take him.

And she did. Every last drop. Everything he had to give. As she swallowed his essence, Faith knew the camera didn't lie. Connor didn't fuck her. He made love to her.

Yet she knew he wouldn't admit it. And she wasn't sure how long she could live with that.

18

"EVERYONE in favor of Connor's proposal?"

The entire board—except Jarvis—raised their hands.

"All opposed?" Jarvis raised his hand.

Another Monday morning and another great initiative bites the dust. Connor made a tick on his agenda. Meetings had gotten to the point where even minor decisions, such as altering a purchasing policy, had to be approved by the board. Jarvis had called three special meetings. All to mock Connor and exhibit his own omnipotence.

Unfortunately, it merely showed that Jarvis was an ass and not above costing the company money to prove a point.

Connor had married Faith for her father's company, yet over time, especially since that Fairmont trip a week ago, his days at Castle had become hell, while his nights at home with Faith had turned into heaven. Something had changed that night, though he couldn't pinpoint what. He only knew that the transformed Faith was infinitely desirable. She was the only thing that got him through the interminable day.

Yet Connor persisted. "We've got one more proposal on the agenda today."

Jarvis, seated at the head of the table as always, raised an eyebrow and glanced through the bifocals perched on his nose.

Preston made a show of shuffling his papers. Connor couldn't tell if the man had even bothered to read the proposal e-mailed to everyone. One of the Finches cleared his throat. Probably none of them had bothered to read since it was a foregone conclusion that Jarvis would turn down any proposal coming out of Connor's office.

Life at Castle Heavy Mining had gone to shit. He'd actually been better off at Green as a minor manager.

"Any statements before we vote?" Jarvis grinned. But for the glasses, he looked like a smiling death's head.

The so-called statement was a mere formality. Instead of wasting time trying to get buy-in, Connor went for the jugular. "Quality on Green products has now dropped off by 50 percent. Ignoring this problem is detrimental to Castle's health."

"I talked to Herman. He's done the testing *you* required"—meaning Jarvis didn't think it was necessary—"and the issue appears to be in the bonding process once the product gets here."

How would Herman deduce that? "That's bullshit, Jarvis."

"Excuse me?" The old man loved raising that eyebrow. He looked at the three ladies, Nina, Alexis Plumley, and Dora.

Connor was damn sure all three had heard the word before.

"Are you calling Hermie a liar, Kingston?"

Actually, he was calling Jarvis an idiot. Would the old man's hatred for Connor blind him to any threat?

Connor drove his point home. "Customers don't come back to Green when *someone's* bonding fails. They come to us. We're the ones looking like shit. It's on our backs, not Herman's."

Branson stroked his chin. "Are you sure Herman's done his due diligence on this issue, Jarvis?"

For several seconds, you could hear the clock ticking on the wall, then the beep of a car remote outside the window.

And Jarvis finally spoke. "He feels it's too coincidental that all the problems began when Kingston came on the scene."

Was that Herman or Jarvis talking out of his ass? "If Herman isn't willing to provide a better answer than that," Connor countered, "there are only two alternatives: find another source or do it in-house."

"That's bullshit." Spittle flew from Jarvis's mouth. "I will not turn my back on a forty-five-year relationship based on a spurious report by *Preston's* VP of Engineering."

"Biddle is *our* Engineering VP," Preston said, his calm voice in direct opposition to Jarvis's higher-pitched diatribe.

Gabriel Finch cocked his head and stared at Jarvis. Branson pushed slightly back from the table as if distancing himself. Nina tapped her lip with a crimson nail, her glance ping-ponging between Jarvis and Connor. The old man had never endeared himself to his family or his board, but Connor detected something new for the first time. Not only was Jarvis disliked, but his competency was in jeopardy.

"What are the details on the alternatives you've outlined, Connor?" Thomas opened his folder and pulled out the proposal.

"I'm running this meeting," Jarvis raised his voice.

"True," Richard Plumley said, "but we can ask questions."

As a whole, the board shut Jarvis down.

"I've outlined two proposals and the estimated costs of each. First, we find another supplier." They should have had a second supplier all along. You *never* have only one source. "We'll have to have new dies made, and there'll be costs involved with certifying a new contractor. That's all in the report."

"And the second alternative?" Preston asked. He'd been studying the numbers.

"We do it in-house."

"That's a huge capital outlay."

"True, but the return on investment is damn good once we're up and running."

"How quickly can that be accomplished?"

"Worst case, six months; best, we do it in three. The plating line will take the longest to set up and train on."

During the discussion, Jarvis sat silent except for the drum of his fingers. He'd tossed his bifocals on the table and regarded them all with narrowed eyes.

Then he smiled. "We've heard enough. Let's vote. All in favor, raise their hand."

"I make a motion to hold the vote until the next meeting while we do investigation." Preston wore his own evil smile.

"I second the motion," Branson added before Jarvis could say a word, as if the two had somehow rehearsed it.

"I don't ratify that motion," Jarvis snarled.

"Sorry, Jarvis, you don't get a choice." Cyril spoke for the first time. He was a quiet guy, but he was the corporate secretary and knew the bylaws. "A motion was put forward and seconded, and the vote will take place at the next meeting."

They'd outmaneuvered the old man. Amazing.

Of course, he'd vote the proposal down at the next meeting.

Unless Connor got his wife's proxies.

FAITH had called him in the meeting, his cell phone vibrating in its holder on his belt. He needed to call her back, but Christ, his head was pounding. In his office, Connor grabbed a bottle of water and downed three ibuprofen. What he needed was Faith's fingers massaging his temples. Or her mouth sucking his cock.

Funny, it used to be he needed a shot of whiskey and some solitude, but he hadn't been to his apartment in weeks, nor had he missed it. Maybe it was time to let the place go.

In the beginning, he'd imagined that handling Faith day in and day out would be the bigger of his problems when he married. Women could be high maintenance, though he'd done his best to choose a woman at the lowest end of that scale.

Damn if he hadn't chosen well, because it was his wife providing the refuge while the company drove him crazy. His desire for her hadn't waned.

Connor reached to his belt for his cell phone, then hit her speed dial.

"What are you doing?" Faith didn't even say hello.

"Just got out of a meeting."

"Are you in your office?"

"Yes."

"Is the door locked?"

"No." He glanced up. "It's still open."

"Lock it."

"Why?" She made him smile. She'd taken to issuing orders in and out of the bedroom. When she got like that, he knew damn well she had something sweet and sexy planned for him.

"I'm so hot, Connor, and my vibrator keeps calling my name, and I want you to talk me through an orgasm." She gave a plaintive little sigh.

He set the bottled water on his desk, idly turning it under his fingertip. "I'll be home soon."

"But Connor, honey, sweetie, baby, I need it now. I'll take care of you when you get home. Just do me over the phone."

His headache was gone. As easily as that. Her voice or her desire; it certainly wasn't the ibuprofen.

"Talk to me," she whispered, "while I stroke myself with my vibrator and put it inside and ride it . . ."

She trailed off. He wanted to unzip, pull out his dick, and start whacking to the sound of her voice.

The snick of the latch climbed his spine like a chill. Nina leaned against the closed door.

"Someone's just stepped into my office, baby. Why don't you keep it hot for me, and I'll be there pronto."

"Connor—" Faith stopped herself. "Can I give myself an orgasm to take off the edge?"

"No."

"Creep."

He grinned. *This* was how he wanted her. Playful, fun, hot. "I'll be home soon, baby. Promise."

She muttered another curse as he hit the end button.

"The wife?" Nina smiled slyly. "Or someone else?"

He liked Nina. She flirted, and if he'd shown an interest in doing her, she'd have jumped on it, but she didn't hold his vows against him. Odd that, since in South America, he'd feared his goose was cooked, or, at the very least, she'd try to make the job a living hell. But no, Jarvis was the one doing that.

"Faith, of course. There is no one else."

She tipped her head one way, then the other, as if trying to read him. Then a breath puffed out her lips. "My God, you're in love with her."

Her words hit him like a wallop to the solar plexus. For a second. Then the sensation melted away. What he had with Faith was far more sustainable than love. It was painless for both of them, all the upsides of hot sex and no emotional downsides.

However, it would be counterproductive to his plans to deny Nina's statement. In fact, admitting it might work in his favor. "You sound surprised."

"I didn't think you had it in you." She laughed. "I didn't think *Faith* had it in her."

Connor narrowed his eyes. "She's perfect. And I don't like people denigrating her."

Her eyebrows shot up. "Ooh. Said like a besotted man."

He wasn't besotted. He was totally in control. But he liked what he had with Faith. In fact, he'd rather be sliding deep inside her than standing here talking with Nina.

"What can I do for you?" He leaned against the desk.

Nina got down to business. "Is Jarvis getting Alzheimer's?"

Hmm, he hadn't expected that one. Not from Nina anyway.

"I have no idea."

"Are we really in danger over this thing with Green?"

"Yes, I believe we are. Individually, the teeth aren't expensive to fix. But in a customer's point of view, when he keeps having to deal with a piddling problem over and over, he gets pissed and walks."

"Why is Jarvis ignoring it?"

Because he hates my guts. "I have no idea."

He'd been here only months, but he'd never seen her without a twinkle in her eye and a flirty comment rolling off her lips. Her chest, which was already impressive, expanded with her deep breath. Then she tapped the door and opened it. "We'll have to figure out how to take care of the problem, won't we, Connor?"

She was gone. He didn't know what the hell that meant, nor did he care. The only thing he cared about was getting home before his wife exhausted herself with her vibrator and there wasn't anything left for him.

WHAT did that mean?

Jarvis wasn't used to hanging back and making himself invisible, yet he scuttled down the hall before anyone saw him eavesdropping.

Kingston and that bitch Nina were planning something. Figure out how to take care of what problem? Faith?

Jarvis ground his teeth. They were having an affair. Kingston was a cheat, a thief, and a liar. It probably started in South America, right under Jarvis's nose, even as the whippersnapper claimed he'd *never* cheat on Faith.

Thank God he'd hired that private investigator. He'd make sure the man got pictures. Faith would be done with Kingston, and somehow, Jarvis would find a way to buy out his contract and get him out of their lives forever.

"I'M on my way home, Preston."

Damn, his office seemed to have a revolving door. Nina went

out, Tybrook came in only a few minutes later. Connor's headache returned.

Didn't these people get it? His wife was waiting at home with her vibrator at the ready. He had a duty to perform.

Connor almost grinned, but managed to keep it to himself.

"This will only take a minute, son."

"I'm not your son."

Preston waved a hand. "Right, sorry, figure of speech."

"What do you want, Preston?" Getting a person out the door as quickly as possible meant no beating around the bush.

"Just a talk, that's all."

Connor pointedly flipped his wrist to look at his watch. "My wife's expecting me."

At that, Preston smiled. "Ah, the little wife. Everything going well in paradise?"

As he'd told Nina, life with Faith was perfect. She was everything he could have hoped for. She didn't nag, and she made no demands. Except for sex. Exactly the way he wanted it.

"Paradise would describe it."

"Well, then, I've a little proposition for you." Without being invited, Preston sat in one of Connor's leather chairs.

Connor didn't make a move to take his own seat. "Preston, this will have to wait till tomorrow."

Again, the man smiled. "It would behoove you to listen to what I have to say now."

Connor crossed his arms. "You have five minutes."

Quirking a half smile, Preston crossed his legs and settled in. "I didn't like you at first."

"And you've changed your mind?"

"Jarvis changed my mind."

"Nice to know. What's the point?"

"Dora and I thought the company would be better off if you went back where you came from, wherever the hell that might be. I even did my share to make sure that happened." When Connor opened his mouth, Preston held up his hand. "A few well-placed rumors at the club about your supposed infidelities."

"So it was you."

Preston grinned. "Yes. But little Faith wouldn't hear a wrong word said against you."

Faith's support warmed his gut and pushed his headache away. Preston didn't seem to have a single compunction about using dirty pool, though. In a way, Connor had to admire him. He wasn't above a little dirty pool himself. "Thanks for the honesty. Now I know who to come to the next time it happens."

"Oh, I'm not the only one. Let's just say there are a few others in our community who wouldn't mind being rid of you. But me"—Preston tapped his chest—"I've changed my mind. I think you and I can be of great assistance to each other."

Where this was going, Connor didn't have a clue, but he'd hear Preston out. "How?"

"Jarvis is going to run this company into the ground."

Connor shrugged. "He could have an agenda none of us understands." Connor had considered that if he himself were out of the way, Jarvis might very well get things back on track.

It was a big if, though, and project overruns had predated Connor coming on the scene. Jarvis had been showing signs of losing his hold on the company for months.

"Jarvis's agenda has always been making sure he is king at Castle. If it's not his idea, it sucks the big one."

The euphemism didn't fit the dapper man before him, but Preston hit the nail on the head. "And your plan to stop him is . . . ?" Connor spread his hands.

"We vote him out and you in as chairman. We give you the five percent you want so you have equal voting power as everyone else on the board with the exception of Jarvis and myself."

Oh yeah. He knew right where this was going. "One big problem, Preston. With his forty-eight percent and the proxies for Faith's five, none of you can outvote him."

"But if Faith gives you the right to vote her shares . . ." Preston trailed off and quirked that half smile again.

"So you want me to turn my wife against her father."

Preston tut-tutted. "Not *turn against*. That sounds so ruthless and devious." Which is exactly what it was. "We just want to do what's best for all of us. You can solve the few issues we have, then wash your hands of the thing once we sell."

Like Pontius Pilate. He might have been shunted from foster home to foster home, but he had at some point learned his Bible tales from watching TV.

"You'll make a lot of money. You can get out."

"Out of what?" Connor asked. Not that he didn't know.

"The company." Preston paused significantly. "And anything else you want to get out of."

The implication being that he could get out of his marriage.

"Otherwise"—Preston spread his hands—"we all get nothing but the fire sale of the assets."

There was that possibility. If Jarvis went unchecked, the company wouldn't be worth more than the cluster of buildings and the assets, and those would just about cover the liabilities.

Granted, Preston was looking out for his own livelihood, but he had a point.

"I'll let you ponder. Talk it over with Faith. She'll see the logic of it. If you like, I can have Dora speak with her."

"No." He wasn't sure which part he was saying no to. In his gut, he knew Faith would never understand ousting her father.

Yet in the face of his vendetta against everything Connor represented, Jarvis had lost all sense of proportion. The tide couldn't be stemmed forever. Eventually, Castle Heavy Mining would pay the price. So would the family. As would Faith.

Preston was offering them all an alternative.

"The rest of the board will vote with you?" he asked.

Preston nodded. "Talk with each of them, if you'd like."

Of course he would. He wasn't simply taking Preston's word

for it. Yet he knew that Nina's questions had been the precursor to this. "And when do you want to do it?"

"We have that meeting scheduled next week."

Connor drew a breath deep into his gut.

"You can walk away with all the money you could need and all the freedom you could ask for," Preston added as inducement.

Why the hell did they all think his only mission was to screw Faith, her father, and the company? *Duh*. Because they all knew he'd married her for her money. Once he had that, what did he really need Faith for?

Except that he did. His goal had never been just the money. He'd be able to walk away from the company, but he couldn't walk away from the child he *knew* grew inside her even now.

Still, if he was to have a shot at getting it all, he had one week to get Faith's proxies. He told himself it was for the good of the company. For Faith. Even for Jarvis. Connor couldn't let Castle Heavy Mining go down the tubes, and if he left Preston to do his worst, the board might actually sell the company right out from under Jarvis.

He just wasn't sure Faith would understand why he needed to overthrow her father using *her* proxies in order to save it all.

Maybe the only way was not to tell her the real plan.

FAITH had grabbed her keys off the hall table and a coat out of the closet. It was short but covered the bare essentials. *Bare* being the operative word. All she wore was the coat.

She'd wanted to surprise Connor by having him find her lying on the bed with her vibrator. Waiting for him. Instead he'd surprised her with a phone call a half hour after she'd called him. Oddly enough, it was easy to do things like that. She was terrified to tell him she loved him, but she could get all sorts of kinky and sexy now with barely a twinge.

When he'd called her back, he'd given her an address and told her to meet him there, and she hadn't given herself time to dress or even put up her hair. It hung about her shoulders in waves. Connor liked it that way.

Driving in the car, she was hot and shivery. It had nothing to do with the weather and everything to do with the mind-blowing event he had planned this time. He'd promised their sex life would be exciting, and he hadn't let up for a moment.

She'd become obsessed. Trinity had called several times, and Faith still hadn't been able to get hold of her. Was that accidentally on purpose? She just knew she couldn't talk about Connor even with her best friend. As for looking at houses, she hadn't done that, either. Her life had suddenly become all about Connor, and she felt paralyzed when it came to anything else.

She stopped for a red light and imagined the guy in the 4x4 next to her could see she was naked under the coat. She wanted to put her hand between her legs and test how wet she was.

The light changed, and she surged forward, clutching the wheel, dying to get there.

She thought about sex all the time. Hadn't she read in some women's magazine that men thought about it every eight minutes? Or was it eight seconds? Whatever, she had them beat, because she thought about doing Connor *every* second.

Turning the corner onto a residential street, she glanced at the paper she'd written the address and directions on, then at the side of the apartment building. This was it. A cream-colored structure with two levels and parking underneath, it had a row of flowers in boxes along the walkway. Faith parked on the opposite side of the street.

As she climbed out and turned to shut the door, a car drove by and air rushed up her coat, billowing it. She quickly smashed it down, then couldn't resist a giggle.

Sitting in a car by a hydrant, a man glanced up from the newspaper he'd been reading. She wondered if she'd flashed him.

Faith had never done anything like this in her life. Connor

had gotten her to go without panties, but without anything at all? Never. She felt like a movie starlet from the forties, draped in mink and nothing else. She couldn't remember the movie or the actress, just the mink pooled on the floor at her feet.

Faith had worn high heels, too.

She crossed the street, glanced at the apartment numbers, and found the one Connor had directed her to on the second floor. Her pulse raced. The beads of her nipples rasped against the coat. Hot, wet, trembling, she put a hand on the railing and climbed the steps.

Could the man in the car see her butt cheeks beneath the coat? God. It gave her the most delicious thrill to imagine he could, and she ascended with an extra sway to her hips.

She was turning into an exhibitionist. Wouldn't Connor be pleased.

The curtains were drawn across the window, yet he opened the door before she even knocked and grabbed her arm.

"What took you so long?"

His lips, spiked with the tang of whiskey, crushed hers. She went up on her toes, wound her arms around his neck, and kissed him hard. Then she felt the rush of air once again up her coat as Connor squeezed her butt.

"You're naked under there."

"You told me to get over here now." She smiled. "I didn't have time to get dressed. My vibrator and I were waiting."

He hitched her closer, using her buns for leverage. "Did you bring the vibrator?"

Damn. She hadn't even thought of that. "No."

He yanked her inside and closed the door. "You never cease to amaze me," he said.

Faith pushed him back into the center of the room with one hand on his chest. She didn't take stock of the room, other than the fact that it had a couch, a coffee table, and an entertainment center, and the walls were bare.

Like her. And Faith had the best idea ever.

Though he'd taken off his jacket, he wore his tie. She pulled on it, bringing his face down to her level.

She licked along the seam of his lips, then locked gazes. "Fuck me, Connor. Right now."

She loved the blaze in his eyes when she talked dirty, when she got assertive, when she told him what she wanted in no uncertain terms.

Then she drew in a deep breath, her breasts rising along the lapels of her coat, her nipples almost spilling out. "Fuck me doggie style," she added in barely more than a whisper.

He pulled her head back by her hair. "Who the hell *are* you?"

She laughed, deep, throaty, husky. "Whoever I want to be. Now fuck me." She'd said the word for him three times.

His gaze smoked. He reached for the belt of her jacket and she twisted his fingers back. "No. Do me with it on."

"Jesus, Faith, you're gonna kill me." Then he pushed her to her knees. She went down on her hands beside him and looked up. His erection raged against his slacks. "Better hurry, or I might have to find someone else to do my bidding."

God, she was hot. So hot. The play was fun, exciting, excruciating. She watched as he went to his knees behind her, then slid his hand straight up her center.

"Christ, you're wet."

She was barely able to contain herself. "And you're hard. No preliminaries. Get inside me."

The rasp of his zipper filled the small apartment, then he shoved her coat to her waist, braced her hip with one hand, and slammed home.

Faith cried out. "Oh my God."

"Did I hurt you?"

"No," she said, pushing back on him. "Do it hard and fast."

And he did, pounding her so hard she felt as if she'd lose consciousness. Colors kaleidoscoped all around her. She curled her fingers into the carpet and held on. Oh God, oh God. His cock filled her, drove her to the edge of the world. There was simply his breath, his relentless thrusts, the clench of her pussy every time he withdrew, and a roaring in her ears. She thought she heard him shout her name, then there was only the slap of his testicles, the pulse of his cock, and the heat of his semen, until she melted into orgasmic oblivion.

19

IT could have been one tick of the clock. It could have been hours. Faith couldn't move, and her head felt woozy. But she was oh so deliciously sated and comfy curled up against him, his body still hot against her flesh even through his clothing. Faith couldn't quite remember how they'd fallen like that, a heap on the carpet, his breath at her ear, stirring her hair.

"When's your period due?" Connor idly stroked her belly.

Her cheeks flushed. She did all manner of kinky sexual things with him, let him touch her everywhere he wanted to, yet some things still embarrassed her. The things one took care of behind a locked bathroom door. The first time she'd told him they couldn't have sex because, well—she'd blushed furiously then, too—it was the wrong time, he'd laughed and said there were so many things they could do despite *that*. Only she'd been so crampy and miserable. Connor made her sweet, hot tea, brought her pills to help, and even a heating pad for her stomach. He was so damn good to her, she'd wanted to cry.

"It's supposed to come next week," she said.

He played with her belly button. "I don't think it's going to start this time."

Tipping her head back, she stared up at him. She adored his gorgeous smoky eyes. "And what makes you think that?"

He trailed two fingers along her abdomen, then cupped a breast in his palm. "They're bigger."

"They are not."

Bending his head, he took her nipple in his mouth, only to let it pop free again. "They are." With his index finger, he circled the beaded nub. "I've sucked them enough to know."

Faith blushed again. How did he make her do that? "I don't think we should get our hopes up, just in case."

"The whole world's ready to crush your hopes under its boot heel, so why the hell should we crush them first? Plenty of time for that later on."

He had the oddest philosophies. They flew in the face of old clichés. "All right." She guided his hand back down to her belly and pressed his warmth to her. "Let's get our hopes up."

God, he really did want to have a baby with her. The thought made her glow inside.

He rubbed his nose against her cheek. "And what gave you the idea to come over naked like this? I almost had to have you out on the landing." He pulled the lapels of her coat together, covering her up again.

So, was that hot and nasty enough for you? That's what she meant to say. Instead, something else entirely came out. "So, was that making love?"

Her stomach tumbled right through the floor.

"Baby, baby, baby," he muffled against her throat. "Everything we do is."

A sigh fell from her lips. At least he hadn't said it was *just* fucking. Her side was starting to ache against the hard floor despite the carpeting. Faith pushed to one elbow. "Whose place is this?"

The couch had seen better days, its beige fabric worn, its springs having lost their bounce in certain spots. Still, it was clean. Nicks and water stains marked the coffee table, and an old TV on a roller stand butted up to the wall in the corner. Not a single picture or painting adorned the walls. No plants, either. The only thing that made it even look lived-in was a single glass of amber liquid on an end table.

Whiskey. She tasted again the pungent smack of whiskey on his lips sometimes when he came home. And Faith started to feel a little sick.

Connor stood, grabbed her hand, and pulled her to her feet. Attending to his own pants, he zipped as he said, "It's my apartment. The one I lived in before we got married."

"I didn't know you still had it." It sounded so innocuous. It just didn't *feel* that way.

Connor shrugged, then reached up to straighten his tie. "I couldn't get out of the lease."

She thought of the photos hidden under her grade books. Were they taken here? Her jacket suddenly wasn't enough to keep her warm despite the heat of a summer evening. She swallowed, but it sounded loud in the quiet of the room.

"Lease is up, though," he said. "I'm getting rid of it. I don't think there's anything here you'll want; it's just a bunch of Salvation Army stuff, but you can take a look."

For the first time he actually looked at her. She couldn't read a thing in his eyes. She couldn't tell if his concentration on righting his clothes was a significant bit of body language, yet there was something in the way he offered her a chance to look around the place. As if he were giving her a message she couldn't quite grasp.

"Is there anything you want to take to our house?"

Had he put a slight emphasis on *our*? "I don't know," she said. "What's here?" Would she find evidence of secrets she'd be much better off not knowing?

Like the little monkeys, she wanted to close her eyes and cover her ears. She didn't want to see, didn't want to hear.

His fingers were warmer than hers when he led her down the

short hallway. Faded brown towels hung on a rack in the bathroom. In the bedroom, the spread was of green chenille. She didn't think they even made things like that anymore.

"Is there anything *you* want to keep?" she asked.

"I don't need this place anymore, Faith. I don't want it, and I don't want anything in it." He put his warm hands to her cold cheeks. "Except you." He smiled. "I'll take you with me."

Okay, okay, he *was* saying something.

"Is the bottle of whiskey empty?"

A tiny light flickered at the back of his eyes. "Yeah. That was the last of it in the glass."

It was all very subliminal and understated, subject to interpretation, but coupled with his talk about her not starting her period, Faith took it to mean what she wanted it to.

Her husband was committing himself to her.

Instead of throwing her arms around him, though, she simply said, "I think we should throw out all the old stuff."

CHRIST, he'd skated through that one. He didn't lie about making love. *Love* was an illusion and *making love* just a term. But she'd delighted the hell out of him, and the moment he realized she'd rushed over naked under her damn coat, he'd wanted nothing more than to bend her over the railing of his apartment building and fuck her for all the world to see.

In the animal kingdom, it was called staking a claim.

Faith was his. It was so much better than love. Been there, done that, gotten screwed, and all the rest of it. What he was creating with Faith was so much better. More solid in that it wasn't based on an illusive emotion that disappeared as quickly as it came.

She got it about the apartment. She understood the sacrifice. He glanced up the stairs of their condo where she'd disappeared only moments ago after arriving home. *Sacrifice* was the wrong word. She understood he was choosing her.

It might have been the appropriate moment to bring up the proxies. Then again, one didn't mix business with pleasure.

Connor smiled to himself. He had the feeling tonight's pleasure was far from over. He'd followed her home, then she'd rushed upstairs, and he didn't think it was to hide her vibrator. He climbed more slowly.

He'd deal with the proxies later. There was plenty of time. He didn't want to ruin tonight. Or tomorrow. Or the week. He had to find the right spiel to get her to accept what needed to be done, but for now he didn't give a goddamn about the company. All he wanted was his cock buried deep inside her again.

He couldn't get enough of her. If she kept creating hot little surprises like she had tonight, he'd never get enough.

She wasn't in the bedroom. He followed the sound of . . . tearing paper? She hadn't quite closed the door of her office. He pushed it open with his fingertip.

"What are you doing, Faith?"

She startled, then jumped to face him, one hand behind her back. Beside her, the desk drawer was open. Looking down, she closed it with her foot, the lower edges of the coat parting to reveal an expanse of delicious thigh he wanted to suck.

After he discovered what she hid behind her back.

"I was just going through some old grade books. Thought I might throw them out."

"You're not a good liar, Faith."

She demonstrated that by looking at the doorjamb over his shoulder. "Why would I lie about a thing like that?"

Three steps into the room brought him to her. "I don't know why. But you and I are far from done tonight, and"—he breathed deeply, loudly—"you still smell like hot, horny woman. So I don't think going through your grade books would be the first thing you'd rush in to do."

She smiled, but he saw through her telltale shifting gaze.

"What are you hiding, Faith?" he whispered in a voice for sweet nothings or dirty talk.

When she didn't move, he slid one hand beneath the jacket to her bare breast while with the other he reached for what she was holding from him.

She clutched tight for a moment, then finally let go.

A manila envelope and a big red question mark on it. And some pictures. For a weird out-of-body moment, he didn't even understand what he was looking at.

"You have porn in your desk?" He smiled lasciviously—until the starkness of her gaze settled in his gut.

She'd already torn one photo to pieces and thrown it in the trash can.

He studied the top picture with a more discerning eye. A couple going at it doggie style. He glanced at Faith but she'd fixed her gaze on the carpet. He turned to another photo, a side view of the couple in action, no faces, just bodies. Red hair, a full breast, a long expanse of flesh from buttocks to thigh to calf spread alongside her partner's leg as he impaled her. And a bracelet around her ankle.

Nina Simon going for the gusto.

"And you think that's my bare ass?" he asked. A knot tied his insides into a not-so-neat little bow.

"No," she whispered, staring at his tie.

"Then why didn't you show me these?"

He heard her swallow.

"Because you didn't trust me," he answered for her.

Godammit. Who? Preston and Nina? Preston admitted to feeding the rumors. But would he send photos? Come to think of it, at his age, would Preston's butt look that toned? Connor grimaced. "When did you get them?"

Faith bit her lip before she answered. "These came three weeks ago or so."

"*These?*" Hell and damnation. "There are others?"

A nod, still without meeting his gaze. "I tore that first lot up." She pulled her belt tighter at her waist. "They came while you were in South America."

He'd kill that bitch. Nina tried to set him up and when that didn't work, she'd used photos she already had. But something struck him. "Did they come *from* South America?"

"Someone left them under the front mat. Both times."

Sonuvabitch. Nina had *another* accomplice. Obviously her male cohort, which he was pretty damn sure wasn't Preston Tybrook. How many people were out to destroy his marriage?

More important was why Faith had hidden this from him.

"That's not my ass." Shit. He shouldn't have to deny it.

"I know."

But dammit, she was talking to his tie. "Look at me."

Lifting her gaze, she rolled her lips between her teeth and looked at him. A misty sheen filled her eyes.

He felt like howling. "If you didn't think that was me, why didn't you show them to me?"

"I just wanted to rip them up."

"But you didn't." He stepped back from her, raking a hand through his hair.

"That's what I was doing just now."

"After three weeks. What, did you take them out every night with a goddamn magnifying glass and try to figure out if it was me or not? All you had to do was ask."

She didn't answer. He gave her his back, anger seething in his chest. Why the hell was he so angry? With the bastard that left her the pictures, yeah, but with Faith? It didn't make sense, yet it roiled inside him. Finally he turned.

Only to find she'd been waiting for him to look at her. "It's not easy for me to ask."

He felt cold suddenly. "It is if you trust me."

Her breasts rose with a deep breath. "Why did you let me think you'd let your apartment go?"

Her question slammed into his gut. "I never said I had."

"But we talked about you bringing your stuff over and you said you'd rather give it away."

Yes. He'd slyly led her to believe the apartment was gone, yet he'd been sneaking back over sometimes before going home to her. "I didn't take another woman there. I haven't been with another woman since before I met you. I kept it because I needed . . ." He stopped, regarded the wing tips of his shoes. "I wanted a place that wasn't yours or your father's, but mine. Somewhere that I could regroup on my own, recharge." Then he looked at her. "I don't need that anymore."

Her gaze tracked his face, from his mouth to his cheeks and finally to his eyes. "After tonight, I'm not afraid anymore that it's you in the pictures. That's why I was tearing them up."

The knots pulling his chest apart eased. In two strides he was at her side. Slipping his hand beneath the fall of hair at her nape, he pulled her up on her toes until his lips rested on hers. "Come fuck the hell out of me, Faith, and we'll forget about the pictures and the apartment. I'm sorry."

He just wanted to be inside her. He didn't like the lingering taste of bad emotions. So he took her mouth, consumed her with his tongue, his lips, his kiss, and burned away the raw edge of emotion.

Tomorrow, however, someone would pay for sending those photos to his wife.

CONNOR wanted her to have his baby. A child wasn't just part of the bargain they'd made, his payment for giving him her father's company. A baby was something he wanted *with* her.

Faith couldn't sleep. Curled up against her husband's warm body, she could only think of all the good things she'd been blessed with. They'd made love in his apartment, then again here at home. He'd hated those pictures as much as she had. Standing in her office, they'd forged a bond. He didn't need a refuge away from her anymore. Things were going to be okay.

"I love you," she whispered in the dark.

He didn't have to love her as much as she did him, because she had enough love for the two of them.

Her heart froze in her chest. What a pathetic thought.

She wanted him to love her the way she did him. What was it Trinity said the day she heard about the engagement? That Faith deserved a man who would make love to her and cherish her.

Without love, she could never be sure he wouldn't tire of her. She couldn't be sure he wouldn't rent another apartment without her knowledge or that the next set of pictures would show his face in ecstasy while he fucked another woman.

"I love you," she mouthed.

What she had would *have* to be enough. Because it was all she was going to get. And truly, he was more than she'd ever hoped to have.

Still, she could almost hear Trinity's voice telling her she was pathetic.

THE following morning, Connor found Nina seated in a cushy leather chair, the dryer hood propped against the wall. He'd called her assistant—why she needed an assistant to make her hair, nail, and facial appointments, he couldn't say—and Nina was right where she was supposed to be at the appointed time.

Legs spread, he stopped in front of her. "We need to talk."

She raised her head from the fashion magazine she perused. Her ultrachic salon came equipped with space-age hairdryers shaped like huge silver bullets, leather seats, and gilt-edged mirrors. Yet it was ultimately still a beauty parlor where women slathered scary-looking gunk on their heads; the hair products reeked enough to bring tears to a man's eyes, and the blast of dryers and screech of voices trying to be heard *over* the dryers set his ears ringing.

"I'm having my hair highlighted, Connor. Couldn't we discuss what's on your mind later?"

She had a way of looking at a man, starting at his mouth, working her gaze down to his crotch, then lower, punctuating it all with a tilt to her mouth, that spoke of pure boredom. A slow inspection designed to cut a man down to size. He was sure it drove her lovers crazy, made them want to do anything to get her to gaze at them fondly the way she used to.

Connor merely grabbed the magazine, tossed it on the pile beside her chair, and yanked her to her feet. "We'll talk now."

She pulled back when he headed toward the front door. "I am *not* going out there. Look at my hair."

Tinfoil spliced her red locks, and two stripes of dye splotched her forehead where her eyebrows were supposed to be. The contrast turned her skin sallow. He could see why she didn't want to step outside, yet she didn't so much as flinch that he'd discovered her in this state.

"Better find us a back room," he said, "or we'll have our little talk right here."

"Oh my," she cooed, "we do have our panties in a wad, don't we?" She batted her eyelashes at him.

He had to admire the woman. She never lost composure. A man would never cow her. He wondered if she had any chink in her armor at all.

He lifted one brow. "Public or private?" Then he pulled the sheaf of photos from his inside jacket pocket and fanned them briefly before her like a deck of cards.

She glanced at them. "Well, hell, *that* took Faith ages." She crooked her finger, led him down a hallway, and stepped inside a tanning room. "We only have a couple of minutes before I turn orange." She flicked lightly at a piece of foil.

"Tell me all," he said once the door was closed.

She rolled her eyes and puffed out a breath. "I was pissed. You turned me down. I thought I'd get back at you."

"Bitch." It came out sounding almost friendly. Her answer was typical of the reasons he'd begun to like her. She made no bones about being a malicious bitch. With Nina, you knew what you were up against, an adversary. She didn't hide her machinating personality behind lies and manipulation. It was goddamn refreshing.

"Thank you," she smiled. "When neither of you made a fuss, I figured it didn't matter anyway."

He flapped the photos at her. "Aren't you worried about these things getting on the Internet?"

She shrugged. "Please. Who cares? Look at Paris Hilton."

He preferred not to. Nina didn't care about much, it seemed, certainly not her reputation. "Who did the hand delivery when you were in South America?"

"A . . . friend." She ran a polished nail over his shirt.

He didn't react. His body didn't react. He simply stared her down.

She folded her arms and leaned against the booth wall. "So why did she pick now to tell you?"

The question was really why had Faith picked last night to tear them up. Because he'd earned her trust or because she'd decided to trust him? There was a big difference in the two things, and the answer eluded him. He wanted to earn her confidence, and he didn't like how that desire had somehow morphed into an obsessive need. For Nina, though, he chose a totally innocuous answer. "Because we're a team."

Nina laughed, half mocking, half disbelieving, then she sucked in a breath of air. "A team? Men and women can't play on the same team, Connor."

"Maybe *you* can't, but Faith isn't anything like you."

"I was thinking more of you." She poked him in the chest. "*You* aren't a team player."

"Hell, yes, I am. Making Castle a *team* is what I've been trying to do since I got there."

"No, it's been you trying to show Jarvis how he's fucked up all these years and you need to come in and save us."

"That's bullshit."

"Is it?" She tapped her fingers on her arm, waiting.

He formulated an answer.

"You took his daughter," she said for him, "you took his company. You told him his best friend was a screwup, and you shoved it down his throat that he's too old to handle it all."

He told Faith what she needed. He told Jarvis what the company needed. Then he'd sought to provide it. He was looking out for their best interests. It wasn't his fault that Green Industries had lost their edge, but did he have to use it like a club on Jarvis's head? Maybe not, but the thought was academic right now. "What the hell does that have to do with your photos on my doorstep?"

She leaned in, her chemical scent wafting up at him.

"It wasn't your doorstep. It was Faith's."

"Same thing."

She shook her head. "No, it's not, Connor."

He suddenly saw himself last night. He'd so magnanimously offered to get rid of his apartment. Then he'd yelled at Faith for keeping the photos from him. He never once asked her how they made her feel. He simply accused her of not trusting him. He'd made the whole episode about *him*.

Just as he'd made the issues at Castle Heavy Mining all about Jarvis's lack of good management.

"Have you told her you love her?" Nina hit him with her best shot.

"I don't." A shard pierced his side. The denial felt shitty. As if he'd said it to Faith herself.

Nina tipped her head, and the smile curving her lips was neither malicious nor seductive. It was almost encouraging. "You can always tell a little white lie to make someone feel better, you know."

"Faith and I don't lie to each other." He winced again. He'd lied about the apartment. He'd considered lying to her about why he wanted her proxies. And why the hell was he listening to Nina, a self-confessed selfish, conniving bitch?

But was he any better?

She laughed again, this time with her eyes wide and her mouth open in total disbelief. "Oh my God. You really are in love with her. I mean *really* in love."

He didn't believe in love, but he wasn't about to deny it a second time. Faith deserved better than that. "All I want to know is who left the pictures for Faith to find."

"You'll have to beat it out of me." She gave him a twinkling smile.

She knew he wouldn't do a damn thing to her. He arrived fully intending to intimidate the answer from her, yet she'd completely turned the tables on him with her simple talk of love and Faith. She'd known what buttons to push.

He shook his head as if it needed clearing. Only one thing mattered at the moment. "Are you for Jarvis or against him?" he asked. Preston claimed the rest of the board would support Connor if he got Faith's proxies.

"I'm for me," Nina answered. "I don't care whether you're a team player or not as long as I get my money's worth." She leaned in once more. "Get my money for me, Connor, buy me out, whatever. Do that, and I'll support any vote you want me to make." Finally, she pulled at a bit of tinfoil. "I think I'm cooked, Connor-honey. So let me out."

Stepping back, he handed her the photos. "You might as well have these back. Souvenir and all."

She smiled and turned them right side up. After a brief study, she tipped her foiled head to him, all smiles wiped clean. "She got these while I was in South America?"

"No. This set came three weeks ago."

Her mouth dropped open, and she huffed. "That bastard. I never said he could use these."

Connor queried with a raised brow. "What's the difference?"

She raised her chin haughtily. "Because he didn't *ask* if he could use them. And besides, I'd changed my mind about the whole thing anyway before we even took these."

He almost laughed. She had an odd code of conduct. It was all right to harass Faith with them, but only if Nina had given her permission. "And might I ask whose ass that is?"

"Honestly, Connor, you're so dim-witted." She flapped the pictures at him. "Hello? Who's hated you from the moment you asked Faith to marry you?"

Shit. He *was* dim-witted. It was so damn obvious.

"Better get that foil out before you turn orange." Then he stopped her with a hand on her arm. "And don't *ever* try to hurt my wife again. Because I won't forgive a second time."

WHILE the country club dining room was fairly empty at three on a weekday afternoon, the bar area was packed. A round of golf, then a beer or something stronger, and the business took place. Connor had never gotten into golf. It was a slow, boring game. He preferred slamming walls in a racquetball court. Really took care of a man's aggressive instincts.

Lance Green had parked his sorry ass in a cushy chair at the edge of the bar and text messaged with his BlackBerry with one hand. A freshly made iced concoction frothed on the side table.

"That didn't take long," he said, still punching buttons on his handheld.

Ah, Nina had sent out the warning. The woman was good at playing both ends with only one goal in mind—her own best interests. Connor couldn't fault her.

He stuck his hands in his pants pockets and struck an idle stance. "Don't screw with me, Lance. You'll lose."

Lance sipped his piña colada. Connor should have known the

guy was into froufrou drinks. "I don't know what you're talking about, Kingston."

Connor smiled. Explanations weren't necessary. He went on in a mild tone. "I can play as dirty as you. Back off Faith, or I will take you down."

"Aren't you already trying to take Green down? Turning Jarvis against us?"

Though there were interested ears all around, the conversation was low-key and imperceptible to even the closest. "All I'm suggesting to Jarvis is that his quality problems will go away with a different supplier." Connor raised a brow. "Or if his current supplier stops using crap material."

Lance tipped his glass and saluted Connor. "We thank you for pointing out that problem. It's under control now."

"Then you don't have anything to worry about, do you?"

"No," Lance said, shaking his head, "I don't. But that doesn't solve all your problems, does it, Kingston?"

"My problems are my concern."

"You and your vendetta against Green made them my concern."

"I don't have a vendetta against you, Lance. But you try poisoning Faith's mind again, and you won't have any doubts about what an asshole I can be."

Lance shivered. "Ooh. I'm so scared." Setting his glass on the table, he rose. "She was mine before you got here, and she'll be mine when you're gone."

For the first time during the interview, Connor struggled for a little calm. "She was never yours, Lance."

Lance smiled with nothing more than his eyes, a bright spark of triumph. "Guess she never told you about how I took her virginity. You know a woman never forgets her first." He straightened his tie. "And she wants it again. Maybe you're the one who has to fear his spouse's infidelity."

Connor wanted to smash his fist into Lance's nose. But he didn't

believe the asshole for a moment. Green was a goddamn liar trying
to set Connor off in any way he could. Faith would *never* be with
this pathetic excuse for a man. Lance just wanted to throw whatever slur he could and see if it stuck in Connor's craw. It would
insult Faith even to ask her about it.

His breath harsh in his throat and his heart beating hard in his
ears, he wrapped his fist around the knot in Lance's tie, slowly,
until his knuckles ached. To their audience, it would look like a
mild altercation. "Don't go near her. Ever."

The bastard didn't even try to shake him off. "Or what?"

"Figure that one out for yourself." As slowly as he'd taken hold
of Lance, he let go.

"I do have Jarvis on my side," Lance said. He fiddled with the
tie knot, putting it back in place.

"Jarvis doesn't matter in this."

"Jarvis will *always* matter in Faith's life." He slipped his Black-
Berry into his jacket pocket. "Even if you think you've got her
under control right now, today, tomorrow, someday, Jarvis will
come between you."

Not if she had Connor's baby.

The thought pounded at him long after he left Lance. Connor's
plans at Castle Heavy Mining depended on Faith's proxies. His
marriage depended on putting a baby in her womb.

For the first time he wondered what his life in Faith's bed would
be like once he screwed over her father.

20

MONDAY'S board meeting had been a disaster. Tuesday, Jarvis had sat at his desk contemplating his navel and possible methods of doing away with Kingston. Today, Hermie had provided an answer, and it wouldn't take murder to accomplish it.

Sitting opposite Hermie in his friend's swank office, Jarvis patted the pocket where he'd stored the damning e-mail printout. "Thank you. It's safe to say, this is enough to terminate him."

Hermie wagged his head, his jowls flopping. "I agree he's an asshole, but I'm sure Kingston thought he was doing a good thing at the time by reducing overall costs." He spread his hands. "After all, he's only an accountant. He wouldn't grasp the implications of using a lower-quality metal."

"Don't make excuses for him. You don't authorize the purchase of material that doesn't meet spec. Even an accountant knows that if he didn't get his college degree off the Internet."

"But—"

Jarvis held up his hand. "And even if he was idiotic *then*, he certainly knows now, and he hasn't owned up to his mistake."

If one read Kingston's e-mails that Herman had had printed off the backups, one discovered the man had deliberately changed a purchase order to bring in substandard materials. He wondered also if perhaps Kingston had gotten a kickback from the vendor. It would explain the irrational act. However, there was no proof. All he had right now was evidence that Kingston himself had caused the whole quality problem.

It wouldn't send him to jail, but it would suffice to vote for his contract termination at next Monday's board meeting.

Hermie tapped a pencil. "How does Faith feel about this?"

He wouldn't tell Faith until it was done. "I know what's best for her."

"But don't you think you should—"

Jarvis slammed his fist on Hermie's desk. "He's a parasite in our midst and needs to be eradicated."

His blood rushed to his ears, and his heart pounded in his chest. For a moment, little spots flitted before his eyes.

Hermie's jowls trembled. "Are you all right, old man?"

He swallowed, his throat parched. "I'm fine."

"You shouldn't get so worked up."

The tips of his fingers tingled. Was it his heart or an anxiety attack? He'd never admit it to a living soul, but recently, he'd experienced a bit of panic. His doctor did the requisite tests and they all came back saying his heart was fine. But his mind . . . He had a lot of worries. With Kingston in his life, they'd gotten worse. The man impugned his intelligence, his managerial skills, and even his love for his own daughter.

He flooded his chest with a deep breath. "He married Faith, and look what he's done to her. Lied to her, cheated on her. A man does what he has to do to save his family regardless of the risks. The end justifies the means."

"And I'm behind you one hundred percent, old man."

Jarvis nodded, deciding to take Hermie's words at face value.

The e-mails would rid the company of Kingston. And the photos sitting on his desk at home would rid Faith of him.

Faith wouldn't countenance infidelity, and Jarvis had indisputable proof. Pictures of Kingston in another woman's arms. His tongue down her throat and his hands grabbing her ass couldn't be explained away by simply saying she was a "friend" or some such nonsense.

Even Faith would have to believe those pictures.

He'd terminate Kingston's contract at the next board meeting, then deliver the coup de grace with Faith right after.

Thank God she wasn't pregnant yet or they might never have gotten rid of the man.

SHE was pregnant. She could *feel* it. Connor had just left for the plant, and Faith stared at herself in the bathroom mirror. Deliriously happy, she giggled at her reflection. Her breasts felt heavy and full, and she was three days late. She was *never* late. She'd started hoping on day one, which had been Wednesday; she'd wanted to burst on day two, but today . . . she wanted to shout but was afraid to. Connor had asked when her period was due, but she'd gotten the exact day wrong. Yet even seeing her mistake, she hadn't told him. He had his hopes up, but she couldn't do the same. It might be Connor's certainty influencing the changes she *thought* she felt in her body.

Every night for the past week, he'd put his hand on her belly and claimed he was touching the baby. He'd kissed her stomach. He'd smile up at her and say he could *feel* a child.

Then he'd make love to her as if he would never get enough of the taste of her in his mouth or the feel of her body milking an orgasm from him. She needed his touch as much as she needed air to breathe, water to drink, or food to eat.

But she wanted to see the doctor first. To make sure she wasn't letting her hopes, *Connor's* hopes, get away with her. Or she could pee on the stick. God, what a euphemism. Couldn't those early pregnancy tests be wrong? She wanted a doctor to tell her. She wanted to be sure. She'd made an appointment for Monday afternoon.

Faith put her fingers to her lips. Okay, okay, she was scared spitless to tell Connor. That was the truth. She wanted him to love her. She was afraid he'd only love the company and the baby, and that what she felt in his arms was an illusion, something she *wanted* to believe rather than reality.

Five nights ago, she'd lain flush against him in bed, his arms wrapped around her, and told herself that he didn't have to love her as much as she loved him.

Now her heart ached for him. She'd been living in Lalaland when she came up with that one.

"Do you realize," she asked the mirror, "that you just went from ecstatically happy to the depths of despair in the space of five seconds?" God. The baby would have a bipolar mother.

In the bedroom, her cell phone rang. Running through the door, she banged her elbow on the jamb, and was out of breath when she answered.

"I told you I'd be busy with my vibrator. What did you forget?" A few short months ago she wouldn't have admitted to anyone she even masturbated, but Connor had helped her lose so many of her silly inhibitions.

Connor was silent a little too long so Faith prompted him. "Hello. Did you hear me?"

"I did, Faith," a female voice answered. "I just don't know how to reply to that."

She almost shrieked as she tore the phone from her ear and looked at the readout. She didn't recognize the number, but the voice . . . the voice . . . "Josie, I didn't realize it was you. I . . . uh, thought it was an obscene phone caller who's been bugging me, so I . . . uh, decided to give him a taste of his own medicine."

"The obscene caller wouldn't be your husband, would it?"

Open mouth, insert foot. She'd have to tough it out. "Busted," she quipped. "I thought you were Connor."

"Well, I'm not, but I do need to talk to you about him."

God. She felt the bipolar disease come over her again as her stomach plunged. "About what?"

"Let's meet, okay? It's easier in person."

Faith didn't like the sound of that. Too many people had been willing to tell her things about Connor. She was getting damn tired of it. "If you're going to bad-mouth him, Josie—"

"I'm not. He's like my favorite guy these days." She stopped. "Well, not favorite in a sexual way, but favorite in an I-like-working-with-him way."

She should have gotten to know Josie better over the years. The woman was kind of . . . adorable. She came off sounding Valley girl, but she was actually sweet and smart.

"So meet me for coffee, okay? There's this little place in Los Gatos that makes the absolute best white chocolate mochas. They use real shaved chocolate, not syrup or powder. I'll buy."

"Josie, I—"

"I try to live on my salary alone without going to Dad, but I can afford it."

"Josie, that's not what I mean—"

"Meet me, Faith. I don't have my own office here, just a cube, and I can't talk about this over the phone. No one will miss me for an hour or so." Then she gave Faith directions.

It was all so mysterious, but if Josie said one bad word, despite whatever she promised, Faith would slam her down. She wasn't going to put up with this crap anymore.

By the time Faith got to the café, Josie had ordered and picked up their mochas, and found them a table on the sidewalk.

"Okay, I'll get right to it," Josie said before Faith even sat down. She pulled her chair closer, and leaned on the metal table. She wore a tight green tank top with a red Chinese dragon on it and low-waist jeans that revealed a strip of skin above the belt. Dangling dragon earrings matched the shirt.

"Your dad has gone bonkers."

"I don't know how to respond to that," Faith said, imitating Josie's reply to her over the phone.

"He's got it in for Connor. Grapevine has it your dad will vote to terminate his contract at the next board meeting."

Rumors, rumors, rumors. She was sick to death of rumors. "Who is the grapevine?"

"My mom and dad. I heard them talking about it when I had dinner over there last night."

"Why would my father want to do that?"

Josie tipped her head and stared at Faith.

After too many seconds of that, Faith felt her cheeks heat.

"Because Connor wants to get rid of Green as a supplier, and your father hates that Connor questions his managerial judgment all the time. They've been at each other's throats for weeks."

"Why would Connor want to get rid of Green?"

Josie blinked. Faith noticed how long her eyelashes were. She was pretty sure there wasn't a speck of mascara on them, either. *And Connor hasn't talked to you about this?* The question was unspoken, yet Faith felt it roiling inside.

Josie jutted her head forward and dropped her mouth open. "Because quality over at Green has taken a nosedive, and Connor's proven we're better off finding an alternate source or setting up our own in-house shop."

Faith had never been interested in the company. She knew what Castle sold, she knew Green Industries' part in the mining equipment, but she didn't pay attention to the intricacies of it.

"Doesn't Connor talk about work at *all*?"

No. He didn't talk about work. He didn't talk about finances. All he talked about was sex. All they had in common was . . . sex.

And the baby she was almost positive grew inside her. Faith put her hand to her stomach. "He doesn't want to bother me with that stuff."

Josie pursed her lips in a round *O* she held for a couple of seconds before she finally said, "So you don't know that your father has vetoed every good idea that Connor's come up with or that the bottom line has been bottoming out for months or that—" She stopped. "You don't know *anything*."

Josie made it sound like Faith had just committed murder and fed the body parts through a wood chipper.

"No," she whispered. Connor hadn't told her. He hadn't shared it with her. And she hadn't asked.

"Well, your dad's going to ax Connor at the next meeting."

"But won't the board stop him?" She put a finger to her temple, closed her eyes, and rubbed. "Except if he uses my votes to over-rule everybody else that sides with Connor."

Josie pointed a finger and shot her. "Bingo. Give the lady a hand. Your dad *hates* Connor, and he *will* use your shares to get rid of him."

Faith wrapped her hands around her coffee cup.

Why hadn't Connor told her any of this?

She thought of all the sweet things he'd done for her in the last week. How wonderful he'd been to her. "How long has everyone known about the meeting on Monday?"

"Since last Monday."

Last Monday. With the weekend left.

Suddenly it all made sense. Connor was buttering her up to get her proxies so her father couldn't fire him.

"WHOA there, Kingston my boy."

Connor didn't have to look to know Preston was on his heels. He was almost to his car, the sun, at its zenith, beating down on his head. Friday afternoon, and he had a blinding headache only a long mountain drive with the windows rolled down could cure.

Or Faith's fingers threading through his hair.

"Just wondering about the mission to secure Faith's votes."

"It's on plan, Preston." He hadn't done shit about it.

The meeting was Monday. He'd never been into avoidance

before, but after days of telling himself the moment hadn't come yet, he realized it would never come. The word was out on the company underground. Jarvis had it in for him. Negligence, fraud, whatever, come Monday, the old man planned to rid himself of his son-in-law, at least from the company payroll, and the last thing Connor wanted was Faith in the middle of their fight.

"So she's signed them over to you." Preston beamed a porcelain smile.

"No."

The man's veneers disappeared behind pinched lips. "My boy, we only have two more days."

"No, Preston, *I* have two more days. After Monday, you and Dora will still have your twelve percent share of Castle."

Connor would have nothing. Not even a job. So why hadn't he asked Faith, beyond the fact that he didn't want to involve her in his affairs of business? He kept Faith and her father in two totally separate compartments. He didn't talk about her father with Faith and vice versa.

He just hadn't figured out why that was so.

"It does concern us, Kingston." A tiny foam speck formed at the corner of Preston's mouth. "You're the one who keeps saying Jarvis is going to run us into the ground."

"Perhaps once I'm gone, Jarvis's head will clear."

"That's bullshit, Kingston."

True. Yet he hadn't formulated a palatable lie to tell Faith, nor was he content with telling her the truth. Maybe he was waiting to find out about the baby. He would have fulfilled his part of the bargain.

He should have bought her one of those home pregnancy tests.

But he didn't want the baby to become a pawn. That was his child and the most important thing in the world.

"I haven't known you long, Kingston, but you never struck me as a sit-back-and-take-it-up-the-ass kind of man."

Connor huffed out a chuckle. No, he never had been. The foster system taught him that you never sat back and took it up the ass or you'd be getting reamed for the rest of your life.

He slapped Tybrook on the back. "Preston, my man, everything is under control. Don't worry about Monday."

The older man rubbed his fingers together. "It's a lot of money we're talking about here."

"I'm fully aware of that."

"It's about Faith, too, you know. If Castle goes under, she'll have nothing, either. We're doing this for her, too."

"Right, Preston." Connor beeped his remote, climbed in his car, and took off before Preston could tap on his window.

It was for Faith. He'd been telling himself that for days. It was for the baby. It was the only way to protect them.

Yet another truth had pummeled his guts, one he wanted to ignore. This fight was all about him. He'd created it by mishandling Jarvis, and now, like a child, he was considering asking his wife to fix it for him. He didn't want to go back to being a meaningless middle manager, a grunt, a tiny cog in a huge wheel. A man without a legacy.

Yet to get what he wanted, he had to screw Faith's father, with her help, unwitting or not. She'd never forgive him. Life would be intolerable living with someone who hated you.

At this point, what choice did he have? He either got her votes or he walked away from it all.

A piece of his gut feared walking away from Faith would be so much harder than walking away from that damn legacy.

FAITH'S first thought had been to run to her father and demand an explanation. Her second thought had been to call Connor and ask him why he'd kept all this from her.

Why hadn't he asked for her proxies so that he could vote down her father? Josie had said the board would vote with Connor, not against him.

In the end, she'd done neither of those things.

Instead, she'd gone to the drugstore and gotten a home pregnancy test. Afterward, she'd clutched the tester in her hand for what seemed like hours, until her fingers started to hurt. She'd have to repeat the test in the morning to be sure, but for those few moments, there was only joy. Beautiful, bursting joy.

The problem was she couldn't ignore everything else for long. Connor wanted her proxies. Her father hated Connor. And she was going to have a baby with a man who didn't love her.

When they started out, that hadn't mattered. Now . . . it did. She wanted their child to have the best life, one *with* his or her father right there. Her child would not pay the price for Faith falling in love with her husband. Connor had done everything he claimed he would. He'd stood up for her, treated her well, taught her to appreciate herself as a woman, and gotten her pregnant. He'd fulfilled the bargain to the letter.

Therefore, at the end of a long day filled with so many ups and downs that she *knew* she needed medication, Faith greeted her husband with a big kiss.

"That was nice." He leaned in, sucking her tongue into his mouth for a long, delicious, wet kiss. "That was even nicer."

Her heart ached. Did he mean that? God, she had to stop questioning. "I've got a surprise for you."

He smiled. Her insides melted like cream cheese frosting every time he gave her that smile stamped with his own special brand of sexiness. Her knees felt weak.

Dipping, he pulled on the hem of her skirt. "You're naked and hot and ready under there, right?"

She fought his fingers, pulling her skirt away. "No. I've planned dinner *out* for us. Go get showered and changed."

His eyes twinkled, yet he held her arms with a tight grip that almost bruised. "Do you have something to tell me?"

She pushed him toward the stairs with the other. "Not a word will pass these lips," she bantered, "until we get where we're going." Yet despite the teasing, she couldn't quell the ache around her heart.

His sigh brushed her cheek as he relinquished his hold on her, trailing a long, lingering gaze over her face before he backed up two steps, then turned. It was the oddest look, as if something was going on in his head that she would never fathom. From the top of the stairs, he waved at her before disappearing down the hall. He was such a contrast. Hidden depths, sexy smile, deep emotions flaring in his eyes, yet laughter curving his lips. She wasn't sure who the real Connor was, but God, she loved him. She wanted to be the anchor he came home to, the safe haven, the woman to whom he poured out all his troubles.

Yet she was little more than a bed warmer. Faith closed her eyes and swallowed. She kept remembering Josie's face when she'd said, "You don't know *anything*."

"Get over it," she whispered, "and stop feeling sorry for yourself." Past. Done. They were united now. The positive pregnancy test changed everything. If it truly came down to supporting her father or her husband, she'd choose Connor.

She might want love from him, but she wasn't going to get it. He wanted lust, he wanted hot sex, he wanted her to let down all her barriers. Finally, after all these months, Faith truly understood what the bargain she'd made really meant. It worked both ways. Her heart might be his, but his body was all hers.

It was time she showed him who was in control.

HE'D been going a little crazy the past hour. He wanted to shake the answer out of her. In the bathroom, with the water running in the shower, he'd actually searched the trash can to see if she'd left any pregnancy test evidence.

Why is it so important that she be pregnant, Connor?

If she was, she wouldn't leave him if he lost the battle with Jarvis. He'd gotten used to living with her. He enjoyed their sex. He didn't want to see all that end just because Jarvis had a bug up his ass.

Right. Convenience and comfort. He would have closed his eyes and sighed if she hadn't made him drive.

"Turn left," she said.

"Yes, ma'am."

She'd decked herself out in the very dress she'd worn the night he met her. She looked gorgeous, her hair down, her lips lushly red, her breasts ripe. She was goddamn edible. He wanted her for dinner. She was all the sustenance he needed right now.

With a few more turns, they headed out of town. Into the hills. He thought of the day he'd taken her by the side of the road, and his cock throbbed. She'd probably planned a cozy dinner at one of the restaurants scattered along the mountain summit. He didn't think he could wait to have her until they got home. He wanted her now, under the stars, under the trees, on the hood of the car.

"Right turn at the next little offshoot."

Shit. His mind suddenly focused on exactly where they were. He hooked a right through the gold-etched, wrought iron gates onto her father's long, winding drive.

She wanted to tell them the news together. He felt cheated, jealous. He didn't want to share her.

"Pull over here," she directed.

The main house was visible through the trees, but they were still a quarter mile off. Connor pulled over, shut off the engine and lights, and sat in the darkness.

"We're here to see my father," she said, looking at the house through the leaves.

Daddy would blab about Monday. "Faith, we need to talk."

She put her fingers to his lips. "No talk. I have something else in mind."

Her tongue was sweet with cinnamon toothpaste. Her open-mouthed kiss rolled him over and sucked him under. She kissed the way he taught her, with her whole body, her breasts rubbing him, her arms hugging him. Oh yeah, he'd taught her, but Faith added her own unique twist, which was nothing more than the synergy in the sigh of her breath, her sweet flowery scent, and a soft moan in her throat.

She undid him physically in ways he never knew were possible.

She wasn't consciously seductive, but sexy from the inside out. She was the genuine article in a place where honesty was just a word in the dictionary. Right here on her father's driveway, the house lights sprinkling through wayward tree branches, he wanted her.

Tunneling his fingers through her hair, he let her retain control. He simply needed to touch the silk. Her hand trailed down his abdomen, and she stroked him through his slacks. He thrust up into her. Reaching further, she cupped his balls, rubbed, caressed.

"You make me nuts," he whispered against her mouth. "So you better stop now or I'm not going to let you stop."

She licked his lips. "I won't stop till you come in my mouth."

His breath snagged in his throat. "Here?"

She laughed, a sexy, cock-grabbing sound. "Of course here."

"Daddy might see," he quipped. It reminded him of the night her father agreed to the contract. That night, Connor had coerced her in the garden. Tonight, she was in charge.

"Daddy won't see." She pulled back, hair mussed, lipstick smudged, nipples hard. "I want you in my mouth now, Connor Kingston. Not later. Not at home. Here. Now." She swiped her tongue along his cheek. "This"—her thumbnail flitted along his cock from base to tip—"is mine," she whispered. "Anyone touches and I'll do serious bodily damage to you both."

Despite the material in the way, he almost came. A shiver coursed across his skin. He truly hadn't belonged to anyone since his father died.

Her gaze locked with his, she unzipped him slowly, the sound racing around the car's interior. Then she reached inside and wrapped her fist around his cock.

"All mine," she whispered.

He'd heard the words before. No, he'd said them. When, he couldn't remember. He simply remembered the need to show her she belonged to him. As he now belonged to her. He couldn't breathe. If he moved, he'd come. She bent her head to him and licked his slit. His body jerked.

"Mine," she said, then her lips closed over his crown.

He arched into her, groaned. Oh Christ, her mouth was good, so sweet and hot and perfect. Her tongue circled the sensitive underside, and he surged up, forcing himself deep.

She sucked hard as he pulled out. Warm, wet woman, that's all he could think. How badly he wanted to come inside her. How hot his come shot would feel.

She circled and swirled and sucked and drove him fucking nuts. He was her prisoner, her victim, her partner, her slave. His body rocked and thrust, his breath rasped in his throat. Squeezing his eyes tightly shut, the colors of the rainbow flashed and sparked.

He thrust deep one last time, shouted her name, and came so hard, his guts tore open and his heart sliced in two. He felt himself fall completely apart and come back together again.

Moments, minutes, hours passed. Or so it seemed. She smelled like come. Delicious. He tasted it on her lips. She'd swallowed it all. She'd taken him. For those few moments, she'd owned him. He wanted to feel that again. Over and over. Despite the terror that threatened to cut off his breath.

"Well, that was nice," she murmured against his throat.

Nice? That was all? His lips couldn't yet form words.

She sighed. "You were right, baby, lust is so much better than all that messy, emotional stuff."

Shit. She was quoting him. And a part of him wasn't so sure anymore that it was true.

Buried in the warm, wet recesses of her mouth, he discovered he didn't want to be just her husband or the father of her child or the CEO of her daddy's company.

He liked belonging to her. He liked being the object of her desire. It wasn't merely *nice*. It was cataclysmic. He wanted her to feel that way, too. He didn't want to be just a cock to her; he wanted more. "Faith, we need to have a serious talk."

She tipped her head back on his shoulder and looked at him. "You're right, we do. I'm going to have your baby, Connor."

A surge of ecstasy rushed through his veins, taking over like a tidal wave. He wanted to grab her, hold her, keep her. Yet a terrible ache around his heart immobilized him. She didn't seem very happy about it. "Faith, are you—"

She put a finger over his lips just as she had the moment before she took his cock in her mouth and his heart in her hand. "I'm going to vote my own shares at the meeting on Monday. And we're here tonight to tell my father that."

He turned, stared at her. She knew about the meeting and the proxies. "Who told you about Monday?"

"Josie bought me coffee."

That little schemer.

"I'm glad she told me, since you weren't going to."

"It didn't concern you."

She glared at him.

He winced. "What I mean is—"

"I know what you meant. There's the part of our bargain that concerned my father and the part that concerned me and never the twain shall meet."

"That was how I thought of it. It's not your problem." He didn't think that explanation was any better.

"The baby changes all that. Whatever happens to you affects the baby. *Everything* concerns *us*."

It was on the tip of his tongue to remind her yet again that he wasn't destitute and that his child wouldn't end up in a workhouse making cheap clothing for twelve cents an hour. But Faith was on a roll.

"My father is using my shares to vote you out, but he and I had an agreement, too. I'm not going to let him back out of it just because he's angry over"—she flapped her hands in the air and shrugged—"over whatever."

"I'll fight my own battles." Hell if he didn't like that she was willing to fight for him, but he couldn't let her do it.

"This *isn't* your battle." She gave him an uncharacteristic glare of total aggression.

"Why not?" He didn't get her logic.

"He's never trusted me to make my own decisions. You heard him after I dissolved our agreement. He called me an idiot."

"I did want to punch his lights out on your behalf."

"Thank you very much, but I won't let *you* fight *my* battle the way you did that day. You're the father of my child, and you're going to run the company that will one day belong to our children. And I won't let my father kick you out."

She was sweet, but a little naïve. Just because she used her shares to save him didn't mean her father would ever work willingly with him.

"Are you with me, Connor?"

He stared at her as if seeing her for the first time all over again. Just as he had the day she stepped into his office and ordered him to go down on her. Sexual confidence energized her then. This time, motherhood turned her into a lioness.

His wife had come into her own. And that wasn't something *he'd* taught her.

He couldn't deny her the right to go up against her father on behalf of her own flesh and blood. Because this was all about the child. Their child.

They'd created a miracle, yet he wanted . . . more.

He wanted a piece of Faith for himself. Asking for it was . . . He couldn't do it. He hadn't asked for anything beyond the physical from a woman since he was eighteen years old. Giving that kind of power to another person could be disastrous.

He might want more, but he wasn't capable of giving anything in return. Except this. Letting her take a stand *she* needed to take no matter how he felt about it. "I'm with you, baby."

She smiled. It tied his stomach in knots.

Wrapping his hand around her nape, her pulled her close. Her lips parted anticipating his kiss. Instead he dropped a hand to her belly.

"For our child," he whispered.

21

ON her father's grand front entrance, flanked by rosebushes and small marble replicas of famous statues, Faith held her face up for Connor's inspection. "Is my lipstick all messed up?"

Connor laughed. "You just blew me, sweetheart. Yeah, I think it's a little messed up."

She was proud of herself. She'd taken Connor boldly, wrenched a gut-deep orgasm from him, threatened bodily harm if he ever allowed anyone else a touch, and forged a link over the baby they'd made.

It would have been perfect if he'd said he loved her, but she was done living for impossible dreams. Reality and good sex. She would live up to her end of the bargain if it killed her.

Her stomach clenched. It just might kill her if she didn't squash her wayward emotions.

She raised her face. "Fix it," she demanded.

Connor smoothed a finger over her lips. "All fixed."

God. His touch. It simply undid her, made her want to beg.

With him standing on the step below her and she with her heels on, she was so much closer to his height, and Connor misinterpreted her look for worry. "Your father and I will work this out, Faith. You don't have to do this."

It was a tidy little lie to take care of her feelings. She was part of the bargain, and with her father shutting him out of Castle Mining, Connor didn't get a damn thing in return except her love . . . something he'd never asked for and had in fact said he didn't want right from the beginning.

She owed him this battle. Dammit, she owed it to herself.

"Okay, I'm ready then." She was Connor's wife first, her father's daughter second. She rang her father's bell, which was the oddest feeling. She'd never rung the doorbell in her life; she'd simply walked in. In a few short months, everything had changed. When the baby came, they would have to rebuild their lives all over again. She better get used to change now.

Connor came to stand at her side. "Will you tell him about the baby?"

"After I tell him about the shares." It was important to gauge her father's reaction about that first. She'd know his true feelings. Over the past few months, she'd begun to wonder if he even loved her at all.

Connor squeezed her hand. "He loves you."

She shot him a look.

"It's written all over your face."

For a moment, she'd hoped he could read her mind. But it was nothing more than her being incapable of hiding her feelings. She'd have to get better about that in the future. No one must know how she felt about Connor. Not even Trinity. She didn't want anyone's pity.

Archie stooped a little as he opened the massive front door. "Miss Faith?"

Faith thought she heard a question mark on the end of that.

Connor took her hand. "Mrs. Kingston." Then he pulled her inside without being invited.

"Your father's in his study," Archie called as Connor was headed there anyway, "and I don't think he's expecting you."

Faith merely waved over her shoulder.

Oh my God, what do I want to say? She hadn't rehearsed. She only knew that she couldn't let her father walk all over her.

Connor let her enter first. Her father sat behind his leather-top desk. Reading glasses perched on his nose, he flipped a piece of paper. His hair was billowy on top as if he'd been drawing circles in it.

"Father?" Damn, her voice quivered.

He didn't shift his head, merely raised his eyes to gaze over the tops of his glasses. "What's he doing here? I didn't invite him."

"You didn't invite me, either."

"I suppose he's come to you with some sob story about how nasty your old father is."

"No, he didn't say a thing." She stepped away from Connor, closer to her father, looking back over her shoulder, her eyes pleading. *Please let me do this.*

Connor merely blinked his lashes at her.

"Josie told me about the vote on Monday. That you're going to fire Connor." *Take a deep breath,* she told herself. "That wasn't part of our agreement, Father."

As if he recognized the change in his designation, from *Daddy* to *Father*, he simply sat there, his head tipped slightly to the side, his glasses now resting almost on the tip of his nose.

Then he circled his hand, the wind-up motion which meant *Get on with it, girl.* She remembered how many times she'd seen it over the years, as if she were always taking too much of his time. With another step closer to him, she was one step further from Connor.

"I can't let you do that, so I'm voting my shares on Monday."

Her father barked out a laugh, ending it with a sharp cough. "Well, I should have seen *that* coming. Should have known he'd manipulate you. Scumbags always do and women fall for it."

"He's not a scumbag."

Her father crooked his finger. Faith almost shivered, but stopped herself before it shot full-body. She would not revert to a childhood reaction.

On his desk, he turned the piece of paper he'd been staring at, then tapped it with his finger. "He's been cheating on you. I wanted to spare you, but it seems I can't do that anymore."

Connor didn't say a word, but his breath came more harshly.

"He has a hideaway you knew nothing about." Her father glared over her shoulder at her husband, his eyes narrowed.

In the photograph, Faith recognized the landing of Connor's second-floor apartment. His door was open, he stood in the entry, his hand on the arm of a woman.

"There's more." Her father splayed several photos over the desktop. "I'm sorry, Faith." But the look he leveled on Connor was anything but apologetic.

He didn't seem to care that he was hurting her as well.

The pictures were in a series. Connor grabbing a woman, pulling her to him, kissing her. Connor reaching down to cup her buttocks, her arms around his neck, her coat rising to reveal a bare cheek under the hem. Her long hair flowed down her back like a bloodred waterfall.

Faith pulled the last photo closer. A grainy, badly taken color picture. "I hope you didn't pay a lot for these. I mean, really, with digital photography, you should have been able to get a good close-up."

Her father gave her a woeful gaze. "Honey, I know how hard this must be—"

He didn't. He hadn't even thought about it. He only thought of how he could get rid of her husband. "You were spying on Connor."

"Only to protect you."

This had nothing to do with protecting her. Her eyes stung. He didn't care. He really didn't care.

"And I've never liked Nina," he added.

"Nina?"

"Nina. Married to your cousin Lionel. Nothing but a floozy. If only he hadn't left her his shares. He should have willed them to the family."

Faith pointed to the photo. "You think that's Nina Simon?"

He waved his hand over the display. "Red hair. Flaunting herself. Of course it's her. She was always a hussy."

"I think she looks extremely seductive," Connor said.

Faith hadn't even been aware of him coming to her side.

"In fact," he said, looking right at Faith, "she's a veritable Aphrodite."

"Listen to his audacity, Faith."

Her gaze locked with Connor's, and warmth spread through her. "That's not Nina, Father. It's me."

"Faith, sweetheart, you don't need to lie to protect him." Her father blinked back what might have been tears. Or phony condescending moisture.

She picked up the picture revealing too much bare flesh, flipped first one, then another, and another until they all faced her father. She didn't even feel self-conscious that it was her father looking at the photos.

"That's me. I went to Connor's apartment on Tuesday. Isn't that when your spy took those pictures?"

He looked down, then back at her. And didn't answer.

"*That* is me. I know about Connor's apartment. He's never used it for secret assignations with anyone but me."

"Faith, please don't delude yourself. It's past needing to lie for him."

She stabbed the picture of Connor kissing her. "That's me. You can believe whatever you want, but that's not Nina."

"But Faith, that woman is—" He looked down, up again, shut his mouth.

"Sexy?" Connor supplied. "Gorgeous?" He leaned close. "Perfect?" He kissed her ear. "That woman is my wife."

Her father didn't pay attention. "He's forcing you to lie for him. You could never be so . . . brazen."

"You don't think I could attract a man the way Nina can. That a man like Connor would want to be with me." She tapped her chest. "But I *am* good enough."

"Honey, I didn't mean—"

"Yes, you did. That's exactly what you meant. I'm not good enough to hold a man in my life. I have to buy him with my father's money." God, it hurt. As if he'd reached inside, plucked her heart out, and stomped on it. All those years, he'd chased men away, said they weren't good enough for her, but the truth was, he'd feared she wasn't enough for them, that they'd stray because *she* couldn't hold them.

"You're twisting what I'm saying."

"You were the one spying on us. How twisted is that?" Her blood throbbed in her ears, and a vein ticked at her temple.

"I'm just trying to show you what kind of man he is. There's more, not just these photos." He yanked open his middle desk drawer to pull out another file.

"I don't want to see it."

He spread the folder. "You have to see. It proves what he really planned to do." He grabbed the top piece of paper, crumpling it in his haste. "This. It proves what he was doing at Green and what he's trying to do to us."

Beside her, she felt Connor withdraw behind stone.

"Read it, Faith," her father urged.

She couldn't make sense of it.

"You see?" her father whispered. "He purchased crap material, then laid the blame for all the quality problems at Hermie's door. I think he planned all along to destroy Green Industries because Hermie wouldn't let him marry his daughter."

"Then he married me instead. Is that what you're saying?"

"I'm sorry, Faith." Her father reached out but didn't manage to touch her. "I'm so sorry."

She didn't look at Connor. She didn't want to see the truth on his face. No, she wanted to feel the truth deep inside where her baby grew. *Connor's baby.* Her hand splayed across her abdomen before she even realized it.

Faith closed her eyes and took three deep belly breaths.

JARVIS stared at Faith. His cheeks were gaunt, sunken, his jowls hung heavy, and a five o'clock shadow grizzled his chin.

Her silence was so long and the quiet in the spacious study so intense, Connor felt deafened by it. Waiting for her to speak, he died a thousand excruciating deaths at the hands of his own demons. His knees felt weak. Did she believe the muck her father had raked up?

Jarvis couldn't seem to wait for her answer, either. "Sweetheart, I just want you to face facts about him. I want you to be happy, and you'll never be happy with him. He's out for numero uno. He's a cancer in our midst."

A chill ran the length of Connor's body, then shot back into his heart, freezing it in his chest. He might not even have been in the room for all the attention Jarvis paid him. The old man's focus was entirely on Faith, as if by concentrating hard enough, he could command her to see what he wanted her to.

Yet Jarvis had just torn him to little pieces and tossed the remains at her feet without a thought. He didn't even care that he'd manufactured some fantastic lie. Maybe by now he'd even convinced himself it was true.

"You're forcing me to choose," she said, her voice low but without inflection, as if Jarvis hadn't even opened his mouth. She leaned both hands on the desk. "I'm voting with Connor, Father. Not you."

Connor didn't realize he'd stopped breathing until she said his name. Then air filled his lungs until he felt high on it.

"You know what that means, don't you?" Jarvis stared at her

with suddenly rheumy eyes. The color leached from his face. "He and the rest of the board will sell the company. If he wins, I'm out and that good-for-nothing family of mine will sell to the highest bidder."

She straightened and crossed her arms over her chest. "So be it. I'm going to have his baby, and I'm going stand by him. If you don't like it, then you don't have to see us. Ever."

Jarvis merely stared. He didn't even react to the news of his grandchild.

Connor's momentary relief died.

She was so cold, so unlike the Faith who'd taken him to the moon in his car. She wasn't even the woman who'd told him she needed to stand up to her father for her own mental health. She was an alien.

If he ever wanted the real Faith, for better or for worse, he couldn't allow her to cut her father out of her life on his behalf and live with himself.

Grabbing one damning e-mail page, he flipped it over. "Give me a pen, Jarvis."

Jarvis handed him a felt-tip.

Connor scrawled across the page, dated it, signed it, then shoved it at Jarvis. "My resignation, effectively immediately."

"I knew you were guilty," Jarvis snarled, and Connor wanted to hit him. Didn't he see what he was doing to his daughter?

Faith stood silent, a statue.

"You wanted to steal my company," the old man said, grinding into Connor's wounds.

"No." Connor turned to Faith. "I wanted to buy my way into your family. But I'm not poor, Faith. I have a good 401K. I've worked the stock market to my advantage. I can support you, pay for a child's college education, and buy a house. A nice house in a decent neighborhood with good schools."

"But the company is our bargain." There was no inflection in her voice, no spark in her gaze. "I get a baby, you get my father's company."

Her matter-of-factness stung. "What about you, Faith? Do I get you?"

"Of course." She tipped her head and regarded him as if he were mentally challenged. "We're married."

Godammit, he wanted more than a marriage certificate and Faith in his bed.

As his dad always said, he'd asked for the moon. Problem was he hadn't given his all to get it. He'd wanted a legacy without facing the lean years or spilling the blood, the sweat, and the tears. He wanted a family's acceptance without granting it unconditionally in return. He wanted a wife without opening his heart or risking any pain.

He wanted the one thing he'd turned his back on when he was eighteen. He wanted to be loved. He'd been reaching for the moon when all he really needed was Faith. He wanted *her* love, and there was only one way on God's green earth he could earn it. By loving her.

With so much that needed to be said, he answered Jarvis's accusations first. "I never bought bad material. If I was idiotic enough to compromise the spec, I wouldn't be stupid enough to divulge it in an e-mail."

Jarvis snorted. "Just like you weren't stupid enough to have a woman in your hotel room with your father-in-law's suite right across the hall."

"Yeah, Jarvis, just like that."

Faith scanned his face as if he'd given an answer to a question he didn't even know she had.

Yet believing the scene was all about him, Jarvis wouldn't let go. "Fine. If you're not guilty, then why resign?"

He didn't owe the old man a thing. All he had to give belonged to Faith. He wanted to touch her so badly, his guts ached. "Do you believe I screwed Herman over?"

She shook her head. "I don't believe you did."

He closed his eyes, breathed her in. "But I have been lying to you, baby."

She worried the inside of her lip, perhaps hoping he couldn't see the action. Connor took her hand, clasped it with his, and held them together against his heart.

"I told you that lust beat out love, and that was a lie." His insides quaked, but he bent his forehead to hers. "Lust is nothing compared to what I feel for you," he whispered.

He felt rather than heard her intake of breath.

"I want you for the woman you are, your sweetness, your kindness, your caring, for the way you touch me."

She subsided against him, and he tunneled his hand beneath her hair, caressing her nape lightly with his fingers. "I will never tire of you," he whispered. "Not now, nor when you're eight months pregnant with my baby. I won't tire of you ten years from now or even fifty. Never."

Turning fully into his arms, she burrowed against him.

He held her tightly. "I don't want to push my way into your father's company if it means forcing you to choose between us. So I resign." He lifted her chin and made her look at him. "I will spend the rest of our lives trying to make up to you for how we began and teaching you to love me the way I love you."

Dipping her head, she muffled her laugh against his shirt.

She was laughing?

"You're always trying to teach me things, Connor."

"That's because you're the best student a man ever had." And he wasn't done teaching her all the things he wanted to.

"Well, you don't have to teach me about this. I've been in love with you from the moment you—" She stopped, looking to her father, then rephrased. "From the moment you found me out in the garden at the country club."

In other words, from the first moment he touched her.

"I just didn't know it then," she finished.

This time, Connor laughed with her, then lifted her in his arms. "God, I love you. And I love our baby."

She pushed away, smiled at him, and held his hand to her stomach as she turned to her father. "Daddy, what do you have to say for yourself?"

The old man simply stared. Something had changed during the minutes Connor had concentrated solely on Faith. A single tear had slipped down Jarvis's face and now trembled on his upper lip. In the next instant, it fell to his chin.

"I love you, Faith. I'm sorry I hurt you." He glanced at Connor and blinked away one last tear. "But I have a gut feeling about him—"

Her glare cut him off. His daughter was a tough woman. Jarvis had taught her that. "Don't spy on me ever again, Daddy."

"It wasn't you—"

She held up one finger to stop him. "Connor and I are a team. What you do to him, you do to me."

Her words wrapped around Connor's heart, as if she held it in her hands the way she'd hold their child.

"I know you don't think I trust you to make your own choices, sweetheart, but I do." Jarvis bent his head. "I just lost sight of things for a little while." Then he raised his gaze to hers. "Please forgive me. I love you more than anything."

"I love you, too, Daddy. I never stopped, even if we've hurt each other." Then Faith held Connor's hand to her abdomen. "Except you're still avoiding the issue. What about Connor?"

"I don't want to lose you, sweetheart." Jarvis eyed Connor critically. "But I'm not sure I can love him even for you."

"But will you *accept* him?"

Connor didn't know what the hell that meant, but after a long moment, the old man closed his eyes and nodded.

"What about the baby, Daddy? Will you love our baby?"

"I do already, honey. I swear it. We're family. And if this one"— he pointed a finger at Connor—"has to come with the package, so be it." Then he picked up Connor's resignation and started to tear it in half.

"No." Connor couldn't let the old man do it. "That's over, Jarvis. We've proven we can't work together." There had to be more trust between them. "But I will take care of Faith." He rubbed her belly, nuzzling her hair and breathing in the scent of her. "I promise you that."

"Connor."

Her voice pulled him back from the heaven of her scent. "Yes, dear?" The smile that rose to his lips wasn't even voluntary.

"Castle Heavy Mining is our baby's legacy."

Damn. She was right.

"He'll be running it someday, so you and Daddy need to keep it in good order."

"What if it's a girl?" her father asked.

"Then *she'll* run it," she said, eyes narrowed. "This is the twenty-first century, you know. Women can do anything they set their minds to."

God, he loved her so damn much his insides ached. How had he missed the way she'd become a part of him? Completed him.

"And Connor's going to vote my shares."

"But Faith—" Jarvis stopped at her steely look.

Turning her with a touch to her arm, Connor said, "You can vote your own shares, Faith."

She shook her head. "I've decided I don't want to. I know you probably think that's sacrilege, but while the company will some-day belong to our children, I'm a teacher. That's what I do. That's what I *want* to do." She cocked her head and smiled. "And some-time after the baby comes, I'll start my own preschool, giving other children a leg up in life. That's what *I'm* good at." She turned back to her father. "So with Connor voting my shares, neither of you can do anything totally on your own. You're a team now."

Connor wanted to haul her up against him, press her close. He'd never told her what he longed for at Castle, yet she understood. Maybe it was woman's intuition. Motherhood. Love. Damn, he was so proud of her. The woman he'd married a few months ago would never have thought of starting her own school.

"Faith, honey . . ." Jarvis's voice trailed off at another of his daughter's ferocious looks. "Fine. We're a team."

"And I want the authority," Connor stepped in. "No more board votes over mice nuts."

"Define how much authority you want," Jarvis countered, crossing his arms over his chest.

And the negotiations started.

22

THE doorbell rang. Connor had left an hour ago to see her father to "strategize" the Monday board meeting.

He'd made love to her all night long. Real, honest-to-God love-making. Then this morning, he'd stood over her as she repeated the EPT. Faith didn't even mind the lack of privacy. Not one bit. When they'd read the positive, he'd swooped her up in his arms and danced around the bedroom with her.

God, how she loved him. She answered the door knowing her joy must be shining on her face. "Trinity!"

Her friend sailed in, long blond hair flying behind her. "I'm sick of playing phone tag. It's been *ages*, and I *had* to see you." She grabbed Faith's hand in hers. "I'm sorry I've been so out of touch. I'm a bad friend, but I love you."

"It's fine, Trin. *I'm* fine."

Trinity stepped back to survey her. "You look beautiful."

Faith smiled and accepted the compliment without question. "I'm going to have a baby."

For just a moment, Trinity's expression was deadpan, absolutely flat, then the look vanished so quickly, Faith was almost sure she'd imagined it.

"Oh my God." Trinity threw her arms around Faith and together they bounced a few steps in the small entry hall. "I'm so happy for you." Then she pulled back. "Are *you* happy?"

"About everything. Trin, I love him. And he really loves me. I know what everyone's been saying—"

Trinity shushed her with a snort. "Who cares what everyone says?" she finished for Faith. "You're the most wonderful person I know and you deserve it. And thank God it all turned out, because I swear, Faith, I really didn't want to have to use my curling iron on him or feed his entrails to the gulls." Trinity beamed a gorgeous smile. "I really do feel like Cinderella's godmother." Then she dipped her head. "Except I should have been around more for you to talk to. I'm sorry."

"I could have tried harder to get hold of you." Faith pulled her into the kitchen. "Sometimes you just have to go through things on your own, Trinity." She set a kettle on the stove to boil. "I love you and I wanted to talk to you, really I did, but I think I really needed to work it out on my own." She held the two mugs she took out of the cupboard to her chest. "Do *you* forgive *me*?"

Just as in the hall, something flitted across Trinity's face, then disappeared. "There's nothing to forgive. You're my best friend. And I love you."

"I love you, too." Trinity was the one to always stand beside her no matter what. "I have to tell you something about your father and Daddy's company."

Then, in the oddest gesture, Trinity put her finger over Faith's lips. "Remember when you said that even if I heard a bad thing about Connor, you didn't want to know about it?"

"Yes, but—"

"This is one of those kinds of things. Daddy was crying last night, and I . . ." Trinity trailed off. "You had to work out your thoughts about Connor on your own and . . . well . . . I think this is something I have to deal with on my own, too."

Faith took her hand. "I'm here if you need me, though. Now tell me how things are going with Harper."

Trinity brightened. "He's absolutely marvelous and do you know where he took me?" And she was off on an enthusiastic tale.

There might be a dark cloud in Trinity's sky, but she was never one to let things get her down for long. And when she was ready for a heart-to-heart, Faith would be there no matter what.

"IF it's a boy, I want him named Jarvis. And if it's a girl, she should be Eleanor after Faith's mother."

"No," Connor said as he opened Jarvis's office door and stepped out into the empty executive hallway.

"Why not?"

"Because Faith and I will choose the name, not be dictated to by you." Baby names. A ghost of emotion whispered through him, and he closed his eyes briefly to savor it.

"You're an asshole, Kingston."

"I know." Connor smiled. "That's why you and I are going to get along so famously. Because you're an asshole, too."

He was sure Jarvis snickered, but the old man tried to cover it with a light sneeze.

Friday night, they'd negotiated a cease-fire. Saturday, they agreed upon the terms of a truce. Sunday, they'd started working together for the first time in months. They'd devised a proposal regarding Green Industries for the Monday board meeting, one they both supported, and in the next few minutes, they'd see how it flew.

"I'm leaving right after the meeting," Connor said. "Faith called a little while ago to say she found a house she wants to show me, then I'm taking her to the doctor."

Jarvis snorted. "In my day, women didn't need so much coddling. Nowadays, the father goes into the damn delivery room with a video camera."

"Welcome to the new millennium, Jarvis."

A hand on Connor's arm, his father-in-law stopped in the middle of the hall. "Take care of her. She's all I have."

"You know, that's your problem. Faith *isn't* the only person you have. You've a whole goddamn family in there." He pointed at the closed double doors of the boardroom.

Jarvis's eyebrows damn near shot to his hairline. "The *cousins?*"

"Yeah, the cousins. Some people have absolutely no one. Maybe you should start valuing what you do have."

Connor had managed that feat. Jesus, he'd even begun to be grateful for his father-in-law. After all, Jarvis had brought him Faith. Without all the shit between him and Jarvis, Connor wasn't sure he'd ever have allowed himself to acknowledge his own feelings for her.

Jarvis shook his head in an absent gesture—whether he'd ever change, who knew?—then grabbed a door handle. Connor did the same, and they entered side by side. A team. Finally. Now, if they could just convince the rest of the board to join.

Preston and Thomas were in various stages of coffee prep at the sideboard. The Finches and Plumleys sat around the table. Dora surveyed herself in the mirror of a small compact. Josie had been invited to join them, too, and perched on the edge of her chair eagerly awaiting the reason why. Nina tapped her crimson nails on the mahogany surface and narrowed her eyes on Lance, who was seated straight across from her.

Yes, Lance and Herman had received invitations also.

"People, let's get down to business." Jarvis shot a pile of agendas to the center of the table, and everyone helped themselves.

Connor sat on Jarvis's right, next to Herman. Interesting. Was it telling that Herman had placed himself on the opposite side of the table from his son? To say that Herman was upset his son had fed him those falsified e-mails would be putting it mildly. He'd been grief-stricken when Jarvis talked with him.

"First on the list," Jarvis began, "we have a new lead project manager."

Josie closed her eyes and bit her lip. Dora, her mouth pursed, looked absolutely horrified.

Pointing his finger at Josie, Jarvis added, "You've got the Dominican job. Don't mess it up."

Connor shook his head sadly. He may *never* change.

"I won't let you down." Josie clutched a fist, shook it lightly, and beamed a high-watt smile at Connor.

"Item number two," Jarvis moved on, "quality issues with Green products." He tapped the folder of proposal copies, but he didn't hand them out.

"Let's all get up to speed here," Lance jumped in. "We've just identified the problem as being in fabrication. Someone"—he turned his gaze on Connor—"purchased substandard materials that didn't meet spec."

Someone had. And if that *someone* wasn't Connor, then that *someone* created bogus e-mails to frame him. At the same time, they'd done Castle Heavy Mining a favor and pinpointed exactly who, what, where, when, and how on the quality issues. It wasn't Herman. He was merely his son's patsy, doing his dirty work without even knowing it.

Connor tapped his mechanical pencil on his agenda. For all the silence in the room, he and Lance might have been the only two present. "That's what we're here to discuss today. Green's responsibilities in regards to the current spate of returns Castle has been experiencing, and how we're both going to remedy the situation."

The corner of Lance's eye twitched. "I think you need to assess your own culpability. My father recently found some e-mails that clearly show where the blame lies."

Next to Connor, Herman huffed out a harsh breath. He'd con-firmed yesterday who gave him the printout. His apology to Jarvis had been genuine, his sense of betrayal revealed by the mistiness in his eyes as he'd helped Jarvis and Connor work up the proposal.

For Lance's benefit, Connor smiled. Widely. With lots of teeth. "Let's not talk about *blame*, shall we? It's such an ugly word. Let's look for solutions." He indicated the proposal he and Jarvis had worked out with Herman yesterday afternoon. "I'll give you all a few moments to read."

As he read, Lance's eye problem became a full-fledged tick. Preston tipped his head slightly to regard Connor. When he'd asked about Faith's shares this morning, Connor merely said he had ev-erything under control, including Jarvis.

Lance stabbed the first page of the proposal with his finger. "After all this mumbo jumbo, it's a fucking takeover."

"Please, Lance, watch your language." Jarvis glared. "We have ladies present."

As if making a statement, Nina's anklets jingled.

"Dad?" Lance held both hands in the air. "What the hell?"

Herman shook his head. "We don't have the working capital to cover the returns."

"So you're just going to let them buy us out?"

"Yes." And that was all Herman said. No other explanation.

"Don't worry," Connor added, "your father will run Green, and in addition, he'll get two percent of Castle. It's a fair deal. Let me point you to page three." Papers rustled. "Here, you'll notice it states that you *won't* remain as vice president."

"You *asshole*."

Jarvis clucked his tongue at Lance. "Language, my boy."

Lance didn't seem to hear. "This is all because of Faith."

"This is all because you bought out-of-spec material in order to reduce costs. You took the easy way out, then lied about it when the product started coming back. If you'd been up-front right away, we could have minimized the damage." Connor smiled. All right, it *was* a tad malicious, but really, he hadn't mentioned anything about Lance creating false e-mails or embroiling his unwitting father in the scheme to accuse Connor. "You're just not VP material in our opinion. We have no objection, though, if your father wants to keep you on as, say, a junior buyer with enough authority to purchase"—he waved a hand in the air, thinking—"pencils. And if you prove yourself with that, we might let you start buying small office equipment, such as calculators."

He admitted he was having too much fun. Time to get the show on the road. "Jarvis, if everyone's done reading, and there are no other questions, would you like to call for a vote?"

Lance jutted his head forward. "Dad, are you really going to let them get away with this?"

Herman rose, patting his jacket pocket. "I'm going out for a cigar while you all vote."

"Dad, you can't let them do this to me."

His jaw tense and steel suddenly in his gaze, Herman leaned forward. "*You* did this to yourself." Then he straightened. "You betrayed my trust. You betrayed the company. Then you used *me* to put the blame on someone else." Puffing up his chest with a big breath, Herman walked out the door and left Lance behind.

And thus he punished his son with a public humiliation. Connor wasn't sure they'd needed to go that far, but Lance had killed something when he fed his father the fraudulent e-mails.

Lance jumped to his feet. "You're going to pay for this, Kingston."

"Thanks for the warning. I'll be sure to watch my back."

"OH, sweetie, you are so not an asshole." Faith leaned over, her seat belt tugging across her breasts, and kissed Connor's cheek. "Want me to beat him up for you?"

He shut off the engine and put the car in park two doors down from the storefront. "Thanks, baby, but I have to learn to manage my own playground fights."

She laughed. He made her smile as easily as he made her come. At the doctor's office, he'd wanted to go right into the exam room with her. She figured he'd even change diapers when the time came. He loved the house she showed him, but being that it was a buyer's market right now, he wanted to see a few more before they made an offer. He also forgave her father and Herman for ganging up on him. And he'd spent all weekend showing her just exactly how much he loved her, desired her, and needed her.

What more could a girl ask for? Nothing. Not one thing.

Turning to him, she tucked her feet beneath her. "So then what happened?"

"Lance very dramatically slammed the door. And the board voted in favor of the proposal. Green has now merged with Castle. They'll be a wholly owned subsidiary with Herman still running everything on that end. Even Preston seemed pleased."

Faith sobered. "What does this mean for Trinity?"

"She'll still be able to afford her hair and nails and salon treatments and country club membership and—"

Faith put her hand over his mouth. "Be nice."

"She'll find she's better off than she was before," he said against her fingers before pulling her hand away. "Did you think I was going to screw over her old man?"

"Do *you* think I thought you were going to screw him over?"

He put his forehead to hers. "I love you," he whispered.

Her cell phone chirped. "Oh my God, it's Trinity." Trinity, as well as Connor and her father, had her own special tone. "I *have* to take this. We've been playing phone tag so much, I just can't let it happen again. Do you mind?"

He smiled and nodded his assent.

"Trinity, where are you?"

"Tahoe."

"Tahoe?" Faith felt a tremor of unease. "What are you doing there?"

"Harper and I eloped. We just got married in Dr. Raymond Love's Chapel of Love."

Faith couldn't say a word.

"Are you happy for me?"

She found her voice, but it squeaked a little. "I'm so happy for you." For Connor's benefit, she added, "Trinity just got married to Harper Harrington."

"The Third," Trinity amended. "Okay, I gotta go. Harper got us *the* best room at Harrah's."

"Trinity—"

"Gotta run. Love you, talk to ya later, see ya, bye."

And Trinity was gone. God. This felt just plain *wrong*.

"She married the numerals?" Connor didn't make it sound like a compliment.

And she was terrified Trinity had made this decision too quickly. "Oh my God, this is all my fault. She was over on Saturday and I knew there was something wrong, but I didn't make her talk about it."

"Faith." He held her chin in his fingers. "She's a big girl, and old enough to make her own decisions. The most you can do is be there for her if things go wrong."

She widened her eyes. "That is so *not* a guy thing to say."

"I know, but I'm trying to be sensitive, and sensitivity isn't my strong suit. Now come on, let's go inside and see this present you want me to buy for you."

Her fears about Trinity had taken the joy out of her own moment. Mr. Sensitive was right. Trinity was a big girl, and all Faith could do was be there, just as she'd said she'd be. She needed to be happy for her friend instead of a doomsayer.

So she climbed out of the car and dragged Connor into the toy shop.

"Are we here for handcuffs?" he whispered in her hair.

"No, I want you to buy me something better."

"I do love the idea of buying you naughty gifts," Connor murmured as she pulled him past the counter with all the sparkly makeup into the depths amid the vinyl and leather outfits.

Stopping in front of the bust-shaped hanger, she pointed. "I want that." She'd coveted the halter top that day, but she'd been too afraid to even contemplate trying it on, let alone wearing it for Connor.

Yet he'd given her the confidence to own her sexuality and to ask for what she wanted.

"Holy hell." Connor reached out to touch the gold coins of the bodice, setting them jangling, fingering them, then letting them cascade off his hand to fall back into place on the hanger. "You should have at least warned me. How am I supposed to hide this hard-on, baby, when all I can think about is doing you in all that gold?"

"They're not real," she said as she turned over the price tag and raised an eyebrow. "Though they do cost a small fortune."

"Then we're lucky that I'm a fortune hunter, aren't we?"

"Very lucky." Especially since he was *her* fortune hunter.

He tapped her arm with his elbow. "I'm so hot I'll have to follow you into the dressing room while you try it on."

She buried her face against his shoulder. She was sure he meant it. "I had this fantasy about starring in a movie wearing just the coins." She looked up at him and fluttered her eyelashes. "Don't you think they'd make great sound effects?"

He wrapped both arms around her and hitched her up against his long and very hard body. "Baby, I'm here to make your fantasies come true."

And he had. Every single one of them.

Jasmine Haynes has been penning stories for as long as she's been able to write. Storytelling has always been her passion. With a bachelor degree in accounting from Cal Poly San Luis Obispo, she has worked in the high-tech Silicon Valley for the last twenty years and hasn't met a boring accountant yet! Well, maybe a few. She and her husband live with their cat, Eddie (short for Eddie Munster, get the picture), and Star, the mighty moose-hunting dog (if she weren't afraid of her own shadow). Jasmine's pastimes, when not writing her heart out, are hiking in the Redwoods and taking long walks on the beach.

Jasmine also writes as Jennifer Skully and JB Skully. She loves to hear from readers. Please e-mail her at skully@skullybuzz.com or visit her website, www.skullybuzz.com. Her newsletter subscription is skullybuzz-subscribe@yahoogroups.com.